THE
FAKE
OUT

BOOKS BY SHARON M. PETERSON

The Do-Over

SHARON M. PETERSON

THE
FAKE
OUT

bookouture

Published by Bookouture in 2023

An imprint of Storyfire Ltd.
Carmelite House
50 Victoria Embankment
London EC4Y 0DZ

www.bookouture.com

ISBN: 978-1-80314-937-0
eBook ISBN: 978-1-80314-936-3

To Carl,
Who, on the occasion of our first kiss,
took me on a hike and with a beautiful
waterfall as the backdrop, turned to me,
stared deeply into my eyes and then...
kept staring for several more moments.
So, I got nervous and yelled, "What do you want?"
Thank you for still marrying me anyway.
I love you.

ONE

Are you from Tennessee, because you're the only ten I see.

—JULIA B.

There was a man sleeping in my library.

Well, not exactly *my* library. The Two Harts Public Library didn't belong to me personally. I was, however, its only employee. Not by choice, mind you. It had been a year ago when the city council in all its brilliance (which is to say, none), led by its fearless (idiot) mayor, decided to slash the library budget to bare bones. As a result, I was a one-woman show. Book circulation? That was me. Afterschool homework club? Me. Genealogy classes? You're looking at her. Hall monitor, light housekeeping, budget maker. Me, me, and me. All that on a salary that would make most people cry.

But, like most librarians, I wasn't in it for the money.

The Two Harts Public Library had always been a special place for me. We'd moved here – my mom, baby sister, and me – when I was ten. The three of us were nothing more than a

huddle of raw nerves and exhaustion after years on the road
with my father, none of them good.

Here at the library, I'd found friends among Anne who
lived at Green Gables, or Laura Ingalls in the Piney Woods. I
didn't have to worry that I was That Girl whose dad was in and
out of prison. Or when he wasn't locked up, doing all the things
that landed him in prison in the first place. No one whispered
about my mama and how she had to work three jobs to get by.
No one felt sorry for me and my hand-me-down clothes. Here, I
was just... Mae Sampson, the girl who liked to read.

As far as I was concerned, the library was sacred ground,
the same way some people felt about a church building or how
most Texans felt about a football field.

So, it really pissed me when I found a man sleeping in the
non-fiction section.

I'd just ushered little Jordan Hunter—age six, big fan of
dinosaurs—into the warm March sun and had given the front
door lock a satisfying click. I kicked my sandals off and groaned
in delight.

Although I loved my job, the hours I spent here added up.
As the one and only employee, I couldn't slack. If I didn't do it,
no one else would. It's not how I'd expected my library career to
go. I'd hoped to find a position at a large library system far away
from Two Harts where I could work as a children's librarian.
The thought of living in anonymity where no one knew of the
Sampson family sounded like a dream. Extra points if it was in
an entirely different state.

But as much as I wanted to believe dreams could come true
in real life and not only in books, the truth was few of us ever
got anywhere close to achieving them.

The book return cart was overflowing so I pulled up my
latest audiobook on my phone, turned the volume up as loud as
it could go, and tossed it on the cart. The historical romance had
come to the first kiss, and I was a bit distracted by the Duke of

Fellows' prowess. The poor bookish second daughter of a disgraced viscount was certainly not complaining.

I turned the corner to make my way to the 600s (Applied Sciences) with a copy of *Old Tractors and the Men Who Love Them*. I'd purchased it after a special request from Mr. Conway, who has since checked it out every couple of months. "To look at the pictures," he said.

And there he was.

A big oaf of a man, slouched in the armchair I'd gotten from an estate sale after old Mrs. Friedman went to the Great Beyond. It should be noted she passed away while sitting in said chair, but I thought that gave it character.

I shrieked. The book slipped from my hand and landed with a thud on the floor.

Shockingly, the man did not budge.

Or at least, it didn't look like he did. It was hard to tell with the baseball cap pulled low on his forehead, dark hair peeking out around his ears. His jean-clad legs were stretched out and crossed at the ankles where he blocked the 750s (Art and Recreation).

Everything about him seemed oversized, in a long, lean sort of way. The arm dangling to the side almost reached the floor. His enormous tennis shoe-clad feet. A hand the size of a dinner plate splayed across the open book on his chest. I didn't recognize him, and he seemed memorable by sheer size alone.

Two Harts was a small dot on the Texas map, about forty-five minutes west of Houston, and this library was the only one for four towns. I knew everyone who visited the library; I knew their reading tastes, their family tree, and (unfortunately for some) their internet search history.

What bothered me the most was that he'd gotten in here without me noticing. This was exactly the reason I'd asked the city council to consider putting in one measly security camera, especially now I was here alone. After all, this man could be a criminal or violent or request to check out a copy of *Fifty Shades of Grey*.

The man shifted a bit, his hat moving enough to give me a glimpse of one dark eyebrow and a jawline dusted with at least a day or two of growth. From where I stood, he looked like he could use a shave and a haircut. But for all his scruffiness, he didn't appear dirty.

Annoyed, I inched closer and nudged one of his giant feet. He didn't so much as flinch. My eyes narrowed on his chest to make sure he was still breathing. The last thing I needed was a dead guy in my library.

Good news. Still alive.

I cleared my throat. "Excuse me."

Nothing. Yet, I was reminded of the millions of times I'd played hide-and-seek with my sister when she was very young and believed that if she kept her eyes shut and couldn't see me, I couldn't see her. Surely this grown man wouldn't be playing the same kind of silly game.

After glaring at him for several seconds, I stomped to a small closet and retrieved a broom. Standing as far back as I could, I poked his arm. "Hey, wake up. Library's closed."

Still no reply.

I stuck a hand on my hip, gripping the broom in the other like some kind of book witch. Oooh. *Book Witch.* I needed that on a t-shirt.

"The Duke's lips trailed along her cheekbone, his tongue traced the delicate shell of her ear," my phone read aloud.

"Oh, crap," I jolted, remembering the audiobook that had been playing the whole time.

"'Fellows, you must stop,' she protested and then, belying her words, leaned into him. 'I'll be ruined if someone see us.' But she didn't pull away when his fingers began to touch—"

My heart racing, I tossed the broom and scrambled to get

my phone from the cart. Frantically, I jabbed at the screen until the audio stopped.

"Now why'd you go and do that? It was just getting interesting," a deep voice said, a touch of humor laced in his words.

I gasped; my gaze darted to the man. Nothing about his position had changed, save for his eye, which was now open, and the corner of his mouth I could see was tilted up.

For some reason, this half-smile irritated me. My spine straightened and I whisper-screamed at him, "Why are you sleeping in my library?"

It should be noted that all librarians learn to whisper-scream. And to shush people.

Lazily, he stretched his arms, taking his baseball cap off to reveal a head of dark hair that was just a shade too long. It curled around his ears and dusted his forehead. The scruff on his face was equally dark. All of that should have made him look unkempt and messy. But it did not. Not at all.

He gestured toward the book he now held in one hand. "Sorry about that. Thought I'd do a little reading."

My eyes darted to the book, and I frowned. "*The American Medical Association Guide to Preventing and Treating Heart Disease?*"

"Knowledge is power," he said, his voice deep and tinged with a drawl of the Southern variety. It drew my eyes right back up to the source, his mouth. A wide grin met me there, still a little sleepy around the edges.

That smile. Friendly. Open. *Charming*.

But I'd spent twenty-six years on this earth. While I knew I still had a lot to learn, I did know one thing: that smile meant trouble and I didn't want trouble. My own mother had spent all my life playing with trouble and all it had gotten her were a world of heartache, a few extra callouses on her feet, and nothing in the bank.

So no, I wasn't impressed with that smile. It didn't cause any sort of tingling anywhere in my body. That was just irritation racing down my spine.

"The library is closed," I snapped. "Didn't you hear the four announcements I made?"

His smile slipped a bit as he sat up in the chair. "I guess I missed them. I honestly didn't mean to."

I waved a hand in the air. "Nap time is over."

He nodded and stood. It took a while because he was about twelve feet tall. And not the skinny, beanpole kind of tall either. The strong, lean, wide-shouldered kind of tall, like he ran five miles a day as his warmup and *then* worked out. He stretched an arm, settled his hat back on his head, and took a curious look at me, from the tip of my toes to the top of my hair. "Nice shirt."

It was my *I Will Dewey Decimate You* shirt—I'd gotten it for myself on my last birthday.

"Thank you, and goodbye." I took a step back so he could walk by.

He shrugged, looking a little confused, but he took the hint and held out the book in my direction. I had to tip my head back a bit to see his face, which was saying something—I was 5'10" barefoot.

"I'm sorry for any inconvenience I may have caused you," he said. His voice sounded sincere.

I blinked, not expecting his words. This close I could see his eyes were a brown so light and warm they reminded me of fresh honey on...

Knock that off right now. I was not waxing poetic about his eyes. They were brown. Normal, brown eyes. The most common of all eye colors. Cows had brown eyes. He had cow eyes. Nothing remotely interesting about that. Unless you were a female cow on the prowl. Which I was not. Obviously.

I snatched the book from his hand. "It's fine," I said, my tone implying it was anything but.

He nodded solemnly but I swore his eyes crinkled at the

corners like he was stifling a grin. I trailed behind as he made his way to the door. On the way, I grabbed my keys off the circulation desk and scurried around him to jam them in the lock. Holding open the door, I waved him through. He paused in front of me, his brow creased like he was trying to figure me out.

No, thank you.

With a shrug, he took a couple of steps and then stopped and turned around. "I did have a question, if you don't mind."

I did mind. I minded so much. "What?"

"So, where do you think that Duke was gonna put his hand? I'm thinking he was about to touch her—"

With a growl, I pulled the door shut. He was still laughing as I locked it.

TWO

Kiss me if I'm wrong, but dinosaurs still exist, right?

—*CHRISTIE L.*

"Oh, canned biscuits?" Miss Mary said, who'd been the cashier at Pappy's Market since I could remember. She'd also been my Sunday school teacher at the Baptist church and Mama's before me. People didn't much leave Two Harts, and they usually wore more than one hat. For example, one of the two attorneys in town was also a taxidermist.

Pappy's, like most things around here, showed its age with its faded store sign and dim lighting. The shopping carts were small and old and every wheel in the place pulled a little to the left.

"Yes, ma'am," I said with an internal sigh. This is why I did most of my shopping at the Walmart twenty minutes away.

She slid on the glasses she kept on a chain around her neck and squinted at the package. "Now that's just something. Always used my grandmama's biscuit recipe, of course. But I've heard these are good." She said the word good like it was synonymous with poison. Or dog poop.

The register beeped as she pulled the can across and set it aside. The other thing about Pappy's—there was no rushing. Miss Mary could move at her own pace, thank you very much. And she did. Captive audience and all.

"How's your mama?" she asked, eyeballing the package of Italian sausage in her hand.

I shifted on my feet and propped an elbow on the tiny checkout counter. I was going to be here a while. "She's doing better, thank you for asking."

"We were all so worried about her there for a while."

"She's a fighter," I said, hoping to move on from this topic and perhaps get home before the next millennium.

"Of course she is, honey. You know the ladies at the church can bring y'all meals any time or help around the house or drive her to doctor appointments." She peered at me over her glasses. "We take care of our own."

Inside, I bristled. Although Mama had grown up in Two Harts, I'd been ten when she'd moved us back here, and I'd always felt like I was on the outside looking in.

Of course, that my father had been arrested many times over in this town didn't help matters either. A large part of me wanted to prove I was nothing like him. I wasn't flaky or irresponsible. I was a fully capable woman who could take care of anything life threw at her.

"We've got it covered," I said, forcing a small smile. It should be noted I didn't have anything covered, but unless I wanted to have a full-on panic attack in the cereal aisle at Pappy's, lying was easier.

Miss Mary patted my hand. "'Course you do, honey. You were always that way."

My cheeks warmed at the surprising compliment. "Thank you."

With a nod, she picked up the next item and inspected it. "Would you look at that. Peas frozen in a bag you cook right in the mi-cro-wave." Beep went the scanner. "That sure is fancy."

By the time I dragged myself home, I'd already forgotten the encounter with the giant sleeping stranger at the library. I kicked my shoes off by the front door and yelled out a greeting.

No one replied but I could hear the distinct sound of someone screaming in agony.

I rounded the corner, knowing exactly what I would find—Mama and her best friend Sue on the couch, eyes glued to the TV. Last week, the two of them had discovered *Game of Thrones* and this viewing party had become a daily ritual.

Quietly, I rounded the sofa and dropped a kiss on Mama's cheek. Nowadays, I never missed the chance to kiss her cheek or hold her hand or spend time with her. Life was precious and quickly lost, as we'd learned the last few months.

"It's almost over, honey," she whispered without turning her head in my direction.

"I'll go start dinner then," I said. "Hi, Sue."

With a wave of her hand, Sue shushed me. I stifled a laugh. After dropping off the groceries in the kitchen, I made my way to my room to strip off my work clothes and throw on some holey shorts and an old, faded t-shirt.

Kevin, our geriatric cat with the social graces of a cactus, cracked open an eye from his position smack in the middle of my bed. Or rather, his bed, which he kindly let me sleep in at night. When Grandma had passed away my last year of college, we'd decided I would take over her bedroom. Kevin came with the room. He didn't care for humans, vacuum cleaners, and shoes. We had a lot in common if I thought about it.

"Hello to you, too," I said.

His reply was to cover his face with a paw and go back to sleep. Typical.

"Holy crap," Sue yelled from the other room, and I grinned.

Sue had been Mama's best friend since before I was born. They'd both grown up here. Sue had done a stint in the Navy after high school and then come back to Two Harts to work as a tow truck driver at the family business. By then, Mama had met my father and he'd taken her on a roller coaster before she moved my sister and me back here. These days, chances were if you saw my mama, Sue wasn't far behind.

In the early days after Mama's stroke when we weren't sure she'd survive, it had been Sue who had taken care of all the practical things—feeding the cat, checking the mail, making sure Iris and I ate regularly. The last seven months had been the hardest of my life and we wouldn't have made it without Sue.

But Mama had pulled through, although the left side of her body was slower to recover. Her health insurance had only covered two months in a rehabilitation center. Then she was released with printed-out instructions of exercises, a wheelchair, and a "good luck."

That's when I discovered how expensive hospital stays and therapy are.

On the way to the kitchen, I knocked on Iris's door. No answer. Frowning, I opened it and peered inside. She had a real funeral-director-meets-death-metal-band-meets-vampire-seethe aesthetic going on in here. But there were hints of the young girl she pretended not to be. Like the corkboard filled with every postcard she'd ever received, or the bookshelf crammed with Babysitters Club books. Or the stuffed animal tucked in the middle of her unmade bed. Kitty used to be yellow and have two eyes. Years of tears and cuddles had left it faded and tattered but very loved.

What I did not find in the room was Iris.

My sister had added this disappearing trick to her repertoire in the last year. Despite being a senior in high school, she'd seemed to make it her life's work to avoid school, home and family as much as humanly possible. I'd already intercepted a phone call from her math teacher who made it sound like it would take a miracle, and possibly a cash bribe, for Iris to pass the class.

I glanced at the photo resting on a table beside Iris's bed, a rare family picture with Dad included. Iris was about ten, all rosy-cheeked, blonde hair caught up in a ponytail. A wide smile was plastered on her face as she stared up at our father. When she was little, she'd been a literal ray of walking sunshine and always a Daddy's girl.

But the last couple of years, Iris had turned to the dark side. Literally. Dyed her hair black then cut into chopping layers, a chunk always covering one eye. Black wardrobe heavy on the vintage band t-shirts. Black lipstick. Black nail polish. Fake lip ring—although I had my doubts it was really fake.

But she did help with Mama, so I tried to give her some leeway. Plus, she was only seventeen, still a kid. I, on the other hand, had been an adult since I was nine—the first (but not the last) time Dad went to prison.

Our agreement was that Iris came home straight from school. Yet, more and more, she'd been conning Sue into staying while she "slipped out" for hours at a time. She'd come home well after curfew, tight-lipped about where she'd been or who she'd been with. But I was dealing with it. Mama didn't need to know about her grades or curfew breaking.

Mama had one job right now: to get better. My job was to take care of everything else.

"Where's Iris?" I said once Sue and Mama joined me in the kitchen.

Mama waved a hand. "Out with friends."

"That girl is slipperier than an eel dipped in jello," Sue said.

"Why would you dip an eel in jello?" I asked.

"Eel jello wrestling, of course. Very popular, I hear."

I laughed. "How long have you been here?"

"Two episodes. You gotta watch it, Mae. It's so good."

"I'll pass." It should be noted I'd love nothing more than to sit and binge hours of TV until my eyes forgot how to blink, but there wasn't time. There was always something to take care of.

"How was therapy today?" I asked as I began to pull together ingredients to make dinner.

Mama smiled, her left side struggling to keep up with the right side. The sight of her smile was bittersweet now. I was glad she was around to do it, but it was a constant reminder of what she'd survived and how close we came to losing her.

"It was hell," she said happily. "But I do feel like I'm getting stronger. Just wait and I'll be through with the chair before you know it."

It was true she was using her walker more and more. By evening time, she often had to switch back to the wheelchair from pure exhaustion. But the therapy was working.

It was also real expensive.

Which is why I had to get the second job, the one no one knew about, and I wanted to keep it like that.

Iris slunk into the house just after midnight, the typical sullen glint in her eyes. I looked up from the book I was pretending to read while I pretended not to wait up for her. It should be noted I was definitely waiting up for her.

"What?" Iris scowled. That was her normal expression these days. She flung herself on the far side of the couch.

"It's past curfew," I said. "Way past curfew. Where were you?"

Iris rolled her eyes, which were ringed in heavy black eyeliner. I'd once asked her if she was taking makeup tips from a raccoon. She was not amused. "Out."

"Iris." I glared at her.

She glared back. "Maebell."

"You can't be out this late. You didn't even answer your phone when I called." And I had called several times.

With a shrug, she picked at the chipped black paint on her nails. "I was busy."

"I talked to Mr. Sullivan. He says you're failing his class. Like you might not be able to graduate. If you want to start at the community college in the fall, you need to get caught up."

She cut me off and threw her head against the back of the couch. "Fiiine. I'll take care of it."

"Plus, you're supposed to be here with Mama until I get home. That's our deal."

Another eye-roll. We'd now seen the extensive collection of emotional responses from Iris—eye-rolls, shrugging, and scowling. "Sue was here."

"Sue wasn't the one who was supposed to be with her."

She yanked the hair elastic from the lazy ponytail she'd put it up in. "I get it. Mom."

"I'm not your mom," I snapped, but we both knew I was more like a second parent than a sister to her and had been practically since her birth.

"Then stop acting like it. You're the oldest twenty-six-year-old ever."

"I am not!" This wasn't a new argument. Sure, I owned a lot of books and had a geriatric cat with an attitude, but I wasn't old.

"I think Mrs. Houser goes on more dates than you."

I gasped. "Mrs. Houser is eighty-seven years old, mostly blind, and routinely leaves her dentures in the church bathroom."

"I know." Iris patted my knee with mocking pity. "And she still gets more action than you."

I shivered thinking of Mrs. Houser doing anything but

sitting in the second row from the front on Sunday mornings, happily singing off-key.

"Whatever," I muttered and held my book in front of my face.

Perhaps thirty seconds later, one black-tipped finger curled over the top of the book and pulled it down to reveal Iris's blueberry eyes.

"Are you pouting now?" she asked.

"No, I am reading."

"I'm sorry, okay?" she said. "I'll call. Or whatever."

"Especially when you're going to be late."

"Fine."

"Thank you." I held the book against my chest. "I just need to know you're safe, okay?"

Ignoring me, Iris pointed to the book. "*The Blue Castle* again. You are so predictable."

"I am not. And besides, it's a good book." Actually, it was a great book, easily one of my top-twenty favorites. I didn't have one favorite book and I didn't trust people who did.

More eye-rolling. "You need to get a life."

"I need to get some sleep, which I can't do if I'm worried about you," I said.

"I need to get some sleep," she mimicked, and then yawned.

"Shut up." I smacked her on the arm.

"You're just jealous because I'm the cool one in this family." She reached over and pulled my hair.

But it was late and neither of us was really giving it much effort. Instead, she settled her head on my shoulder and I kissed the top of her head, which we would pretend never happened. We were, of course, mortal enemies. Mortal enemies did not cuddle.

"You're a brat, you know that?" I said. "I don't know why I put up with you. I should have sold you at that garage sale when I had the chance. But no, I had to have a conscience."

I shrugged to get her attention, but she didn't respond. Her eyes were closed and judging from the open-mouth breathing, she was asleep. Another of Iris's talents, falling asleep anytime, anywhere.

"Alright then," I muttered. But I stood up and, as gently as I could, laid her head on one end of the sofa, slipped off her shoes and swung her feet onto the couch.

She immediately curled up into a ball. It reminded me of when we were younger and I'd wake up in the middle of the night with her curled like that in bed with me. My heart squeezed at the memory.

I wasn't sure what Iris planned on doing with her life. If I took a guess right now, I'd say she planned to run for president of the local witches' coven. (Did covens have presidents? Head Witch in Charge, maybe?) But I knew she had dreams, and I wanted to make sure she had every chance to reach them.

I tucked a blanket around her and clicked off the light. Just as I walked away, I heard her mumble, "Love you, Maebell."

THREE

Is that a mirror in your pocket? Because I can see myself in your pants.

—CHRISTINE K. H.

The Sit-n-Eat Café was a Two Harts' institution. It had been around forever and, like a lot of places here, it had been passed down through the family. Its current owner, Ollie Holder, had never married or had any kids of his own. He was roughly three hundred years old, and no one quite knew what would happen to the Sit-n-Eat when he passed.

"How's the meatloaf?" I asked, hopping onto a stool at the counter. It was Friday. Friday's special was meatloaf. Monday was fried chicken, Wednesday was brisket, and so on. If you tried to order anything else, you still got the daily special *and* a dirty look from Ollie.

"Good." Ollie was a man of few words; I liked that about him.

"Do you ever think about changing things up sometimes, Ollie? What about Sushi Saturday?" I asked, to mess with him.

Behind me, someone chuckled. Probably one of the handful of old men who spent their afternoons in the café.

The Sit-n-Eat opened every day from precisely ten to two. Breakfast wasn't served. Neither was brunch or dinner. You came here for lunch. And the friendly service, of course. Despite all that, the café seemed to have a steady stream of customers such that a HELP WANTED sign hung permanently in the window.

Ollie ignored me. "One or two?"

"Two, please."

"I expect that other one is coming, then?"

See? Isn't he charming? He wasn't a very tall man and with his shiny bald head, dark bushy eyebrows, and friendly disposition, he gave off very strong "get off my lawn" energy.

I grinned. "You know her name is Ali—she worked for you two summers in college, and she comes in at least three times a week."

He shrugged and shuffled behind the partition that separated the front counter from the kitchen.

My best friend, Ali Ramos, was usually late. Although she made her own schedule as a virtual assistant, she often was last seen falling down some internet rabbit hole. Or dreaming up her latest revenge fantasy. Three months ago, after four years together, Ali's boyfriend Alec dumped her, claiming he was tired of their long-distance relationship.

You'd think he would have known his tech-savvy ex-girlfriend could stalk him online and find out he was dating again—seventy-two hours after they broke up.

It should be noted that Ali had not taken that lying down. I bet Alec was still trying to get the smell of rotten fish out of his car and figure out how his profile and email address showed up on a "Furries Looking for Love" website.

"I love meatloaf day," Ali said when she arrived in her "work" clothes—yoga pants, an oversized Star Trek t-shirt, her dark hair piled atop her head haphazardly—a bit sweaty from her walk.

Ali didn't drive—refused to, actually—so she walked most places. She lived off the main strip of town and could get to most places in minutes. As a result, she was often in a permanent state of sweatiness. Texas was not a state made for walking.

With a grin, she slid onto the stool next to me. "Hit me, Ollie."

We'd been friends since I'd moved here in the fifth grade. Ali knew all my secrets.

Well, most of my secrets.

I mean, the ones I told her about.

Ollie grunted and slid two overfull plates in front of us. Ali wasted no time in taking a generous bite of her meatloaf.

"So good," she moaned. "This is why I love you, Ollie."

Ollie grunted but I could have sworn his cheeks pinked as he shuffled off.

Ali stopped inhaling her lunch long enough to point at me with her fork. "Did you hear?"

"Hear what?" I asked.

She rolled her eyes. "I swear you are on another planet sometimes."

"I am not."

"Yes, you are. I'll prove it. Do you know who Chris Sterns is?"

I shook my head. "Should I? Did he go to school with us?"

"There were sixty people in our class, and you were the yearbook editor. You know he didn't go to school with us. How are we friends?"

"I think you followed me home from school one day."

"You're hilarious."

I grinned. "Probably another reason we're friends."

Ali huffed, waving her fork between us. "I am the zany,

unpredictable one in this relationship. You are the serious, responsible one. Stay in your lane."

She wasn't even a little bit wrong. Ali had a way of attracting trouble. It didn't help that she had a deep sense of justice, which presented itself in creative ways. Often involving shaving cream, water balloons, lock-picking kits, prank calls, sophisticated catfishing schemes, replacing hair conditioner with glue, once a clown, that time she hired a petting zoo, and anything else that came to mind. She was kind of the MacGyver of revenge.

The lesson here: never, *ever* get on Ali's hit list.

"I need that on a t-shirt." I waved a hand across my chest. "*The Serious, Responsible One.*"

"Trademark forthcoming," Ali said.

I laughed. Which was another thing I loved about her: she could make me laugh. "So, who is this Chris Sterns you speak of?"

"He's only one of the most famous football players in the entire world."

"So what?"

"So what? I'll tell you so what. He's here. Like, in Two Harts."

I scoffed. "Why would a world-famous football player come here?"

"The word is he's rented out the Wilson place for a few months for a little peace and quiet."

The Wilson place didn't belong to the Wilsons anymore. It had been bought several years ago and renovated. Now it was rented out as a vacation home. Although, why anyone would want to vacation in Two Harts, I wasn't sure. Don't get me wrong, I liked Two Harts. But I also hated Two Harts. It was a complicated relationship.

"Well, may he rest in peace."

Ali gave me the stink eye. "I don't think you fully understand the significance of Chris Sterns. Mae, he's dead sexy."

With a snort, I cut off a piece of meatloaf. "I thought you were giving up men."

"Pu-lease. He is not a mere mortal. He is a god. I'm not talking about normal sexy. I'm talking *People*'s Sexiest Man sexy. On top of that, he's like, a good guy. Donates to charity, visits kids in the hospital, helps out animals." Leaning closer, she dropped her voice slightly. "There's this one picture of him online where he is shirtless and he's holding a pu—"

"Puppy. I'm holding a puppy," a voice said behind us.

Ali jumped and whipped around. Her jaw moved up and down before she finally got words out. "Holy crap. It's him. It's you. Y-you're Chris Sterns."

"One and the same," he said, a trace of humor in his words.

Something about the voice hit me strangely, like I'd heard it before. Which was ridiculous because I'm certain I would have remembered meeting a professional football player. I turned slowly and looked up, way up, past long jean-clad legs and a gray t-shirt with a faded logo of some sort on it. All the way up until I discovered a scruff-covered chin and the baseball cap pulled low to cover what I knew were eyes the color of warm hon—

"You."

He rocked back on his heels and pushed his hat back, a small smile on his lips. "Nice shirt."

This one read *Librarians Do It Better*. I liked librarian t-shirts. Everyone had a weakness; this one was mine.

"Stop looking at my shirt," I snapped.

He wasn't doing anything wrong, per se. Except his eyes... twinkled.

I frowned. They did *not* twinkle. They were *not* honey-colored. They were normal brown eyes just like a...

"You have cow eyes," I blurted out. Just as quickly, I

slammed my mouth shut so hard my back teeth ached with it. What was *wrong* with me? I did not blurt things. I was calm, cool, and collected. Ali was right. She was the one who got us into trouble; I was the one who rescued us.

"Whoa," Ali murmured. "Where did that come from?"

Chris, God of Football, pushed his cap back to reveal said eyes more fully, a glint of mischief shining. "Well, now, cows are pretty special animals."

My back straightened, and despite what I'm sure were the flaming red cheeks only a natural redhead could produce, I tried to appear dignified. "Is that so?"

"Sure. You know they sleep over half the day, even while standing up, and they have a real good sense of smell." He tapped his nose. "Plus, cows never like being alone. They like to have a friend to hang out with."

"That's a lot of facts about cows," I said.

"Boy Scout. I got my Bovine Knowledge badge."

"There is not a cow badge."

"Sure is." He smiled, big and warm with a flash of white teeth, a smile that sent a tingle of awareness down my spine.

I scowled, starting to understand why Ali had been singing his praises.

"Also, a Goat Call badge, a Famous Barns of America badge, and a Zombie Apocalypse Preparedness badge."

Ali slugged me in the shoulder. "I thought you said you didn't know who he was."

"He was sleeping in my library yesterday."

Ali laughed, having recovered from her initial shock. "Dude, I bet you got in trouuuble."

He held out his hands, grinning. A dimple flashed. I hadn't noticed the dimple. It was disturbingly distracting. "Hey now, I was resting my eyes."

With a harrumph, I crossed my arms and was about to reply when yet another voice interrupted me.

"Ladies, I see you've met Chris."

I growled. Yes. An actual growl. If every supervillain joined forces, found a way to combine all their DNA and used it to create a mutant baby in a lab, then gave it dark-blond hair and the cold, dead heart of a politician, it would be this man—Peter Stone.

Once upon a time, I'd thought him handsome and charming with his swoopy hair, broad shoulders and commanding presence. I'd thought the little paunch he'd developed after college and even his penchant for cowboy boots and too-tight Wranglers were all adorable. I'd even dreamed of marrying him and having his little Wrangler-wearing babies. I'd tried to give a relationship with Peter a real chance. In the beginning, it had been nice, fun even. But like most everything that started out good in my life, it hadn't lasted; *he* hadn't lasted.

Now I hoped one day he got lost in the woods and a pack of ravenous coyotes devoured him. I guess Ali wasn't the only one with revenge fantasies.

Actually, this was a good thing. Seeing him reminded me that pretty packages often have ugly insides.

"I thought it was meatloaf day, not meathead," Ali said. She was a good and loyal friend so she hated Peter, too.

"Alicia, I see you've been working on your grown-up words," Peter said, clearly taking his life in his hands.

Ali arched a single dark eyebrow, already planning how she'd make Peter eat those words.

"We met yesterday," Chris said to Peter, but his next words were for me. "Thanks for book recommendation. I did finally figure out where that Duke put his hand."

"You're welcome," I said in a syrupy-sweet voice. "I'm just glad to know you can read."

He leaned a hip against the counter next to me, that dang twinkle back in his eye. He was enjoying this. Which was irritating.

"Maybe we could have ourselves a book club? I'll pick the next one though." Then he winked. See? Irritating.

"Let me guess. Book Club badge?"

"Obviously."

"Maebell, I'm glad I saw you," Peter cut in. "I had a question about the library budget and hoped we could find a time to talk about it."

"Uh-oh," Ali whispered.

Did I mention Peter held the auspicious title of Mayor of Two Harts, Texas? He took up the mantle from his father, who took over from his father. I know a mayor is an elected official, but when no one's willing to run against you, it was basically a dictatorship.

"Maebell?" Chris said, drawing the word out. "That's cute."

"I am not cute," I snapped. Which was true. Puppies were cute. Tiny doll furniture made to scale was cute. Ali was cute in a messy, nerdy way that a surprising number of men found attractive. At least until they got on her bad side.

Peter cleared his throat and my eyes jerked back to glare at him. "What is it you want to talk about?"

It had been Peter who'd convinced the city council to slash my budget so drastically last year. 'Cause he was a jerk like that.

"I have ideas about how we could cut some corners," he said in his cheerful, baby-kissing politician voice. "Turns out the new football stadium is going to cost a little more than we planned, and we're asking everyone to chip in a little."

"You're joking, right?" I said.

"Let's not do this now. You think about it. I'll have Maria call and set up an appointment." He waved at someone over my head. "Ed, how are you? Had a question for you."

As I watched him walk away, my fists curled at my sides. Maybe he could get lost in the forest but with honey in his pocket and find a bunch of really ambitious bears.

"You gonna eat that?" Chris was now sitting on the stool beside me, looking at my meatloaf with interest.

I pushed the plate his way. I wasn't hungry anymore. "No, go ahead."

Ali shoulder-bumped me. "You okay?"

"I hate him."

"I know. I hate him, too." See? Good and loyal friend. "Anytime you want to take action, you let me know. I already have a few ideas."

"Ali," I said on a sigh.

"Do you know what a glitter bomb is?" Excitement sparked in her eyes.

"He hasn't changed much," Chris said. Ollie brought him over a glass of sweet tea, and he nodded his thanks.

"You know him?" I asked.

"Played football in college together. He was a blowhard then too." He dug into the meatloaf with abandon. "This is good."

Ali leaned forward to see around me. "Is it true you're staying in town?"

Chris nodded. "For now."

"Why?"

He set his fork down and took a long pull of his tea. "I have a little work to do in Houston. Thought I'd check it out."

A glance at my phone told me I needed to get back to work. Although the library closed early on Fridays, I had to run home and change before the forty-five-minute drive into Houston. For my second job. The one I needed time to psych myself out for.

I stood and gathered up my things. Ollie slid a to-go carton across the counter.

"I didn't order this," I said.

"You need to eat." He walked away before I could thank him. Ollie was good people.

"I'll call you later," I said to Ali.

She nodded and scooted over to my stool to sit next to Chris, eager to get closer to the sun, I guess.

"Have fun in Two Harts," I said to Chris.

I was halfway to the door when he called out. "Oh, hey, Maebell, cowboys or pirates?"

"What?"

"For our book club? Cowboys or pirates?" He grinned. "You know what? Never mind. I'll surprise you."

FOUR

Was your mom a beaver? 'Cause damn!

—ALLISON A.

"Don't you look nice," Mama said. "Another night out?"

I shot her a small smile. "Yep."

Nope. At least not the kind of night she thought.

After the bills started arriving, I knew we were in trouble and the only way out I could see was to make extra money. But I'd refused to tell Mama about the money or the job. The former because I didn't want her to worry; the latter because I knew she'd try to talk me out of it.

I tugged on the fitted sparkly tank top I was wearing, something I wouldn't normally be caught dead in because its itchiness far outweighed its cuteness. But to keep up the facade, I had to dress the part. As painful as that might be. Like these ridiculous high-heeled boots peeking out from under my jeans. I wanted to burn them. Instead, I would be wearing them all night.

"I'm so happy you're getting out and having fun." She shuffled to the small dining table and sat down slowly and carefully.

She'd insisted on making a simple dinner of chicken and rice tonight. Sometimes she pushed herself too hard just to prove she could do it. But tonight, she seemed steady on her feet and the pinched look she often got around her eyes when she was tired was missing.

"You're too young to spend your Friday nights with your mother."

"I like spending time with my mom." I pressed a kiss to her forehead before checking the time on my phone. Where in the heck was Iris? "Can I get you anything before I go?"

"No, I'm fine." She patted my cheek. "I love you, Maebe-Baby, and I'm so proud of you."

The front door slammed, and Iris clomped into the kitchen in her black army boots and knee-high socks dotted with tiny skulls. "I'm here."

"Hi, sunshine," Mama said, patting Iris on the cheek when she was near enough. Mama refused to admit her little "ray of sunshine" had turned into something closer to a bleak, cheerless landscape.

"Sorry for being late," she said as she wandered over to the fridge. "The car was acting weird."

Oh, great. We did not need car troubles right now. Mine was already twenty years old and held together with duct tape and prayer. Mama's car was newer and more reliable, so Iris drove it for the time being.

"Weird how?" I asked, already moving money around in my brain to cover the cost of fixing it.

"The battery light came on a couple of times." She grabbed a pitcher of grape Kool-Aid from the fridge and set it on the counter.

Mama shot me a worried look.

I rushed to reassure her. "I'm sure it's nothing. I'll take it into Joe's on Monday when he's open, and Iris can drive my car."

My sister grunted behind an oversized plastic Scooby-Doo cup. "Your car is a piece of shit."

Mama whipped her head around. "Iris, how many times do I have to tell you? Watch your mouth."

"I am almost eighteen," she said, grabbing a handful of animal crackers.

Mama narrowed her eyes. "As long as you live in my house, you're going to watch your mouth. I don't much care when the government decides you're an adult."

"Whatever. I'm going to do it eventually. You don't want me learning it on the streets, do you?" She tossed a cracker in her mouth and turned to me. "I hate your dumb car. The AC doesn't work."

"Roll down a window."

"It's hot," she whined.

"You won't melt."

She wiped purple Kool-Aid from her top lip and flung herself at the table next to Mama. "Whatever."

"You're my favorite sister," I said.

"I'm your only sister."

I ruffled her hair as I headed out of the kitchen. "That's good news for you or your ranking would probably not be quite so high."

"Be safe tonight," Mama called as I passed into the living room.

"Yes, ma'am." I poked my head around the corner and sent Iris a pointed look. "You'll be here all night, right?"

She rolled her eyes. "Mama and I are gonna watch TV."

As I was leaving, I heard Mama say, "What do you want to watch?"

"There's a new Swedish police procedural about a serial killer terrorizing a small lake town. It's filmed with one camera and all in black and white," Iris said. "Don't worry. It has subtitles."

"That sounds... fun," I heard Mama say as I pulled the door closed behind me, almost grateful I had to go to work and miss it.

Forty-five minutes later, I was sitting in my car, giving myself a pep talk. In front of me, Chicky's Bar and Grill stood in all its glory.

"You can do this, Mae. You are strong and smart, and you can do anything you put your mind to." I stared at myself in the visor mirror, shuddering at the image.

It was bad enough I had to cake on the makeup—"a Chicky's girl always shows the world her best face"—or that I have to wear my contacts instead of my glasses—"a Chicky's girl has an image to uphold"—but my strawberry-blonde hair was now in two braided pigtails that hung to past my shoulders. Each tied with red gingham ribbon.

Furthermore, the braids were the *least* offensive part of the Chicky's uniform as far as I was concerned.

Four months ago, when the medical bills started coming in, it became painfully clear we were in a whole lot of trouble. Even with the decent health insurance she'd had through her job as a nursing assistant, the deductible and out-of-pocket expenses were shockingly high. Besides, she'd had to quit her job since she wasn't physically capable of performing it. Just like that, we were down to a one-income household.

But this was what I was good at: being the person in our family who could figure things out. It was Ali's cousin who'd given me the idea. She had worked at Chicky's and often bragged about how much she made in tips even though she only worked a couple of nights a week.

Still, I was not Chicky's Girl material.

Then I learned how much Mama's medications would be each month.

After a little liquid courage, I went online and applied. The application required a photo and after some debate (and more wine), I found a photo of me in a bathing suit from college. It wasn't entirely accurate. I'd gained a little bit since then but I'd never been thin to begin with.

Granny, when she was alive, used to say I was "pleasantly plump with junk in the trunk and girls in the front." It always made me laugh. I wasn't petite, that was for sure. My pants said size 16 or 18 and I felt comfortable in them. That's all that mattered to me.

I didn't expect a callback for an interview. But when it came, I pieced together an outfit, then forced myself into the car. By the time I pulled into the Chicky's parking lot, I'd convinced myself this was the right thing to do. Until I sat down across from Shane Sullivan.

He was the worst.

That was apparent right from the beginning when all his interview questions were directed to my chest. Halfway through, he made me try on the uniform—Daisy Duke cutoffs and tiny gingham shirt that buttoned (barely) and tied far above the waist. I felt naked.

"'Course, you're a little thicker than most the other girls, but I think you'll work out." He leered. He was leering. My skin crawled.

I was two seconds away from launching into my rant about the size of an average American woman, and how the media had so distorted our expectations that anything bigger than a size 4 was plus-sized, and exactly where he could take his stupid comments and creepy staring and his ridiculous job.

But I needed the job and it wouldn't be good to tip my hand about my propensity to share my opinions. He'd figure that out in time.

I'd been working here every Friday, Saturday, and Sunday evening for three months now and still I had to talk myself into walking into the building every single time. But I reminded myself that the tips I made over the weekend would cover all of Mama's therapy this next week and a little toward the medical debt. Mama was worth it.

"Just a heads-up," Amanda, a Chicky's veteran server, said. "There's a bachelor party tonight."

I groaned. I'd like to say the customers of this fine establishment where of a discriminating variety, but they weren't. While we did occasionally have families come in, most customers seemed to be slight variations of Shane. But the bachelor parties were the worst. Aside from being loud, they had the nasty habit of getting a little touchy-feely. On top of that, they never left decent tips. All work and no reward.

"Let me guess? It's one of my tables?" I began reciting another pep talk in my head. The one where I convince myself that someday I'll look back on this experience fondly.

Amanda patted my back in sympathy. "Maybe they won't be idiots."

They were idiots.

Most of them had clearly been drinking well before they'd even arrived. The groom was wearing one of those stupid hats with the built-in drink holders and straws, which he thought was hilarious, and he refused to drink any other way. Another man insisted on making a speech for each new round. He'd blather on and make everyone in their vicinity cheer for the "dude getting married."

"Hey, Saaamantha," the drunk guy at the end of the table yelled at me, waving his arm.

It should be noted I played a game with myself when I worked at Chicky's. I imagined I was a character in a novel. Her name was Samantha (as my nametag read), and she was a shameless flirt. Samantha had started out a shy, innocent country girl until I realized shameless flirts made better tips.

"Hiya," I said, laying on the Southern drawl a little thick. Because better tips. "What can I do for you, handsome?"

He crooked a finger. "Come here."

Tucking an empty drink tray under my arm, I leaned down. "Yes?"

"Little closer, babe."

Babe. Ugh. I bent closer, until I was only a few inches from his face. His breath was hot and rancid with alcohol. I bit back the strong desire to gag.

Samantha plastered on a smile; inside, Maebell seethed.

"I just wanted to put this"—he held up a folded piece of paper—"right here." With a wink, he tucked it in the back pocket of my shorts and gave my backside a squeeze.

I froze. Samantha shook her head and stepped aside for Maebell.

"You did not just do that," I said, my voice quiet.

His grin was sloppy. "Call me."

"What should I call you?" I straightened, gripping the tray in my hand with all the rage in my body. Which was a lot at this point. I hated this job.

I hated a lot of things lately.

He tried to wink but it looked like he was having a seizure instead. "You can call me anything you want, babe."

"How about jackass?" I said sweetly. The next thing that happened was completely not my fault. I was trying to get away, honest. Could I help it if his head got in the way of the tray?

Shane didn't see it that way either.

"Mae, this is the third customer who's complained about you this month," he said when he cornered me at the end of my shift. To my chest. My height plus these stupid high-heeled boots put me a good six inches taller than him. But that didn't have anything to do with it. He was just a pig. A short pig. A short pig with all the power.

"So, I'm improving?" The month before I'd had twice as many complaints.

"Look, if this happens again, I'm going to have to let you go."

My heart thumped against my rib cage. I couldn't lose this job. "I'll do better."

For once, he met my eyes. "I'm serious. I can't have this. We have a reputation to uphold here at Chicky's."

"Got it. I'll be on my best behavior."

As he walked away, I fantasized about putting a pig in his office. Just for fun.

FIVE

Do you like raisins? How about a date?

—ADLIR A.

"Where were you last night?" I asked Iris on Wednesday morning as I brushed my teeth at the bathroom sink. Which she ignored when she barged in and announced she was taking a shower.

One day, I will live in a house with two bathrooms and no Iris.

She shrugged. "Out."

It had been after midnight again before she'd slunk into the house. I know because I couldn't sleep until I knew she was home.

"With who?"

"With whom."

"What?"

"It's 'with whom'?" She flipped on the water and started to disrobe. The mirror began to steam up immediately.

"Are you correcting my grammar?"

Grinning, she hopped into the shower. Without her gothy makeup, she looked young and approachable. "I am getting an A in English, you know."

"That's great. More time to focus on passing math now. Have you gone in for tutoring? You can't fail that class."

"Sure thing," she yelled over the water.

Right. Like I believed that.

"Don't forget Mom has that appointment this afternoon," I shouted, slathering on SPF moisturizer. Curse of the redhead—the pale, freckled skin of my people was prone to baking in the sun.

Her head appeared around the shower curtain. She saluted me. "Yes, ma'am. I'm on it. Don't worry about a thing."

"You don't have to be so sarcastic about it," I snapped and pulled my hair into a quick ponytail.

"Well, you don't have to be so bitchy about it."

I narrowed my eyes. Wisely, her head disappeared behind the shower curtain.

When I got to work, the mail was already waiting. To keep Mama from dealing with the stress, I'd had all the bills sent here so she wouldn't see them. I cringed at the latest bill from Mama's neurologist, the amount of which was enough to weigh my soul down.

Stomach twisting, I made a mental note to call and make payment arrangements. I already had similar arrangements with four other medical establishments. At this rate, I would be the only eighty-year-old woman working at Chicky's. "Hold my dentures" didn't seem like a great way to make tips either.

Last night, I'd laid in bed long after Iris got home and fretted over how I was going to make this all work. It was when I did my best planning. At night, when I should be sleeping. I liked plans. I liked to know what was going to happen or what I needed to do or how I was going to get there. And I didn't like to veer from my plans. They were a lifeline to me. Without them, everything felt like chaos.

At the library, I booted up the computers and unlocked the door at 9:30 a.m. on the dot. There was no great rush of patrons but at eleven, the little ones started arriving with their parents in tow for story time.

"Mae-Mae." A little girl of four with dark hair threw herself at my legs and hugged me.

"Lily, how are you, my friend?"

She seemed to contemplate her answer. "It's been a good day so far. I got pancakes for breakfast."

"Pancakes are the perfect way to start the day." I directed her to the table where I'd laid out coloring pages and crayons. "Why don't you go color? We'll start story time soon."

Her mom, Tonya, gave me a weary smile as she bounced a sleeping infant in the sling on her chest.

"How's the little one?" I asked, gazing at the tiny six-week-old peeking out. My chest ached at the sight of the downy blond cap of hair and rosebud mouth. One of these days, I wanted one of those. I just wasn't sure I wanted the man that I'd need to get one.

"I'm exhausted. So, so tired," she said, looking on the edge of tears. She forced a smile. "I mean, it's great."

Or I could just watch babies from afar. Be the cool aunt. Did vampires reproduce? I'd have to ask Iris.

I escorted Tonya to the rocking chair I kept for just such visitors. She sat down with a sigh. At 11:30 on the dot, I clapped my hands and the kids raced to the magic reading carpet.

We started with a rousing rendition of "Wheels On The

Bus" before moving on to "Five Little Speckled Frogs." It was during the "Name Game Song" I noticed the new presence in the room: Chris Sterns.

I stumbled over little MacKenzie's name when I saw him take a tiny kid-sized chair, plunk it behind the children and take a seat. He looked ridiculous, his knees practically touching his chin. I frowned; he grinned.

A few of the moms glanced over at him, probably attracted by the godlike pheromones he naturally secreted. Not that I had noticed. One gasped and slapped the woman next to her. Another ripped out the hair tie securing her messy bun, ran her fingers through her hair and rummaged through her purse to find a tube of lipstick, all while bouncing a baby on her knee.

I cleared my throat and moved on to the final song in our repertoire, "Old MacDonald Had A Farm." The kids wiggled with excitement as I pulled a small box from under my chair.

"Old MacDonald had a farm. E-I-E-I-O," they sang cheerfully off-key. "And on that farm, he had a..."

They bounced with anticipation as I reached inside the box and brought out a puppet at random.

"CAT!" the kids screamed. "With a meow, meow here, and a meow, meow there..."

When we finished that verse, I tossed the puppet to a small boy with bright-red hair in the front row. He squeezed it to his chest like it was the best gift he'd ever received. His little face melted some of my bad mood.

The second verse started without pause except now a warm baritone joined in from the back. Chris grinned when I glanced his way, just as excited as the kids when the next puppet I drew was a horse. On the final verse, I tossed out the last animal to a little girl in the front row and situated myself to read our book.

"Where's my aminal?" Lily said, her eyes welling with tears. "I didn't get an aminal."

"Oh, honey," I said. "I'm so sorry. It looks like we ran out."

She climbed to her feet. "But I didn't get one."

I knew we were about 2.4 seconds away from full-on meltdown.

"Do you want to help me turn the pages?" I asked.

She shook her head. "I want my mommy."

But one look at her mother, Tonya, proved that might be tricky. She'd fallen asleep, mouth slightly open. And was that drool? Houston, we have a problem.

"You can sit with me," Chris said. He scooted off the ridiculously tiny chair to the ground and patted the spot next to him. "I didn't get an animal either. I'm kind of sad too."

Lily, clearly under the Chris Sterns spell, promptly smiled and sat right next to him. By the end of story time, she was leaning on his knee and giggling like they were best friends.

This day had taken a strange turn.

After, several of the moms got photos with Chris and Tonya finally woke up. I was helping the last of the children check out their book selections when the library door was wrenched open.

Peter Stone stormed up to the circulation desk. "I need a word."

Ignoring him, I leaned over to speak to Mariah, a tiny girl who'd just placed a stack of books on the counter. "I'm so sorry. This mean man jumped right in front of you, didn't he?"

Mariah frowned. "Mommy says people who cut in line are rude and have to go to the timeout corner."

Peter looked down at the girl. "Yes, well, I'm very busy. Do you mind if I step in front of you and speak to Mae?"

"I'm busy too. I gots to check out these books and then go home and eat lunch." She patted her stack of books.

Biting back a smile, I glanced away, my eye catching on the man sitting over by the magazines. Chris Sterns had been in that very spot for over an hour, deeply engrossed in a paperback. But the real-life drama unfolding before us seemed to have caught his attention.

Peter cleared his throat. "Sometimes we have to make exceptions to rules, especially when important issues arise."

Self-important jackass. Even when we dated, he'd always given the impression we should all be grateful to be in his presence. What had I been thinking? Two years wasted on him.

Mariah put a hand on her hip. "But I got library books. That's the most importantest."

Peter crouched down to her eye level. "Look. This is city business. I'll only be a minute. You can be patient for a minute, right?"

She scowled.

I coughed to cover up a laugh. "What important city business did you need to take care of?"

"What is this?" He pulled a folded-up paper from his pocket and slammed it on the counter.

I didn't need to pick it up to know what it was. "Due to recent budget cuts, I'm afraid I've had to call in all the outstanding fines."

It should be noted that I forgave 99.9% of the fines. But Peter? He was the 0.01% who I planned to hold to the fire. Passive-aggressive? Yes. Then again, I was dealing with the pettiest man to walk this earth.

Also, I think Ali was rubbing off on me.

His eyes narrowed. "Really? Two hundred and thirty-seven dollars and twenty-five cents' worth of library fines?"

I turned to the computer and pulled up his account. "It looks like you checked out a book thirteen years ago and haven't returned it. At five cents a day, that adds up."

"What book?"

"It says here it's called *The Dummy's Guide to Manscaping.* Does that sound familiar?"

"What's manscaping?" Mariah asked, her expression puzzled.

I patted her head. "Ask your mommy later. Tell her you heard Mayor Stone talking about it."

Splotchy patches of red overtook Peter's face. "That is ridiculous."

"The fine amount or the book title?"

He snatched the paper off the counter. "This whole situation. Don't think I don't know what you're doing."

"My job." I crossed my arms and kept my voice steady. "That's what I'm doing."

"Don't get too comfortable with your job." He jabbed a finger in my direction, and I showed an amazing amount of restraint by not grabbing it and twisting. "Things are changing around this town. Just wait."

"What does that mean?"

"You'll see." With that, he spun on his heels and sailed right out the door.

"My mommy really needs to talk to his mommy," Mariah said.

"Seriously," I muttered.

Later, after most of the kids cleared out, Chris ambled up to the front desk.

"*The Dummy's Guide to Manscaping*?" he asked by way of greeting. "I'm impressed."

"I have no idea what you're talking about."

"Sure." With a grin, he plopped a small bag from the local bookstore on the counter. "This is for you."

I poked it with a pen. "Is something gonna bite me when I open it?"

"Are you always this mistrusting?"

"Yes." I pulled the bag toward me and peeked inside. "I thought you were joking."

"I never joke," he said with a voice that indicated the exact opposite.

Warily, I pulled out the paperback from the bag. On the cover was a scantily clad woman in the arms of an even more scantily clad man. A pirate specifically. The title emblazed across the front read *The Pirate's Booty*.

Hastily, I flipped the book over to hide the cover. "Um... I don't know what to say."

"The reviews are good. I've already read the first two chapters, so you better catch up."

With a deep breath, I pushed the book toward him. "No."

His brow creased in confusion. Maybe he wasn't used to not getting his way.

"I appreciate the offer, but I'm going to have to pass."

With that, I turned away and began typing aimless questions into the search bar on my computer—Do bearcats really smell like popcorn? (yes), Is *Die Hard* a Christmas movie? (no), How tall is Chris Sterns? (6'5", *holy freaking cow*) while I waited for him to take the hint.

He did not take the hint. "Come on, think about it. It could be fun."

"Why?"

"Why what?"

"Why in the world would you want to start a book club..." I leaned closer to whisper. "A romance book club, no less, with a person you hardly know?"

A frown tugged at his mouth. "Well, I like to read, and I like you."

"You don't even know me." I rolled my eyes. "I could have the bodies of the last three people who asked me to be in a book club buried in my backyard."

One side of his mouth kicked up in amusement. "Do you?"

"Would I tell you if I did? No, because we are not friends. Especially not friends who share where the bodies are buried."

"Aren't you the librarian of this fine establishment?"

Glaring, I crossed my arms.

"And isn't the primary goal of a librarian to encourage literacy?"

I huffed in reply.

"And," he continued with conviction, "wouldn't a book club do exactly that? You'd be encouraging me to read. You'd be expanding my mind."

"You are full of crap," I said.

A grin slid across his face. "Fine. The real reason? You haven't cared at all about who I am. It's kind of nice. You remind me of my sisters."

I cocked an eyebrow. "You read romance novels with your sisters?"

"*They* read them. I never have. But it seems like a good way to get to know a new friend."

"A new friend?" I had no time for *new* friends. Ali was about all I could handle after Iris and Mama.

"I'm an excellent friend to have. Would you like references?" He pulled his phone out and started scrolling through his phone book. "Here's Sherrod. Great guy. He's on the team with me. I could call him. Or Phillip Monaghan. Been one of my best friends since fourth grade when he dared me to lick a slug and I did it. I've helped him out the last two times he moved. I'm the kind of friend who helps you move. There aren't many of us."

"Okay, I get it." I nibbled my bottom lip and looked down at the book. The sexy pirate romance book. Then I studied his face. With the shaggy hair and the hopeful, determined smile, he had an almost boyish quality. A very stubborn, irritating boyish quality.

"You aren't going to leave me alone until I agree to this, are you?"

He rocked back on his heels. "Nope."

I sighed. "Fine."

"Excellent." He held his hand out to shake on it. I slid my palm across his and something terrible happened. A tingle started at my fingertips and went right up my arm. Like a jolt. I pulled my hand back and stared at it.

If he'd felt it, he didn't react at all. "I'm glad you came around to my way of thinking."

"I have a rule," I said quickly.

"Go ahead."

I cleared my throat. "No one needs to know about this book club, okay?"

Most people knew me as practical, no-nonsense Mae Sampson. I suspected they all saw me as a "serious" fiction reader, not wasting my time daydreaming about sexy pirates on the open seas. But I did.

Still, I kept it a secret from everyone, almost embarrassed by my love of romance. It wasn't the kissing (and the other, ahem, stuff) that drew me to a good romance. It was that romances were, in the end, about hope. Even when it seemed impossible. Despite having seen love destroy my mom bit by bit, I guess I still believed in that hope.

"Understood," he said solemnly, but the corners of his eyes crinkled in amusement. He turned to leave but when he got to the door, he snapped his fingers and jogged back. "So, can I have your number?"

"Was that a pickup line?" My eyebrow arched. "I expected better from God's gift to women."

He preened. "I think dreamboat is more appropriate, don't you?"

"I'm guessing you did not get the Humbleness badge."

He laughed. "And that was not a pickup line. You'll know when it's a pickup line. Give me your phone."

Against my better judgement, I tugged my phone from my back pocket, unlocked it and handed it over. With a wicked little grin, he began typing.

"This is my number. I texted myself. If we're going to be book club friends, we have to be able to talk about the book, right?" He handed the phone back. "Now, get reading. You're already behind."

SIX

Are you made of ice cream? Because you bring "sun" to my "dae."

—HOLLY JO E.

A week later, Mama and I were watching *Wheel of Fortune.* Or she was watching. I was deeply engrossed in a sexy pirate romance so that my new book club friend, the superstar football god, and I could discuss it tomorrow at lunch.

My life was getting stranger by the minute.

"What are you reading?" Mama asked at the commercial break.

I tore my eyes from the page with a sigh. I was in the middle of a very swoon-worthy scene. Dang it. Holding up the paperback I'd wrapped in a book cover, I said, "A memoir."

"Your cheeks look awfully red. It must be good reading."

Not quite looking her in the eye, I tucked it in between the sofa arm and my body. "How was therapy today?"

"It went so well. Guess what?"

"What?"

"I buttoned an entire shirt on my own. I swear it took me longer than a one-legged man in a three-legged race to finish, but I did it." She grinned her sweet, lopsided grin.

"That's wonderful," I said, feeling a tightness in my throat that I swallowed down.

Mama's blue eyes settled on my face. "I wanted to talk to you about something."

"Alright." I turned toward her, tucking a foot underneath me. "This sounds official."

"You've always been such a big support for your sister, and now with..." She waved a hand down her body.

"I want to help."

"Oh, I know you do. It's how you were made. Never had to worry about you making poor choices or acting first before thinking things through."

To be fair, I'd never much had a chance to rebel.

She patted my leg. "You were like that when you were little, too. I think you had more sense than me when you were five. Never caused a second of trouble."

I tilted my head, trying to figure out exactly where this conversation was headed.

"I've never had to worry about you wandering off to go find yourself or getting in trouble like your father." She spit out the last word like it was spoiled milk and pressed her lips together until they turned white around the edges.

Ah, my father. There wasn't anyone I wanted to talk about less. When you're a kid and don't know any better, your parents are the focus of your whole world, the sun, the moon, the stars, the smartest, bravest people you know. But my father had shown me who he really was when I was young, and by the time I turned ten I'd lost all respect for him. He'd only spent the ensuing years making it worse.

It was hard enough having a criminal for a father, especially one who landed himself in trouble so often. But the truth was he was a terrible criminal.

One time, he'd been arrested after trying to rob a convenience store. While using a zucchini as a gun. When asked why he went with a vegetable, he said he didn't have a concealed carry permit. Another time, he'd broken into a house, fixed himself something to eat, rummaged through everyone's belongings and then fallen asleep in a bed. Like Goldilocks, except the three bears had called the police when they'd got home.

But his real claim to fame were the cons he ran. With his boy-next-door looks, warm smile, and natural charm, people gravitated toward him. Worse, they trusted him. He took full advantage of that. Robbing old ladies of their savings with fake stories about helping them invest in an "exciting opportunity." Convincing investors he'd discovered hidden treasure if only he had the equipment to dig it out. Selling the latest fad from companies with very pyramid-shaped business plans. Backroom poker games, betting rings, you name it, he'd at least tried it. Despite his track record, he never could stop himself from targeting what he called an "easy mark."

The gas stations, elderly couples, and vegetables of the world weren't safe when he was around.

"But Iris," Mama said, cutting into my thoughts, "she's different from you. She always was a Daddy's girl."

Which was ironic since she'd probably only spent a handful of weeks in his presence. In the early days, after we moved to Two Harts, he'd show up every now and then, con Mama into letting him back in the house, spend just enough time getting Iris's hopes up that he'd stay, then just as quickly disappear.

Come to think of it, maybe that's exactly why she was a Daddy's girl. She'd missed out on the years on the road, moving from hotel room to shabby apartment. When she was just a few months old, Mama had brought us to Two Harts, and we'd moved in with Granny. It was the first time I'd had a home for longer than six months and it was the only home Iris had ever known.

"I worry about her," Mama went on. "I don't know if she's ready to be out in the world on her own."

"Iris will be fine," I said with more confidence than I felt. But I would just have to make it so. Maybe I could put a tracking device in her lip ring?

"She will, eventually. But Iris has always been one who needs to see for herself instead of listening to what everyone else tells her." Mama rested a hand on my knee. "She said she wants Dad to come to her graduation."

I sucked in a breath.

"You and I, we cover for him. We always have. But it's time she sees him for who he is." She paused, eyes narrowing. "I can't say he was a mistake because he gave me you and Iris, but I could go the rest of my life never seeing his face."

"Me too," I grumbled.

"This is important to Iris."

"Do we even know where he is?"

"He calls every now and then, to check up on you girls." Her cheeks reddened. "And me too."

"Mama."

She held up a hand, her voice firm. "I'm not interested. Trust me. Been there, done that, didn't even get the t-shirt. This is for Iris."

I hesitated. This was all new information. I liked to mull things over before weighing in. "Are you sure that's a good idea?"

"I don't want her to resent me because she thinks I kept her from him." Mama heaved a sigh. "But I don't want you to resent me either."

"I won't," I said quickly. But maybe that was a lie.

She held up a slip of paper, "I think you should call him."

"Me? Why?"

"I've already called and left a message. Iris, too. We aren't getting a response. I think it would be good if you tried."

"Mama," I sighed.

She picked up my hand, placed the slip of paper in the palm and wrapped my fingers around it. "Please. For Iris."

With a shake of my head, I stood and stalked to my bedroom, a sour taste in my mouth. I threw myself on my bed and screamed into my pillow like I used to when I was a teenager. This was not how I imagined my life as an adult. Yet here I was. In my bedroom angry with my father and worried about how the next bill would be paid.

I turned my head to the side and Kevin glared from the pillow beside me.

"Sorry to disturb you," I muttered.

His ear, the one with the notch in it from some cat equivalent of a bar fight, twitched. He stood and rearranged himself so his butt was in my face.

"Such a gentleman. Thank you."

My cell phone buzzed with a text notification.

Dreamboat: *Did you fall from Heaven? 'Cause I think you're an angel.*

It had been a week since Chris had first texted. It had taken me a minute to figure who Dreamboat was and why he was sending me random cheesy pickup lines. If I were being honest, his texts were becoming something I sort of looked forward to. Not that I would ever admit that to him or anyone else.

Me: *Were you born on a highway? I hear that's where most accidents happen.*

Dreamboat: *You are savage.*

Me: *Thank you.*

Dreamboat: *We're still having book club meeting tomorrow at lunch, right?*

Dreamboat: *I'm on chapter 10 and I have questions.*

Dreamboat: *That thing they did in chapter 9 on the plank. Is that even physically possible?*

Me: *Maybe you don't have a good enough imagination.*

I almost threw the phone across the room when it rang.

"Excuse me, I have a great imagination," Chris said as a greeting. "I was even voted Most Imaginative in high school."

"Your parents must have been so proud."

"I'll prove it to you. I'm imagining what you're doing right now."

I rolled my eyes. "I'm talking to you, dummy."

"Shut up. I'm imagining here." He had a nice voice, deep but smooth. "Yes, I see it. You're on your bed and there's a cat."

I sat up. That was a little creepy. "Why a cat?"

"Because you are definitely a cat person," he said with certainty.

"Why does that sound like an insult?"

He chuckled. "It's not. Cat people are discerning. They're very selective in who they choose to hang with. You never want to mess with a cat person. They might seem quiet, but you never can tell what they're thinking. For instance, you could be planning my murder right now."

"Keep that in mind, Sterns. Let me guess, you're a dog person?"

"I think that's obvious. For one, I'm adorable. I'm willing to do a lot of things for food and I'm very loyal."

"Don't forget you both like to play with balls."

His laughter was immediate and warm. Long after I hung up and crawled into bed, I could still hear it.

SEVEN

One actually great one I overheard at pirate day at the Renaissance Festival:

> *"Damn, milady, you're putting the curvy in scurvy."*

—@INFIELDFLYGRL

"You cannot be serious." I stared down at the new proposed budget Peter had slid across his desk.

He leaned forward in his ridiculous oversized leather chair and steepled his fingers under his chin like he was the freaking Godfather. "I think you'll find we've been fair."

"Fair? You want to cut the library to twenty-five hours a week." Which was also reflected in my new proposed salary.

"Do we really need it to be open more than that?" He took a sip from the coffee mug on his desk which read WORLD'S BEST BOSS. He'd probably bought it for himself.

I was momentarily stunned into silence. Don't worry. It didn't last long. "Plus cutting my book budget by half?"

He frowned and ran a finger over his soul patch. No one should wear a soul patch, least of all a man-child with a weak chin. If I could go back to the day when I decided Peter was the man for me, I would kick my own ass for being infatuated with this guy.

"Maebell, everyone has to give a little." He directed my attention to the oversized, full-color blueprint for the high school football stadium he had on an easel beside his desk. "This football stadium will put our little town on the map."

I hated him and his stupid stadium.

"You cannot cut my budget." I crossed my arms. "This is asking too much. Especially after last year."

"Look, everyone is chipping in. The police department is willing to cut back on overtime."

"I feel safer already."

He scowled. "The city maintenance department has come up with some cost-saving measures."

"Great. I bet it will take twice as long to get a light bulb replaced now. Is the city going to cut back on drinking water, too? I mean, who really needs to stay hydrated? That's junk science."

"Are you done?" he snapped.

I smiled. At least I'd gotten under his skin.

"Not by a long shot." I stood and snatched his idiotic budget proposal from the desk.

"It's pretty much a done deal. City council will vote on it in eight weeks."

I leaned over his desk and was pleasantly surprised to see him shrink back in his seat. "I guess I have eight weeks to figure out how I'm going to make sure this doesn't happen."

Then I dumped the entire contents of his coffee mug on his lap.

"He didn't," Ali said with a justifiable amount of outrage. "I hate him."

"Thank you," I said into the phone. "I don't know what I'm going to do if the library hours get cut."

I'd gone straight back to the library after my meeting with Peter, fuming mad. But as the anger had worn off, it had been replaced with overwhelming anxiety. The kind that had forced me to sit down and take slow steady breaths. It hadn't worked; I still felt like either throwing up or throwing something.

"I know a guy who can help me get my hands on an ostrich," Ali offered. "We could put it in his office and, you know, let it play out."

"That's very kind of you, but I'll pass." I hesitated, picturing a terrified Peter cowering under an evil-eyed ostrich. The scene had real merit. "Who exactly is this guy? No, never mind."

"You're going to figure it out," Ali said, her voice sure.

I appreciated the vote of confidence, but sometimes I wished people didn't think I was so competent. It would be nice, just once, for someone else to swoop in and solve my problems.

"Yeah, I'll figure it out. Somehow."

The library door burst open, and Chris Dreamboat Sterns was suddenly standing in front of me.

He was very... sweaty. That should be very unattractive. It was not. Neither was the fact he was wearing one of those shirts with the sleeves cut off at the shoulders that looked stupid on mortal men. On him, it highlighted the muscles in his arms. There were a lot of them, and I noticed. I promised to have a long introspective discussion with myself about this later.

"Ali, I have to go," I said, my voice sounding almost breathless. With a scowl, I hung up and crossed my arms. "Did you run all the way here? You know they have cars for that."

He shrugged and leaned an elbow on the counter, his bicep bulging. "It's only four miles."

"Only four? Light day for you, I guess."

"Yup. But it's off-season; I can go a little easy." He tapped the belt bag at his waist. "I brought the book too. Where are we sitting?"

"Come on then." I put the OUT TO LUNCH sign on the front door and directed him to my small office/break room/copy room. He sat down at the table there while I pulled out the lunches I'd picked up from the Sit-n-Eat on my way back from seeing He-Who-Must-Not-Be-Named. Peter's smug face popped into my brain. I slammed the to-go boxes on the table and threw myself in a chair across from Chris.

"You doing okay?"

"I'm fine." But I wasn't fine; I was angry.

"You don't seem like you're fine." He opened the Styrofoam container in front of him. Ollie outsourced to Juana Fernandez who made the best tamales this side of the border for Tamale Thursday. "Wow."

"I got you a double serving," I said, my eyes drifting to his arms. "Because you're big."

He almost smirked but seemed to change his mind when he saw my face. "You sure you're okay? You seem grumpy."

I arched an eyebrow.

"Grumpier than usual," he amended and dug into his tamales with relish.

"It's nothing." I poked at my lunch. "Maybe you're too dang happy. Like a puppy."

He brushed the top of my hand, which was resting on the table. Such a small touch but my skin grew warm right in that very spot. "If you need someone to talk to, I have four sisters. I'm pretty good at listening, I won't ever tell you to calm down—I learned that lesson the hard way, and I can kick someone's ass if you need me to, no questions asked."

The kindness in his voice gave me pause. Sometimes it was easier to wallow in anger. Anger had done well for me—kept me fight-ready and that helped me survive. But it was also so exhausting. Which was the last thought I had before I opened my mouth and blurted it all out.

"Fine," I huffed. "Your good friend Peter—"

Chris shook his head. "Don't lump me in with him. I went to college with the guy. We're barely acquaintances."

"Fine. Your *not-friend* Peter has informed me that he plans to cut the library budget yet again. If he succeeds, it will affect my salary and decimate our book budget among many other things." I picked up my straw, tore the wrapping off like it was one of Peter's limbs, and shoved it in my cup. "That man is the absolute worst."

"Is there anything I can do to help?"

"No, it's my problem. I'll fix it," I said firmly and pushed around the rice on my plate. "But thanks. For, you know..."

My voice trailed off, not exactly sure what I wanted to say, but strangely grateful he was here.

"No problem. Now, this book. I have questions." From his belt bag he pulled out our sexy pirate romance novel. Sticky notes dotted the edges and the cover looked used and abused.

I tugged it from his hand and flipped through the pages. "You highlighted? You took notes in the margins?"

"I even committed most of chapter ten to memory."

I flipped to the chapter and discovered a scene that left very little to the imagination. With a huff, I tossed the book on the table. Chris picked it up and began thumbing through it. My eyes moved back to his arms. His muscles tensed with each motion he made. I had a strange desire to touch them, just to see what they felt like. Were they warm? Would they give under my hands?

I bit back a groan. Completely and totally inappropriate. I needed to get more sleep. That must be the reason for all this.

"You okay? You look like you're a little warm," Chris asked, sounding concerned.

Mortified, I jerked my eyes back to his face. "Sorry. I was lost in thought."

"About?"

"Ah, octopuses." Smooth, Mae. Smooth.

"Octopuses?"

"Yep. Lot of tentacles. Think they get in the way sometimes?" I didn't let him answer that because I sounded like an idiot, and inside I was panicking a little and I wasn't quite sure why. I snatched my copy of the book from my desk. "I have thirty more minutes left of lunch; we should probably..."

"Of course." He cracked open his book. "Now, after reading the first ten chapters, I had a question. Do you think the character of the first mate is the author's commentary on the struggle of the everyday man in the early nineteenth century?"

I blinked. Twice.

"And can we talk about chapter fourteen? Doing the deed in a crow's nest? Sounds kind of uncomfortable. At the very least, there'd be a whole lot of splinters in places you do not want splinters. What are your thoughts?"

EIGHT

If you were an open fire and I wanted to cook over you, so I had to adjust the grate to the right height and do the hand test and see how hot it was, I would only be able to hold my hand there for one or two seconds.

—BRET AND KRYSTALYNN B.

Dreamboat: *Hey, babe, what's on your mind?*

Me: *Very, very naughty thoughts.*

Dreamboat: *Really? Like what?*

Me: *Like where I can hide a body so no one can EVER find it.*

Dreamboat: *Wait. Am I the body?*

With a snort, I stuck my phone in my locker and stared at myself in the tiny mirror hanging there. It was Saturday and another shift at Chicky's. Time to give myself one last pep talk.

"You are going to be charming and helpful. You aren't going to worry about money or Mama, or if Iris is thinking about joining a cult. You're going to focus on the task at hand. You are not going to hit anyone, even by accident."

"Are you talking to yourself again?" Amanda asked, suddenly beside me.

I blushed. "Let's pretend you didn't hear that."

"Not a problem."

I liked Amanda. She was, like a lot of the women who worked here, just trying to get by. Her deadbeat ex-husband could not be counted on. Which meant she'd had to find a way to take care of her kids. She'd been at Chicky's for over two years. How she'd managed to never whack a customer over the head with the nearest heavy object, I'd never know. I guessed she probably made better tips than me.

Amanda opened her locker and grabbed a tube of lipstick from the shelf. "If you haven't heard, there's some bigwig coming in tonight."

I groaned. We didn't get celebrities often but, when we did, it amped up my anxiety tenfold, along with everyone else in the restaurant. "Who?"

"I have no idea. But Shane is having heart palpitations over it." She smacked her newly painted lips together.

"Poor Shane," I muttered, closing my locker.

"Don't worry, he'll put Heather on their table."

"Of course." Heather was the perfect Chicky's Girl. Perky, looked great in virtually no clothes, never complained about the handsy patrons, and kissed Shane's butt like she was permanently attached to it. It also meant she was given the "special" tables when the need arose. Sure, these tables almost always came with better tips, but they made you work for it. I just wanted to lay low, do my job, and get out of here.

The evening rush hit hard. It seemed like every man with too much time on his hands had wandered into Chicky's for hot wings and to watch an inning or two of the Astros' double-header. I preferred it like this. It made the evening fly by. My autopilot switch flipped on and that kept me from thinking too much.

My tables kept me too busy to even think about our esteemed visitor. Snippets of excited whispers here and there made it to me, but I didn't have time to piece them together. I was waiting on an order by the kitchen window when Heather popped up next to me, her soft brown eyes and slightly vacuous smile on full display.

"Would you mind helping me getting these out?" she asked, pointing to the line of plates under the warming lamps. "It's a *special* table and I want to make sure everyone gets their meals at once."

Special table, pu-lease. At least I would get to see what all the chatter was.

"Sure, lead the way." I grabbed a folding table, tucked it under my arm and balanced three plates.

If I hadn't been trying to be as careful as possible, I might have gotten a clue sooner. Maybe I would have noticed the guy at the end of the table.

But I didn't.

Not until right about the time he noticed me.

Chris Sterns was in the building.

NINE

First job asking clients at my work, "Do you want any cream or sugar with your coffee?" One guy answered, "No, just put your pinky in it and swirl it around. That'd be sweet enough for me." Eighteen-year-old me was swooned off my feet with that line.

He's now been making me coffee for forty-two years.

—LIZA C.

I froze. Like a deer in headlights, if deer wore pigtails and the headlights were twinkly brown eyes.

Chris's gaze moved over me. I sucked in my stomach in some vain attempt to fold into myself and become invisible. Then he glanced away. Maybe that worked? After all, I was dressed like Hillbilly Barbie, and he couldn't have been expecting me to be here.

As quickly and quietly as I could, I set up the folding table, keeping one eye on the job at hand and the other on Chris. Four other men and a woman were seated around the table; none of them seemed to notice us servers. At Heather's direction, I slid plates of food in front of two of them and shuffled around the table to serve the last one. It put me closer to Chris. I held my breath.

Don't notice me. Don't make eye contact.

But when I risked a glance, he was staring right at me.

He squinted.

I rocked back on my heels.

He raised an eyebrow.

I shook my head.

He grinned slowly.

Of all the terrible restaurants with half-naked waitresses and he had to come into mine.

My hands started to shake. Unfortunately, I was holding an order of chicken wings. I watched in horror as the plate teetered and the contents slid off, landing on the lap of a middle-aged guy in a gray suit. Then I watched in slow motion as the bowl of Chicky's dipping sauce took the same journey, leaving a blotchy red trail on the man's hair, his face, his white shirt.

He swore loudly.

"Oh, I'm so sorry." I hurriedly set the plate down and snatched a napkin off the table. With a wince, I rubbed at Chicken Wings Guy's head like it was a genie's bottle and I could wish this whole situation away. Yeah, that didn't work.

He batted at my hands and yanked the napkin off his head.

"What the hell? You idiot!" he bellowed, his thin face turning almost purple.

I froze and was shocked to discover the backs of my eyes began to burn. I did not cry, and I would not now.

"This is a two-thousand-dollar suit!" He cursed again, throwing out a few choice words about my mother, my intelligence, my weight, my apparent sexual promiscuity, and my cat. I don't know how he knew I had a cat but no one, *no one*, talked about Kevin like that.

My hands curled into fists. I opened my mouth, not exactly

sure what was about to spill out, only mostly sure it would get me fired.

Before I could, Shane appeared by my elbow. My eyes swung to the side and caught on Chris. He frowned slightly; his head tilted to the side as though he wanted to say something. I shook my head and begged him silently to keep his mouth shut.

"I'm so sorry about this," Shane said. "We'll get you some towels. Please, let me take care of your meal today as an apology." He pinched my elbow and growled through gritted teeth. "It's coming out of your tips. Go get towels. Now."

I snatched up the now empty folding table, ready to make a mad dash for the kitchen or possibly right out the back door to catch a shuttle to a different planet. Could I do that? Volunteer to repopulate Mars, or something? I'd have to research it.

How was this my life?

Chris's voice stopped me. "It was an accident. No need to get angry. Nothing that can't be fixed."

His eyes moved between Chicken Wings Guy and my boss, a friendly smile on his face. But his voice had a firm, no-nonsense quality to it, like he meant business.

"Besides, that was an ugly suit anyway." He grinned. "You did him a favor."

Did he find this funny? This was not funny. This was my life. I glanced down at Chicken Wings Guy just as a glob of sauce dripped down from his hair to his nose and chin. Maybe it was a little funny.

I took a deep breath. "I am sorry. It was absolutely my fault. I'll pay for the dry cleaning."

Chicken Wings Guy opened his mouth, but Chris cut him off. "Nah, I'm sure Douglas understands that these things happen. He'll take care of it but, Doug, you're gonna need something to change into." He swiveled his head around until it landed on the wall of Chicky's merchandise—keychains, license plate holders, shot glasses, mostly stuff with sparkly letters and silhouettes of women in braided pigtails with large front and back carriages. Your run-of-the-mill money-grab merchandise.

Chris smiled widely. "I know exactly what you can do to help us out."

In the next ten minutes, Chris dragged Doug to the bathroom. Shane gave me another hurried speech about getting my act together, and I cleaned up the mess while Heather put in for another order of chicken wings.

My mind raced as I sopped up the barbecue sauce. There was no good way to explain this away to Chris. He may be a football player, but it was becoming very clear he was a *smart* football player.

I pressed a hand to my stomach, overcome by the desire to puke my guts out. How had he managed to learn two secrets about me in such a short time? Secrets I'd worked hard at keeping hidden from every other person in my life.

I stood up from wiping the floor in time to see Chris leading Doug back to the table. Doug was free of chicken wings, sauce, and his fancy gray suit. It had been replaced with a pair of black sweatpants with *Chicky's* sprawled up one leg in sparkly pink letters. It paired well with the pink t-shirt bearing the famous Chicky's silhouette.

A manic laugh bubbled up and I pressed my lips together to stave it off.

Chris shot me a smile. "See? All taken care of."

Doug did not look amused. Doug looked like he wanted to do me great bodily harm.

"I—I'm taking a fifteen-minute break," I said to no one and scrambled into the kitchen. I slumped against the nearest wall. My breath sawed in and out like I'd run a marathon.

"You okay?" one of the cooks asked. "You look like you're gonna be sick."

I pushed off the wall, mumbling something about going to the bathroom. Once inside the ladies' room, I splashed a little water on my face. One of my stupid fake eyelashes was hanging a whole lot lower than the other one. I looked like I was in a permanent state of winking.

"You'll be fine," I said to the mirror. "You made a mistake and yes, Chris Sterns showed up, a-and..." I paused, pulled in a deep breath and steadied my voice. "Shane hasn't fired you yet. Just get back out there and do what you need to do. You got this."

Good plan.

Solid plan.

With a renewed sense of confidence, I pulled open the door and there he was. Waiting. For me.

Fine. New plan. Without stopping, I grabbed Chris's hand and yanked him down the hall to the only place we could have a chance of privacy—the supply closet. It was mostly shelves and a small space to store a mop bucket and vacuum. Still, we managed to cram both of us in there, and Chris was a whole lot bigger than a vacuum.

There was just enough room to breathe if he leaned back against the door. I pulled the string dangling down and a weak light snapped on.

I crossed my arms. They brushed against his chest. I uncrossed my arms. What the heck should I do with my arms?

"What are you doing here?" I demanded.

One dark eyebrow rose. "You're asking *me* that?"

I ignored him and plowed ahead. "I was almost starting to respect you. Why would you come to a place like this?"

My mouth said that, but my mind skittered somewhere else. Mostly thinking about how good he smelled. He wasn't encased in a cologne burrito like most of the guys who came in here. It was a clean fragrance, like he'd just gotten out of the shower—and then my brain briefly struck on the idea of Chris Sterns in the shower even though it did not have my permission to go there. I stopped that immediately. These wayward thoughts had no place in my life. It was already crowded enough with jobs and bills and a stupid mayor/ex-boyfriend on a mission to ruin my library. Besides, I was Chris's *sister-friend*. Geez. Get a grip.

He shrugged. "Doug's my agent. He picked it."

"Your agent is a sleaze."

"I know. That's what makes him a good agent," he said. "My turn."

"For what?"

"A question." He frowned. "Where are your glasses?"

"Really? That's the question?"

"I like your glasses. They suit you." His eyes roamed my face then dropped lower. I wanted to cover up the copious amount of cleavage happening down there, but I forced myself not to. "I'm not sure this suits you, at all."

I straightened, feeling almost offended. "Excuse me? I'll have you know I can pull this outfit off just fine."

He smirked. "I don't think I said that."

"You implied it."

Now he crossed his arms, coming dangerously close to the ladies. He muttered something under his breath about four sisters and patience. "Let me try again. Why are you working here? Is this some sort of fantasy you've always had?"

"Yes, I've always dreamed of wearing Daisy Dukes while serving drunk guys overcooked food. I can die happy now. So glad we had this talk."

He rubbed a hand over his chin, his eyes crinkling in the corners with amusement. "Hmm."

"Hmm, what?"

"You should consider wearing this at the library. It could be very popular with a segment of the population who usually aren't big readers—they're more video watchers, if you know what I mean."

"Shut up."

He ignored me. "What about a story hour for adults? Hot wings, beer, you reading a selection of, ahem, adult literature?"

"I'm so glad you find this amusing."

He flicked one of the braids resting on my shoulder. "These are a nice touch. I like them."

"Are you done?"

He rubbed his thumb along his bottom lip like he was deep in thought. "I think so."

"You are the most irritating person I have ever met. Do you know that?"

Judging from his expression, he wasn't bothered by this observation at all. "It's a gift."

I took several deep breaths to curb the anxious rhythm of my heart. Irritating or not, he knew something about me I didn't want anyone else to know.

He sighed and unfurled his arms. Gently, he cupped my shoulders. His voice was soft when he spoke. "Is everything okay?"

I stared up at him, at the concern in his eyes. It was like he could see straight through me, and I was almost overcome by the strangest desire to press my head right against his chest and tell him everything—my mother, the stroke, the medical bills, the library, Iris, my father's possible return. Maybe he'd pull me close and rub my back and tell me it would be okay and that he'd help me figure it all out, and I would believe him.

But the thing is, life didn't work that way. Heroes didn't swoop in out of nowhere and solve your problems. Life wasn't a romance novel. Life was more like a never-ending literary novel. Literary fiction never had happy endings, just real endings.

My eyes dropped to the buttons on his polo. "I'm fine. Just trying to earn a little extra money on the weekends, that's all."

He didn't reply. Instead, he squeezed my shoulders and let go. But I felt the slightest touch on my cheek. It wasn't weird except it was weirdly comforting, and I was shocked to discover tears were forming for the second time that night.

I cleared my throat and met his eyes with resolve. "Can you not tell anyone about this? Please?"

The twinkle was back in his eye and that was good. Turns out Gentle Understanding Chris was on my list of potential downfalls. "It'll be just between us, *Samantha*."

"Thank you. Now, I need to get back to work. So..." I waved a hand to encourage leaving. "Open the door. Let's go. Chop-chop."

With a grin, he rested his hand on the doorknob. "Although, if you wanted to wear that shirt to our next book club meeting, I would not be unhappy about it."

Ignoring his laughter, I marched back to work.

TEN

Quick! Somebody call 9-1-1 'cause you just took my breath away.

—NONIE S.M.

I spent the next few days getting even less sleep than I normally did. On Wednesday, I woke up exhausted, my head aching.

Iris frowned when she saw me. "You look awful. Worse than usual, even."

"I didn't sleep well," I mumbled as I shuffled to the kitchen and the coffee.

"Seriously." Her face scrunched in concern. "Maybe you should stay home."

"I'll be fine." And that's exactly what I kept telling myself as I dressed and dragged myself to the library. But by eleven, the headache had gotten so bad I felt nauseated and sapped of energy. I canceled story time and seriously considered laying in front of the 200s (Religion) and dying.

My phone buzzed.

Dreamboat: *Hey, sweet cheeks, wanna meet up for lunch. Just Me-N-U. Get it. Menu. Me-N-U.*

Me: *Ugh.*

Dreamboat: *That's all you got? I'm disappointed.*

Instead of replying, I buried my face in my arms on the counter. A minute later, the phone rang.

"Why are you calling?"

"I was worried," Chris said. "You didn't insult me. I thought you might be in danger and trying to tell me you needed help."

"Sorry to disappoint you. Just not feeling well."

There was a pause. "You sound terrible."

"Your pickup lines are getting better and better."

"No, really. What's wrong?" he asked, and I could hear the concern in his voice which was kind of nice.

"I think I'm going to go home and crawl under the covers and cry myself to sleep." That sounded like a great plan.

"I never imagined you as a crier," he said. It was weird to think he'd thought about that. Had he thought other things about me? Was I taking up a tiny little space in his brain? If I were honest (with just myself), he was in my head a little too much.

I cleared my throat. "Excuse me, I broke my arm in the sixth grade. I cried."

"Thank God, you are human. I was starting to wonder."

"I'm hanging up now."

"One last thing. Don't die. Funerals are so depressing."

* * *

The house was empty when I got home, a rarity. But Mama had a couple of back-to-back doctor appointments at the medical center in Houston. Then she and Sue were making a day of it with lunch and shopping at the Galleria.

I tracked down some pain reliever and took a hot shower. Kevin kindly made some space for me on my bed, and I was half asleep when a knock on the front door came. I ignored it and snuggled down under the covers, unwilling, and possibly unable, to move. But the knocking continued.

"Go away," I muttered, not that whoever the intruder was could hear me.

They did not go away.

With a dramatic sigh, I wrapped myself in a blanket and stumbled to the front door. I was expecting a delivery guy, a Jehovah's Witness, a guy trying to sell me steaks from his trunk, but nope, it was worse.

"Wow. You do look like you feel bad," Chris said.

"Again, how are these pickup lines working for you?"

He held up a plastic sack. "I brought you soup."

"Soup?"

"Yeah, Ollie sent it over."

"Ollie sent me soup? It's Wednesday. It's not soup day."

It was never soup day.

Chris shrugged. "I guess he likes you."

"How do you even know where I live?" Pulling my blanket tighter, I eyed him skeptically. "Are you stalking me?"

"Yes, I am. The soup is all part of my plan to lull you into a false sense of security."

"Soup is the best you could do?"

"Also, I saw Ali at the café, and she asked me to check on you. She would have done it herself but she, and I'm quoting here, can't stand you when you're sick."

My eyes narrowed. Ali and I would be discussing this later.

"I didn't have anything else to do." He jiggled the bag. "Can I come in?"

"Why?"

"Because you don't feel good, and I brought you soup."

Crossing my arms, I leaned against the doorjamb. "I appreciate the offer but... no."

His smile deflated as he handed over the bag. "I get it. I thought you might want some company, but I understand. Hope you feel better. I'll see you later."

Shoving his hands in his pockets, he turned and headed down the porch steps. Shoulders slumped, he walked slowly, stopping to kick a rock. He looked like he'd discovered someone had stolen his new puppy, his best friend was moving away, and no one remembered his birthday all at once.

"You're pathetic." Without turning around, he shrugged in response. I sighed loudly. "Fine. I guess you can come in."

With a grin, his long legs carried him back to the door. "It works like a charm every time."

Of course it did. "Before I let you in, remember we don't have any filthy rich football players living here. Please adjust your expectations accordingly."

"I see being sick hasn't made you any less sarcastic."

I stepped aside for him to pass and watched him give a cursory look around. Our home was clean but small and stuck firmly in the early 1990s, baby-blue carpet and fake wood paneling included.

Chris took two steps inside and stopped. "This is a lot of rabbits."

He was right; there were a lot of rabbits. Granny didn't do things by half. There were hundreds, lining shelves, tucked into crevices, covering tables. Rabbits were painted on the magazine rack and stenciled around the room as a border. There was framed rabbit art and a footstool Granny had covered in the same rabbit-themed fabric she'd made the curtains in.

"My grandma liked them," I said, my voice a tad defensive.

"I'm not judging. Just observing." He held his hand out. "Give me the soup."

"I'm fine. You don't even know where the kitch—"

"You look like a drowned kitten and about as strong as one. You sit." He pointed to the couch. "I'll get you soup."

I scowled; he scowled right back. But his was scarier. If that's what his opponents saw on game day, I bet they just tossed him the ball and walked off the field. I handed him the soup.

"I can find the kitchen. Sit."

I sat.

When he returned, it was with two bowls of soup and a glass of water. He found the TV trays Granny had used religiously and set one up in front of me.

"Eat up." He stared at me while I took a slurp of soup before he sat and tucked into his meal.

After a long stretch of silence, I set my spoon down. "This is weird."

His forehead wrinkled. "What? Is it the soup? Is it warm enough?"

"No, I mean, it's weird you're here."

He shrugged. "Got nothing better to do."

"Your concern is touching."

"You're welcome." He ate a spoonful of soup, but his eyes were busy taking in the living room, the floral couch and loveseat, TV, coffee table. More rabbits. He picked up one of the throw pillows next to him. It featured bunnies playing baseball. "Rabbits are kind of creepy. If you look at them close enough, they sort of look like giant rats. You know they sleep with their eyes open?"

"I did not." Despite Granny's obsession, we'd never had a pet rabbit. "Let me guess, another Scout badge?"

"Nah." He picked up a framed photo of Granny, Mom and us girls that was sitting on the little table next to the couch. In it, I was about fifteen and sullen and very not-smiling. "Future Farmers of America. I raised rabbits one year."

I hummed and took another spoonful of soup; it was good. I tried to remember if I'd even eaten anything today. Maybe that made it taste even better.

"This is your mom and sister and grandma?" Chris tapped the photo.

"Yes. Granny passed away my last year of college. Cancer. I miss her." I frowned, hearing the sadness in my words. Why in the world was I telling him this?

Chris, perhaps sensing my mood, was polite enough not to offer empty platitudes. "Who is this very angry teenager?"

I tried, and failed, to snatch the photo from his stupidly long arm. "It was a phase."

"You're kind of intense here. I wouldn't have wanted to get on your bad side."

"Thank you. Exactly what I was going for."

Back then, I'd been angry at my father, Mama, life, the world. I bet Chris had been popular and upbeat and came from a nice family which did not include a felon. We would never, in a million years, have been friends.

He stared at the photo a beat longer before putting it down. When I finished my soup, he took our bowls in the kitchen and I heard the water run. Then, "Why is there duct tape on your dishwasher?"

"To keep the door shut, obviously."

He paused at the entrance to the living room, hands on his hips. "That's not how dishwashers work."

"That's how they work here." In a house with three women on a very limited budget, that is. I wasn't completely useless, and I'd tried to fix it after watching forty-three YouTube videos and reading several how-to articles. But I'd run into a problem without having the right tool, and I was worried I'd break something else in the process.

Anyway. The duct tape worked fine, thank you very much.

Chris shook his head and sat back on the couch. "Wanna watch something?"

"I guess?"

He found the remote and started flipping through channels before coming to a stop. "*Gilmore Girls*. This is a good episode, too."

I scoffed. "Oh, right. I'm supposed to believe you watch *Gilmore Girls*."

"I told you, four sisters. They had marathon weekends all the time and I guess I got roped into the story."

I narrowed my eyes. "Okay. Name one character."

"I'll name you two: Luke and Lorelai."

"Really?"

"Sure. I liked how he was sort of mad all the time and she was optimistic. Somehow, they worked."

"Ah, the grumpy/sunshine trope."

"What's that?"

"It's a theme you find in stories, especially romances. Grumpy/sunshine is a big one."

He rubbed a thumb across his bottom lip while he mulled this over. Maybe I watched a little too closely. He had a very nice... thumb. Thumbs don't get enough credit. They are opposable, after all.

With a smirk, he slid down and flung an arm over the back of the couch. The tips of his fingers grazed my shoulder. "I guess in our friendship, I'd be the sunshine and you'd be the grump."

"Excuse me?"

He gestured with a hand between us. "You're the grumpy, and I'm the sunshine. You know, the whole cat/dog thing."

Then, like they'd secretly met earlier and planned this whole elaborate setup, Kevin sauntered into the room and stood before the couch, surveying his choice of humans. He hopped into the space between us and then regarded me with narrowed yellow eyes before waltzing himself right over to Chris and settling in his lap.

Kevin. The cat who hissed at me this morning because I touched the pillow he was laying on. The same cat who had once so terrified the air conditioner repairman by jumping on his back and clawing his way down that the man had refused to come back. The very one who was at least seventeen years old and so set in his ways he'd been known to sit directly on my face if I was late to get him breakfast.

"I can't believe you chose him, you furball."

"Stop. He'll hear you." Chris covered Kevin's ears with his hands. "So grumpy."

"I'm not grumpy. I am tired."

Chris arched one dark eyebrow, a cheek dimpling. "Sure."

"Oh, shut up." With a huff, I wrapped a blanket around me, ignoring the warm, rankling sound of his laughter.

ELEVEN

There's only one thing I want to change about you: your last name.

—MELANIE K.

I woke up to Iris laughing, low and devious.

"Go away, I'm sleeping," I grumbled and snuggled close to the warmth wrapped around me.

"Leave her alone," my mom whispered. "You know she doesn't sleep enough."

"I'm taking a million pictures," Iris said. "Then I'm putting them all on Instagram."

"Please don't do that," another voice said, deep and rumbly. So deep and rumbly, it was like I could feel it through my whole body.

"She won't, I promise," Mama said in a reassuring tone. "Thank you for coming to check on her. I knew she wasn't feeling well. She works herself to death."

"She's kind of bitchy when she's sick," Iris said.

That pierced through my sleepy brain fog.

"Iris Marie, watch your mouth." Mama said. "Go and get my chair, please."

My heart thudded against my ribs as I tried to work out exactly what was happening here. I was laying on my couch. Except I wasn't laying on the couch exactly. Unless the couch had started breathing and grew an arm to wrap around me and smelled clean and...

My eyes snapped open.

I was laying on a couch made of Chris. How had this happened? I took a shaky breath.

"I'm sorry. Do you need some help?" Chris said from very near my ear.

"Oh, no, honey, you stay right there," Mama said. "I just overdid it today."

"Here, Mama," Iris said, presumably returning with her wheelchair. There were a few seconds of rustling after which Mama released a long sigh.

"Young man, I didn't realize you and Mae were friends."

"We're good friends," he said. That's when I felt the hand he'd had resting on my back slide under the blanket. It made its way down my arm, raising goosebumps, where it landed on my side. Then he pinched me.

With a yelp, I rolled off the couch and fought my way out of the blanket. "Why did you do that?"

"Do what?" Chris asked, all dark innocent eyes, but I saw the teasing twinkle.

"Mae, honey, how are you feeling?" Mama asked.

"Yeah, Mae, how are you feeling?" Iris repeated, not even bothering to contain her amusement.

I stood and wrapped the blanket around me like a cape. "I'm fine, thank you. I had a little headache, is all. And"—I pointed at the couch—"this is not what it looked like. I must have... have..."

"She fell asleep. Just tipped right over against me and fell asleep," Chris said. "I figured it was better to let her rest than wake her up."

"That's very kind of you," Mama said.

"You're a real prince," I snapped and pulled the blanket even tighter around me.

"She's not very nice when she doesn't feel good, is she?" Chris asked Mama, his smile amused.

"Oh, she's terrible," Mama replied. "Been that way since she was a little girl. Too busy to be sick."

"Excuse m—" I tried to interrupt and was ignored.

Chris nodded sagely. "That, I can believe."

"That's my little Maebe-Baby."

"Maebe-Baby," Chris repeated and shot me a half-grin.

"One time in high school," Mama said, "she insisted on going to school and ended up passing out in the middle of gym class because she was so feverish and dehydrated."

"You remember that time she broke her arm and refused to tell us?" Iris said.

"Took me two days to realize what was wrong." Mama's smile was a little sad.

"She really needs to slow down," he said.

"I agree. Rest is important."

"Are the three of you done gossiping like church ladies at a quilting bee?" I cut in.

Mama appeared to be holding back a smile when she nodded.

"I'm going to bed." I stood as tall as I could and turned to Chris. "Thank you very much for your help, however unnecessary it might have been. I'm sure you can see your way out."

A grin crawled slowly across his face. "That's alright. I'm not in much of a rush. I could tuck you in."

"You are incredibly irritating," I said, and trudged to my bedroom.

I was halfway there when he called out, "See you later, Maebe-Baby."

Later, much later, hours in fact, I lay in my bed, tossing and turning because I couldn't get comfortable. I punched my pillow, kicked the blankets off, and annoyed Kevin so much he moved off the bed to my laundry basket.

I had cuddled with Chris. Cuddled. It wasn't my fault. It didn't count because I was sleeping. It was gravity, really. That's right. It hadn't been purposeful cuddling. Accidental cuddling meant nothing. There, see?

I groaned and pulled a pillow over my face. Cuddles aside, Chris was a puzzle I couldn't figure out.

At first, he'd seemed like any other pretty boy I'd had an acquaintance with—flirty, a little arrogant, used to getting his way with a smile. But his actions were an entirely different story. There was a solidness to him, not physically—although, yes, that was also solid—but a solidness of character; he'd shown himself to be thoughtful, understanding, trustworthy. This, more than big, strong muscles or twinkly eyes, was scarily attractive.

In all, it was hard not to like the guy. As a friend. *Only* as a friend. There was no room in my life for any other messy feelings.

After another twenty sleepless minutes, I tossed the covers off and stomped (but not too loudly as to wake up anyone) into the kitchen for a glass of water and promised myself I would not think about What's His Name again. Good plan, Mae.

Under the soft glow of the light above the stove, I leaned against the counter, taking sips of water. That was when I noticed it: the dishwasher.

Someone had fixed it.

TWELVE

I wish I could be your derivative, so I could lie tangent to your curves.

—*MARIA S.*

From: Peter Stone <Peter.Stone@cityoftwohearts.gov>
To: Maebell Sampson
<Maebell.Sampson@cityoftwohearts.gov>
Subject: Cease and Desist

Maebell,

It appears someone has signed me up to receive a subscription to a magazine called *Girls and Corpses* and then had it delivered to my office. It scared Maria half to death when she opened it.

Tell Alicia Ramos to knock it off.

Peter

Ali got points for creativity. I pulled out my cell phone and shot off a text.

Me: *Girls and Corpses?*

Ali: *Hey, it wasn't a glitter bomb. I think I showed real restraint.*

Me: *I'm supposed to tell you to stop.*

Ali: *Duly noted and ignored.*

Me: *You're a good friend.*

Ali: *I know.*

I set my phone down and unlocked the library door for the morning crowd. By the time I returned, I had another text.

Ali: *Did you see this?*

The link she'd added was to a gossip site called Let Me Spill the Tea. The post at the top caught my eye immediately.

OKLAHOMA STARS' CHRIS STERNS' VEGAS BIRTHDAY WITH A SPECIAL GUEST

Chris Sterns has a reputation for being a team player on the football field and an Eagle Scout off it (no, really, he's an actual Eagle Scout). He's been very vocal about using his platform for good and spends his free time fundraising and visiting sick kids in hospitals.

But the Oklahoma Stars' defensive end has always been hush-hush about his dating status and the personal deets about his life. Aside from an occasional red carpet walk with a model or actress, he's never been photographed with anyone. Anyone!

Until now. Gather round and let me tell you.

In early February, Chris celebrated his twenty-eighth birthday with several of his fellow Stars' teammates Las Vegas-style. A little gambling, a lot of drinking, and, it appears, the company of some special new dancing friends. Clothing was optional, it seems.

If the rumors are true (*and girl, there is evidence!*), Chris Sterns was seen entering his room with one mostly naked woman draped on his arm at a certain high-class Vegas hotel.

The woman has currently not been identified but a contractor hired for the party did confirm Sterns and the mystery woman were seen together multiple times. Did I mention there is a video? Although this happened six weeks ago, the video recently surfaced from an anonymous source.

While this may seem like typical NFL player behavior, it's very out of character for Sterns. The Children's Heart Fund, which Sterns acts as the spokesperson for, is already starting to send out some indications they may be trying to distance themselves from any possible scandal. I guess strippers and sick kids is not a good look.

As for Chris Sterns? No one knows exactly where he is right now and he's being awfully close-lipped about the whole situation. But don't worry, he can't hide for long.

And there *was* proof. The video showed a long-legged blonde draped all over Chris's shoulder, a small blanket draped around her. Although someone had blurred out the important bits, it was clear she wasn't wearing much of anything. Except for some very high heels and some bunny ears.

Even though the photographer wasn't especially close, it

was still easy to make out her giggled, "Oh, my stars, Chris. I can't believe you're here."

Chris mumbled something too low for the camera to pick up. When they got to the door to a hotel room, he steadied her while he dug around for his key. Chris ushered her inside. Just as the door closed, he could be heard saying, "Now let me take care of you."

"Of course." I muttered and tossed my phone down, a heaviness settling in my chest. If I'd learned anything in life, it was that most men were not what they seemed. Look at my father, Peter, even Ali's ex-boyfriend.

But somewhere in the last three weeks, I'd grown to tolerate Chris, even like him. As a friend. I mean, sure he was a little annoying and kind of arrogant and flirted with abandon, but he was sort of sweet and thoughtful and smart.

Also, those opposable thumbs should not be overlooked.

Worst of all? I'd started to *respect* him. I'd even started to think there were guys out there who weren't like my father or Peter. There was hope for mankind. Hope for me, to one day find a good man because they existed.

Clearly, they did not. I rubbed my chest, recognizing the feeling for what it was.

I was *disappointed*. Kind of like when you finally realize Santa isn't real.

Apparently, the Chris Sterns I'd gotten to know wasn't all that real either.

THIRTEEN

Are you my appendix?
  'Cause this feeling in my stomach makes me want to take you out.

—*STEPHANIE R.*

Just before closing the library for lunch, Sabrina Olsen waltzed in. Sabrina had been a couple of years ahead of me in school, one of the popular girls with blonde highlights and manicured nails.

"I'm here to pick up my library holds. If you don't mind," she said with a wide smile that showed too many teeth. Like a barracuda. I'd always kind of hoped she and Peter would get together and when she grew tired of him, she'd eat him and save me the trouble of having to dispose of his body one day.

"Not at all." I searched the hold shelf and pulled out her stack of books. I'd been surprised when I'd gotten her requests. She'd never requested any before.

Long, red-tipped fingernails tapped on the counter as she

waited. She gazed around the library with disinterest. "Quiet in here."

"That's how we like our libraries." I set her stack of psychological thrillers on the counter. Maybe she *was* getting ideas for how to dispose of a body.

She hummed and flipped her long hair behind her shoulder. "I would hope more people were making use of these resources."

"They do," I said, hearing the defensiveness creep into my voice. I pulled out a calendar of events and slid it across the counter. "We have preschool story hour and homework help after school. I teach a genealogy class and Internet 101. Lots of things going on here."

She gave the paper a cursory glance. "I know *you* know we're voting in a few weeks to cut the library budget. Such a shame."

It should be noted Sabrina was also on the city council.

I ground my back teeth. "We don't know the outcome of that vote yet. I have faith in the good people of the council to make the right decision."

"Oh, honey, bless your heart. I think we all know how it's going to turn out."

With an overbright smile, I handed over her items. "Here's your books. Due in two weeks."

Hopefully she could deduce what I didn't say: You're the worst.

"Thank you. I'm sure I'll enjoy every one of them," she said in a sugary-sweet voice and turned to leave.

That's when the door opened, and Chris walked in, wearing khakis and a blue chambray button-down shirt, sleeves rolled up halfway, revealing muscly, sun-touched forearms.

It is a truth universally acknowledged, as Jane Austen would say, that there's something about a man's forearm that makes a woman's heart skip a beat. How that part of the male anatomy can be so dang sexy without even trying is a mystery. But there you have it.

With a gasp, Sabrina put a hand on her chest. "Chris Sterns. I'd heard a rumor but... I'm so pleased to meet you."

Chris ducked his head and shot her a smile of the aw-shucks variety. "It's nice to meet you."

"Could I get a photo?"

"Sure thing," he said.

Sabrina pulled out her phone and handed it to me. "Would you mind, Mae?"

"Of course not."

She wasted no time situating herself at Chris's side, practically burrowing under his arm until he lifted it and put it around her shoulders. I almost laughed at his pained expression, especially when I was ninety-nine percent sure she'd given his backside a good feel-up.

I briefly thought about cutting their heads off in all the photos but, in the end, I was a good girl. Before she left, Sabrina gave him her business card and offered her services for *whatever* he needed.

"She's scary," Chris said, when the door shut behind her.

"It's the teeth. Very pointy." I gave him my very best imitation of her smile. "You're dressed all fancy today."

He pulled at his collar. "Yeah, I had a meeting this morning."

For what? I wanted to ask. But it was none of my business. At all. Remember that, Maebell Sampson. "Book club, then?"

With a nod, he followed me back to the office/copy room/break room and set a bag of takeout on the table. "It was my turn to bring lunch. I know we planned on the café, but I was in Houston, so I stopped for barbecue."

I paused, then pulled the takeout carton toward me. "Oh, okay. That's fine."

"It doesn't sound fine."

"I planned on something else, that's all. I like to know things ahead of time." I glanced up to find him staring at me, lips pressed together. "Are you laughing at me?"

"A little bit. It's lunch. I didn't buy you a house."

"There's nothing wrong with wanting to have a plan," I said, my voice taking on the same edge I used with the kids who sometimes came here after school and hid in a corner to giggle over scenes in some racy novel they'd found.

"Nothing wrong with being a little spontaneous either. Some of my best decisions have been made in the spur of a moment."

"Agree to disagree."

"Deal. Let's get back to the *Pirate's Booty*. More like the Pirate's Booty Call, amirite?" With a wicked little chuckle, he pulled his book out. Somehow it looked even more tattered and worn than the last time we'd met. "Did you finish?"

"Yup." I tucked a paper napkin in around my neck.

"So," he began, flipping to a page he had marked, "what did you think about the whole proposal?"

"Who doesn't like a good marriage of convenience trope."

He set his book aside. "What do you mean?"

"Guy needs something from the girl. Girl needs something from the guy. Marriage seems the easiest way to get it. They're both going into it clear-eyed, no pesky feelings." I paused and took a bite of my sandwich.

"So, it's a contract of sorts." Chris watched me thoughtfully.

"Exactly. Pretty cut and dry. It sounds boring, but"—I held a finger up—"this is a romance novel, so... You put two people in close proximity by circumstance. They can't leave. They can't ignore each other. They're married. It's either kill each other or fall in love."

"Sure. Sure," he murmured.

"There's always a happy ending in romance novels." I took a sip of my tea. "That's why we readers can believe a marriage of convenience is even a thing. I mean, in real life, this would be a disaster."

Chris's head cocked to the side. "You don't think it could work in real life."

With a huff, I set my cup down. "No. In real life, no one gets a happy ending."

"That seems pretty cynical."

"I'm not a cynic, I'm a realist."

"You honestly think people can't have happy endings?"

"Not really. Life is way too messy and unpredictable. No one can truly be happy always waiting for the next bad thing to happen."

"Wow." He rubbed his bottom lip, but I wasn't distracted by his stupid opposable thumb this time. Not today, Satan. "That's kind of sad."

I shrugged. "It's a fact of life. Like the sky is blue and cats are the best pets and... and... hair keeps growing after you die."

"Well, actually..." he cut in.

"Seriously? Was there a Mortuary Sciences badge?"

He grinned. "Yes."

"Liar."

Silence fell as we both tucked back into our food. After a few minutes, I returned to the reason for our lunch.

"Since this is a romance, the whole marriage of convenience thing worked out for Elizabeth and Lord Hastings. He was accepted back into the peerage, she was protected from her father. They both found some new places on that ship to, you know, explore their relationship. I didn't think it could get weirder than the plank, but..." I paused, eyeing Chris across the table. He was staring intently over my shoulder where a poster of a cat wearing glasses and reading *Purr-ide and Prejudice* hung. "Hello? You still here with me? You seem miles away."

He blinked slowly. "Oh, yeah. Sorry, thinking about something."

"So, they fell in love, our Elizabeth and Hastings. There for a moment, it didn't seem like it would work out. But he managed to pull off a grand romantic gesture. They got back together. Lived happily ever after. The end."

I finished off my sandwich and waited for him to comment. He did not. It was clear he was anywhere but in the room with me.

"You know, we don't have to do this today if your mind is on other things."

As soon as the words were out of my mouth, he began cleaning up his food, tossing napkins in the empty to-go box. "You don't mind?"

"No."

"Great." He stood and tossed his garbage in the trash can. "Thanks for lunch. I have to go take care of something. I'll see you later."

Then in a very brotherly way, he gave me a pat on the shoulder and left.

FOURTEEN

I'd like to take you to the movies, but they don't let you bring in your own snacks.

—SARAH M.

"Seriously, Kyle," Amanda said. "They're your kids. Carson's growing like a weed. He needs new shoes, and I can't do this without—"

It was Friday night and I'd just popped into the changing room at Chicky's for a quick fifteen-minute break. I wasn't trying to eavesdrop but, besides Amanda, I was the only other person here and it was not a big room.

"I hate him," Amanda growled and tossed her phone on the counter next to me. Her eyes glistened with unshed tears.

"Ex-husband?"

"What did I ever see in him?" She grabbed a tissue and carefully dabbed under her eyes. "He quit his job. Said he was just working to pay for child support so why bother. Meanwhile, I'm working two jobs just to pay the rent and keep the lights on."

"I wish I could help in some way." And I meant it; Amanda was good people.

"Maybe some poor drunk soul will get sloppy and give me a five-hundred-dollar tip." With a tired chuckle, she pushed off the counter and pasted on a smile before walking out the door.

Another name to add to my list of Reasons to Avoid Men At All Costs. It included: my father, Peter, Ali's ex-boyfriend, and now Amanda's deadbeat ex-husband.

I'd just finished calling Mama to check on her when Amanda returned. "There you are. That guy from last week is back."

I stared at her in horror. "The guy I spilled the food on?"

"No." She hopped on the tips of her high-heeled boots. "The hot one. The football player. What is his dang name?"

"Oh." My relief was short-lived. "Wait. He's here?"

"Yup," She smiled broadly, flashing straight white teeth and a single dimple. "He asked specifically for you. He's at the bar."

What could he possibly want? If he was here to make fun of me, he had another thing coming. I didn't have the time or patience for games. He'd have to understand not all of us were sports heroes with fat paychecks and no problems.

I'd gotten myself good and riled up by the time I spotted him at the bar. He was laughing at something Kara, the bartender, was saying to him. With a giggle, she leaned over the counter (conveniently giving him a very good view of her cleavage) and playfully smacked him on the shoulder.

I had a momentary desire to rip that arm off Kara's body and throw it in the nearest meat grinder. Which was ridiculous. I liked Kara. She was funny and smart (currently in her second year of law school). If she wanted to flirt with Chris, she could have him. I did not care a whit. I was whit-less, indeed.

Witless was more like it.

How had my life gotten so weird? Here I was, marching

across a crowded restaurant dressed as a show extra for *The Dukes of Hazzard* to a real-life football god.

When I was about ten feet away, Chris turned and saw me. His smile widened and, for a split second, I faltered under the full wattage of it. A powerful weapon, that thing was. Not to mention the rest of the package wrapped in faded jeans and a t-shirt, baseball cap firmly in place. The whole slightly scruffy, casual clothes thing worked for him.

It was sure working on Kara.

"What are you doing here?" I asked.

Chris's smiled dimmed a little; two little tick marks appeared between his brows. "Is this a bad time?"

"I am at work."

"Sorry. I need to ask you a question."

"And you have to do it right now?"

"Yes," he said, his voice earnest. "Well, no, not exactly, but it seemed like I should do it immediately."

"What could possibly be this important?"

"I won't take much of your time. After our lunch the other day..."

From the corner of my eye, I saw Kara's curious gaze move back and forth between us.

"Wait. You have to at least order something." I pulled my order pad from the tiny apron we all had to wear.

"Fine." He picked up the menu next to him. "What's good here?"

"Nothing," Kara and I said at the same time.

"Is a burger safe?" he asked.

"What do you consider safe? Will it kill you? It's unlikely. If you're asking if it's really beef? I'm legally not allowed to answer that question as per my employment agreement." I clicked my pen. "With or without cheese?"

"Why don't I put this in for you?" Kara glanced back and

forth between Chris and me like she was at a particularly vicious game of pickleball. "You two can talk."

After she left, I rounded the bar and stood across from Chris. Mainly to look busy in case Shane came out of his office and wanted to get yell-y. About five seats over, an older guy with a bad combover was bellied up to the bar and staring at the baseball game.

"So, what's this very important question?" I found a towel under the bar and started wiping at the space between us.

Chris straightened, his expression earnest in that Eagle Scout way he had about him. "What happened to your mom?"

I threw down the rag. "No offense, but first, it's none of your business and second, why do you care?"

"We're friends and, well, it's for a good reason. Just trust me. Please?" His eyes were all warm and soft and so sincere.

I crossed my arms. "She had a stroke about eight months ago."

"I'm sorry. That must have been terrifying."

"Yeah, it was. But she's doing better now. She's in therapy and getting stronger every day."

"I bet therapy is expensive."

I picked up the towel and began wiping down the very dry bar again. "We're doing okay."

"That's why you have the second job. Medical bills." It wasn't a question.

He watched me closely like he was waiting for some kind of reaction. Was he expecting me to break down into tears and confess how horrible life was? 'Cause that was not happening.

I stared right back. "Like I said, we're fine."

He opened his mouth to say something else, but Bad Combover started waving his hand. I marched down to him, glad for the reprieve.

I stole a glance at Chris as I refilled the guy's glass. He was bent over the bar a little, spinning his mostly empty glass

absently, his profile displaying the strong line of his jaw that I
knew softened when he smiled. Which he was not doing now.

In fact, now that I took a moment to study him, he had all
the earmarks of a man in trouble. Hunched shoulders, tired
eyes, grim expression.

I wandered back to him. "What's wrong with you?"

His eyebrows jumped in surprise, then he sighed. "I need
your help."

"My help?"

"Did you hear about the Vegas thing?" he asked, and I swear
he started to blush.

I nodded.

"I know it looks bad but it's not true, the things they're
saying."

It wasn't my job to act as a lie detector. "It isn't my business.
We barely know each other."

He frowned. "Well, then this will be awkward."

"What's that?"

"I have an idea," he said slowly. "A proposition."

"Proposition? Again, with the bad pickup lines?" I looked
down my nose at him. "You can't afford me."

His mouth tipped up in a small smile. "Proposition might
not be the best word. Maebell Sampson, would you do me the
great honor of agreeing to be my wife?"

FIFTEEN

Do you have a map? Because I'm lost in your eyes.

—KIMBERLEY

I did what any other adult woman would do in the face of such a question. I gasped. I stared. Then I ran.

Ran might not be the best word; I definitely scurried though. And I avoided the bar area, but, as hard as I tried, I knew Chris was still there. He didn't approach me, but he did send Amanda over to tell me he'd stay until the end of my shift to "talk."

Then I told Amanda to go back and tell him I wouldn't be off for hours and he probably shouldn't wait.

Then Chris sent Amanda back and told her to tell me he didn't have anything else to do.

And then I tried to send Amanda back with another message, but she got annoyed and told me that we weren't ten-year-olds on a school playground and to give him the message "my damn self."

So, at the end of my shift, I changed out of my uniform into shorts and a t-shirt. After stalling as long as possible, I finally skulked to the bar, backpack tossed over one shoulder. Amanda had taken Kara's spot bartending. Chris perched on the same barstool.

"I'm leaving," I announced.

"Let's settle up your check." Amanda scooped up his credit card. "I'll be right back."

Chris turned my way, his eyes settling on my face. "You look tired."

"It's almost one a.m. I'm exhausted and some weirdo proposed to me out of the clear blue sky earlier tonight." And my feet ached, and I still had a forty-five-minute drive back home, and then I'd have to get up and do this all over again tomorrow night. "Do you do this a lot?"

"What?"

"Propose?"

"No, this is a first."

"Huh." I rested an elbow on the bar.

"What do you think? Wanna get engaged?" he asked as though he was asking if I wanted paper or plastic.

"You cannot be serious." I hitched up my backpack and turned to leave.

"Wait." He stood and took a step toward me. "Can you just hear me out? It won't take long."

Over his shoulder, I saw Amanda coming back our way; I thought of the phone call I'd overheard earlier. "Okay, fine. You give Amanda a five-hundred-dollar tip and I'll listen."

His eyebrows shot up. "Five hundred dollars?"

"Yep. That's what I said."

With a grin, he held out a hand. "Deal."

Cicadas sang to us as we walked across the parking lot. The air was sticky and warm, but tolerable. There were only a handful of cars left, belonging to employees finishing up the night and prepping for tomorrow. I stopped beside my car, unlocked the door, and tossed my backpack inside.

A hand on my hip, I let my impatience show. "So, let's talk."

"Do you want to sit, or something?" He gestured toward my car and frowned. "Maybe not there. I don't know if I can fit. Come on." I followed him to his truck near the edge of the parking lot. He flipped down the flap to the truck bed and tapped it. "We can relax and enjoy the scenery."

The scenery in question was a patch of neglected land adjacent to the parking lot. Even in the dim light of the moon and parking lot lights, the empty beer cans, plastic grocery sacks, and occasional chip bag littered the overgrown grass. "Not exactly prime real estate."

"We can look at the stars." He patted the truck. "Hop up."

The truck was one of those big half-ton deals with extra-tall tires. I eyed the distance between the ground and the truck bed. "I'll stand."

"I feel like you're going to fake me out and run away."

"I'm not going to run away. I am an adult." And kind of mad I hadn't thought of that myself.

Chris narrowed his eyes and then a grin curled one side of his mouth. "This isn't because you can't get up there, is it?"

"No, of course not." I eyed the lip of the truck bed. I could get up there. Probably.

He smirked. "You know, you could ask for help."

"I don't need help."

"Okay, fine. No help being offered."

To prove my point, I tried to hoist myself up. That didn't go well. I side-eyed Chris, who looked like he was holding in a laugh. Fine. Whatever. I tried pulling myself up again, but it wasn't working.

"Are you sure?"

"I got it." My only other option was to hook a foot onto the truck and pull myself up. Not only was it a completely graceless move, but I almost fell on my butt. With my head high, I straightened and turned back to Chris. "You know what? Standing is fine."

"You are stubborn." Chris moved toward me, determination scribbled on his face. He stopped within a few inches of me, his eyes twinkling.

"Um, excuse me," I said. "You're in my personal bubble."

"This will only take a second."

Then before I had a chance to gather a reply or understand what was happening, two large hands wrapped around my waist and hoisted me on the truck bed like I weighed no more than a toothpick when I was a solid two hundred pounds. I landed with a surprised squawk.

His hands lingered a few seconds, tightening on my waist before sliding away to rest on either side of my hips. "See? That wasn't so bad, was it?"

"You manhandled me," I said, my voice full of righteous indignation. But truthfully, a tiny secret part of me was a little, I don't know, turned on at the display of caveman strength, at a man who was taller than me by several inches, and so strong.

"You're welcome." He tapped on my nose before easily hopping onto the truck.

I patted at my overheated cheeks. Because it was hot outside. That's why. "Alright, let's hear it."

"Right. A few of the guys on the team talked me into going to Vegas for my birthday. It was a good time and then it got to be too much." He cleared his throat. "I don't drink a lot. I'm kind of a lightweight. So, I had a couple and that was it. The rest of the guys? Like it was their last night on earth."

"Classy."

"Then the strippers showed up and everything got a little crazier."

"So, you decided to help a mostly naked stripper out?"

"Yes." Pause. "Well, no." Another pause. "There's something else."

Good grief. What else? Was she pregnant with his child?

"I need you to keep this between us. No matter what." He paused and put his hand on my arm until I turned to look at him, his eyes serious.

I nodded. "I promise."

He blew out a breath. "That woman in the video? She's my sister."

"Oh," I whispered.

"She lives in L.A. We're close. She has a little boy who just turned three. His name is Oliver." He pulled out his phone and showed me a photo of a little boy with dark hair and bright-blue eyes.

"He's adorable."

"I know. Looks like his uncle, right?"

I rolled my eyes.

"Anyway, I don't get to see her often so when she asked if she could drive over and see me when I was in Vegas, I was all for it. Soon as she got there, I could tell something was off. The next thing I know she's guzzled half her weight in rum and Coke and is stripping off her clothes and dancing on tables and taking dares to recite the preamble to the Constitution while standing on her head. I got her out of there as fast as I could."

"Is she okay?" I asked.

"We had a long talk and she admitted things have been really tough, and she's been drinking more than she should. I found her a rehab where she could bring Oliver with her, and she stayed there for a few weeks. She's doing better. It's kind of a one day at a time sort of thing. She's fragile right now and I don't want anything to derail her." He pulled off his baseball cap and ran his fingers through his hair in frustration. "I try to keep my personal life out of the spotlight. The media is a beast and once they get a hold of something, they won't leave it alone."

"Which is what would happen if her name got out."

"Yeah." He smacked the cap on his knee and then yanked it back on his head. "When that video came out and they all assumed she was one of the dancers, it seemed like the easiest way to keep her name out of all this." His shoulders slumped. "But now the Children's Heart Fund is threatening to sever ties over it. They don't think that video is the right image for a children's charity."

"Well..."

"A lot of responsibility comes with this job and I take it seriously. I've been so careful where and who I hang out with, what words come out of my mouth when I do interviews. I don't want some little kid asking me about naked dancers the next time I do a hospital visit."

He flopped back on the truck bed with a frustrated growl and stacked his hands under his head. I absolutely did not notice the sliver of skin that peeked out at the bottom of his t-shirt.

I tucked a knee under me so I could see his face. "Is it really the end of the world if you have to find another charity to work with after this all dies down?"

"Yes." He frowned. "My youngest sister, Millie, was born with HLHS, hypoplastic left heart syndrome. Basically, a part of her heart wasn't formed correctly. Instead of four chambers like you and me, hers only had three. I was fourteen when she was born, and it changed our whole family."

"Is she okay?"

"She still has regular check-ups, and she'll need more surgery as she gets older. But she's doing okay." He stared up into the inky sky, where the stars were just visible despite the light pollution from the city. "Anyway, I decided I wanted to find ways to help other kids and families who have to go through this."

I rubbed at my chest where a small pinching feeling had settled. "That's very admirable."

He sat up suddenly, his face very close to mine, close enough to smell cinnamon on his breath. "Do you believe me?"

His sincerity was so evident that it was impossible not to. I nodded slowly. "But I have no idea what this has to do with me and a marriage proposal."

"I probably could have approached that differently. My team has a plan to fix all this bad publicity."

"Your team?"

"My agent, publicist. The team."

Of course, he had a team. "Okay."

"They say we need to create a distraction. Something that would help my image. What's better than a fiancée? Not any old fiancée either: a small-town, salt-of-the-earth librarian. You're smart, you're the right age, you aren't otherwise engaged, right?" He frowned as if this thought may have just crossed his mind.

"Well, no, I'm not."

He clapped his hands. "You're perfect. It's like the book. Except we won't have to get married. It's an engagement of convenience."

I huffed a laugh. "That's a terrible idea."

"No, it's a great idea. I need your help and you could use mine."

"What exactly do I need help with?"

One dark eyebrow rose. "You need money."

"Excuse me?"

"You're working seven days a week. Your mother has a lot of medical bills. Ali told me about the situation with the library, and how you're worried about your sister and paying for college." He sat back, a satisfied smile smeared on his face.

I wanted to wipe that smile off his face even if he was correct about everything he'd listed.

"Ali has a big mouth," I snapped.

"Think about it. Please."

"You cannot be serious."

"I am. I really am." Those honey-colored eyes of his gazed into mine with so much dang sincerity.

"I can't believe I'm even giving this space in my head. I don't have time for this. And who in the world would believe you would propose to me, of all people?" I wagged a finger in his direction. "So many things could go wrong. You're fixing a lie with another lie. What would your mother think?"

That was a shot in the dark. I had no idea what his mother would think but I felt certain if there was a Mama Sterns somewhere, he would care what she thought.

He winced. A-ha. Bull's-eye. "I'm a little worried about that myself but if we do it right, my mother will never need to know it was all for show."

"Why doesn't that make me feel any better?"

"I know this is a lot to take. Think about it. Please. But I need an answer soon. By Monday."

I shook my head. "I can already tell you my answer. It's a no. A big, fat no. Very loud with lots of exclamation points."

He sighed. "I understand."

"Good." I hopped down from the truck. "I should get going."

I was halfway to my car when his voice stopped me. "Mae, one more thing. It pays a hundred thousand dollars."

SIXTEEN

Do they have a fire extinguisher around here? 'Cause you're smokin'.

—JOCELYN S.

I couldn't sleep.

Not my normal, run-of-the-mill, anxiety-fueled insomnia either. Although that was present and accounted for. This tossing and turning led straight back to that conversation with Chris.

A fake engagement? That stuff only happened in romance novels for a reason. Not in real life and not to people like me.

No. I couldn't do that. I couldn't spend the time and energy convincing people I was happily engaged to anyone. To freaking Chris Sterns, football god.

But also... $100,000.

Of course, I should probably be offended he thought I could be bought off. Then again, I wasn't in a position to be offended. That kind of money was life-changing.

I sat up and flipped on the lamp on my nightstand. From the drawer, I withdrew a notepad and pencil I kept there. Sometimes, when the anxiety got too bad, I'd make a list of good things in my life to help me get through it. Every now and then, it worked.

I found a fresh sheet and divided it in half, labeling one side PRO and one side CON.

CONS

  —The lying
  —The pretending
  —The fake-ness

PROS

  —$100,000
  —Money to pay off Mama's medical bills
  —It bears repeating: $100,000

With a groan, I tossed the notepad aside, disturbing a sleeping Kevin. This earned me a scathing glare. His tail whipped around in righteous kitty anger.

"Well, excuse me," I grumbled.

"Don't do it again," his eyes said.

"This is ridiculous. I can't even believe I'm considering this nonsense." I flipped off the covers and quietly stole away to the kitchen. Maybe a snack would help.

Decisions usually came easy to me and once I made one, I stuck to it. Even when quitting might have been better for my mental health and well-being. Case in point, the summer I nannied for the Colson Triplets. They were *monsters*. I still had an occasional nightmare about that last trip we took to the zoo. It should be noted that no one, not even the zoo staff, could figure out how Connor got into that prairie dog exhibit. But I stuck it out until the bitter end.

I was almost to the kitchen when I heard a soft clunk coming from the general area. When I turned the corner, I found my mother sitting at the kitchen table eating ice cream straight out of the carton.

"Mama?"

She startled and her spoon clattered to the table. "Goodness, you scared me to death."

"Can't sleep?"

"What gives you that idea?" she asked, picking up the spoon and digging back into the carton.

"Could be that it's two in the morning. Could be that you're speed-eating ice cream." I dug around in the silverware drawer for a spoon and sat next to her. "Hmmm. Chocolate Pecan. I didn't know we had any."

She pushed the container between us. "That's because I hide it, so you and your sister don't find it."

I snickered and took a bite. Under the dim light of the overhead above the stove, I studied my mother's face. There was a pinched look around her eyes and the corners of her mouth.

"Are you feeling okay?" I asked.

With a sigh, she shook her head. "I'm fine. You?"

"Just the usual."

Mama set her spoon down and straightened, fussing with the collar of her floral housedress. "I'm glad you're up."

"Oh?"

She reached into her pocket, pulled out an envelope, and slid it across the table. "I got this today. It's a bill from my neurologist."

Oh, no. Oh. No. Bills were never supposed to be delivered to the house. I grabbed at it and saw it had been opened. With a heavy feeling in my stomach, I pulled the bill from inside.

"I'll save you the trouble," Mama said, an edge to her voice as she told me the figure: $7,393.47.

"Mama..."

"Why am I just seeing this?" She jabbed a finger at the bill in my hand. "In fact, why haven't I seen more of these bills? There must be more."

"Mama..."

She kept talking over me. "This is my fault. I don't know why I haven't been looking for them."

"Mama..." I said again.

"Maebell Sampson, do not lie to me," she said, her voice raised. "Are there more of them?"

"It's under control. I swear."

She pressed her lips together, the left side of her mouth listing downward, and I was again reminded she could have *died*. I might not be sitting next to her in the kitchen in the middle of the night because she almost *died*.

Carefully, I folded up the bill and slid it back into the envelope. "I don't want you to worry."

"How can I not worry? How many other bills are there?"

I shook my head and lied some more. Really, I was getting very good at all this lying. "This is it, and I'm working with the clinic to get it reduced." I turned to her and looked her in the eye. "I have it all under control. I promise if there's anything I need, I'll let you know."

"Maebell," she sighed.

I stood and dropped a kiss on her cheek. "Don't worry, Mama. I have a plan."

When I got back to my room, I sent the text even though it was almost 3 a.m. It was short and sweet.

Me: *Yes.*

Setting the phone aside, I climbed under my covers, shivering a little even though it was a warm spring night. When the phone dinged back, my whole body tensed like one enormous charley horse. My hand shook when I grabbed for the phone.

Dreamboat: *Thank you.*

SEVENTEEN

Is your name Google? Because you have everything I'm searching for.

—ASHLEY

Chris's rental house was known locally as the Wilson place. A few miles outside of town off a dirt road, it was a sprawling ranch-style home with a little red barn in the back and a front porch that stretched across the entire front of the house.

I pulled into the driveway and parked between Chris's truck and a BMW. My hands gripped the steering wheel as I sat, giving myself a pep talk. "You can do this. Sure, it's lying but it's lying that pays a lot of money."

Someone knocked on the driver's side window and I shrieked. Chris grinned and pulled the door open. "Are you talking to yourself?"

"No."

His grin grew two sizes. It was clear he didn't believe me. Whatever.

I grabbed my purse and climbed out of the car, trying to hide my nervousness.

Chris led me to the front door and hesitated before opening it. "Ready?"

"Nope."

His eyes were gentle. "Thank you for this."

I cleared my throat, touched by the sincerity in his voice. "I'm just using you for your money, you know."

"I wouldn't have it any other way." He put a hand on my lower back and ushered me into the house.

Although I'd never been in the house before or after the renovations, I had in mind something simple that would appeal to a variety of potential renters.

I was wrong. So very wrong.

The front door opened to a large entrance hall, and I gasped. Rustic wood covered all the walls and complemented the reclaimed barn wood floors. A large oval mirror fashioned out of what appeared to be ropy pieces of tree branches hung over a side table, the legs of it made of thin tree trunks. While all that together made me feel like I'd walked into a log cabin, it was not what made me gasp.

That was because of all the eyes staring at me. The eyes didn't belong to people. They mostly belonged to all the deer. Not just one or two: there were six mounted deer heads proudly on display. On the side table next to a cheery bouquet of wild-flowers, a stuffed fox perched, one paw permanently raised as though it was waving hello to visitors.

"Um," I said, my gaze fixed upon one particular deer whose creepy stare seemed to be following me. "This is a lot."

"I should have prepared you. Whoever decorated this place was really into hunting. You should see the elk head in the master bedroom."

"How do you sleep like that?"

He leaned closer and I got a whiff of clean, warm Chris. "I put a towel over its eyes. I can't handle it watching me all night."

An image of the big, strong football player cowering in bed because of an elk head amused me.

As I followed Chris through the rest of the house, I took in the gobs of dark wood paneling, the oversized leather furniture, the many, many paintings hung on every possible wall, probably with names like "Alert Dog in Field Who Just Spotted the Mailman" or "Ducks. A Whole Lot of Ducks."

And. So. Many. Stuffed. Animals.

"Is that a beaver?" I asked as we passed a wall of built-in shelves. "And a squirrel and, oh, an armadillo."

"It gets worse."

We stepped into the dining room, and I understood what he meant. There was an entire wall devoted to guns, antique and otherwise. A bobcat perched on a sideboard, its teeth bared. A trio of stuffed mice rested on a shelf. Someone had taken time to arrange them around a miniature table that resembled the big oak one in the middle of the room. One of the mice wore a tiny felt hat.

I hesitated. Chris put a hand on my back and pushed me forward. He pointed to one of the two people in the room; he was razor-thin with quick pale eyes who liked to yell at servers for accidentally spilling barbecue sauce on them. "This is Doug McGill, my agent. You probably remember him."

"Her?" Doug asked Chris. So much incredulity packed into one little word.

"Hi," I said. "Nice to see you again."

Frowning, he inspected me from head to toe.

The woman next to him didn't wait to be introduced. With her cap of sleek dark hair and shrewd eyes in a short, compact form, she radiated a "I'm nice but do not mess with me" attitude. She held out a hand. "I'm Piper Connor. I'm Chris's publicist."

"Nice to meet you."

Piper clapped her hands. "Why don't we all have a seat and get started."

Doug scowled. "Chris, can I talk to you for a minute? Alone."

The two walked through a swinging door I imagined led to the kitchen. Piper indicated the chair at the front of the table, and she took one at the other end.

"So, you're a librarian?" Piper asked.

"Yes, I—"

A loud thump interrupted me, followed by muffled, raised voices behind the door. I flinched.

"Don't worry about them. They have a love/hate relationship, heavy on the hate on both sides. Between you and me, I have never understood why Chris stays with him," Piper said, her voice brisk but friendly. "Can I get you anything? Water? Tea?"

Someone, I thought Doug, yelled, "I'm done."

"Um, I'm good," I said.

The door flew open, and Doug tore into the room, his face a storm cloud. With a huff, he threw himself in his seat next to Piper. Chris followed, looking for all the world like he'd just been on a leisurely evening walk. He took the seat beside me.

Ooo-kay.

"Let's get this over with," Doug snapped and slid a packet of paper down to me.

I grabbed it and read the top: "Non-Disclosure Agreement." A pen came flying down next.

"Doug, knock it off," Piper said, and I liked her even more.

"Sign it." He wagged a finger in my direction. "Remember, it's legally binding. You break it, you'll pay for it."

"You're a real charmer," I muttered. I picked up the pen and began scanning the document. Unsurprisingly, I'd never even laid eyes on an NDA. It was four pages front and back. "This is a lot. Am I signing over my firstborn child?"

"Keeping all this a secret is very important," Piper said. "You won't be able to tell anyone. Not even your family. Everyone needs to buy it."

I glanced at Chris to find him studying me. He appeared relaxed but one of his hands rested on the table and he was rubbing his thumb across his fingers repeatedly like he was nervous. Was he worried I'd back out? Should I back out?

"Am I the right person for this? I'm sure there are any number of Brazilian swimsuit models who would mud-wrestle for the chance." Swallowing, I put the pen down. "Or actresses who are, like, professionals at, you know, acting."

Doug threw his hands up in the air. "That's what I told him. But he won't listen."

Chris shook his head. "I choose Mae. She can handle it."

"But why? Who would believe it? You with someone..." Doug waved his hands in my direction "...who looks like her."

Chris leaned forward. "What does that mean?"

I knew exactly what he meant. I held up a hand. "I got this."

"Go for it," he said, amused. "Let me know if you need to tag me in."

Then I turned my attention to the weasel at the end of the table. "Someone who looks like me?"

Doug glared at me. "Like you said, you aren't exactly a swimsuit model."

Piper sighed. "Doug."

I pushed my chair back. "You know what? You're right. I sure as hell am not the right person for this. Because if it means spending another second in your presence, I might end up in prison for twisting you into a pretzel trying to stick your head up your ass."

From my vantage point, I could see Piper roll her lips together, dark eyes dancing.

Breathing hard from anger, I stalked to Doug and towered over him until he had to tilt back in his chair to see me. "I'll have you know, if I wanted to be a swimsuit model, I would be. I know you weren't implying there was anything wrong with my body, were you? Because I sure don't need your approval."

Everyone's eyes were on me, including the stuffed bobcat, two of the three mice, and a bird I'd just noticed in the corner. Twenty whole minutes, and my mouth was already getting me in trouble.

As much as I'd have loved to walk out the door and pretend I'd never given this whole plan a second thought, the truth was I needed that money. Not for me but for Mama and Iris. I closed my eyes and took a deep breath before turning toward Chris. Time to save face. But the look on Chris's face surprised me. He looked almost... proud.

His smile unfurled slowly. "Like I said, I choose Mae."

EIGHTEEN

I hope our love will be like the number Pi: irrational and endless.

—DERNA

"Who doesn't like Monopoly?" Chris asked, outrage in his voice.

"Me. I hate it," I replied.

He grunted and continued to flip through the pages in front of him. After the meeting yesterday, Piper had given us homework: a huge packet of questions meant to help us get to know each other fast. It had taken hours to fill out.

"Wait. You're afraid of frogs?" He dropped the packet, eyebrow raised. "You're joking, right?"

"I do not joke about frogs."

The questions ranged from the benign to the intimate. Nothing was off-limits, including perfect first date, saddest memory, childhood best friend, and preferred underwear style (which I refused to answer, and Chris did—boxer briefs).

He flung an arm around my shoulders. "I solemnly swear to protect you from all frogs, both foreign and domestic."

"You are hilarious."

"If you'll look, I believe you'll see I listed 'great sense of humor' under my best traits."

"Along with excellent physique, good hair, and humble attitude. And your fears?" I searched for his answer. "Nothing. You wrote the word, nothing. I'm glad you're taking this seriously."

Piper entered the dining room impeccably dressed in a sharp red pantsuit and mile-high heels. I was beginning to think of this as Command Central for Operation Faking It and Piper was the general in charge. Doug had scurried back to his office in New York earlier in the day for which I was hugely grateful.

"Alright, lovebirds. You can go back to that in a bit. We need to look at the contract." Piper passed me a manila folder.

"Contract?" I hesitated to open the folder.

Piper smiled reassuringly. "It's pretty standard."

"Do you organize a lot of these fake engagements?"

"More than you think."

Right.

"Before we go over this," Piper said, her expression serious, "is there anything you need to let us know about?"

My stomach twisted. "Like what?"

"Are you secretly married?" she asked.

"No, of course not."

"Have you been engaged? Dated any men who might try to cause problems?"

"No engagements." I squirmed in my seat. "I don't think my ex will be an issue."

"Who's the ex?" Chris asked, turning toward me.

With a sigh, I closed my eyes. "Peter Stone. We dated for two years."

The ensuing silence was broken by Chris's snort of laughter. "No kidding?"

"I would not kid about that." I would, however, love to erase it from my memory.

"Huh? What happe—?"

I held up a hand. "Nope. Not talking about it."

Piper cleared her throat. "Have you spent time in prison?"

An image of my father flashed in my mind. I hesitated for the briefest of seconds, but it was enough for Piper to zero in on me.

"We've done a background check. The results will be here later this week. If there's something we need to know, now's a good time."

"I've never been to prison, but my father has. Several times."

Piper picked up a pen. "His name?"

"Do we really need to talk about him? I haven't seen or heard from him in three years. He could be anywhere at this point." Hopefully a Mexican prison. "I don't want anything to do with him."

"His name?" Piper repeated.

"Dale Sampson." I turned to Chris. "I didn't think about saying anything sooner. I understand if this is a dealbreaker."

I wouldn't beg. I was doing fine on my own before all this came into my life and I'd be fine after it disappeared. But for one moment it had seemed like I was going to get a break.

Without looking away from me, Chris said, "Piper?"

She clicked her pen. "It shouldn't be a problem."

"Good." He picked up the forgotten contract. "Let's get back to this."

Slowly, I filed through this new packet. Our engagement would last approximately three months, or until my services were no longer needed. I would be required to do interviews, like on television, if the need arose. I couldn't be seen with any other man (obviously). All transportation and other expenses would be paid. I'd get the money at the end of the three months.

I paused at one of the clauses. "I have to quit Chicky's?"

"We'll need you for weekends," Piper explained. "Plus we're going for small-town librarian, not Daisy Dukes and push-up bras."

"But I need that income." I rubbed my forehead with my fist. "If I'm not getting paid for three months, what am I supposed to do until then?"

"I'll pay you upfront for the time off," Chris said. "Will that work?"

"I guess so."

"You don't have to quit. You can take a break. I'll talk to your manager. We'll work it out."

I frowned. "No, I'll talk to my manager. My job, my responsibility. You aren't here to rescue me. We're both getting something out of this. It's a mutually beneficial relationship."

Chris straightened in his seat. "I don't see why putting a word in would be a bad thing."

"No," I said firmly.

We went back to the contract, but I couldn't quite shake the feeling that Chris didn't get it. I had always taken care of myself. The men I'd had in my life sure hadn't done it. First, my father. Then Peter. I wasn't being stubborn; I didn't need anyone else's help.

"The PDA Clause?" My eyes darted to Piper.

Piper folded her hands and placed them on the table. "You're engaged. You need to do engaged people things."

My stomach dipped. "Like?"

Her gaze moved between the two of us, a patient expression held there. "Well, kids, when two people love each other, they do things like hold hands, touch here or there, kiss."

Kissing? My brain caught on that word and started to send panicky signals everywhere. Of course, you idiot. You're fake-engaged. Kissing is what real-engaged people do. Unless they're part of those weird cults who save their kisses for their wedding day. I wonder if I could convince them I'm in one of those?

"How much PDA are we talking?" I asked.

Piper leaned back in her seat. "I don't know that it's something we can really quantify, to be honest."

"Let's try," I said. "To quantify it, that is."

"I would hope every time you're seen in public."

"That seems fair." Chris nudged me with his shoulder. "Am I that repulsive? I promise I brush my teeth at least once a week and I'll stop eating garlic cloves but if we come across any vampires, that's on you."

The problem was all this intimacy was kind of alarming and *not* because it would be awful.

Let's face it. Chris was no slouch in the sex appeal department (hello, *People*'s Sexiest Man). The problem was that I might kind of, sort of, enjoy it. And that would be terrible. This was purely a business transaction. I was his friend. Anything more than that was not happening. No, sir. Not on my watch.

I looked down my nose at him. "You are slightly revolting, but I'll figure out how to get through it."

He smirked. "Besides, this is all for show. It's not like it means anything."

"Right. No feelings involved. It'll be like kissing my brother."

"Exactly," he said. "It's business."

"Whatever you have to tell yourselves," Piper said. "We want you to cause a little stir. Enough to get your photos in the blogs and take the attention away from the bad press. So, I need you to be adorably, sickeningly in love. Which leads me to this week. Our first goal is to get this town to see you fall in love."

"Is that all?" I muttered.

Chris rubbed his hands together with something like glee. "Let's do this."

It was going to be a very long week.

NINETEEN

I grew up in a ranching town. One night at closing in our town's only bar, two cowboys asked my sister and me, "Y'all want to go pig hunting?"

—*KERRY C.*

"I've been thinking about your library situation," Ali said about four seconds after sitting across from me at the café on Monday. Fried chicken today.

"Let's hear it." The library budget had been put on the back burner while I was getting fake-engaged. My stomach had been in knots since I'd said yes to this whole scheme.

That morning I had checked one thing off the list though. I'd called Shane at Chicky's and explained I needed a few months off for personal reasons. Surprisingly, he'd been willing to take me off the schedule without too much groveling on my part. He was probably relieved he wouldn't have to comp any more meals due to my "attitude." At least for a while.

"We need a fundraiser. Something that attracts people and

gets them to donate. Or maybe a bake sale? Or a fun run? I haven't worked out all the details yet, obviously."

"Obviously." I grinned.

"Wanna come over tonight, and we can brainstorm? I'll buy the pizza if you bring the beer."

My eyes dropped to the tabletop, and I traced a water stain left by a glass long ago. "I can't tonight."

"Why? You gotta date?" She scooped up a forkful of mashed potatoes and stuffed it in her mouth.

"Well, yes."

There. I'd lied. It was official. The first lie of many lies. I was doing this.

"No way. You haven't been on a date in, like, a long time."

"Pot meet kettle," I muttered, giving her pointed glare.

"We aren't talking about me right now. Spill it. Who is it? Do I know him?" She gestured wildly with her fork. "Oh, my gosh, is it the new guy at the feed store? He's cute if you don't mind the missing teeth."

"It's, ah, Chris Sterns."

Ali's eyes grew so big, I was worried they might pop out of her head. She gave a tiny little anemic squeal. Then nothing. Not a sound. Just my best friend staring at me like I had grown a second head and it was playing the flute.

"Say something."

"D-did"—she paused to clear her throat—"did you say you have a date with Chris Sterns?"

I nodded, my face growing hot. "Yeah."

"*The* Chris Sterns?"

"Yes, that one."

With the back of her hand pressed to her forehead, Ali collapsed against her seat. "But... but how? When?"

I shrugged and stuffed a bit of chicken in my mouth to avoid talking.

She blinked slowly before a wide grin overtook her face. Ali had a big smile normally, but this was her special smile, the Danger Smile, I called it. She was thinking things when she smiled that smile. Usually, it leads to questionable situations that often lead to, well, danger.

"I knew he was into you. He's been asking me all kind of questions about you and..." Suddenly, she gasped. "YOU ARE GOING TO MAKE OUT WITH CHRIS STERNS."

And now the entire café had gone silent.

"Ali!" I whisper-screamed and cradled my forehead on my hand.

She winced and had the decency to look apologetic. Half-standing, she waved at the restaurant, which mostly consisted of the regular bunch of old men and chess boards. "Nothing to see here, people. Just ignore us."

I groaned. "I can't believe you."

Ali soldiered on, disregarding my embarrassment. "How did you... I mean... oh, I don't even care. But you had better call me, text me, send a smoke signal, whatever, as soon as you get home tonight. The very second. Do you understand?"

"Okay. Okay."

"What are you wearing? Something that shows off your legs. Don't wear any of those librarian t-shirts. Or that ugly jacket with the weird stripes on the sleeves."

I liked that jacket. "What if I get cold?"

"Duh." The look she gave me could only be described as incredulous. "You'll have a big strong man to warm you up."

"Oh, right." I was positive my face was on fire.

Ali winked. "Now we're talking."

TWENTY

Wanna be my date to my wedding?

—*KERI*

Mama, Iris, and Sue were waiting for me when I got home. The three of them sat side by side on the couch, facing the front door. The television wasn't even on. I guessed I was the entertainment. The thing about small towns is that news travels fast, gossip faster. So, when your best friend yells about your evening plans at lunchtime, you can assume your family knows by dinner.

I should have remembered that.

"Hi." I slowly slid out of my shoes and put my purse down.

Iris scooted over to make a space between her and Mama, a space Mama patted. "Come sit with us, Mae."

I bet this is what the victims of the Inquisition felt like. Except, you know, higher stakes.

I sat.

"Honey," Mama said, putting a hand on my knee and squeezing. "How are you?"

"Yeah, how are you?" Iris repeated with a smirk.

"Got any big plans tonight?" Sue asked.

Subtle, they were not. "I guess you heard."

"What would that be?" Mama asked, barely keeping her smile at bay.

I sighed. "I have a date."

Iris tried to look bored. "I heard it was with Chris Sterns."

"Yes."

"Huh." But I could see she was interested, even a little impressed. "He's kind of hot."

Mama put her arm around my shoulders. "He's such a nice young man. Do you know he fixed our dishwasher? Only took him a few minutes."

"All I know is that he is one fine specimen," Sue said. "Though I haven't seen him up close yet. When's he picking you up?"

"Six thirty."

"Excellent." Sue rubbed her hands together.

"Maybe I should make up some cookies? Or some banana bread?" Mama said. "Something to offer him. You think?"

"A boy like him must eat an awful lot." Sue helped Mama to her feet and handed her the walker. The two of them shuffled toward the kitchen. "Maybe we should make him a meatloaf. He needs protein."

"Do not make a meatloaf," I yelled at their receding backs. "Or anything else. He'll only be here for a few minutes to pick me up."

Sue turned. "Well, now, we need to make sure he keeps his strength up for that goodnight kiss."

Seriously. How was this my life?

I tried on three different outfits before deciding on a soft green knee-length sundress, a pair of cowboy boots, and gold hoop earrings. With a bit of makeup and my hair braided loosely, I was ready fifteen minutes early. That gave me plenty of time to stare at myself in the mirror for far too long. I switched out the earrings and left my hair down. Then I got annoyed at myself for wasting this much energy on a fake date.

Mama and Sue managed to whip up a batch of brownies and a veggie tray. The three of them piled back on the sofa by the time Chris knocked on the door.

"You want me to answer?" Sue asked.

But she looked so comfy sitting on the couch, eating a bag of popcorn with a slightly deranged look of excitement on her face, I told her no.

With a flourish, Chris whipped out a bouquet of roses from behind his back when I opened the door. "For you, madam."

"Oh, thank you." I took them and stood back so he could pass by. "Enter at own risk."

He brushed by me, that same clean, warm smell hitting me immediately. I introduced him to the welcome committee, although he'd met two of them.

"Oh, my. Did you bring flowers?" Sue said. "Those are beautiful."

A dozen, gorgeous dewy pale-pink roses just beginning to unfurl. I wondered where he'd gotten them. They were most definitely not grocery store flowers.

Iris smirked. "Mae hates roses."

"Iris!" I turned to Chris and hesitated ever so slightly before I put a hand on his arm. PDA, Mae. PDA. "They are lovely. Truly. I'll go put them in water."

As I rushed to the kitchen, I heard Mama offer Chris brownies.

"I don't want to spoil my dinner," he said.

"Come on now," Sue said as I returned. "Just a brownie or two so you can keep your strength up."

I sighed. "Just do it or they won't let us leave."

He took a brownie, ate it in three bites, and smiled. "That was great."

Sue elbowed Mama. "Did you hear that, Lucy? He said it was great." She turned her attention to me. "Mae, he's a looker, for sure. I'd let him get to second base, at least."

"I might let him go for a home run, if you know what I mean," Iris said, just in case we didn't.

"Iris," Mama snapped. "Watch yourself."

Iris rolled her eyes. "I would."

"Baseball gets all the good innuendos," Chris said. And then he winked at them.

Which caused my mother to giggle and Sue to mutter something that sounded like, "Batter up."

"Time to go. We are going." I pushed Chris toward the door. "I'll be home in a couple of hours."

"You can keep her out as late as you want, Chris," Mama called. "Don't rush back on my account. You two have fun."

When I closed the door behind us, Chris stopped on the porch and grinned down at me. "You don't like roses?"

I shrugged. "Nope. But you didn't know."

"What's your favorite?"

"Tulips. Carnations. Lilies. Gerbera daisies. Irises. Peonies. Wildflow—"

"So pretty much any other flower except roses?" Smiling, he brushed a piece of hair from my cheek.

The movement was done so casually I wasn't quite sure how to react. My cheek buzzed in the spot his finger had touched me though.

"Why did you do that?" I asked. My voice more an accusation than a statement.

"What?"

"Touch my cheek."

"PDA Clause."

"We aren't in public." I waved a hand wildly around. "There's no need for a display of affection at the moment."

He leaned down and whispered. His breath smelled like toothpaste and cinnamon gum and the thought drifted through my brain that I liked that combination an awful lot. Irritated, I reminded my brain I was not interested. At all. "Pretty sure someone is spying on us from that front window."

I whipped around just in time to see the curtain flutter. "Can we go?"

When we got to his truck, he opened the door for me. "Let me get this straight. You don't like roses, frogs, or Monopoly?"

"That about sums it up." I climbed into my seat.

"You are full of surprises." He leaned a little closer, a smirk lingering at the corners of his mouth. "And, by the way, I like your dress. It suits you."

"Thank you." I clicked the seatbelt into place and ignored the curl of pleasure in my stomach at his compliment. "Now let's get this over with."

TWENTY-ONE

My name must be John Deere. Because I'm a-tractor-ed to you.

—LAURA B.

"Why do you hate roses?" Chris asked after five solid minutes of awkward silence on our drive into town. It should be noted I was mostly the awkward part.

The quiet had given me time to get used to my surroundings. New-ish truck, fancy satellite radio, a chain with a cross hanging from the rearview mirror. Otherwise, it was spotless. I guessed he had people who took care of that for him.

"I just do."

Chris glanced my way. "You know, if we're doing this, we mind as well have fun and get to know each other."

I crossed my arms. "I don't like lying to my mom."

"Don't think of it as lying. We are going on a date. There will be an engagement ring on your finger."

"But none of that is real."

He reached across and wrapped his fingers around on my leg. "I know. It's a lot." With a gentle squeeze, he took his hand back and put it on the steering wheel. "But if we're doing it, we should get to know each other, smile, laugh, enjoy each other's company."

"Smile, laugh." Apparently, I was a parrot now.

I turned to look at him. He had on a red polo shirt, the slim fit kind that curved over his relevant body parts nicely, and a pair of tastefully distressed jeans. So, in other words, he looked awesome without even trying. He could probably wear a onesie and a bonnet and still manage to look awesome though.

He flashed me a smile. "Exactly."

I knew the stakes were high for him. Otherwise, why would he go through all this? But he seemed so laid-back about it. Maybe he was a good actor, better than I gave him credit for.

"Let's start with dinner, okay?" I said.

The Taco Truck was aptly named because it was, well, a taco truck. It was a quiet night, being a Monday, and only a couple other tables were filled. But if our goal was to be seen, I'd make sure we were seen. We ordered and I made sure to introduce Chris to Ana Casarez, one half of the couple who owned the Taco Truck. Ana was known for two things: her taco plate and her quiet but thorough dissemination of information (AKA gossip). I didn't miss the way she discreetly snapped a photo of us with her phone.

We found a seat at one of the picnic tables dotting the patch of dirt in front of the truck. Although it was early April, the air was heavy with humidity and the promise of summer heat. An umbrella protected us from the direct rays of the setting sun. String lights had been draped throughout the area, but it wasn't yet quite dark enough to see them.

I stopped Chris the second before he was about to dig into his taco plate.

"You can't come to the Taco Truck without trying the hot sauce. If you're man enough to handle it."

Chris set his taco down. "Excuse me? Did you just call me a wimp?"

"I think I *implied* you were a wimp." I pulled the condiment basket on the table toward me. It contained three plastic bottles. "You have three choices."

"Why don't these have labels on them?" he asked, his eyes narrowed with suspicion.

"Because they're homemade. For example, this green one is just regular old hot sauce." I tapped the yellow bottle. "This one is the medium sauce, what we call 'Not Your Mama's' sauce. And lastly, the red bottle is lovingly called the 'Wish You Were Dead' sauce."

He leaned back and rubbed his bottom lip with his thumb. I caught myself following its path and jerked my eyes away. "This feels like a test."

"Just having a little fun."

"Alright." He nodded slowly, a glint of mischief in his eyes. "How about this? Each of us tries them. For every sauce we taste, we get to ask the other person a question."

I paused, considering the ramifications of this. "Any question?"

"Everything is fair game. In the spirit of getting to know one another, of course."

"I'm assuming we have to answer honestly?"

He raised an eyebrow. "That was implied."

"Just making sure." The rational part of me pointed out that this was probably a bad idea. The other part of me, the curious part, had questions. "Fine. Let's do this."

We each grabbed a chip from the basket we were sharing and started with the green bottle, dripping out a few drops on our respective chip. With a count of three, we downed them at the same time. This sauce wasn't much more than a typical, run-of-the-mill hot sauce. Sure, it had a bit of a kick, but it went down well enough.

"Pretty good," Chris said. "Ladies first."

I thought about it for a moment. "What do you want to do after football?"

"I want to go into medical research."

"Really?"

"I know you only want me for my body, but I have a brain too." Playfully, he batted his eyes until I cracked a smile. "My undergrad degree is in biology and my plan has always been med school, then a residency in research. I'd like to work somewhere I can study congenital heart defects."

I was impressed and I realized it made his work with the Children's Heart Fund even more important to him. "Do you know where you'd like to go to school?"

He held up a finger. "That's another question."

"Fine," I grumbled. "Your turn."

"So, Peter? How did that happen?"

"Wow. You came out swinging." I picked out a tortilla chip and began breaking it into tiny little pieces. "We started dating my third year in college. He'd already graduated. Granny was going through cancer treatment, I was commuting to school and working as many hours as I could between helping out with Iris."

I paused and nibbled on my bottom lip, trying to decide how much of this story I wanted to tell. When we started dating, I'd been twenty and had never been in a serious relationship. More than that, I'd felt so very alone, longing for someone I could lean on a little. But I chose wrong. Really, really wrong.

"Anyway"—I brushed the chip crumbs off the table—"I thought he was a good guy, but he seemed to be confused by the definition of monogamous. I caught him in the act of cheating the day of my granny's funeral. So now, I hate his guts and sincerely hope one day he is attacked by killer bees and that it's all caught on video so I can replay it when I need a pick-me-up."

"Ouch." His eyes were kind, which I sort of hated. I didn't want his pity. "He really did a number on you."

"It's over now. It could be much worse—I could still be dating him." I shuddered at even the thought. "Ready for round two?"

He picked up the yellow bottle. "Let's do this."

We popped our respective chips in our mouths at the same time. The initial taste was sweet, almost fruity. And then...

"What. Is. This?" Chris coughed, his eyes widening. After chugging half his water bottle, he wiped his mouth with the back of his hand. "Why are you not reacting? I can feel it burning my stomach lining."

It was hot, that was no lie. But one, I liked spicy. Two, I'd done the Taco Truck challenge before, several times. Probably, most of my taste buds had been burned off at this point.

I smiled sweetly. "It wasn't too bad."

"Wasn't too bad? Are you a witch?" He held up his hand. "Don't answer that. I don't want to know. Go on, ask your question."

"Do you have any pets?"

His eyes lit up, a boyish smile exposing his dimple. That dimple. That smile. It did something to my cold, irritated heart. Which I ignored.

"Yep. Three dogs and a tortoise." He pulled his phone out. "Wanna see?"

"Sure." For the next ten minutes, he scrolled through his phone showing me photos of three rascally-looking dogs (all rescues) and his Russian tortoise posing in front of a Barbie-sized kitchen with a tiny chef's hat on its head that made me laugh.

"Now, my question. Why do you hate roses?"

I glared at him. His questions were far more personal than

the ones I'd asked. I opened my mouth to say something vague and vaguely untrue, but Chris interrupted me.

"Remember, we said we'd be honest."

My mouth snapped shut. How had he known?

"Fine. Roses are supposed to be a symbol of love, but mostly they get used for insincere apologies. Give someone roses and all is forgiven. Roses heal all wounds, blah, blah, blah." I was stabbing the table with my finger now. "Anyone can buy roses. Just like anyone can say the words 'I'm sorry' and not really mean them. Roses and apologies, both aren't worth much as far as I'm concerned. People might believe what you say, but they always believe what you do."

Every time my father had come home, it had been with a bouquet of roses and apologies, only for him to repeat the process over and over like the worst kind of déjà vu.

"Sorry," I muttered, my cheeks flushing.

"No roses. Got it."

I cleared my throat and changed the subject. "Ready for round three?"

With a grunt, he eyed the red bottle. "I think this might kill me. If it does, make sure to delete the history on my laptop before my parents see it, okay? For no real reason."

"Searching up baby animal pictures again?"

He nodded sadly. "I knew you'd understand."

Both of us loaded up a chip with three careful drops of hot sauce. Chris counted us down and then there was no turning back. I swallowed quickly and then schooled my face, so it showed as little reaction as possible. Was this mean? Eh, maybe. But I was still going to enjoy every minute.

Chris took his time chewing, which was a real mistake. His expression moved from hesitant and thoughtful to alarmed and pained in under fifteen seconds. His eyes widened and he made the mistake of sucking in a deep breath. The heat was always worse on an inhalation. He beat a hand against the picnic table.

"Why is your face like that?" he demanded, and then poured the rest of his water down his throat with shaky hands. I almost felt bad. But it wasn't permanent. Eventually, it would pass. Eventually.

"Why is my face like what?" I asked, holding back a cough, and calmly taking a sip of water. The heat had bypassed my mouth and gone directly for my throat. My eyes began to water, and I blinked to staunch that.

"Y-you're not..." His accusation hung there as he began to sweat. "I need more water."

He lifted the bottom of his shirt to swipe at his forehead. My gaze snagged on the swatch of abs it revealed. His face was covered so I could look and not feel (too much) like a perv. I had to imagine it took hours and hours of hard work, training, and dedication to have abs like that. Hours in the gym, running, doing crunches, lifting weights getting all sweaty and...

Okay, *now* I sounded like a perv.

I averted my eyes and uncapped my water bottle. Chris snatched it from my hand.

"Hey!" I tried to grab it back, but he was much faster.

He emptied it in two gulps. With narrowed eyes, he swiped the back of his hand across his mouth. "How many times have you done this?"

I crossed my arms, but it was hard to keep the smile in check. "I don't know what you're talking about."

With a grunt, he got up and stalked to the Taco Truck window. When he returned, it was with four more bottles of water which he clutched to his chest like they were bags of gold. Instead of sitting across from me, he pulled out the chair next to me and sat. He was close, close enough that his leg brushed mine. Close enough his arm, warm from the sun (and probably the hot sauce), nudged my shoulder as he ripped the cap off the first bottle and downed it in seconds.

The look he gave me was so disgruntled and grumpy, so

unlike the Chris I knew, I couldn't stop the laughter. He pressed his lips together and glared at me for a couple of beats. His lips began to twitch, and a hint of a smile touched the corners. Slowly, he leaned closer until his mouth was next to my ear, his breath warm on the side of my face.

"You have made a grave mistake," he said in a low voice.

"Oh, yeah?"

"I have a motto."

"What's that? Smile and the world falls at your feet? Or no, wait! Don't drop the sportsball?"

His chuckle was evil. "I don't get mad, I get even. Now it's on."

This time I winked at him. "Bring it."

I think for a first date, it went pretty well.

By the time Chris drove me back home, a half-moon was nestled in the bruised purple sky. Suddenly, he banged his palm on the steering wheel. "I didn't ask my third question."

"Why was that again?" I asked, grinning.

He shot me a dirty look. "You got a mean streak, book lady."

"Ask your question then."

The driveway to the house was dark and the tires crunched on the gravel. He parked near my car. "What do you want to do when you grow up?"

I unbuckled my seatbelt and turned in my seat, curling one leg under me. "I'm already grown up. But I always thought I'd leave Two Harts and live somewhere big. Don't get me wrong, there are good parts about living here. But I've always felt a little like an outsider. We didn't move here until I was ten and I guess I never quite felt like I fit in."

"It seems like you fit in just fine."

"I'm not going anywhere for a while. Got to get Iris through college and, with Mama needing help, I'll be in Two Harts for the foreseeable future." I tapped my chin with a finger. "I guess I have one more question, don't I? I am reserving the right to ask this question at a later date."

"Bold move. I like it."

I grabbed the door handle. "I guess I'll see you later this week?"

"Hold on." He jumped out of the truck and pulled my door open. "A gentleman would walk a lady to her door at the end of a date."

"Even a fake date?"

"Especially a fake date when someone is spying on us from the window."

"Again?" I glanced behind me just in time to see the curtain flutter. "I'm going to kill whoever that is."

"Don't do it on my account."

At the front door, he turned so his back faced the window, his body effectively protecting me from prying eyes.

"So. Thanks for dinner," I said, trying to ignore the relationship between my stampeding heart rate and his proximity.

"I'll send you the bill for the case of Pepto-Bismol I'm going to pick up on the way home."

I laughed. "That's fair."

"You ready?" His arm wrapped around my waist, heavy but not unpleasant. "Gotta make this look good."

"Maybe I don't kiss on the first date," I pointed out, feeling myself tense.

The porchlight illuminated his twisty little grin of mischief. "I promise not to kiss and tell."

"Just do it."

"Such sweet words." His head dipped and stopped close my ear, his breath warm and, even though I didn't want to, I shivered a little. "You smell like cookies."

"Vanilla extract behind the ears. Nothing fancy," I said, irritated my voice sounded breathless.

"I like it. It suits you." He pressed a soft kiss to the corner of my forehead. It was a nothing kiss, more a press of lips than anything, feather light, and yet it felt oddly intimate.

He straightened. I frowned; he grinned.

"See you later, book lady."

"Yeah, sure." Then, without moving an inch, I watched him walk back to his truck and drive off.

TWENTY-TWO

Someone spelled fruit right. 'Cause they put U and I together.

—*AARON Q.*

The next morning, Mama was already up, dressed, and a breakfast of piping-hot apple cinnamon oatmeal (my favorite) was waiting for me. She sat across from me at the table, sipping her coffee and watching me over the top of her mug with a smile.

"What?" I asked. "Is there something on my face?"

"No, honey. You look adorable. Is that a new t-shirt?"

I glanced down and frowned. It was not a new t-shirt. It was a t-shirt I wore all the time. My *Librarians are Just Like Regular People, But Cooler* t-shirt. "No, it's not new."

She hummed.

I took a cautious bite of my oatmeal.

Mama set her mug down and propped her elbows on the table, chin in her hands. "So how was your date? How was that goodnight kiss? Do I get any details?"

"Mama! I thought that was Iris peeking?"

She grinned. "Afraid not. All me."

"Seriously? I can't have a single secret?"

She tilted her head, her eyes narrowing. "Maebell, I suspect you have more secrets than I can even begin to know."

Without looking her in the eye, I stood. Was I finished with my oatmeal? No. Was I finished with this conversation? Yes. It was time to leave before she started to get those secrets out of me.

For a good reason. It's for a good reason, Mae, don't you forget.

I leaned down and gave Mama a kiss on the top of her head. "Have a good day. Not sure if I'm doing anything after work. I'll call. Is Sue coming over?"

"Of course, honey." I'd almost made it out of the kitchen when she stopped me, the teasing note gone from her voice. "Have you called your father yet?"

The knot in my stomach tightened. "No."

"Please, Mae. Please just call him."

With a sigh, I nodded and left for work.

"You want me to call him?" Ali asked. "See if he answers? I could ask about his car's extended warranty."

"Ha. Ha." I dropped my forehead to the table. We were eating lunch in the backroom of the library today. "This is serious."

Ali squeezed my arm. "I know. I'm sorry for joking about it. And car warranties? Such low-hanging fruit. I need better jokes."

I took a bite of my PB and J. "I don't want to see him or talk to him. Ever. But then I don't want Iris to be hurt if he doesn't show."

And maybe that was the worst part, knowing that at the end of all this, Iris would be crushed. I hated my father and that he put us in situations like this over and over. For years, Mama and I had hidden Dad's screw-ups, his broken promises. We'd made excuses and tried to make up for his absences. Maybe that had been the wrong strategy but it's hard to look at a six-year-old and tell her that her father didn't show up like he promised because he got arrested for his involvement in a fake lottery ticket scheme.

I rubbed my chest, the pressure there heavy. It never really left. I'd learned to live with the constant worry. Most of the time, it was manageable. Other times, it grew so extreme, it felt like a physical thing. I'd never talked to Ali directly about my anxiety, but she'd known me a long time and she knew the signs. Like always, she made it her mission to make me feel better.

Ali stood and bounced back and forth on the balls of her feet in a fighter's stance. "You got this." She hopped behind me and rubbed my shoulders. "You call that number and you give it your all. Because who are you?"

"Mae," I muttered, holding back a smile.

"Louder. Really put your heart into it."

"Mae Sampson."

"That's what I'm talking about." She danced back in front of me, throwing a few imaginary jabs with each word. "And. What. Are. You?"

"I'm a librarian?"

"With confidence!"

"I'm a librarian," I yelled, full-on laughing now.

"Not just any librarian. You're the badass librarian of Two Harts, Texas. Books are your superpower. Children want to be you when they grow up. You will not be intimidated by some stupid phone call."

"You are so weird. I love you."

"I know." Ali grinned. She picked up my cell phone and held it out. "Now call the man."

With a sigh, I pulled up his number and dialed. It rang. I bit my lip, heart pounding. But then it rang again and again and again before a generic voicemail recording kicked on.

I didn't leave a message.

TWENTY-THREE

This conversation happened about two weeks into dating, but it's still good. My now-husband asked me during a date where I wanted to eat. I told him I could find something I like anywhere. His reply: "You know, you're the easiest girl I've ever dated."

—J.L.T.

"Alright, everyone," I said, standing in front of the Save the Library Committee who were tucked into the tables in the small library conference room. "We all know the situation. The library is in danger of losing more funding."

When I'd advertised a meeting, I wasn't completely sure who to expect. But five people and a dog had shown up right on time.

"A crying shame," yelled out Horace Otismeyer, who was a retired train conductor with a penchant for urban fantasies. "This is all because of that Peter Stone."

"Now, it's not exactly Peter's fault," Melinda Douglas said. "He just wants to help our little town grow."

Melinda was contractually obligated to make such statements seeing as how she was Peter's great-aunt.

The group took this as open season to debate on the merits of Peter and his plan for Two Harts. Stanley, the half-terrier, half-throw rug rescue dog that belonged to Abel Sanchez, belly-crawled to my feet and stared up at me with huge mournful brown eyes.

"Yes, yes. I don't like it when they all talk at once either," I said.

Stanley half-barked in agreement and then slumped to the side. He wasn't dead or anything. Just lazy.

"Can we please get back to the meeting?" I bellowed.

Mrs. Katz, who had been my sixth-grade teacher, shot me a sharp look. "Really, Mae, did you have to yell?"

I bit the inside of my mouth and prayed for patience. "We need a plan. This mess the library is in requires a good plan."

"Is it true Stone wants to cut the budget by a hundred thousand dollars?" Saylor Bridges, a mother with two young children, asked. She also happened to be the youngest member of the committee. By decades.

"That's what I heard too," Horace said. "A hundred thousand dollars is a lot of money."

It's an entire fake engagement worth, actually.

"Between last year's cuts and these new proposed cuts, it will be close to that amount," I said. "It's going to be catastrophic to the library if this new budget gets through the city council."

"What can we do about it?" someone asked.

"That's what this meeting is for," I said.

"How about we hunt down all those council members and tell them what for?" That was Sarah Ellis, who weighed eighty pounds on a good day and with her white curls, orthopedic shoes, and pearl necklace, was also our oldest member.

"That council will do whatever Peter says." Horace pounded a fist on his palm. "Maybe we could rough up Peter."

"For God's sake, Horace," Mrs. Katz huffed. Horace and Mrs. Katz got along about as well as oil and water. If the oil was a salty retired teacher and the water was a crotchety old man with too much time on his hands.

Abel Sanchez, who was generally a silent observer, piped up. "My son knows a guy."

"We should probably stay away from anything illegal," I said. Although secretly I thought the idea had some merit.

Mrs. Katz raised her hand (because teacher) and waited for me to call on her. "Back in my day, we used to raise money with a silent auction. We'd get local businesses to donate and then let people bid on them. 'Course, the biggest draws were always the donations that came with a man."

I choked on a cough. "I'm sorry, what?"

"Years ago, it started with a lunch auction. The ladies would make a homemade basket lunch. The meals would get auctioned off along with the company of the woman who made them. But it seems the ladies are better at fighting over the men."

"That seems a little sexist," I said.

"But it's the truth. There was once a four-way bidding war over a man that ended with a donation of over five thousand dollars."

I bit back a laugh. "So how did this work, exactly?"

"A man would volunteer—"

"Or be volunteered," Horace cut in, shoulders slumped like he'd been there himself.

"A gentleman would offer a skill or service." Mrs. Katz strolled to the front of the room and faced the crowd. "Things like three hours of handyman work, or enjoy a home-cooked meal by Juan Fernandez. That man made the best fajitas. It was awful easy on the eyes to watch him make them, too."

"You would like his fajitas," Horace muttered.

Mrs. Katz shot him a scathing look.

Sarah nodded. "Years ago, Joe Price was the hot ticket. You remember that?"

It should be noted Joe Price was in his seventies and was permanently clothed in coveralls and grease as he owned an auto shop.

"I do, indeed." Melinda sighed. "He was known to be very good with his hands."

"Of course the quality of the man is important." Mrs. Katz gave Horace a once-over. "Isn't that right, Horace?"

"What's that supposed to mean?" he demanded.

Mrs. Katz cocked one eyebrow. "Oh, I don't know. I seem to remember some of the packages weren't big sellers."

"Just because no one appreciated learning about a fascinating topic..."

Mrs. Katz barked a laugh. "Fascinating topic? The history of railroads in Texas?"

"...doesn't mean it had anything to do with the quality of the man."

"If you say so."

He crossed his arms. "I do say so."

Stanley winced and threw his paws over his eyes. Same, puppers. Same.

"So, it's decided then?" I said, before Mrs. Katz could reply. "We're holding a silent auction."

Horace frowned. "Maybe we could have some rules for this thing? Minimum bids and such?"

Mrs. Katz snorted. "Yes, and rules for the items donated. Nothing train-related, perhaps?"

Horace crossed his arms, shooting a glare at Mrs. Katz.

Although we didn't call for a formal vote, it seemed everyone agreed.

"It will be a regular meat market, I expect," Horace grumbled.

"Cheer up, Horace," Sarah said. "Maybe someone will pay more than twenty dollars for you this time."

TWENTY-FOUR

On a scale from one to America, how free are you this weekend?
  (This one is best on July 1–3.)

—JASON A.

Dreamboat: *Girl, you must be a library book because I can't stop checking you out.*

Me: *Groans. Loudly.*

Dreamboat: *What are you doing after work today? Because it would be both a "Crime and Punishment" if you didn't let me take you out.*

Me: *I might still be recovering from these pickup lines. Wow.*

Dreamboat: *I've been sitting on those for a long time. Feels good to get them out. I'll meet you at the library around 5:30. Will that work?*

Me: *Indeed.*

Dreamboat: *It's a date.*

"So, where are you taking me?" I asked as I locked the door to the library.

Chris slid on mirrored sunglasses. "On a walk."

Weaving my purse strap over my head and shoulder, I waved a hand in front of us. "Alright then, let's walk."

The sun warmed my back as we set off down the block toward Two Harts' main drag. April was sort of a toss-up in terms of weather. Some days, the temperature climbed dangerously close to a hundred degrees. But not today. Today, it was warm but not sweltering, a breeze teasing my hair. The perfect day for a walk.

And for getting noticed.

Joel Reading, who owned the only drycleaners in town, froze when we strolled by. Silvia Salas—a voracious reader of horror—smiled broadly when she saw us and called out a greeting. A group of teenage girls sitting together at a table in front of the ice cream shop stared as we passed. Chris waved, causing them to break out in giggles and one young lady to drop her ice cream cone on the sidewalk.

With a snicker, I bumped him with my shoulder. "Someone has a fan club."

"Jealous?"

I grinned. "Obviously."

Most of Two Harts' quaint little town square was specifically designed to draw in the weekend day-trippers that came in from Houston. It included a mismatch of antique stores, a couple of cafés, and upscale boutiques that no local could afford to shop at and thus they swapped names and owners regularly. Scattered among these touristy shops were necessities like a tiny outdated post office and the slightly larger but still outdated City Hall.

Lastly, the other big draw, Stone Pizzeria (as in Peter Stone's family), a massive and recently renovated brick building with an enormous billboard on the freeway that drew in customers for its famous Spicy Texas Pizza. I refused to go there on principle.

"Does it ever get busy here?" Chris asked.

"We have a busy Founder's Day weekend in the summer. Plus, we get some weekend visitors for the shopping. It's mostly pretty quiet."

A woman I vaguely recognized stared at us from across the way; I waved. Chris turned his head slightly and, a moment later, his fingers skated down my arm and tangled with mine. His hand was warm and dry and so very big.

"PDA clause," he said.

I swallowed. "Of course."

"Piper says we have a photo of us already floating around the internet."

"Really?"

He nodded. "From the Taco Truck."

"Before or after you cried like a baby from the hot sauce?"

"I did not cry," he said with pretend outrage.

"If you say so."

He grunted and tugged me to a stop in front of Bookmarks, the small used bookstore that had been around for years.

"I thought we could look for our new book club selection." The bell tinkled as Chris held the door open. "After you."

I was hit by the comforting smell of musty, used books and something there wasn't a word for—the pure, sweet essence that people who loved books the world over knew and loved.

"Maebell, I haven't seen you in a while," Miss Linda said from behind the long, cluttered book counter at the rear of the store. She was a round woman with a contagious laugh and a penchant for loud, gaudy reading glasses. Today they were orange sprinkled liberally with sparkly crystals. "Chris, it's good to see you again."

"First-name basis?" I asked.

Chris removed his sunglasses and hung them from the collar of his t-shirt. "I've been here a few times."

"More than that," Miss Linda said. "He's keeping me in business all on his lonesome."

Chris's cheeks reddened, and he ducked his head in that charming, ah-shucks way he had. It was, of course, adorable. "I like to read, is all."

Oh, brother. My brain must be slowly dying from lack of sleep. Adorable?

"I mainly come to hear Linda share stories of you when you worked here," he said.

"All good, don't you worry." Miss Linda laughed. "Well, except for the incident when the police were called but we were all on your side, Mae. That man deserved to be slapped upside the head with *On Golden Pond*. He should have thanked his lucky stars you didn't pull from the Russian literature section."

"I'll be sure to watch my manners when around the books," Chris said solemnly, eyes twinkling.

"And don't you forget it." I elbowed him in the gut and, though he grunted, I knew it hurt my elbow more than it hurt him.

Chris put a hand on my lower back and guided me through the aisles until he came to a stop at the romance section. "Let's pick a book."

"Another romance?" I asked. "We could find something else. What about a biography or a nice horror?"

"Turns out I like a good romance."

I cleared my throat and blindly pulled a book from the shelf in front of me. "Right. Well, here's one."

"*The Farmer Picks a Wife: A Single Father Amish*

Romance?" Chris pressed his lips together and flipped the book over. "Josiah Smucker is a hardworking widower with six curious children. Sarah Olsen is a wisecracking, single English woman. Will the two defy the odds when Josiah decides it's time to pick a new wife?" He shot me a pointed look.

"What's wrong with a good Amish romance?" It sounded kind of terrible, not that I would admit it. "The Amish deserve love, too."

With a sympathetic nod, he reshelved the book. "I know, but I'm not sure I want to read about it right now."

"Fine. You pick."

He rubbed his hands together. "I was hoping you'd say that."

While Chris studied the shelf in front of us, I studied him. He wasn't wearing his baseball cap today and dark hair curled at his back collar and around his ears—he really could use a haircut. His t-shirt had the washed-a-million-times look about it and I bet it was the perfect level of softness. It was currently doing an excellent job of stretching across his back, tapering at his waist and although it wasn't particularly tight, it was easy to see his shoulders flex as he searched the shelves. My stomach dipped. Forget about firefighters. Hot guy plus books... where was *that* calendar?

Yes, I was pathetic.

"This one," he said in triumph. "There's even two copies."

"Let me see."

"Nope. It will be a surprise."

"But..."

"It's a surprise."

I glared at him and then made my move, lunging at the books in his hand. But that didn't go as planned at all. Instead of being quick and stealthy, my momentum carried me forward.

Chris caught me around the waist with his free hand, holding me against him. To his credit, he didn't budge, take a step back, move an inch. He was solid as a tree. About as big as one too. It was sensation overload to the nth degree. Strong arm, solid body, broad chest, *those opposable thumbs*. My brain short-circuited and a wave of heat not altogether caused by embarrassment started on my chest and worked its way up my neck to my cheeks.

I should move. It should be noted I did not move. It felt way too nice. Like wrapping up in a blanket fresh from the dryer.

Which was yet another reason I should move.

He was so tall, I had to crane my neck back to see him. He blinked slowly, his eyelids heavy; honey-brown eyes met mine. He wasn't smiling though; it was some other expression in between, almost confusion.

"I'm sorry. Let me just..." I slid my hands between us and felt his heart thump against my palm. I pushed gently on his chest but there wasn't any give. His arm didn't loosen; I was stuck. "Chris?"

He hadn't moved a muscle, his gaze still intense on me. Although the look there had shifted to curious, alert. Something was going on behind his eyes that made me... nervous.

So, I pinched him. Or tried. Pinched implied there was an extra bit of fat to do something with.

"Are you going to let me go?" I asked, exasperated.

He opened his mouth as though he planned to say something (likely mildly flirty and wholly annoying) but instead, he frowned, brow creased. A lock of hair dipped in front of his eye, and I had the strange desire to brush it away.

"Well, look at this. Exactly who I was searching for," an overly loud voice said from the end of the aisle. "Go ahead, don't let me interrupt you."

Peter.

"Great," I muttered and tried to straighten again.

But to my surprise, Chris pulled me closer, his hand settling around my waist. A wide smile—the one he normally wore—

spread across his face as he turned to Peter. "Hey, I guess you did catch us having a moment."

"I was actually looking for Mae there. Was hoping to catch her at the library, but I can see she has plans this evening." Peter rocked back on his heels. While he didn't look uncomfortable, he did look almost confused. "I didn't realize the two of you were friends."

Chris grinned. "Sure, friends."

If a wink had a sound, it was Chris saying the word friends.

For a moment, Peter looked too flustered to say anything. Then he pulled himself together and got to the point. "Mae, I know you've been concerned because you had to let go of your library assistant."

I straightened but Chris kept ahold of one of my hands, the contact both heady and weirdly comforting.

How was this my life?

"I think what you mean, Peter, is that you decided to cut the library budget so deeply I had no choice but to let my assistant go. But do go on."

"I've solved your problem." His smile was friendly, and it creeped me out.

"That you created." I waved my hand at him impatiently. "How exactly did you solve my problem?"

"There's a young man, a senior at the high school, who's looking to do some, ah, volunteer work and I thought he'd be a good fit. I hear he's real good with computers."

"Volunteer work?" I asked, turning this information over in my mind, looking for the loophole. There was no way Peter was offering me this unless there was a reason. It was just like when we dated. He was a tit-for-tat sort of guy. If he gave me something, even small, he expected to get something in return that benefited him.

I guess he was always destined to be a politician.

"Yep. I'll have him report to you on Monday after school. Sound good?"

Yes, and that was the problem. This could only mean one thing: there was something he wasn't telling me. "What's this kid's name?"

"Aidan Bustos."

I narrowed my eyes. "Any relation to Carmen Bustos?"

Carmen owned a chain of laundromats around the county. She was also a member of the City Council.

"Aidan is her nephew. He's come to stay with her to finish out the school year."

"That seems strange, especially when it's his senior year and all," Chris said. My eyes darted up to his, startled. I'd almost forgotten I was practically hanging all over him.

I pointed a thumb in his direction. "What he said."

Peter pulled absently at the collar of his shirt. "He needed a change of scenery."

Chris dropped my hand and turned toward Peter, arms crossed, his mouth set in a firm line. It was kind of football-player-who-moonlighted-as-a-police-detective-and-could-smell-Peter's-lies-from-miles-away pose. It was a good look.

I tried to mirror his energy. "Give it up, Peter. What aren't you telling me?"

"I told you the truth," Peter said. "He needs volunteer hours. It so happens he needs them to complete the community service hours the courts have mandated he do."

I sputtered. "You're giving me a juvenile offender as a library assistant?"

Peter straightened and somehow managed to look smug, damn him. "You're welcome."

TWENTY-FIVE

Are you a parking ticket? 'Cause you have fine written all over you.

—JULIA B.

Next morning, I woke to Iris sitting on my bed, staring down at me. Which was a little terrifying. For a split second, I thought I was dreaming.

"Hi?" I rubbed the sleep out of my eyes and hunted blindly for my glasses on the nightstand.

My sister nudged me. "Move over."

I slid my glasses on and stared at her for a long moment. "Why?"

"Because I wanna lay down. Geez, why can't you just do it?"

I scooted slowly. No sudden movements. I didn't want to scare her away. "Okay?"

She slid in next to me and laid down, stacking her hands behind her head.

"Is everything okay?" I asked.

"I'm thinking of going back to blonde," she announced. Holding up a piece of unnaturally black hair.

"Huh." Maybe I was still sleeping. Or in an alternate dimension? Was I dead? Had she finally succeeded in turning me into a vampire?

"I mean, the black is getting kind of old and maybe I need a change, you know?"

"Yeah, right." Must seem disinterested or she'll get spooked, and this sweet sisterly moment will be over, never to happen again.

"I am going to college next year and all."

"Yep." Keep talking. Please don't stop. Iris used to talk to me all the time. She'd been a regular chatterbox.

Another long moment of silence.

"How was your date with the football player?" she asked, turning on her side and propping her face on her hand.

"It was fun." And that wasn't even a lie. It had been fun. At least until Peter ruined it. I was seriously considering siccing Ali on him now. He'd earned it. Which reminded me. "Hey, do you know a kid at school named Aidan Bustos? He's a senior. He's new."

She shrugged. "Not anyone I know."

More silence. Except she was staring at me. We'd moved on from sweet sister chat to just plain weird.

I cleared my throat. "Did you need something else?"

"Have you heard from Dad?" she blurted out. "I've left a bunch of messages but then I wondered if maybe they accidentally got erased or something and maybe that's why he's not calling back..." Her voice drifted off, but her eyes were bright with hope.

With a groan, I put an arm over my eyes. "I called. No answer."

She sighed. "Yeah, I get it."

The gentle ring of hope in her voice made my chest tight. I

sat up and peered down at her. "You know sometimes Dad can be kind of hard to nail down."

Understatement of the year.

She shrugged and picked at the black polish on her fingernail. "I know. I just thought it's my graduation and it's a big deal."

"I don't want you to get hurt."

She scowled. "Please. I am practically an adult."

I swallowed back a bitter laugh. Someone should tell her that being an adult does not exempt you from pain. "I'll keep trying, okay?"

TWENTY-SIX

I like your shirt. I'd like it more on the floor next to my bed.

Dreamboat: *Are you tired?*

Me: *Why?*

Dreamboat: *I know you spend all day making shhh happen.*

Me: *Wow.*

Dreamboat: *You like it, and you know it.*

Me: *Why are you bothering me?*

Dreamboat: *'Cause I know how much you miss me.*

Me: *I saw you two hours ago at lunch.*

Dreamboat: *You don't have to admit it. I know it in my heart.*

Me: *What do you want?*

Dreamboat: *I have a question.*

Me: *???*

Dreamboat: *How do you feel about getting dressed up?*

Me: *Why?*

"This is not what I imagined when you said 'getting dressed up.'"

Chris laughed, low and a little evil. "I think you look hot."

"That's because I am hot." I attempted to pat at the sweat on my forehead with a giant paw. It did not help. "It's got to be a million degrees in this thing."

Not even in my very active imagination would I have put myself at the children's hospital in Houston wearing a rabbit suit on a Thursday evening. Not some sexy little playgirl number with bunny ears and a little tail either. This was a head-to-toe costume from the tip of the very long, sticky-uppy ears to the oversized bunny feet. In between all that was a round, fluffy body covered in a polka-dotted pink dress. My grandmother would be so proud.

Chris adjusted my bunny nose with its mile-long whiskers before taking a step back and giving me the once-over. "I think you are the very embodiment of Harriet the Heart Hare."

Harriet the Heart Hare was the mascot for the Children's Heart Fund and, as such, she showed up at all their events. While a woman named Molly usually did all the gigs in the Houston area, she was sick. So, I'd volunteered.

Was volunteered? Something like that.

"I think I'm ready." I took a step forward and almost fell flat on my face.

"Whoa." Chris steadied me and hooked his arm through one of mine. "We don't want Harriet to look like she's been knocking back margaritas all day. You hold onto me and we'll make the rounds."

"Easy for you to say," I grumbled and picked up one over-sized foot and winced as it slapped down on the linoleum hospital floor.

With a chuckle, Chris guided me down the brightly painted hallway toward a larger room the staff called the game room. Chris explained this wing was for kids with heart issues. Many were returning guests and often stayed for weeks at a time.

"Chris," said a woman in jeans, an Elmo t-shirt, red high-top Converse and an ID badge swinging from her neck. "It's good to see you."

"Hey, Dr. C." He held up his hand. "Nice shoes."

Grinning, she gave him a high-five as we passed.

"She's a cardiothoracic surgeon. One time, with the family's permission, I got to watch her put a heart stent in. It was amazing."

"You mean you hadn't already done that to earn your Surgery badge?"

"Funny. Can we pick up the pace a little here? I'd like to see the kids before they graduate from high school."

"Well, excuse me. It feels like I'm walking around inside a seven-hundred-pound sauna." I batted away one of the rabbit ears dangling in my face. "I don't get to strut around wearing a football jersey and shorts."

And looking very good in them, of course. The jerk.

We passed a couple of nurses who called out greetings, a mother coming out of one of the rooms who Chris paused next to and gave a side hug, and a woman pushing a cart full of cleaning supplies who he stopped to ask about her son in college.

"So, do you come here often?" I asked.

"Now who has cheesy pickup lines?"

I scowled, which only made my bunny nose twitch and Chris laugh.

"At least twice a year. Usually around Easter. Then around the holidays when I can get away, I lay on the guilt and get a bunch of the guys from the team to visit. We have a big party. All the kids are invited, even the ones who aren't currently patients. There's a ton of food and games and a visit from Santa. Oh, and karaoke, which I am awesome at."

"I can imagine," I said in a dry voice. "Is this the only one you visit?"

"I try to get to others when we're at away games if I can sneak off for a couple of hours. I visit the one in Oklahoma City more because my sister has spent a lot of time there."

"Ninety-five," a voice yelled as we passed a patient room with the door propped open. It was the number on the back of Chris's jersey.

With a grin, he stopped and backtracked taking me with him. "Yo, Carmichael."

I hovered by the door while Chris walked over to the hospital bed where a young kid was laying, a toothy smile stretched across his thin face. They did a complicated hand-shake and Chris sat on the edge of the bed while the boy began to chatter excitedly. My heart did a funny sort of flip that was hard to ignore. I tried to, of course.

"You aren't Molly," a woman said beside me.

I jumped (oh, the irony) and struggled to turn my entire bunny body to see her. The tall Black woman clutching a generic cup of hospital coffee smiled at me. "Nope, not Molly. She couldn't make it."

She tilted her head toward Chris and the boy. "That's my son, J.J. I'm Erika."

"Nice to meet you. I'm Mae. I would shake your hand, but..." I held up a paw.

With a chuckle, she took a sip of coffee and winced. "I swear this stuff is watered-down bayou sludge. I'm glad Chris stopped by. When we heard he was coming, J.J. was upset the doctors wouldn't let him go to the game room. Too many germs at once."

"How's he doing?" I flushed. "Oh, gosh. I'm sorry. You don't even know me. I didn't mean to pry."

"Oh, no. It's alright." She patted me on my bunny shoulder. "He's on the mend now. He had a setback but that's expected. He had a heart transplant earlier this year."

"That's good to hear."

"Chris has been a big support through all of it." She smiled widely. "About two years ago, things were looking grim with J.J. My husband was laid off and, on top of that, our car died. One morning, I look outside and there's a minivan in my driveway, paid in full. I know it was from him. Never would confess to it though."

"That's... wow." A warmth spread through me that had nothing to do with how hot this rabbit suit was.

"Exactly... wow." With an affectionate smile, she gave me another pat on the shoulder. "I'm gonna go say hi. It was nice to meet you. Maybe I'll see you again sometime."

After she disappeared into the room, I hobbled to the nurse's station and leaned on it for support. Chris found me there and offered me his arm.

"Where's your jersey?" I asked.

He shrugged. "Gave it to J.J. I have plenty more where that came from anyway."

"This is really important to you, isn't it?" I asked, my voice quiet.

"Yeah, it is."

I'd always believed a person's actions spoke louder than their words. My father had shored up that lesson for me early on. Chris's actions were telling a story. These kids, this place, were his passion.

Chris paused about ten feet from the game room. In the doorway, a little boy with two missing front teeth and giant blue eyes gripped an IV pole and hopped on the tips of his toes with excitement. Chris waved.

He turned me to him, his expression stern. "I need to say something serious right now."

"Don't mind the rabbit suit. I have my serious face on." I twitched my nose for effect.

"Harriet the Heart Hare is a very nice hare. She brings happiness to sick little kids and their families."

"I get it," I said, trying and failing to reach an itch on the back of my neck. These giant bunny paws were useless. The Easter Bunny did not get enough credit.

"That means," he continued, "you're going to have to push aside your natural inclination to being a grump."

"Excuse me." I stamped one of my bunny feet. "I do not have a natural inclination to being a grump. I am a perfectly nice person."

Chris gave me what could only be called a dubious look. "I don't know. The other day I'm pretty sure you threatened to shove my phone in a place it did not belong."

"It was one in the morning, and you wouldn't stop texting me."

"Don't turn this around on me. My point is, you need to be nice to the children. If you make any of them cry..." He shook his head.

"I am not going to make anyone cry," I snapped. "I work with kids every day."

That dimple popped out on his cheek. "I know. I just like to mess with you. You kind of have a quick temper there, Freckles."

I released a big enough breath that my whiskers bounced in response. "You are so irritating."

He tapped me on my bunny nose and offered me his arm. "Let's hop to it."

"Har, har." I laced my arm through his. "And don't call me Freckles."

TWENTY-SEVEN

May I use your phone? I want to call God because an angel fell from Heaven.

—ELIZABETH F.

The following Monday, I was fighting with one of the computers that had been giving me fits for days. Yet another thing I needed to replace at the library. If Peter had anything to do with it, I might as well invest in some stone tablets and a chisel because that was about all I could afford.

"Please don't tell me we got another virus." I pounded on a couple of keys hoping something would happen. It did not.

"I could help you with that," said a voice behind me.

I jumped in my seat. Standing behind me, I found a young kid, maybe seventeen, wearing khaki pants with creases down each leg and a button-down shirt that was tucked in. His dark hair was neatly parted and combed. A pair of round wire-framed glasses rested on his nose.

"Who are you?" I asked, standing.

"I'm sorry if I startled you, ma'am." He held out a hand.

"I'm Aidan Bustos. Mr. Stone said I was to report to the library today."

Tentatively, I held out my hand to shake. "Right. You would be the kid who is here doing community service hours."

With an almost inaudible sigh, he dropped his eyes and stared at the floor. He wasn't quite as tall as me, and he was thin in that way teenage boys often are. "Yes, ma'am, that would be me."

I kind of felt sorry for the kid, to be honest. He didn't seem like he had it in him to do anything that would get him in trouble with the law.

I took a step back from the computer. "Do you think you really can fix this thing?"

"Absolutely." He was already pulling out the chair and settling in. "Give me twenty minutes and I'll get this all straightened out for you, ma'am."

"Have at it. But if you call me ma'am one more time, we are gonna have problems. Mae is fine."

He grinned up at me, and I caught a glimpse of a crooked tooth, which made him look like a little kid instead of the almost grown man he was. "Yes, ma— I mean, Mae."

I'm not saying I trusted the kid, but he spent the rest of the afternoon doing exactly what I told him to do and doing it well. After fixing the computer (take that, blue screen of death), I showed him around the library, and he picked up on it pretty quickly. In short, Aidan Bustos was not what I expected at all.

By 4:30 p.m., and maybe for the first time in months, I was all caught up. Everything was where it needed to be. I was just waiting for the end of the day. So, I told Aidan he could work on homework, if he had any, for the next thirty minutes until we closed.

I answered a few emails, and when I walked by him next, I saw him bent over a calculus book. "That looks heavy-duty."

He blushed. "I'm pretty good at math. It's my favorite subject."

"No kidding."

I sat down across from him at the table and folded my arms. "What kind of grades do you get, if you don't mind me asking?"

Aidan set his pencil down and leaned back in his chair, crossing his arms in the same way I had. A spark of interest flashed in his eyes. "I was on track to be valedictorian at my old school."

"What happened?"

"I did something I wasn't supposed to do. But I'm not sorry I did it." He looked me dead in the eye when he said it, too. I liked this kid.

I shook my head slowly. "I won't ask you for specifics. But I will ask if you got in trouble because someone got hurt."

Aidan picked up his pencil and started writing again. "Nobody got injured, if that's what you're asking. But the right people got what they deserved."

I know I said I wouldn't ask him what he had done, but the question was still on the tip of my tongue. And I probably would have asked him point-blank except that was when my cell phone dinged with a notification.

My heart did this silly little half-beat it did these days whenever I heard that notification. Because that notification almost always meant I'd gotten a text from Chris. I liked getting texts from Chris.

I was kind of disgusted with myself.

But it wasn't from Chris. It was from Piper, his publicist. And it was one sentence:

We need to talk.

TWENTY-EIGHT

At a bonfire with friends, I once had a guy ask if I had any Irish in me. I responded with no and he asked, "Would you like some?" Mind you, I was sitting on my boyfriend's lap at the time.

He left shortly after that.

—ASHLEY H.

"We have a problem," Piper said.

I blinked and tried to keep my attention on her, but she stood in front of an enormous stuffed moose. I mean, enormous. It had to be almost nine feet tall. How had they gotten that thing in here?

After work, I'd come right over, and had been ushered into an open living area at the Stuffed Animal House (sounded better than Creepy Taxidermy House). The room was huge with a vaulted ceiling accented with wooden beams. All dark wood and leather and so much space for critters of all kinds.

Chris nudged me with his shoulder. "Right?"

"What?"

Piper frowned. "This is serious."

"Sorry. That moose has such sad eyes." Like the poor guy had just wanted to decompose naturally like a dead moose should. "What's going on?"

"One of the gossip blogs released an exclusive interview from an anonymous source who gave a tell-all about Vegas," Piper explained, handing over her phone so I could watch.

This source was nothing more than a shadowy figure wearing a hoodie with an altered voice. He claimed to know the identity of the woman Chris was with and went on to imply the two of them were then and now "very, very, *very* close" and not in the brother-sister way.

"Do we know who this guy is?" I asked.

Piper's jaw ticked. "Not a clue right now. I'm working on it."

"You could clear this up with one statement," Doug said. He lounged in an oversized chair covered in what I suspected was actual cowhide, an ankle resting on his knee. He had, thankfully, not been around much at all but he'd made a special trip so we could "all be on the same page."

Ugh.

"I'm not revealing who she is, if that's what you mean," Chris said. I could feel how tense he was even with two feet of couch separating us.

"That's not what I meant," Doug continued, picking at invisible lint on his suit jacket sleeve. "I think we should go with their story. You had a little fun. Who cares? You're a grown man. Think what it could do to your image."

"I don't see how that would help his image at all," I said.

Doug shook his head in disgust. "You wouldn't. You don't know how these things work. But Chris here gets some notoriety and then he's getting endorsement deals with the big companies. He'd make money, hand over fist. Instead of all this charity work or whatever the hell he wastes his time on."

"Being bad makes him more marketable?"

"Exactly."

I glanced at Chris, saw his jaw tighten, watched the fist resting on his knee curl. He hated this idea.

"That's just stupid. No, absolutely not. Chris is not doing that." I felt the weight of Chris's gaze and wondered if I'd misread him.

Doug snorted. "It's so very convenient that if he did do it, he wouldn't need a fake fiancée anymore, would he? You'd be out of a job."

I decided at that very moment that I hated Doug. I hadn't liked him before but now we'd moved on to a different level. A level even Peter Stone had not reached. I opened my mouth to explain to him exactly where he could shove his opinion of me.

And just as quickly closed it when Chris slid his hand on top of mine and spoke. His voice had an edge of steel in it. "That's enough, Doug."

The two men stared each other down like they were about to have a shootout, spaghetti western style.

"Knock it off, you two." Piper took a seat across from us. "We have a plan. We're getting tons of engagement and views on the updates we've been posting online. A lot of positive attention. I think it's time we take this to the next level."

That sounded foreboding. "What does that mean exactly?" I asked.

"We need to bring the attention right back to you two love-birds." Piper smiled at us. "I think it's time for a trip to meet Chris's family and announce the engagement."

Meet his family? Meet. His. Family. Announce the engagement. My brain wasn't sure which one I should latch onto first and freak out about. I forced a smile, but a wave of panic hit me. Were my hands shaking? Was I dying? That sounded nice. *That's what you think,* the eyes of the stuffed moose seemed to say.

"Deep breaths." Chris moved closer until I could feel his thigh touching mine. He placed a reassuring hand on my back, rubbing small circles, calming me just by being nearby.

It occurred to me that this was Chris all the time. He didn't rattle easily. I don't think I'd ever heard him raise his voice. Right this instant, it's what I needed. His calm calmed me.

Which was confusing and terrifying all by itself.

"What if they don't like me?" I whispered.

"This is ridiculous," Doug muttered.

"Shut up, Doug," Piper said, her voice mild.

"They'll like you," Chris said.

I shot him a glare. "You can't know that. What if they figure out we're fakes? What if they secretly hate Texans or redheads?"

The hand on my back slid around my shoulders and pulled me against his side. I didn't resist. I was too busy wondering how in the world my life had gotten this weird.

"Having known them all my life, I don't know of any anti-redhead opinions they may hold. I feel confident they'll like you, despite the hair." The trace of amusement in his voice irked me, even if I was being ridiculous.

"Don't laugh at me."

He grinned. "I'm not laughing at you."

"Yes, you are."

In reply he squeezed my shoulder. "They already know all about you. They'll be excited to meet you."

"How do they…"

"I told them."

He told them? *What* had he told them? I squeezed my eyes shut and took a deep breath. "Right."

"We'll leave right after the library closes on Friday and get back early Monday morning. You'll be tired but you'll be back at the library to open it."

"That seems like a lot of driving for less than forty-eight hours. Maybe it's not worth it?" Please.

"Chris has access to a private jet through the team," Piper said. "You'll use that. It's not a long flight."

"We're flying?" I asked, my voice at least three octaves higher.

Seriously, could this get any worse?

TWENTY-NINE

During COVID, someone asked me,
   "Is it hard having a smile that contagious during a global pandemic?"

                                                    —SAVANNAH D.

Yes, it could.

"Please tell me you aren't wearing that shirt to dinner," I said, catching a glimpse of Iris in my bedroom mirror where I was attempting to apply makeup with a mostly shaky hand.

To say I was not ready for tonight was like saying the Atlantic Ocean was a mudpuddle. But Chris had insisted.

"It has to happen," he'd said, and no amount of arguing or bartering on my part was going to change his mind.

Iris glanced down at her shirt. "What's wrong with this?"

On a normal day, I wouldn't say a word about her t-shirt, the one that read *Dead Inside* in bold white lettering. But today was not a normal day, and that was saying a lot after what had been a few weeks of really not-normal days.

I met her eyes in the mirror, saw the mulish set of her jaw, and decided it wasn't worth the battle. "You know what? Wear it. I don't care."

"Not that I needed your permission," she muttered as she skulked out of the room.

After brushing on one last coat of mascara, I pulled on the black pencil skirt and a dark green shirt with shoulder cutouts and three-quarter sleeves. I slapped on a necklace and earrings and slid into a pair of strappy black flats. I took a few steps back and inspected myself in the mirror. Aside from the panic in my eyes, I thought it was a decent enough outfit.

After all, if a woman's lucky, she'll only get fake-engaged once in her life and she'll want to look her best when it happens.

In the living room, Mama and Sue were sitting on the couch, Mama in a yellow and cream dress and Sue in what she called her "fancy" khakis.

With too much nervous energy, I paced. Adjusted a couple of rabbit figurines. Straightened a picture on the wall. Thought about getting in my car and not stopping until I hit the Mexican border. "Where's Iris?"

"Right here." She shuffled in from the kitchen, glass of Kool-Aid in hand. "What the hell is with you? You're freaking out."

"Iris," Mama said, a warning in her voice.

"Oh, come on." She stuck a fist on a hip. "I can't say hell? Seriously?"

"Hell is a gateway word that leads to other more serious words, and I would prefer you didn't use it in this house."

"A gateway word? Geez. Wait, is geez okay? It could lead to things like gosh darn it and that's one step away fro—"

"Young lady..." Mama said in her "do not mess with me" voice.

I was almost glad when Chris knocked on the door. Almost. My heart rate tripled. I flipped around to face all three of them.

"I am not freaking out," I snapped in a very freaked-out

way. Closing my eyes, I took two deep breaths. "Everything is fine."

When I yanked open the door, I was met by the largest, most vibrant bouquet of flowers I had ever seen.

"Those are gorgeous," Mama breathed from behind me. "Move, Mae, let him in."

The arrangement barely fit through the door, but Chris managed it. He set it on the coffee table, right in between a rabbit candy dish and a tabletop book called *Bunnies in Action*, and brushed his hands off on his khakis. He'd dressed up for this occasion too—a dark-blue button-down shirt and a tie.

"Not a single rose in sight. I told them to put in one of every flower they had but no roses."

"They're beautiful." Smiling, I touched a bright-yellow gerbera daisy. "Thank you."

Without any warning, he wrapped an arm around my waist and tugged me to his side. I tried to keep a respectable distance between us, but it was no use. It was either hold on or fall on my backside. I was a sensible woman; I held on.

Chris grinned. "Nailed it. Didn't I?"

Stealthily, I tried to pry myself from under his arm. His hold on me tightened as though he'd anticipated my attempt. I briefly thought about slamming my foot down on his, but, to be honest, my heart wasn't in it. There was something calming about the weight of his arm and the steady rhythm of his heart under my ear. And it was all part of the plan. We were supposed to be in love.

I pushed up and kissed his cheek. "You did great."

Iris groaned. "Gross. Get a room."

Without taking her eyes off Chris and me, Sue whapped Iris upside her head.

"Ouch." Iris rubbed at the spot.

Mama ignored them both. "Dinner's about ready. Mae, why

don't you take our guest to the table?" She turned her head to glare at my sister. "You can help me get the food out. Now."

Iris groaned but did as she was told, Sue following behind muttering something about "respect" and "next time I'll smack you harder."

Mama smiled widely. "It will be just a minute now."

With the coast clear, I exhaled and wiggled out from Chris's arm.

"You okay there?" he asked.

"No," I whispered. "I am not okay. My stomach is in knots."

He smirked. "I think that's supposed to be my line. I am the one who is about to ask your mother for her blessing to marry her daughter."

I groaned, twisting my hands at my waist. "This feels so wrong."

"Hey." With a gentle touch, he stilled my hands and waited until my eyes met his. "There's still time if you want to back out. It's okay."

Oh, no. Gentle, Understanding Chris. Danger. Danger.

His eyes were kind and patient and sincere, and I knew, I *knew*, he would put the brakes on it all and walk right out that door. But I also knew he had a lot to lose—a sister to protect, a passion for helping those kids and families—and I didn't want to be the reason he lost it.

Also, I wasn't a quitter, dammit. I straightened, adjusted my glasses, and poked my finger in his chest. "Don't think you're getting out of this, buddy."

Shaking his head, he held up his hands. "Wouldn't dream of it."

"Good. Now, let's go lie our faces off."

"How did that go? What did she say?" I asked when we were safely tucked away in Chris's truck and driving down the road.

His grin was devilish. "She offered me a dowry of forty rabbit figurines and one geriatric cat. She promised you would be a meek and obedient wife. Oh, and something about good birthing hips."

Laughing, I smacked him on the shoulder. "What did she really say?"

He tossed me an amused look. "She said it seemed a little sudden but she trusted your judgement and if you said yes that was enough for her."

"Oh, that's sweet." A wave of guilt washed over me. "She's going to be sad when we break up."

Chris reached over and put his hand on my knee. We drove in silence for ten minutes before I asked where we were headed.

"You'll see."

Another fifteen minutes, and we pulled in front of a quaint little bed and breakfast. Chris hopped out, came around the truck, and helped me out.

"What's going on here?"

"Don't look so suspicious." He grabbed one of my hands and pulled me through a side gate and around the back of the house.

When we turned the corner, I gasped. The garden was a riot of spring flowers, most allowed to grow wild in patches. Crape myrtle trees lined the cobblestone path. It led straight to a gazebo, painted white with twinkly lights twined around it. As we got closer, I saw the table set up in the middle of the gazebo. Candles flickered and a bucket held a bottle of champagne or wine.

It was beautiful; romantic, even. A flutter started in my stomach.

"What's going on?" I asked again. "D-did you do all this?"

"Mostly."

Somewhere around the gazebo, someone snorted and that's

when I saw Piper. "Are you kidding? You know damn well I did all this."

"Well, I paid for it all," Chris grumbled.

"But why?" I asked in confusion.

Piper made her way toward us. "We can't let you get engaged without a photo of it, can we?"

"Oh, right." That absolutely made sense. Except why did I feel strangely disappointed?

"For you." Piper held out a jewelry box to Chris. "You owe me big time after what I had to do to track this down."

Chris popped the box open. I gasped and gazed down at the most beautiful engagement ring I'd ever seen. For a moment, I almost forgot to breathe, staring down at the large opal stone, a rainbow of colors under the sunshine, surrounded by tiny diamonds in a white-gold setting.

"Piper, you did good." With one of his giant football hands, Chris picked it up and gently slid it on my left ring finger. "Fits perfectly, too."

My chest tightened as I looked at the ring on my finger. I'd never been one to dream about weddings and flowers, but I'd also never seen a ring like this before. A sudden punch of longing hit me hard. "I— Thank you. It's beautiful."

Piper turned to me, hiding a smile. "We'll take a couple of photos. I'm taking them with my phone. We'll be quick and dirty and then you can go on about your evening. Pop that ring back off and put it in the box."

I should have expected this. It made perfect sense, and yet that flutter I'd had died a slow and painful death.

Pushing the feeling aside, I tugged the ring off and handed it back to Chris. "Let's get fake-engaged."

"You're getting married," Mama said, her eyes shining.

"Y'all are gonna have some mighty fine children," Sue said,

making large, unidentifiable shapes with her arms. "Big, strapping children."

"Thanks?" I said.

"I'm not wearing a gross bridesmaid's dress," Iris said. "Unless it's black."

"Excuse me," I said. "Who said you were a bridesmaid?"

"Um, duh." She leaned forward suddenly, a dangerous sparkle in her eye. "Could we get tattoos for your bridal shower?"

"You are not getting a tattoo while you live in this house, Iris Marie Sampson, even if it's for your sister's wedding," my mother said.

"Mom."

"No."

Iris crossed her arms, her expression mutinous. "So stupid."

Ignoring them, I plowed ahead. "This weekend we're going to his parents' house."

Mama bit her lip and, for the first time, concern began to shine in her eyes. "This all seems so fast. I want to make sure you don't feel rushed."

Iris rolled her eyes. "He's, like, a bazillionaire football player. If it doesn't work out, she can divorce him and get a ton in alimony."

"Wow. Thanks for the support," I said.

She shrugged. "It's the truth."

I took a deep breath, pushing down the desire to spill all my secrets right there on the living room floor. "I l-love Chris, and I'm excited to marry him."

Mama tugged on my hand until I half stood, half leaned over the table, so I was eye level with her. Using that super X-ray vision that only mothers have, she stared into my eyes for a long moment before nodding with a smile. I wondered what she'd seen there.

"Alright, Maebe, we have a wedding to plan, don't we?

Come give me a hug." I let myself linger in her arms, breathing in all the things that made her my mama—the lemon lotion she loved, her strawberry shampoo, and plain old comfort. The backs of my eyes began to sting, and I willed myself not to cry.

Everything was fine.

Everything. Was. Fine.

THIRTY

Did you sit in powdered sugar? 'Cause you've got a sweet bum.

—CHELSEA C.

"Are you sure this pilot is licensed?" I asked. "Like, you've seen his credentials?"

"Sure. He graduated top of his class from Acme Pilot and Cosmetology School. After we get to cruising altitude, he'll come back and give you a blowout."

"Funny." Glaring at Chris, I yanked on my seatbelt for the twenty-third time. I'd never been on a plane before. Or out of the state of Texas. It was natural I'd be a little cautious.

We sat facing one another at the middle back of the plane (according to my research, the safest place to sit on a plane when you're plunging to your death and want any chance of survival). Piper and Doug were on the plane too, but Piper had work to do, and Doug grumbled about needing a nap.

Chris leaned forward and covered my hands with his. "It's going to be fine. I promise."

I blew out a deep breath. "Okay."

The flight attendant, a slender blond man with pink highlights, stopped at our seats. His nametag read Elvis. "Y'all get buckled up. Pilot says we have about five minutes until takeoff."

My stomach roiled as panic shot through me. "Not okay, not okay."

"Is there anything I can help with?" Elvis asked, crouching by my seat.

Chris unbuckled his seatbelt and switched seats, so he was sitting right next to me. "Just a nervous flyer. We have it under control."

"Alright then." Elvis stood and smiled. "You let me know if I can help."

"Elvis," I called when he was about five feet away.

He turned. "Yes?"

"When our plane crashes to the earth somewhere over East Texas, will you try and save me first? Before him?" I shoved a thumb in Chris's direction.

He grinned. "I'll do my best."

Chris buckled up and pulled up the armrest between us. He scooted a little closer, so we were hip to hip. While that probably should have annoyed me, instead I felt a bit of tension drain off me.

"Why are you over here?" I asked.

"I'm going to distract you."

"How?"

"The usual ways."

"Which are?"

"First, I'll share one of my most excellent pickup lines with you and you'll say something sarcastic about it. If that doesn't work, I'll tell you about the time I got stuck in a tree in my neighbor's yard naked and had to be rescued by firemen. To be fair, I was six and it was a dare."

I snorted.

"So, then I'd move on to putting my arm around you, and telling you to lean in and hold on as tight as you want when we take off because I won't break. Which you will do, even though you'll tell me you don't need any help."

The plane engines began to rev; my heart rate followed suit. "This is happening. This is really happening. Skip to the third option."

"It will be over before you know it," he said in a disgustingly chipper voice as he curled an arm around my shoulders and pulled me to him.

The plane began to race down the runway, picking up speed. I turned my face into Chris's chest and closed my eyes, breathing in laundry detergent and warm, clean skin.

I knew this was ridiculous. I was a grown woman, for Pete's sake. I had a college degree. I ran the only library in four towns. Sometimes I checked the mail barefoot in the summer in a hundred-degree weather. I was not a weakling.

Chris ran his fingers through my hair and that was kind of nice. He pulled me closer yet. Just then, climbing into his skin seemed like a very good idea. It was then I heard the singing, the words to "Hush, Little Baby" sung close to my ear. It was not good singing. In fact, it was terrible.

I lifted my head and looked up at Chris. "What are you doing?"

"Singing. It's to soothe you." He launched into another verse.

Laughing, I shook my head. "Please don't."

He halted mid-verse. "Excuse me? This is good stuff. I practiced."

I laughed harder. "Stop it. You know you sound terrible."

With a huff, he took his arm from around my shoulders and crossed them over his chest. "My mom thinks I have a nice singing voice."

"So, your mother is tone-deaf too?" I asked, but I was

laughing so hard at this point, I'm not sure the words made sense.

"This is the kind of thanks I get for helping you."

I swiped at the tears. "Yes, you're right. Of course. Sorry."

"Well, good." He jabbed a thumb in the direction of the window. "Because we're already in the air now."

"We are?" I leaned around him, taking in the fluffy white clouds. "I did it. Oh, my gosh, I did it!"

He tapped me on the nose, his eyes warm. "You sure did."

THIRTY-ONE

Do you watch Star Wars? *'Cause Yoda one for me.*

—JEREMY S.

"I have questions." I tucked a leg underneath me, turning toward Chris.

He was in the driver's seat of the SUV he'd rented at Tulsa Airport where we'd left Piper, who was visiting friends in the area, and Doug, who was headed back to New York. From the airport, it was about an hour's drive to his parents' house in a little town on Lake Eufaula.

"About?"

I pulled a folded piece of paper from my purse. "I did some research. I've never known anyone who had their own Wiki-pedia page."

"Oh, great," he grumbled.

"Ahem." I smoothed the paper and glanced through my questions. "I read that your favorite movie of all time is *Aladdin* and that, for three years in a row, you dressed up as Aladdin for

Halloween. In middle school. I hope your mom has pictures of that."

"Don't worry, she does," he muttered. "And the only reason I dressed like Aladdin is because my sisters begged me."

"Whatever you need to tell yourself. Here's another one. It says you took a goat to your senior prom? They're KID-ding, right? Get it. KID-ding. A baby goat is called a kid."

He groaned. "Yes, fine. I took a goat to my senior prom."

I paused, waiting for the story that went with such a statement. "And? I need to know how this came about."

"I lost a bet."

"With who? A really devious farmer? A cow with a gambling problem?"

His eyes sliced to me, then back to the road. "You're enjoying this, aren't you?"

"Absolutely." I glanced at the paper. "Oh, this one might be my favorite."

"Yes, I took ballet lessons," he said in a grumpy voice. "Coach said it would help on the football field."

I smirked. "That's not my favorite one; although I did want to ask if you had to wear a leotard?"

"Yes. I mean, no." He shook his head. "What's the next one?"

"Just one more. Is it true you still sleep with a stuffed dog named Spot? Please tell me that's true. Please."

"Ha. That one isn't true. See. You can't believe everything you read on the internet. Especially when it's Wikipedia and you have four sisters who love to find ways to torture you."

I laughed, delighted. "I can't wait to meet them."

"I was afraid of that. Don't listen to anything they say. Don't look them directly in the eye. Or feed them after midnight. Or say any of their names three times while looking in a mirror."

"Because bad things will happen?"

"I don't know, I've never been crazy enough to try," he said, but I heard the edge of affection in his voice.

"You love them a lot, don't you?"

A dimple flashed in his cheek. "I really do."

A fissure of unease hit me as I picked at an imaginary string on my shorts. These people were important to him and suddenly I wanted them to like me more than anything. What if they thought I was too opinionated or too fat or too tall or too something?

Or worse—that I wasn't enough?

And the craziest part of it all was, in the end, it didn't matter. Because this wasn't real.

"I've told them all about you. They can't wait to meet you," Chris said, like he could read my mind. "They're going to like you."

"I'll try my best," I said, not quite smiling.

He reached over and put a hand on my leg, his fingers curling around my thigh and squeezing gently. "You don't have to try; just be you. I promise they'll love you."

A large boulder seemed to be lodged in my throat. "Thanks."

He squeezed my leg again but left his hand there, warm and reassuring and dark against my pasty white skin. That dang opposable thumb taunted me.

It was five solid minutes of silence later when Chris spoke. "It's a bear, not a dog. His name is Chub, and I don't sleep with him; I keep him on the nightstand."

THIRTY-TWO

Did you scrape your knees crawling out of Hell? 'Cause, damn, you're hot.

—*KARA R.*

The Sterns' property started long before we saw the house. Flat, endless fields of grass dotted with spindly oak trees. We reached a fork in the road with a sign that pointed left for LAKE and right for HOUSE.

"You have a lake?" I asked when we turned down a winding dirt road toward the house. "How big is this place?"

"About eighty acres," Chris said.

"Did you grow up here?"

He shook his head. "I grew up just outside Oklahoma City. My dad grew up around here and always wanted to come back, but five kids made that hard."

"Plus a sick baby," I murmured.

"When Millie was older and needed the doctors less and I could help them, we all picked this together." Finally, he turned down a driveway, each side lined with bright white and pink crape myrtles against a wooden fence.

"You bought it for them?"

"It wasn't charity," he clarified. "They sacrificed a lot for me. Hours of driving me to football practices and going to games. Visits to specialty doctors when I needed them, uniforms, being the team parent, putting up with other guys on the team, all that. I wanted to do it for them."

I thought about Mama and how I wanted to give her everything so her life could be easier. "I get it."

We passed by a banner hung between two fence posts. Someone had painted crudely, but clearly, in giant letters: WELCOME HOME, ELMER.

"Who's Elmer?" I asked, pointing as we passed.

Chris grunted. "No one."

I would have grilled him on that more because I could tell he knew exactly who Elmer was, but we turned a bend in the road and there it was. Two stories with a wraparound porch, the red-brick house was surrounded by flowerbeds bursting with color. An enormous oak tree stood in the front with a swing dangling from a branch.

A white picket fence surrounded it all behind which three dogs barked with excitement as we drove right by.

"Wait. Isn't that the house?" I asked.

"That's my parents' house. Mine is back here." He drove around another bend to reveal a much smaller one-story house.

"Oh." I frowned. "I guess I assumed you had an apartment or something on your own."

"This works out pretty well." He pulled the truck in front of a small, detached garage. "I get my own privacy but I'm still around."

"Sooo." I twisted my hands in my lap. "Exactly where am I staying?"

Instead of answering, he hopped out of the truck and

rounded it to open my door. "Oh, I have bunk beds. Since you're the guest, I'll let you have the top bunk."

I glared at him. "You are a twelve-year-old boy in a man's body, you know that?"

With a grin, he took a step back and held out a hand. "Fine. You can have the second bedroom."

"Chrisss," a voice yelled. A blurry figure raced across the football field-sized lawn between the houses, a dog following closely. A dark ponytail passed me without slowing as its owner threw herself in Chris's arms.

"Whoa," he said, but caught her up in a hug easily enough. When he set her down, he was laughing.

She looked about the same age as Iris, and that was where the similarities ended. This girl with the bouncy ponytail and twinkly eyes (like Chris) gave off big Sunshine Energy (also like her brother).

"Aggie, this is Mae," Chris said.

Aggie bounced over and threw her arms around me. "I can't believe you're here. He's not shut up about you." She took a step back and picked up a piece of my hair. "Your hair is gorgeous. The pictures online do not do it justice."

I smiled because it was hard not to smile around her, that much was obvious. "It's nice to meet you. Are you the one who likes to keep his Wikipedia page up to date?"

With a grin so much like her brother's it was almost disconcerting, she linked arms with me. "I see you know my work. I have so many more things I could tell you. I have photos. *I have video.*"

"You know, I'm your favorite brother, right." Chris called from behind us.

Ignoring him, Aggie pulled me toward the house, talking slightly slower than the speed of light. "Now, let's go meet everyone else. Mom wanted to play it cool, so she sent me over."

"No one ever plays it cool in this family," Chris muttered. "Prepare yourself, Mae."

I faltered. "For what?"

"The Sterns."

Margot Sterns was a pretty woman with dark hair and an infectious smile. A bit shorter than me, she was curvy with twinkly dark eyes. Like Aggie, she didn't even wait for an introduction before drawing me into a hug.

"When Chris told me about meeting you, I just knew you were special." She pressed a hand to her heart. "I could tell from his voice my boy was in love. I'm so excited you're here."

"Oh, thank you?" My eyes darted to Chris, who seemed to be finding his phone very interesting.

"When you know, you know. The first time I met his daddy, I knew. Of course, it took that man a whole lot longer to clue in. But thirty-three years married this summer." With a bright smile, she pulled a chair out at the little round kitchen table and gestured for me to sit. "Can I get you anything? Coffee? Tea? Oh! I have some strawberry lemonade, too."

"Water sounds good."

"Of course." She shooed Chris to the side on her trek to the refrigerator. "I have some leftover cheesecake. Now, I don't want to ruin your dinner, but a little cheesecake doesn't count, am I right?"

This was logic I could not argue with.

"Hi, Mom." Chris spread his arms wide. "Your baby boy is home."

Margot patted his cheek on the way back to the table. She set a glass of water and an enormous piece of cheesecake in front of me. "Yes, yes. I love you. Why don't you go find Millie and say hello? Go with him, Aggie."

"But I wanted some lemonade and cheesecake," Aggie whined.

Margot looked her dead in the eye and said, "No."

Chris's eyes narrowed. "Are you trying to get rid of us?"

"Why would I do that?" She sat across from me and beamed a smile at him. "Now, go away."

Chris turned slowly, a little bewildered, and headed out of the kitchen. He paused next to me and dropped a kiss on my cheek. I gave him one last desperate look before he was gone.

And I was alone.

With his mother.

HOW WAS THIS MY LIFE?

I rubbed my damp palms on my shirt and searched my brain for something to say. "I love your kitchen."

That was a low-stakes conversation starter, and I wasn't even lying. It was lovely, airy and bright with lots of windows and white cabinets that stretched to the ceiling. The walls were a sunny yellow, the curtains red gingham, and the floor slightly scuffed wood. There were a few dishes in the sink and photos dangling from magnets on the fridge. A loaf of bread on the counter. A bag of chips left out. It wasn't a magazine kitchen; it was a family kitchen, and something about that put me at ease more than anything Margot could say.

"Don't look too closely at it. I've been on Luke to fix some things around here but, you know how it is. He spends all day fixing things for other people; he doesn't want to do it when he gets home. I keep saying what will the neighbors think when I have to hire a handyman and my husband is a contractor." She pushed the cheesecake toward me, and I took a bite. "I'm sorry. I'm talking a million miles a minute. I do that when I'm excited. Tell me about your family." Margot placed her elbow on the table and her chin in her palm, her warm brown eyes giving me all her attention.

I took a sip of water to stall. "It's just my mom and sister and me."

Her eyes turned sympathetic. "Chris told me about your mom's stroke. I can't imagine how difficult that's been for your family."

"We're doing fine." Because that's what I always said.

She reached out and patted my hand. "Oh, honey. I'm sure it hasn't been at all fine. You know, when I was ten, my mother was hit by a car crossing the street. She passed away that evening and my father was left to raise my brother and me. It was a hard time. We all had to pitch in to help any way we could, and we only had each other. I guess what I'm saying is that I know it can't have been easy for you. Sometimes we need to not be okay. Do you ever get to do that?"

"Um..." Very smooth, Mae. I stuffed an enormous forkful of cheesecake in my mouth.

Margot smiled sweetly. "I hope this weekend you can have a bit of rest and relaxation. Don't think you need to impress me by offering to help or being on your best behavior. You're a part of the family now, and we take everyone just the way they come."

The backs of my eyes began to prick, my nose stung. In horror, I realized I was half a second from crying. How had I gotten here? All I'd said was she had a lovely kitchen.

The back door opened and a young woman half fell into the kitchen. "Is she here?"

She looked about twenty-two or so and was built like her mother, tall and round, her hair cut into a short bob and dyed bright pink. With her nose ring and mini jean skirt and her Chucks, she had a boldness to her that appeared to come naturally. But it was those dark eyes that stood out the most. They shone with intelligence. I guessed this was the second Sterns' sister, who I knew was a teacher.

With a foot, she closed the door and held out her hand. "I'm Betsy, Elmie's favorite sister."

"Elmie?"

"Yeah, it's our nickname for him. We all have nicknames, so he had to have one too."

I must have looked as confused as I felt. Her face lit up as a huge smile transformed her from pretty to gorgeous. "He didn't tell you, did he?"

"Tell me what?"

Betsy rubbed her hands together and sat herself at the table with us. "Our parents named us all after relatives in the family tree. Way, way back in the family tree."

"They're classics," Margot said.

Betsy rolled her eyes. "Eleanor, Elizabeth, Agnes, and Millicent, but we all go by nicknames because... obviously."

"And Chris?"

"Chris is short for Christian but that's his middle name." Betsy's eyes danced with delight. "We like to say he got the most special name of all."

"He did," Margot protested. "He's named after a great-great uncle on your father's side who was an Oklahoma State Representative. An elected official and a patriot."

"So, what is it?" I asked.

"Elmer."

"No."

"Elmer Christian Sterns is a very strong, dignified name," Margot said.

I pressed my lips together to keep from laughing.

Betsy pulled the plate of cheesecake toward her and loaded up the fork with a big bite. "This is going to be fun. I have so many things to tell you."

THIRTY-THREE

Do you have a name, or can I just call you mine?

—AMANDA H.

The dining room was as cheery and bright as the rest of the house. Sunlight shone through the oversized picture window, touching on the large table and matching sideboard. On the opposite wall, framed photos took up almost every inch.

Baby photos, school photos, fancy dress dances, candids of the family romping in a lake, or with Mickey Mouse ears, one of Chris dressed as Aladdin (which I needed to figure out how to steal), even a few of Millie in a hospital bed smiling widely with a devious glint in her eye. I recognized everyone save a tall, gangly girl with dark hair and big blue eyes. This had to be Ellie, although based on the Vegas video, she was a blonde now.

Although the subjects might be all over the place, there was one overarching theme: happiness. People don't realize how blessed they are to have that sort of childhood. To have a child-hood at all. I'd had to grow up fast. While I knew things had been tough for the Sterns, they'd had each other to lean on. I sighed, feeling a little sorry for myself and went in search of Margot to help with dinner.

At mealtime, I met the oldest and the youngest Sterns.

Unlike the rest of her family, Millie was petite, which Chris explained had to do with her heart condition limiting her growth, with blonde hair and an impish glint in her blue eyes. She bounced into the room and rounded the table to the only empty seat, which happened to be on Chris's left side. I sat on his right.

"Hey"—she smacked her brother on the shoulder—"move over."

Chris frowned. "Why?"

"Because I want to talk to Mae and you're in the way." With a hand on her hip, Millie stared down at him and waited.

"Yeah, Elmie," I said. "Move over. I want to sit next to your sister."

"They told you. Great." Grumbling like the long-suffering brother he was, Chris moved over to the empty seat. "Good to see you, too."

"Oh, please. I see you all the time." Millie slid into the empty chair and smiled at me. "Mae, on the other hand, I have never seen."

I'd never had a big family dinner like this. The closest I'd gotten was when Granny was alive. Most of our meals were eaten in front of the television, yelling out answers to *Wheel of Fortune* puzzles. But the Sterns were talkative and loud. They teased each other and chatted about their day. There were smiles and laughs.

I didn't expect to enjoy it; I didn't *want* to enjoy it. None of it was real. Or at least my part in all of it wasn't. This would likely be the only time I'd be welcome here and I knew it was strange after only spending an afternoon with them, but that thought made me incredibly sad.

"Ellie called yesterday," Luke said, his voice quiet and thoughtful. "She sounded better than she has in a while."

Chris nodded. "We talked this week too. She's got a new job."

"I've been so worried about her," Margot said. "I wish she'd just move back home. Then I could see Oliver and pinch his little chubby cheeks all the time." She turned to me. "I'm sorry. Ellie's our oldest daughter, three years younger than Chris. She lives out in California. I suppose with five kids, the odds are pretty high that at least one is going to move away from home."

Luke put a hand on his wife's arm to comfort her. "Maybe it's time for another visit to see her."

Millie pushed her empty plate to the side and sat back in her chair. "So, Mae, how much did my brother have to pay you to go out with him?"

I choked. On what, I wasn't sure. Air? My tongue? How could she possibly know about our deal? I fumbled to pick up my glass of water. "H-he didn't... I mean... well..."

Chris sighed. "It was one time. One time. And I was eleven."

"Wait... what?"

"Tell the story, Betsy," Millie said. "You're so good at it."

"As you wish." She made a big show of standing and clearing her throat.

"Betsy was a theater kid." Chris met my eyes over Millie's head with a reluctant smile.

"Chris was in the sixth grade. Back then, he was still a shrimp." Betsy held her thumb and forefinger up with perhaps an inch of space between them.

"I was not."

"Yes, you were," Margot said. "You were the cutest little bug."

The sisters snickered at Chris's pained expression.

"It was the week of his first dance, and he had a crush on an eighth grader. What was her name?"

"Cora," Chris said quickly, falling right into Betsy's trap.

Betsy smiled slyly. "Yes, that's right. Cora. She was tall, had long red hair and was super smart; always had a book with her."

The entire table's eyes swung to me.

Margot smiled widely. "Would you look at that."

"Guess he has a type," Aggie said.

Chris winked at me. "Maybe I do."

"Anyway, Chris spent days working up the courage to ask Cora to the dance. When he finally did, Cora told him she already had a boyfriend. There are rumors he cried when he got home."

"I did not cry." Chris leaned toward me and lowered his voice. "At least not in front of anyone."

Margot cut in. "But the very next day, he arrived home from school and declared he had a date to the dance. He's always been one to bounce right back up when he gets knocked down."

"His date was the coolest eighth grade girl in school. She skipped classes, bragged about kissing boys, had been caught smoking cigarettes behind the football stadium, and she'd had her ears pierced. Twice." Betsy leaned down so her face was next to Chris's. "The whole school was talking about it. There was no way Vanessa Snow—see, even her name was cool?— would *ever* have been seen with a sixth grader.

"But she showed up to the dance and spent the whole night with Chris. I heard she even forewent her cigarette break to dance a slow dance with him. He became a legend that night."

"Cora danced with me twice, thank you very much," Chris said. "My plan worked."

"Oh, it worked. But it cost Mr. Hot Stuff here his entire life savings," Betsy said. "Didn't it?"

"Fifty-four dollars and eighty-six cents," Chris said. "Every last cent I had."

I shook my head, confused. "But why?"

Aggie piped up. "He paid her to go to that dance with him."

I tried to swallow my laughter but was not successful. "No, he didn't."

Betsy nodded. "He sure did."

Chris sprawled in his chair, hands behind his head. "It was a good business decision. Besides being my first date, I also got my first kiss."

"What did that cost you?" I asked.

"Not a single dime." His smile was downright wolfish. "She gave that to me for free."

THIRTY-FOUR

How much does a polar bear weigh? Enough to break the ice.

—*KAILEY H.*

After dinner, Millie asked me if I wanted to go on a walk with her. She and I moseyed down a path that took us to a pasture on the other side of the house.

I noticed two brown dots off in the distance. "Are those horses?"

Millie nodded. "One is named Custard and the other is Pudding."

"Do you get to ride them?" I asked.

"Not as much as I want. The rule is someone has to ride with me."

"I bet being the youngest is the worst."

"It's not so bad. Being born with a broken heart on the other hand..." Her smile melted as her voice trailed off.

What was I supposed to say to that?

Millie blinked her baby blues. "I made it weird, didn't I? I'm sorry."

"No. No," I reassured her. "Of course not."

Grinning, she turned around, so she was walking backward. "I totally did. My mom says I know exactly how to get the sympathy vote. It's a talent. You should see how many times I get to choose the movie on family nights with a little cough."

It was hard not to smile back at her. "You are diabolical."

"Thank you." She took a deep bow. "Some people get really freaked out when I say stuff like that. You spend a lot of time in hospital beds when you're a kid, you find ways to amuse yourself."

We continued our ambling walk along the fence line as the orange sky melted into the horizon.

Millie paused and leaned against the fence. "We had a sister meeting."

"A sister meeting?"

"Yup. Just the sisters. Right before dinner."

"I bet Chris hates that he's not allowed to come."

"Sometimes we hold meetings even when we don't have anything to talk about. Just to annoy him." Millie grinned. "At this meeting, we voted on you."

"Me?"

"Sure. We do this with all of Elmie's lady friends."

"Oh, are there a lot of these lady friends?" I asked casually. Because I wasn't at all interested in the answer.

It should be noted I was lying to myself.

"Not really. And honestly, we haven't liked any of them. Most of them act like they're better than us. It's gross." She brushed her hands off on her shorts. "But we've voted, and I was chosen as spokes-sister to let you know that you've been approved."

"Thank you. I'm honored." I think.

"You're welcome." She linked her arm through mine, her voice downright chipper. "But you should know we love that big idiot a lot. He's the best brother. He paid for all of Betsy's school, helps out Ellie, and set aside a college fund for Aggie. He bought this house for my parents. And even though none of them think I know, having this heart is expensive, even with insurance. He pays for all that, too. But it isn't the money stuff. He takes care of all of us. Little, quiet things that nobody thinks of."

My heart squeezed at the fierce, tender way she spoke of her brother. "You all are lucky to have him."

"You're right, and you have him now too, so please hear me loud and clear: if you hurt him in any way, we will find you. And then they won't find you."

I froze. "Did you just—"

"Threaten you? Sure did. But don't worry. We'll make it a quick death." Millie tugged on my arm to get me moving. "Come on. Let's go eat some ice cream and watch a movie."

After we returned from our walk, Chris and his dad wandered off when it became clear we planned on watching a romcom. I hung out with Margot and the Sisters (big S, because I was beginning to think they may be an organized crime syndicate).

As soon as the men left, Margot brought out a huge stack of wedding magazines. "I thought we could look through these. I've been collecting them for a few years. I thought for sure I'd have had to pull them out for Ellie by now... Well, anyway, one day for her. But you, we haven't talked about the wedding, have we? Have you all set a date?"

I hesitated. "Not yet."

"Oh, a spring wedding would be lovely. The season will be over for Chris. Do you want a church wedding or outside?"

"Outside? Maybe?"

"I think outside would be beautiful in spring."

I tried to look excited. After all, this was my (fake) wedding my (fake) future mother-in-law was discussing. But the lie, the big fat lie, was taking up more and more space inside me. Growing like... like fungi.

Yes, mushrooms were the guilt of my heart. I hated mushrooms.

"I know you have your mom and sister at home, so I thought," Margot continued, "maybe we could plan a weekend where the girls and I could come down and we could go dress shopping. If we're going for a spring wedding, we should find something soon."

"Okay?" Not okay. The mushrooms expanded twofold.

"Mom, chill. You're going to freak her out," Aggie said.

Margot wrapped an arm around my shoulders. "Don't mind me. I'm just so excited. I have prayed for a woman to come along who would get ahold of Chris. But the right woman. One who'll appreciate his heart instead of the football and the fame and all that. That kind of stuff doesn't last."

I cleared my throat. "To be honest, you hardly know me."

She waved a hand. "I know my boy. You know, he called that very first day he met you and told me about the pretty librarian who yelled at him."

"He did?" I couldn't keep the surprise from my voice. The day he met me? That would have been long, long before our arrangement. He hadn't even known my name yet.

"Sure did. I've heard the way he talks about you. And now, I've seen the way he looks at you."

"How does he look at me?"

"Like you're his favorite thing in the whole world," Aggie said.

I wondered how I looked at him.

But I was too afraid to ask.

THIRTY-FIVE

Are you less than ninety degrees? 'Cause, girl, you are acute.

—SHELBY M.

The next afternoon, we all piled into the rented SUV for the half-mile trek to the lake the Sterns' property butts up to. Margot packed us a fried chicken dinner and sent us off with strict instructions to make sure Millie took breaks. The beach on their property was quiet and secluded. A long dock jettied into the lake where two boats were parked under an awning. Chris pulled the car next to a picnic table and a small blue shed.

"Come on, I'll show you the pool house. It's not much but it has electricity and a bathroom," Aggie said. It took her a moment to unlock the padlock on the door. It was one room. A smallish bed pushed into a corner, a mini fridge and microwave, and a tiny but functional bathroom.

It was a beautiful day, about eighty-five degrees with a light breeze. While Chris unloaded the car, we dragged beach chairs that were stored in the pool house and set them up in a line.

Millie announced she was going to take one of the tubes and float on the lake.

"Sunscreen first," Betsy said.

"Hurry up or the good tubes will be gone." Millie tugged her t-shirt off and stood with her back to Ellie.

"Cute suit," I said to her. My eye immediately dropped to the scar that peeked out of the top of her swimsuit.

Millie raised a hand to cover it.

My face reddened. "I'm sorry. I didn't mean to make you uncomfortable."

"No, it's not that." She pursed her lips and I swear her eyes grew three sizes bigger. "It's just there's always a reminder that I was—"

"—born with a broken heart," her sisters said in unison. "Yeah, yeah. We get it."

"She pulls that card all the time," Aggie said. "Like we haven't figured it out already."

Millie put a hand on her hip. "Hey, it works on Mom."

"That's not saying a lot." Betsy was rocking a two-piece that matched her pink hair perfectly. "I'm pretty sure Mom still believed in Santa Claus until a few years ago."

"Wait, Santa's not real?" Chris said, from right behind me.

I turned to say something sarcastic, but my breath sort of fizzled out like a dying balloon.

Chris Stearns was a world-class athlete. He wasn't some guy you knew from high school who used to play basketball. Nor was he one of those dudes who worked out for forty-five minutes before work and hogged all the weight machines at the gym. It was in his job description to take care of his body, keep it strong and lean and healthy.

Obviously, Chris was good at his job.

How did I know? He was shirtless. Let me say it louder for the people in the back: he did not have a shirt on.

He should really come with a warning label. Something like

CAUTION: When seen shirtless, this model may cause momentary memory loss, particularly of one's own name, as well as body temperature spikes and extreme amounts of gawking.

"All done," Betsy announced, and I ripped my eyes away from Chris.

Millie took off down the dock. "Last one in gets the wonky tube."

Betsy moved on to Aggie and, when she was done, she tossed me the bottle and presented me with her back.

"You two have each other, right?" She pointed between Chris and me.

"Yeah, sure. Be right in." I waited for her to wander off to the water. I shoved the bottle at Chris, who had donned mirror sunglasses. "You can do your front."

Without waiting to see if he planned to follow directions, I trotted to the pool house, whipped off the cover-up Betsy had lent me, and stuffed it in my bag.

Chris was mid-chest rub when I returned. For a half-second, his hand stilled when he saw me. Or at least I thought it was because he saw me. Those sunglasses made it impossible to see his eyes. Wish I had a pair.

Betsy had lent me a bright-red one-piece suit with a halter top and a slim skirt on the bottom, very 1950s glamour.

I adjusted the strap. "Your sister let me borrow it, since someone forgot to tell me to bring one. Does it look stupid? I usually stay away from red. The whole red on a redhead thing."

He cleared his throat and went back to slathering his arms with sunscreen. "It suits you."

"Thanks."

An awkward, heavy silence fell between us. I swear I tried not to watch him rub that lotion all over himself. I swear it. I looked at the ground and my fingernails and the picnic table, but my eyeballs were under some strange spell that made it impossible not to look at him.

Why did he have to be so dang beautiful? Not the outside either, although the wrapping was sure nice. It was all the other stuff. I saw the way he treated his family, how much he loved and respected his parents, how generous he was with his time and money, and how he risked his reputation to protect a sister. HE VISITED KIDS IN THE HOSPITAL IN HIS SPARE TIME.

He was a good guy.

Why? Whhhy?

Why couldn't he be arrogant and selfish and smell like salami all the time? It was making everything so much more complicated in my head.

I didn't want to like him as anything more than a friend. I couldn't. My heart wasn't available. It had already experienced enough disappointment and pain from the people who were supposed to love me, and I wasn't foolish enough to go through that again. Nope. No way. In fact, there was a tiny little sign hanging on my heart that read: CLOSED UNTIL FURTHER NOTICE.

"Can you do my back now?" Chris asked, pulling me from my thoughts.

I swallowed, took the bottle from him, and squirted some in my hand. "This might be cold."

I tried to be a professional about it all. At the very least, not creepy. I think I even succeeded until I found the two-inch scar on his right lower back. Without thinking about it, I traced it with my finger.

"Skateboarding accident when I was thirteen," Chris said, his voice low.

"Did you have to get stitches?"

He shrugged. "Probably, but I snuck out of the house to go skateboarding and I was too afraid to tell my parents about it. I learned my lesson, that's for sure."

"I thought you were an Eagle Scout."

"Even good kids bend to temptation every now and then."

Don't I know it. I bit my lip and ran my hands over his back again, up to his shoulders and neck. I'd already coated everything once so now I was definitely making things creepy.

"All done." I turned around and held my breath, waiting for him to start.

He made quick work of it. In fact, he was so fast, it was obvious he hadn't been nearly as affected as I was. A wave of embarrassment was quickly followed by resolve. I could act like that too. Just watch me.

He hesitated. "I'm going to get under your strap, okay?"

"Yep."

His finger slid under the halter strap around my neck and a shiver raced down my back. I ignored it.

"All done?" I didn't even wait for him to answer. I spun around and almost fell face first into him.

He grabbed my shoulders and steadied me. "Slow down there, Freckles."

"Don't call me Freckles," I snapped. There, that was better. Let's get some irritation in my voice. Much better than confusing feelings I wasn't ready to feel.

A corner of his mouth hitched, and he tapped my nose gently. "But there are just so many of them. Like sprinkles. Makes me crave something sweet."

I crossed my arms. "My freckles give you a hankering for dessert?"

A slow smile spread across his face. He waited a long beat. "Something like that."

"What does that mean?"

With a low chuckle I felt in my belly, he walked around me and headed to the water without answering.

THIRTY-SIX

In high school, I seriously had a boy come up to me, reach around to the back of my shirt, and when I said, "What the hell are you doing?" he responded, "Checking your tag to confirm you were made in Heaven." I burst out laughing, which I suppose was his intention.

—*DILIANA D.*

After a few hours enjoying the water, we ate a late dinner. Around 7:30 p.m. we decided to pack up and head back to the house. I claimed the bathroom to change back into my shorts and t-shirt. While I was in there, I heard someone open and close the front door followed by a rumbling around in the tiny kitchen area.

It was there I found Chris, the cooler of drinks in his arms. He had his shirt back on and his sunglasses dangling from the collar.

"Would you mind grabbing that bag of chips and opening the door?" he asked.

"Sure." I squeezed around him, this really was a tiny room,

and headed for the door. But when I twisted the knob and pulled on it, it didn't budge. So, I tried again. And, again, it didn't open.

I set down the stuff I was carrying. Maybe I wasn't pulling hard enough? With all my might, I gave it a good yank and almost fell flat on my butt when my hands slipped.

"It's not opening?" Chris frowned. "I'll do it."

He said it with such confidence that relief flooded me. Surely Mr. Muscles would have no problem, but three minutes and multiple attempts later, that door was stuck tight. Chris frowned and ran his thumb over his bottom lip.

It was fine. Everything was fine. There were three other people just outside that door. They'd get us out.

"Hey," I yelled, thumping my fist on the door. "Aggie, the door won't open. Can you help?"

I listened hard but there was no answer.

"Betsy? Millie? Anyone? Hello?" I banged on the door.

Chris ran a hand through his mostly wet hair, leaving it standing on end in some places. "They're gone."

"They wouldn't leave us here," I said with the dawning realization they could just leave us here.

The only windows in here were small, slanted vents of sorts, up high and out of reach. I climbed on the bed and flipped open the vent. Even then I had to stretch to peek out.

"The car is still here." I hopped off the bed. "Maybe they decided to take one more dip in the water?"

Chris leaned against the wall with a resigned look on his face. "It's only a ten-minute walk back home, and this has all the markings of one of Millie's plans she talks everyone else into executing. She's a menace."

"B-but they just left. They locked us in here and left?" I pulled my t-shirt away from my body and released it. "It's hot in here. Isn't it hot in here?"

Chris cocked an eyebrow. "You okay there, Sprinkles? You're looking a little pale."

"I'm pale all the time. I'm basically what would happen if mayonnaise and a ghost had a baby, and don't call me Sprinkles." I flung myself on the bed. "What do we do?"

"We wait."

"That's a stupid idea. We need a plan. Oh, my phone." I scrambled to my bag and dug through it, finally dumping all the contents on the ground. "It's not in here. It should be in here."

"Where'd you leave it?"

Frowning, I sat on the floor. "I set my bag in here."

"You let it out of your sight. Last time I did that, one of them borrowed my phone and changed every single contact to MOM. Took me weeks to sort it all out. Should have kept that safe. Rookie mistake."

"Thanks for telling me that *now*. Where's your phone?"

"I was smarter. I locked it in the glove compartment in the car."

I groaned. "So, we're stuck?"

"Until they decide to unlock the door, yes." He held out a hand and helped me off the floor. "This is home, sweet home."

THIRTY-SEVEN

Do you believe in love at first flight?

Because when I look into your eyes, I see my final destination.

—*DANIELLA H.*

"This is weird."

"I told you I'd sleep on the floor," Chris said.

He had, several times. But I wasn't mean enough to do that to the guy. Still this bed was only a double. Chris and I, we weren't double-bed-sized people. His shoulders seemed to take up more than half the width of the bed alone and he had to curl up or dangle his feet off the side to fit.

"You know, if you didn't insist on this pool noodle divider, we'd have more room."

I patted the stack of noodles at my side. "No, thank you. You might take advantage of me."

Or vice versa. Because I'd seen things today I could not unsee—Chris without a shirt on, all wide shoulders and lean muscles, that tiny little scar on his back that fascinated me. I closed my eyes and shivered.

Chris grunted. "This bed is ridiculously uncomfortable."

"Maybe we should try to sleep."

"Good idea. Night."

"Night."

I turned to my side and faced the wall. I'd gotten stuck on the inside, and with the metal headboard and footboard on the bed and a giant football player on the other side, I was basically boxed in. Good thing I wasn't claustrophobic. Or scared of the dark.

Because it was dark here. Real darkness. There were no streetlamps or passing cars or soft glow from the neighbor's house. Outside was nothing but lake and trees and grass and probably some other living things I didn't want to think about.

I sat up. "Are there frogs out there?"

"What?"

"Frogs? Are there frogs?"

"Do you want the truth?"

"If the answer is yes, then no. Lie to me."

"Fine. There are absolutely no frogs in and around that large body of water mere feet from this shed." His fingers brushed my arm and trailed down to my palm, leaving goosebumps. He squeezed my hand. "Better now?"

"No." But I laid back down and tried to think about happier things. Like mice or rats or the plague. Anything but those green, slimy things. I shuddered and turned to face the pool noodle divider.

After a long moment, Chris sighed. "Why frogs?"

"Because they're gross."

"Alright." He waited a beat or two. "But frogs? It seems a little irrational, doesn't it?"

"That is the definition of a phobia."

"It had to have started at some point."

I huffed. "Fine. In seventh grade, we had to dissect frogs in science and one of the boys thought it would be funny to throw frog guts at me. Some of it landed in my mouth. I puked. The end."

More silence.

"I did promise to protect you from them. I am a man of my word." I could hear the laughter in his voice.

"Shut up and go to sleep."

I spent the next few minutes trying to find a comfortable position. After a while, I gave up and pretended there wasn't a spring digging into my hip.

"Are you asleep yet?" I whispered. When he didn't answer right away, I asked louder. "Hey, are you awake?"

He grunted. "I am now."

"Oh. Sorry. I'll let you get back to sleep."

"It's alright. Go ahead. Did you think of something else you're afraid of?"

"Ha. Ha." I pushed up and rested on my elbow, head cradled in my hand. "I really like your family."

He said in a quiet voice, "They like you, too."

"I'm worried about what happens when we're done with this. It's not just affecting us. My mom, your mom. They'll be hurt."

A long pause. "I know."

"Plus I'm pretty sure your sister will put a mob hit out on me."

"Millie?"

"Yes. She's kind of scary."

The bed shifted. I could just make out the shape of his face. We were only inches apart. Thanks for nothing, pool noodles.

"Sometimes I think all her medical problems make her brave in strange ways. She's been through surgeries, weeks in the hospital at a time, close to death more than once. She's fearless."

"She's going to hate me when this is all over. They all are."

My words hung heavy in the air. I wished they weren't true. But I'm pretty sure my fake fiancé got to keep his real family in the breakup.

"What if..." he said, his voice soft. My breath stalled when I felt his fingers move a piece of wayward hair from my face and tuck it behind my ear. His hand lingered and I had the strangest desire to lean my head into it like a cat.

I waited to see if he'd finish. I wanted him to finish. It seemed of the utmost importance that he finish, in fact. "What if what?"

The bed rocked as he moved away. "Nothing."

"They love you a lot. Millie told me all about you paying for everyone's college and her medical bills and the house for your parents. They're so proud of you."

Another long, heavy silence.

"I want them to be proud of me." He sighed. "I hate all this lying and twisting words."

"You're kind of good at it though."

He sat up. "I'm a good liar?"

"I'm just saying you are very convincing." I pushed myself up too.

"That is not a compliment," he said, his voice clipped.

I winced. He was right; this was coming out all wrong. "I didn't mean it like that. It's just... I don't know... you've even made *me* believe we're in a real relationship sometimes."

He threw himself back on the bed so hard the headboard slammed into the wall. "I'm going to sleep now."

And he did. Without another word. Rude.

I flipped on my side and curled around my pillow, which was almost comfortable. But my arm started to tingle from being in a weird position.

It was hot in there. Chris had opened all the vents and there was the tiniest of breezes, but I was so far away from it. I hated being hot. I kicked off the sheet.

I drifted to sleep for a little bit only to wake with a start, heart pounding as I sorted out where I was and who was next to me. Somehow I'd breached the pool noodle divider enough that my arm now rested on Chris's chest, his big hand curled around it. When I carefully tried to extract it, his fingers tightened.

The steady beat of his heart lulled me back to sleep.

The next time I woke up I was almost kissing the wall, my back screaming about how unhappy it was going to be tomorrow. Looking for some relief, I flipped so my head was at the foot of the bed and tried to think happier thoughts. Like Chris without his shirt. That was nice. Another of when we were in the water, and he'd snuck up on me and grabbed my legs. I emitted such a scream I was sure Margot heard it back at the house.

Then he had popped out of the water, all laughs and wet, warm, golden skin and I almost forgot to be angry. The urge to touch him had been overwhelming. Instead, I swam away in a huff.

What if...?

What if I *had* reached out and touched him? Would he have pulled me against him, whispered something sweet? Maybe his lips would start at my jawline, tiny, sweet kisses, creeping closer and closer to my mouth and...

Yes, it was entirely too hot in here and now I had to pee.

Moving slowly, I climbed over Chris's feet and felt my way to the bathroom. Returning to the bed was harder. I pointed myself in what I hoped was the direction of the foot of the bed and shuffled along.

A hand reached out and grabbed me, stealing my breath. One second my feet were on the floor, the next I was on the bed, flat on my back, and Chris was looming over me.

My words came out in bursts. "I'm sorry. Did I wake you?"

"Why are you up?" he asked, his voice all grumbly with sleep.

"I had to go to the bathroom."

"Oh." He didn't move.

Heat radiated from his body and my breath went a little... wonky. "Um, can you let me go?"

"Sorry. I was having a dream about you. Kind of blended into reality for a minute."

I made a choking noise. "You were dreaming about me? What was it about?"

"You were yelling at me."

"Oh, well, sorry for yelling at you."

He released his hold on me and I scrambled back to my side of the bed. "I'm pretty sure you can't control someone else's dream."

"Go back to sleep. Maybe you'll get to yell back at me."

He mumbled something I couldn't quite hear and, just like that, he was quiet again. I forced my eyes shut and tried to take slow, deep breaths, maybe trick myself into falling asleep, but it didn't work. I flipped over on my stomach to get more comfortable. I wished I had my phone. I could call Ali, who was usually up at all hours of the night. Just to hear a familiar voice, something that hadn't changed in my life recently.

More tossing and turning. My brain began churning.

How had this become my life? Two months ago, I was a librarian with an angry cat and a second job at Chicky's. Now I was sleeping in the same bed with my fake fiancé.

I had not had that on my BINGO card this year.

How would the next few months of my life unfold? With the money, I'd pay off Mama's medical bills, set aside some for things Iris might need for college. Maybe we could find her a decent, inexpensive car.

With a grunt, I turned on my side.

"Stop," Chris groaned. "Every time you move, the bed moves. It's like trying to sleep on a trampoline during a kid's birthday party. Go to sleep."

I winced. "I'm sorry. I'm not great at sleeping. My brain keeps going and going even when I'm exhausted. At home, I have a routine. I take melatonin and use a weighted blanket; even then it doesn't always work. I'll just lay here silently, won't move a muscle, I promise."

Chris sighed and began to toss pool noodles across the room.

"What are you doing?" I asked.

"Helping you sleep."

"How are you going—?" I squeaked when he hauled me across the bed.

"I don't have melatonin, but I can be a stand-in weighted blanket." With that, he circled my waist with his arm and sort of wedged me under him, his leg over mine. Suddenly he was everywhere.

I froze.

"Relax," he said, his mouth close to my ear.

"Sure. No problem." It should be noted, it was a problem. A big one. A big, huge, jumbo-sized human problem. My one free hand flailed around for someplace to lay. Tentatively, it settled on Chris's arm.

"You're heavy," I breathed.

"That's the point, isn't it?"

I turned my face into him and inhaled. I might never be able to smell sunscreen again without equating it with Chris now. I wondered if they made sunscreen-scented candles.

Slowly my body relaxed. My eyelids grew heavy. It was getting hard to keep them open.

"Are you okay?" Chris whispered, his voice soft.

"Yes," I whispered back.

"Good. Now go to sleep."

"Okay."

And to my amazement, I did.

THIRTY-EIGHT

Did your license get suspended for driving all these guys crazy?

— *TENNAYA B.*

"Awww. Look how cute they are." That was Aggie.

"See? I told you this was a good idea. They got to have a little alone time." That was Millie.

"Somehow I doubt they're going to see it that way," Betsy said.

"Go away," Chris mumbled. His arm tightened around my waist.

I cracked an eye open and just as quickly shut it against the sunlight streaming in through the open door. We were free. But I didn't want to move from this spot where I was warm and comfortable. That had been the best sleep I'd had, maybe ever.

"Yeah, well, Mom might kill us if she finds out," Aggie said.

Ellie nudged the bed. "Get up. Piper's been trying to get ahold of you. She finally called Mom. Now Mom's frantic because she can't find you."

Chris rolled over on his back, taking away my human blanket. I kept my eyes closed. "Go. Away."

"Sure thing. I'll leave Mae's phone right here on the bed," Aggie said. "Because I happened to find it. Mae, you should be careful about leaving your phone lying around. But don't worry, I kept it safe. I even charged it for you. Remember that when you're picking a maid of honor."

Chris growled. "Put down the phone and leave."

"For the record," Betsy said, "I knew nothing about this scheme. I am innocent."

Aggie gasped. "Did you just throw Millie and me under the bus?"

"No. I removed myself from the road entirely. You know the revenge for this will be..." Betsy's voice drifted off and the door slammed shut.

A moment later, Chris rolled back over and dangled my phone in front of my face. "You can stop pretending. They're gone."

"I wasn't pretending." I took the phone just as a text notification came through.

I blinked the sleep from my eyes and asked Chris to hand me my glasses. When I saw how many missed calls and texts I had, I gasped. All of them were from Piper.

Piper: *Hey, give me a call. A great opportunity just opened and I wanted to make sure you were on board.*

A half-hour and two missed calls later:

Piper: *Really need to talk to you for a quick minute.*

Two hours, five text messages, and seven calls later:

Piper: *Where the hell are you two? I can't get anyone to respond.*

The last text from just before midnight:

Piper: *Fine. A decision was made for you. Be at Chris's parents' house by noon tomorrow. You're taking engagement pictures.*

Oh, crap.

Chris and I grabbed all our stuff and hightailed it back to his house. He left me to take a shower, which gave me plenty of time to panic about the photos.

It was one thing to lie about being engaged or wear the ring or be cute and cuddly in public, or even the couple of cell phone pictures Piper had taken of the "actual" engagement. But professional photos?

There was something so very real about the idea. If we were engaged, one of those photos would end up on a Save-the-Date card and we'd have another framed because it would be our very favorite, that one photo that captured just how we felt about each other.

But this was not, I repeat, *not* real.

"How is this my life?" I said to no one at all. I dragged on a pair of shorts and a tank top and walked over to the main house, my mind spinning.

The second I opened the front door, I was overcome by the sheer amount of people and stuff in the house. Racks of clothes greeted me in the living room. The dining room table had been pushed aside and an entire shoe store was laid out by size and color. When I made it to the kitchen, I saw Margot chatting it up with a pretty woman in jeans and a t-shirt. Sitting at the table were Betsy and Millie and yet another woman I didn't recognize.

"Mae." Margot waved, face bright with excitement. "Isn't this all something else? When Piper told me the whole family got to be in the photos, I couldn't believe it. It's been so long since we've had a family portrait. I only wish Ellie was here. But, you'll get to be in them."

My heart sank. Family photos too? This had all gone too far. "Do you happen to know where Chris is?"

"He went off with Piper." She clapped her hands like a giddy three-year-old with an unlimited supply of cupcakes and no parental supervision. "Let's go find Sergio."

"Who's Sergio?"

Margot put her palms on her cheeks. "Oh, he's amazing. He's the stylist. Did you see all those racks of clothes? They're for us."

"A stylist?"

"You'll see." She hooked her arm in mine and pulled me along to a bedroom. She knocked. "It's Margot and Mae."

The door flew open and a man held his arms out. "It is Mae? She's here."

"Mae, this is Sergio," Margot said.

He was a slight man who wore a black kimono-style dress over black leggings. His bleached-blond hair swooped over one eye. With the eye I could see, he was inspecting me carefully. He held a finger up and indicated I should twirl. So, I did. With the same finger, he tapped his mouth, clearly deep in contemplation. Every now and then, he hummed or muttered under his breath.

After a solid minute of this, he smiled widely. "Yes, you will do very nicely. So lovely and soft. Between you and me, those thin models are like hangers for the clothes. If I wanted to work with hangers, I would have a job at the Gap. But you"—he put his fingers to his mouth and kissed them—"you will make the clothes sing with your curves. Perfection."

"G-great."

"Come, come. No time for talking. We have work to do. Let us go find you the perfect outfit."

That turned out to be more complicated than I expected. I counted five racks of clothes in the living room, but Sergio pointed out two specifically. "These are for you, my love. No one told me you were a redhead." More tapping of his mouth. "For you, we will look for yellow, or maybe..."

He wandered off to one of the racks and began flipping through them. When he noticed I hadn't moved, he waved me to the other rack. "Go on. Look through it. There is a dress that would be beautiful on you, I think. It is aqua green and long and very dreamy. You will look like a seductive wood nymph."

I was pawing through a rack of dresses when Piper found me. "There you are. Are you all caught up?"

"I'm currently looking for a dress that will make me look like a seductive wood nymph. That's all I got right now." I held up a dress. "Is this the one, Sergio?"

He scowled. "That is not aqua green; that is turquoise."

"Right. Silly me." I put the dress back.

"I know this is all sudden," Piper said. "But we were able to get Charles Thackery to take your photos."

"Should I know who Charles Thackery is?" I pulled another dress off the rack. It was green and it had a lovely flowy feel to it. "This one?"

Sergio shook his head in disgust. "That is seafoam green. Did you not learn your colors as a child?"

"Not that one, then." I turned to Piper. "How exactly did you find a Sergio on such short notice in the middle of Oklahoma?"

"Honey, I can work miracles even Moses would think twice about." Piper grinned. "Charles Thackery is a hotshot wedding photographer. He happened to be shooting a wedding in Oklahoma City yesterday for some richy-rich oil baron's kid. But I was able to talk him into doing this for us."

I glanced around the room and moved closer to Piper, dropping my voice. "But doesn't this seem like a lot for a fake engagement? These pictures are going to be useless."

She shook her head. "No, they're not. They'll help us get some great press out there. That anonymous jackass has not shut up yet. At this point, he's making stuff up just to piss me off."

"You still haven't figured out who he is?"

Piper's eyes got hard. "Not yet. But when I do, I swear I'm going to punch him right in his lying mouth."

"Here it is, darling. Here it is." Sergio held up a green dress. "This is aqua green, and it will be perfect on you. I know these things. I am a style magician. Come. Come. It is time for magic."

THIRTY-NINE

There's something wrong with my phone. Your number isn't on it.

—*LINDA E.*

By the time we were to begin the photo session, I'd been poked, plucked, and pinched to within an inch of my life. But when I looked in the mirror, even I had to admit I looked good. The dress was the perfect shade of green for my hair and skin color. Long and flowy, it cinched at the waist and fell to almost the ground where it touched a pair of simple gold sandals. Sergio was right; I did sort of feel like a seductive wood nymph.

I hoped Chris liked the dress and the hair and the whole package. It was foolish, but it mattered what he thought. I wanted him to like me. In a purely fake way.

Yeah, I know, I was even lying to myself.

With a deep breath, I went in search of the Sterns. All the sisters were in the kitchen. We spent several minutes gushing over each other. As one does. Luke Sterns arrived next, dressed in khakis and a yellow button-down shirt that complemented his blue eyes and graying hair. He made his rounds, telling all his daughters (and me) how nice we looked, but when Margot arrived, he only had eyes for her.

She did a twirl and smiled at him. "Do you like it?"

"It suits you," he said, his eyes warm.

"Love you." Margot planted a kiss on his cheek.

It suits you. Chris said that, often even. I guess I knew where he'd gotten it from. Although it was clear it meant something much deeper when Mr. Sterns said it to Mrs. Sterns. But Luke and Margot were in a class all their own. If happily ever afters really existed, they seemed to have found the closest thing to one.

A petite woman dressed all in black and a harried expression entered the kitchen. "I'm Louisa, Charles's assistant. He's ready to begin now. Some rules first. Follow all instructions. Don't look directly at the camera. No rabbit ears of any kind; they make him angry. Understood?"

We all nodded.

"You with the glasses." She pointed at me. "Those must come off. Charles doesn't allow glasses."

"I can barely see without them."

She snapped her fingers. "Off. Now. Let's go."

Reluctantly, I slid them off and tucked them in a pocket. The world grew blurry around the edges, like a filter on a photo. Everything felt a little surreal. Maybe this was the best way to get through this whole experience.

"Where's Chris?" I asked Aggie as we walked into the backyard.

Oak trees framed the open grassy area. Back here was also surrounded by the white picket fence. A flower garden took up a quarter of the yard and right now, colorful tulips and daffodils danced happily in the breeze.

"Right there," she said. I squinted until I could make out a tall blue and khaki shape standing at the far end of the yard. I waved; I think he waved back.

Charles Thackery had a large camera and a stern expression. We learned quickly that he didn't talk to us directly but used Louisa as his spokesperson. As such, she was never more than two feet away from him, shouting orders out.

The Sterns took family photos first and I waited on the edge of the lawn until I was summoned. I slipped my glasses on once or twice when Louisa wasn't looking and admired how they all looked together.

"You." Louisa pointed at me. "Come. We'll start on the pictures of the two of you now."

Nervous energy zipped down my arms and I shook it away.

This was not real. This was not real. This was not real. So why did it *feel* so real?

I set my resolve as I walked toward the blurry figure of Chris. I'd get through this the way I did everything else. With whatever it took.

He frowned. "Where are your glasses?"

I squinted up at him. "Charles doesn't do glasses."

"Really?" Without any explanation, Chris turned and stalked over to Charles. The two men had a conversation that involved a lot of hand motions from the photographer and a lot of glaring on Chris's part.

A full minute later, Chris returned. "You can wear your glasses."

I hesitated. "I don't mind not wearing them. Whatever gets us through this whole thing the fastest."

"I mind. I'm not letting anyone take another picture of me unless you have on your glasses."

"Oh, good grief. Don't go all weird alpha male on me now." I pulled the glasses from my pocket and slid them on. "Better?"

He smiled. "Yes. They suit you."

Did my heart forget to beat for a half-second when he said that? Yes, yes, it did. Did I pretend it didn't? Also, yes.

"Let's get this over with," I said.

"There's that sunny disposition I know and love."

"Charles would like Mae to stand in front of Chris," Louisa said with lot of exaggerated hand gestures in case we were slow on the uptake. "Good. Yes. Now put your hand around her waist and rest it on her stomach. Excellent. And now, Mae, turn your head and look up at Chris. No. No. No smiles. Be very serious. Better."

"Woohoo," Betsy called from the patio where all three sisters watched. "You two look hot."

"Go away," Chris yelled back.

"No, thanks!"

And it went on. More and more positions which probably looked great in the photos but made me feel like a human pretzel. There was one where we had to sit on the ground and wrap ourselves around each other. It was complicated and strangely clinical. Like putting together IKEA furniture but with hand positions and head tilts.

An occasional catcall or round of applause burst from the patio. One of the sisters got paper and markers and they all began to rate our poses from one to ten like we were Olympic competitors.

Betsy acted as announcer. "The newly engaged couple have been asked to do the Sit-Squat pose. It looks simple, but has a high level of difficulty. The judges will be looking closely at form. Let's watch."

"Stop it. I have to be serious," I yelled. "Charles said so."

Betsy ignored me. "And let's see the judges' scores."

"I give them a nine," Aggie said.

Millie held up a 6.5.

"Ouch," Betsy the Announcer said. "There's always a judge

from East Germany and she has spoken. Let's see what the Sterns-Sampson team do next."

"Charles is almost done, but he would like to do some photos of the couple kissing," Louisa announced.

"What?" I turned around so fast my dress got twisted in my legs, and I was about five seconds from a Grade A faceplant on the Sterns' lawn when an arm grabbed me around the waist and caught me.

"Whoa," Chris whispered. "Watch out, or someone will think you don't want to kiss me."

"I don't," I insisted, righting myself.

His eyes narrowed. "I guess you'll have to suck it up."

Louisa showed us the spot Charles wanted us to stand in. "Now, turn to each other and hold hands."

Our fingers entwined; our eyes met. That's when every single thought I had about staying objective flew out of my head. Because it was a powerful, heady feeling to stand like this. Although we stood several inches apart, I couldn't bring myself to look him in the eye. I stared at his neck, studied the edge of his jaw, and his bottom lip which looked soft and full.

I swallowed and closed my eyes.

"Get closer." Louisa stomped up to us, put a hand on each of our backs and shoved. The inches between us disappeared. "Better. Now put your forehead to her forehead. No, don't pay any attention to Charles. He'll be walking around you while he's taking photos. Perfect. Don't move."

"This might be worse than that mattress last night," Chris whispered.

"No talking!" Louisa said. "Look deeply into each other's eyes. More. More. Look deeper, dammit."

"Yeah, look deeper," I said, holding back a laugh.

"Do you think she had a career in the military before this? Maybe drill sergeant?" Chris said.

In my periphery, I could see a black shape slowly walking around us.

"Now, Mae, turn your head toward me," Louisa said. "And rest it on his shoulder. Yes, that's good." She directed Chris to put a hand on my back and told us not to move.

Judging by the ratings the sisters held up, this was not going to be a good photo.

"And now, let's get the photos of you kissing, please," Louisa said.

I leaned back and met his eyes. "Let's just do it and get it over with."

Chris grinned. "I'll make it fast."

Before I could blink, his lips pressed against mine and... he was done. It barely met the dictionary definition of a kiss.

I was sad. Sad because that wasn't the kiss I wanted. And confused because I shouldn't want a kiss. And then mad because I was sad and confused.

"What was that?" Aggie yelled. "That was the worst kiss I've ever seen."

"Boo. Negative ten points from me," Millie said.

"Well, it looks like the judges are very disappointed with what's just happened here and, ladies and gentlemen, their scores are reflecting that," Betsy the Announcer said. "Will they try again for a higher score? Let's watch and see what happens."

Millie faked a yawn. "I thought Chris would have more game than that, but I'm not really surprised."

"Shut up," Chris growled. "Why do I have so many sisters?"

"'Cause you're lucky," Betsy said.

Louisa clapped her hands, demanding attention. "Can we have some quiet, please? Charles would like you to try it again but slower and with more passion."

"I can do passionate," Chris said.

He lifted my head and gazed down at me. Something was

happening behind his eyes. Something different. Something serious. And it was mesmerizing.

He slid my glasses off, carefully folded them up, and slipped them in his shirt pocket. One of his hands slid around my waist and settled low on my back. He pulled me closer.

My fingers curled into the front of his shirt. Instead of speeding up, my heartbeat grew slow and lazy.

With his other hand, Chris cupped my cheek. "Try not to enjoy this, okay?"

"As if."

It started out slow and sweet, a brush of his lips to the corners of my mouth, then one right in the center. Tiny, whisper kisses. Almost-there kisses. Teasing me with kisses like he did with his words.

Frustration built in me. I tried to take control. My hands slid from his chest to around his neck, fingers twisting into his hair. I pulled him closer, begging for a proper kiss without uttering a single word.

He smiled against my mouth.

I growled.

Just like that, the kiss changed. This kiss had purpose. The people and sounds around us faded and it was just Chris and me. A wave of relief tore through me, some secret knowledge that this was always meant to happen. This wasn't just pleasure; there was a rightness to this, a missing part of me clicking into place.

Mine, I thought. Mine.

But there was also an edge of desperation. Like we both knew it wouldn't ever happen again.

Because this was for show; it was fake.

But fake had never felt so real.

FORTY

*My son, Roman, age ten, said his pickup line is going to be,
"You can't have ROMANce without me."*

—JEANNIE Q.

There are many epic battles: good versus evil; man versus nature; pepperoni versus pineapple. But not one of them compared to the battle that had been taking place in my head the last few hours. It was like an MMA cage match up there.

On one side, the sensible, logical part of me, the Me who made plans, who took care of people, who made choices with realistic expectations in mind. The other side? That Me was apparently ready to throw both caution to the wind and myself at Chris.

Hours later, my lips still remembered that kiss. It played like a scene from a romance novel and my stupid romantic heart remembered every detail—his hand on my cheek, the feel of his hair in my fingers, the press of his lips on mine. It was all I could do not to start writing sonnets about the whole thing.

Who even was I anymore?

After the photos, we'd been whisked away to change, pack, and eat a quick dinner with the family. Then Piper had driven back with us to Tulsa and we'd all hopped on a 2 a.m. flight back to Houston. What we hadn't done was talk. Probably because I'd pretended to sleep the entire flight.

Piper parted ways with us and that left Chris and me, alone in his truck for the hour drive back to Two Harts. One hour. Sixty minutes. 3,600 seconds.

I couldn't stand it.

"About the kiss," I said five minutes after we got on the freeway. "We should talk about that."

"Alright. Let's talk about it."

"I know it was for show, so I want to make sure things won't be awkward between us. It was simply a kiss. No big deal."

It was such a big deal. The biggest of big deals. But I waved my hand in the air like I was shooing a pesky fly.

In the flickering glow of the streetlights, I saw him frown.

I plowed on. "We are contractually obligated to engage in public displays of affection. We were honoring our contract. Was it awkward? Absolutely."

One of his eyebrows arched. The one hand resting on the steering wheel tightened. "Was it?"

"Of course it was. We're friends who were practically forced to engage in an activity neither of us wanted. It's not like you woke up this morning with the intention of having your tongue halfway down my throat by dinner."

"Huh." He rubbed his thumb on his bottom lip. Stupid, stupid opposable thumb.

"What?"

"Let's say, for argument's sake, I wanted to."

"Wanted to what?"

"Put my tongue halfway down your throat, as you so eloquently put it."

I huffed a laugh. "Yeah. Right."

"For argument's sake, of course."

I looked away, fiddled with my seatbelt. "I would remind you we're in a business arrangement. It's finite. It has an end date. The more we get tangled in each other's lives, the harder it will be to untangle."

"What if we didn't have to... untangle? What if...?"

What if...? He'd said the same words that night in the pool house. *What if* scared me to death. Because what ifs never ended well. A what if had made my mother fall in love with a con man who had wrecked her life. A what if had made me think Peter Stone cared about me. I couldn't stand the thought of another what if going wrong. Especially if it involved Chris. Because I knew with the same certainty I knew my name that when things went badly with Chris (and they would), I might not survive it.

"There can't be a 'what if.'"

"Huh." He patted my knee with his free hand. The touch traveled through my body with lightning speed. "It's alright. I understand."

"That's it." I half shrieked.

For a long moment, he rubbed his lower lip with his thumb because he was truly trying to drive me insane. "That's it."

I stared at his stupid handsome profile. "You are the most irritating man on this entire planet."

The rest of the drive was done in silence, although he kept smiling to himself.

And that made me nervous.

FORTY-ONE

You know what my shirt is made of? Boyfriend material.

—TAYLOR A.

"We got another one." Aidan set a gigantic floral arrangement on the circulation desk in front of where I was standing.

"Wow. This is very... big." They were so tall I couldn't even see Aidan on the other side of them.

A disembodied hand floated in the air. "Here's the card. I'm going to finish updating the computers."

"Sure." I opened the tiny envelope and read the card.

Please accept this gift as our heartfelt congratulations on your coming nuptials.

We want to offer you our services for what is sure to be the wedding of the year. We provide the freshest flowers in the most unique arrangements. Feel free to contact us any time to set up your free consultation.

With love,

Just Flowers of Houston

I put the card with the rest of the "offers." Three other florists had also sent along arrangements, which had now found homes on various tables and bookcases around the library. In my tiny office, there was practically a full-service bakery with all the cake samples.

It had been over a week since we'd taken the engagement photos. Piper had given rights to a big-name magazine to release the first photo. One simple, tasteful photo of Chris and me smiling at the camera. Since then, stacks of offers had poured in from wedding planners, photographers, caterers, wedding invitation designers, and bridal shops. I had to give them credit for tracking me down so quickly.

The phone rang. I ignored it. Piper said to be prepared for phone calls. The first few days, I'd attempted to answer them until it got too much. There were emails, too. A guy from college I went out with for one and a half dates. My lab partner from a bio class I took. My childhood pediatrician who had retired to Florida but was hopeful I'd send him a wedding invite.

After the second day of me growling at my computer, Aidan had worked out some fancy filter on my email that got rid of anything mentioning the words "wedding" and "congratulations."

I don't care what he'd done in his past. That kid was a good egg.

An egg I couldn't quite figure out. Aidan dressed like a mid-level accountant; I swear he even had a pocket protector one day. He was polite, helpful, proactive, and a complete mystery.

He was also good at math, which had given me an idea. 'Cause I knew someone who was failing math.

"Why am I here?" Iris asked one day after school. She leaned a hip on the table on which I'd set up a display of recommended horror novels. Today she had on black tights, black-and-white-striped board shorts, a t-shirt, a pair of vintage Doc Martens she'd found at a thrift store that I knew were a size too big, and an apathetic expression.

"Hello to you, too." I waved her to follow me to my office. "I talked to your math teacher. He says you have a month to get your grade up or you won't pass his class."

She plopped down in a chair with a groan. "I hate math. And do you know why? This is because I've grown up in an educational system that favors boys over girls in STEM subjects. I've basically received a subpar education. I am a product of their own making. Is it any wonder I'm failing math?"

"Or it could be that you're out until midnight every night, you don't do your homework, and you failed your last test."

She scowled. "Whatever."

"I think I have a solution for you." I called for Aidan. "This is Aidan. Aidan, this is my sister, Iris."

Iris cocked an eyebrow. "Okay. Why?"

"Aidan is really good at math, and he's agreed to tutor you two days a week after school right here in the library."

"I said I'd take care of it," Iris ground out.

"And now you don't have to. I did it for you. That's the kind of sister I am."

Aidan stuffed his hands in his pockets. "Cool shirt. I like My Chemical Romance."

"Seriously, you?" Iris asked incredulously. "You're dressed like the President of the Future Proctologists' club."

He smiled. "And you're dressed like a knock-off emo kid from circa 2007, but I'll still tutor you."

Iris sputtered and I held in a bark of laughter. I had to give the kid credit. He didn't appear to be intimidated by her in the least. Maybe this would work out.

"See?" I grabbed a box of cake samples and shoved them in

Iris's direction. "You're getting along famously. Now, go eat some cake and figure out which two days a week you'll be here after school."

Aidan strolled out, leaving Iris behind. She hitched up her backpack. "Thanks for making my life the worst."

I hugged her and after I refused to let go, she finally hugged me back even. "You're welcome."

With yet another eye-roll, she trudged out of the office and then poked her head back in. "Have you heard from Dad?"

I'd tried to call him no fewer than four times. I'd left two messages. I'd even attempted to reach out to Uncle Gary, Dad's brother, who was only slightly less criminally minded than my father. No luck. "I haven't. I promise I'm trying."

"Yeah, okay." But I didn't miss the hurt creeping into her eyes.

This is exactly why I hadn't even wanted to contact him. All he'd ever done was disappoint us, again and again. I could deal with it; but Iris was different, softer than she pretended to be. Like a coconut.

And we were setting her up for a broken heart.

FORTY-TWO

Are your parents bakers? Because you're a cutie pie.

—JULIA B.

"I can't believe I let you talk me into reading this." I stared at the cover of our latest book club read, a serial romance called *Checking Out the Librarian*.

"Come on, you liked it." Chris took a bite of his second double cheeseburger.

The weather had been especially nice today. So, we'd decided to pick up some takeout and I brought him to the little park just outside town, locally famous because it was home to the Legacy Tree, a Two Harts' historical site.

"Did not," I said out of stubbornness.

With a stern look, he pointed a French fry at me.

"Fine. It wasn't that bad."

"I knew it." He grinned, his dimple making an appearance. "I like it when she yelled at him in the middle of the library. Scandalous. Yelling in the library."

"If you want, I can yell at you at the library."

"You yell at me enough as it is." He balled up his napkin and tossed it on the table.

"I do not!"

"See?"

Glaring, I stood. "Are you done?"

"You sure are bossy."

"It's part of my charm." Usually, I tried to tamp it down but lately even I'd noticed how I hadn't bothered to censor my words around Chris. I was comfortable around him. It was yet another instance of him worming his way into my life. It was a problem.

We cleaned up and started down the well-worn trail until we reached the old oak tree in the heart of the park.

"So"—Chris pointed at the crown jewel of Two Harts— "this is it."

"Yep." The long arms of the oak tree twisted and bent. At some point, this tree was climbed by most every kid that came through Two Harts; it was a rite of passage. "This is the Legacy Tree. Most of us call it the Hart Tree."

"I'm guessing because of all the hearts?" He was referring to the hundreds upon hundreds of hearts and initials carved into it. Another tradition.

"Yes and no. As the legend goes, Joseph and James Hart came from Georgia and settled here after they lost everything in the Civil War. They staked their claim on what is now most of downtown Two Harts. The brothers worked hard, and within ten years had built a decent little settlement. More families moved in. Then a general store, a church, a school, the essentials.

"Joseph, who was the oldest, decided he wanted to get married, have kids, carry on the family name and all that. So, he got himself a mail-order bride from back east. Emily made the journey here and when she was set to arrive, Joseph sent James to pick her up. The story is that Joseph and Emily were married right here in front of this very tree. See the big heart right there in the middle?"

"J plus E. That must be them."

"Officially." I walked closer to the tree. "Emily and Joseph were married, had three children, and by all accounts, lived a long, happy life."

"But?"

"Sometime in the late 1940s, a Hart descendant found a journal that belonged to James Hart. In it, he detailed meeting Emily for the first time, falling in love almost at first sight. He claimed the feelings were returned but she was promised to his brother. He stepped aside. James never married. He stuck around, lived in a little house on the property by himself the rest of his life."

"That sounds lonely," Chris said, now standing beside me, both of us staring at that heart.

I traced the J and E with a fingertip. "And this carving? Emily passed on first, then Joseph. James lingered another ten years, and that's when this was carved. Joseph couldn't have done it. I think James spent his whole life loving Emily. Never seemed able to get over her."

"What would you have done?" Chris asked. "If you were James?"

I answered immediately. "The same thing. Family comes first. As long as they're okay, I'm okay."

Chris tilted his head and inspected me like he was trying to figure out how my operating system worked. "But he lost out on a chance to have happiness."

My phone buzzed in my back pocket. I let it go to voicemail. "You don't know that. Maybe convincing Emily to run off with him would have been the worst mistake of his life."

"You've got to be the most unromantic romance reader in the world."

"I told you. Romance novels are not real life. Sure, they're fun to read but they are fiction. Real people make choices, and they have to live with them. There's family, hard work and, if we're lucky, we're content with what we have."

He stepped closer and tucked a piece of flyaway hair behind my ear, his fingers lingering there. "I think you can find happiness. I think you might even deserve happiness."

A funny little twinge pinged in my chest.

"Oh, you sweet, naïve unicorn of a man. Happiness is never a guarantee. Was there some kind of Optimism badge you earned when you were twelve?"

My phone vibrated again. This time I pulled it out of my pocket and saw it was Ali. It was the second time in five minutes that she'd called. She was more a texter, but I sent it to voicemail again.

"Unicorn of a man?" He smirked. "That makes me pretty rare."

"If you make even one joke about having a horn..."

For the third time, my phone vibrated. Ali again. This time, I answered.

"Thank God," Ali said. "My phone is about to die."

"Why are you whispering?"

"I'm in a bit of a bind."

I sighed. "What did you do?"

"You can lecture me later. Right now, I need help."

"Where are you?"

"Oh, hold on." I was met with the sound of rustling and heavy breathing for a long moment. "That was close."

"Ali."

"Okay, fine. No yelling."

"No promises."

"I'm at City Hall."

I pulled my phone from my ear to check the time. "It's after seven p.m. Isn't it closed?"

"I'll explain later. Just come get me."

"Where are you exactly?"

"That's the thing..."

"Ali!" I repeated, but louder. "Spill it."

"Fine. I'm hiding in the closet in Peter's office."

"What did you do?" My mind began racing with visions of ostriches, water balloons, and shaving cream.

"There's another thing. Peter just came back to his office and—"

That's when her phone died.

FORTY-THREE

A man once told me, "I want to lick you, stick you, and send you first class."

He thought he was being charming.

—*MARTA L.*

"What's the plan again?" Chris asked as we parked two blocks over from City Hall. It was located in the thick of downtown and given the time, locked up tight.

"Distract Peter, get Ali."

"That's not a very detailed plan," Chris said as we began walking to our destination. "Shouldn't we at least be wearing black?"

"We aren't ninjas. Ali's Uncle Joe is on the way, and he at least has keys to the building. We'll figure it out when he gets here."

Joe worked as head of the city maintenance department and was accustomed to the "don't ask, don't tell" policy required to be part of Ali's circle of friends and family.

"What do you think she did?" Chris asked as we passed

window after window of antique shops and boutiques locked up for the night.

"I have no idea." We paused at a corner that allowed us a view of the building.

The hall was a one-story brick building, circa 1960. It was U-shaped with a courtyard in the middle and a few benches. The front of the building was, unfortunately for us, made entirely of windows, so there was no sneaking up on this place. The main lobby had security lights (and probably a camera or two) but most of what we could see was shrouded in darkness except for a hallway toward the back where a faint light was shining.

"It could be almost anything. Two weeks ago, Peter came to the library to tell me someone had wedged raw chicken in the back of the bottom drawer of his filing cabinet. It took at least a week to find it. Blamed it on Ali."

From all accounts, the smell had been so awful they'd had to clear out that wing of the building for the day to get it aired out and cleaned up.

"It was her, right?"

"I never ask outright. Plausible deniability and all that. I merely pass on the information."

"Smart," he murmured.

"Last week, someone replaced all his office supplies with bananas and put the real stuff in the women's bathroom. He was very upset about his stapler, for some reason."

Truly. Ranted about it for two entire paragraphs in the email he sent me.

Chris laughed low and quiet. "Should I be scared of Ali?"

"Yes." I turned to him. "You know, you don't have to help. I would completely understand. If we get caught, Peter will not let us off easily."

When I'd explained Ali's phone call, he hadn't even batted an eye. Just marched us to his truck and asked for directions.

"I want to help."

I crossed my arms and stared down at the sidewalk. "Well, thanks."

Uncle Joe showed up a few minutes later. A stocky man with a booming voice, he immediately started in on the sports talk with Chris. Once I got him steered back to the situation at hand, a plan began to form. I'd go with Joe around to the back door where there weren't any working security cameras. Meanwhile, Chris would find a way to get Peter out of his office. If everything went as planned, we'd meet back at Chris's truck and Peter wouldn't be any the wiser.

"How are you going to distract him?" I asked Chris.

"I thought I'd ask him to be a groomsman at the wedding."

Surely he was joking. Joe stood about ten feet away, doing something on his phone, so I grabbed Chris's hand and half dragged him to a streetlamp where I could see his face.

"Are you kidding?" I whispered.

Chris moved closer and I realized I was still holding his hand. I'm sure if Joe looked over about now, he'd think we were in the middle of a quaint couple moment. "You're doing that whisper-yell thing I like. Do it again."

I ignored him. "Even if we were getting married, *which we are not*, Peter Stone would definitely not be in the wedding party."

"Well, I don't know." He shrugged. "He did kind of introduce us in a roundabout way. Seems only fair he should be in the wedding party. He could give a speech at our reception."

"Absolutely not." I poked him in the chest. "This is the hill I will die on. He will not be at our wedding."

He grinned slowly.

With a huff, I shook my head. What was I even saying? We weren't even real-dating, let alone real-engaged, and we sure weren't getting real-married.

"It's so easy to get you riled up, Sprinkles." He tapped the tip of my nose and I batted his hand away.

Joe cleared his throat. "We ready?"

With one last dirty look in Chris's direction, I said, "Let's go save Ali."

"Ali?" I whispered into Peter's empty office.

It was a spacious room with dark wood paneling and a heavy solid oak desk. Built-in shelves lined the back wall, and it was full of books chosen for their aesthetic qualities rather than their content.

Carefully, I pushed the door until it almost clicked closed. "Ali? Where are you? We don't have a lot of time."

A door hidden in the wall paneling swung open and Ali popped out, dressed in black. Like a ninja. "Thank God. I was so worried I was going to have to spend all night in here."

I waved a hand. "Well, I'm here. Let's go. I don't know how long Chris can keep Peter busy."

Ali smiled. That made me nervous. "I can't leave yet."

"Excuse me? Yes, you can." I marched across the room. "We are leaving now."

"Yes, of course." Ali patted me complacently on the arm. "I just need to do one thing first."

"Ali..."

But she was already moving behind Peter's desk. "I was about to do this when I heard Peter and had to hide."

I glanced nervously toward the door, straining to hear anything that might indicate Peter was returning. "Do what?"

Ali didn't reply and when I looked over, she was furiously typing on Peter's computer.

"What are you doing?"

"It will take me fifteen minutes at the most."

"You have got to be kidding me." I paced back and forth,

wringing my hands. I could hear the low rumble of voices, not close enough to make out the words but close, nonetheless.

"I just have to remap a few of the keys on his keyboard. Last time I was here, I made sure I got his computer details and I've been practicing." She grinned and wagged her eyebrows at me. "This is going to be epic."

I paused at the gap in the door and listened intently. Had the voices gotten louder? Panic fizzed through me. "Seriously. You have to hurry."

"I'm going. I'm going," she muttered. "Stop interrupting me."

I eased the door open a bit and peeked out. Peter and Chris were standing at the end of a long hallway, still too far to make out actual words. Thankfully, Peter's back was toward me. I tiptoed out into the hallway and waved a hand, trying to get Chris's attention.

We made the briefest of eye contact. I switched from waving to stretching my hands apart and pointing to my wrist in what I hoped translated to "more time." He scratched his head and, yes, there—a thumb's up.

"You have five minutes," I said to Ali once I was safely inside.

"That's perfect." Furious tapping on the keyboard. "I'm almost done. This may be my masterpiece. I could retire after this."

"That sounds like an excellent idea."

"I'm kidding, of course." More furious tapping. "Done. Come and see my genius."

"Can't you tell me about it later?" But I was already scurrying to the desk.

Ali popped out of the seat and gestured for me to sit. On the computer, a blank word document was open, cursor blinking. "Type Peter's name. Go on. Do it."

I quickly did as she asked. At first nothing happened until I hit the R. I gasped when, "I am a giant cucumber," appeared instead of his name.

Ali laughed *à la* evil scientist. "Isn't it amazing?"

I typed PETER one more time just to make it happen again and held back a laugh. "We have to go now."

"Right, right." She leaned around me and closed a few windows. "Let us be off. I have to pee anyway."

After opening the door with sloth-like speed, we crept into the hallway. I gave Chris a wave, grabbed Ali and dragged her to the back door. As expected, Uncle Joe had already left, his part in the plan finished.

Ali giggled as we pushed the door open and started to jog away from the building. "That was amazing. Epic. I am the master. Do you hear the *Rocky* music playing, or is that in my head?"

When we made it back to Chris's truck, Ali leaned against a door, a wide smile stretched across her face. "So, how did you do it?"

"Uncle Joe. He brought his key," I said. "How did you do it?"

"Uncle Joe. But he doesn't know I have a copy of his key so don't tell anyone."

I huffed. "Ali. You have to stop doing stuff like this. One of these days, you're going to get yourself in too much trouble and nobody's going to be able to help you."

She shrugged. "Maybe. But it's so fun, and I have so little fun in my life."

"Stop that. You could have a perfectly fun life if you wanted to."

Ali tilted her head back to look at the night sky. "Eh, I'm fine."

She was not fine. Not really.

When Ali was sixteen, she'd had her first grand mal seizure. It had come out of nowhere. The doctors hadn't been too concerned with the first one. She was a student athlete (soccer) and it had been extremely hot that day. Likely she was dehydrated. But a month later, seizure number two happened. She'd been officially diagnosed with epilepsy, and it had changed her life in so many ways. Her parents refused to let her play sports or drive. She wasn't allowed to be alone. Medication was prescribed, probably for life.

But when the car accident happened six months later, Ali started to change too. Ten years later, she was mostly back to normal but there were permanent changes. Because of the accident, she refused to drive (even though she was allowed). Her brother, already the black sheep of the family, had been blamed for the accident and left the state. Ali hadn't seen him since. She'd also closed herself off to anything more than a surface-y relationship with most anyone. I was an exception. Alec, her college boyfriend, had been too. Then he'd broken her heart.

I wrapped an arm around her shoulders and hugged her. "Thanks for making Peter's life miserable."

"You're welcome. But if anyone asks..."

"I know nothing."

Chris strolled up to the truck five minutes later, looking none the worse for having had to keep Peter busy.

"All go okay?" he asked.

I nodded. "And you?"

"No problem. I got him talking about himself and that football stadium. I don't think he even took a breath the whole time." Chris unlocked the truck and opened the passenger door. We climbed in, Ali in the back.

"Thanks for helping me out." Ali leaned forward. "It means a lot."

"It was nothing," Chris said. "Besides, I had a question to ask Peter anyway."

I gave him a sharp look; he grinned and patted my leg.

"Good news. He said yes; he'd love to be a groomsman."

FORTY-FOUR

Even if there was no gravity on earth, I'd still fall for you.

—ELENA S.

"The silent auction is three weeks away," Mrs. Katz said. "We have a few items donated but we need more. No one's going to get overly excited about a dozen donuts from the Sweet Spot with an estimated value of eight dollars."

The Save the Library crew had been hard at work over the last few weeks. A dance had been planned at the Sit-n-Eat to celebrate after the auction, another attempt to draw a crowd. The date and time had been set, the fliers distributed. The newspaper had printed a small article about it. We'd talked a big game about this silent auction but, as yet, our donations had only dribbled in.

Horace raised his hand. "I've been talking to Cliff down at the tractor supply store and he thinks he could probably donate a wheelbarrow and some seed packets."

"People," Mrs. Katz said, using the same voice that could put the fear of the Lord himself into a room full of sixth graders.

"If this is going to be a success, we need more than donuts and seed packets."

"It doesn't make any sense why we haven't got more donations," Sarah Ellis said.

Melinda squirmed in her seat. "I heard a rumor."

All eyes turned to her.

She rose to her feet, wringing her hands. "Apparently, Peter has been asking people not to donate. He's been bribing them with season tickets to the high school football games next season."

"He wouldn't, that little louse," Mrs. Katz said.

"I'm afraid he did." Melinda sat back down, head hanging. After all, she was related to that louse.

After Ali's last prank, he'd surely do any number of things. The next day, he'd stormed into the library—face purple with rage—and had demanded I put an end to these antics. When I'd explained that I wasn't responsible for them, he'd only grabbed at his hair with both fists and stormed right back out.

I heard later it had taken him half the day and several emails announcing he was a cucumber before he'd realized what was happening. Then another three days to find someone who could fix it. He'd also insisted a security camera be placed outside his office door, and he'd sent a certified letter to Ali demanding she put a stop to it all or she'd be looking at criminal charges.

The next day, he'd received a package; in it was a t-shirt with a giant cucumber on it.

Horace shoved a cookie in his mouth and spoke around it. "Now what are we going to do?"

"Good grief, Horace." Mrs. Katz glared at him. "Were you raised by animals?"

He replied by stuffing yet another cookie in his mouth.

"Like I told you, my son knows a guy," Abel cut in.

"No," I said.

"I have an idea," a voice from behind me said.

"Oh, Aidan, I forgot you were still here," I said. He'd asked to stay to work on homework. "Please tell us your idea."

"What about all those businesses who are giving you free stuff? The flowers and cake and all that." He pointed to the two fresh floral bouquets sitting atop the circulation desk. "Maybe they'd be willing to donate?"

Mrs. Katz slapped a hand on the table she was sitting at. "Sir, that is an excellent idea."

We immediately got to work composing a list of businesses and the committee assigned each member a few to contact.

"This is good," Mrs. Katz said when we'd finished. "But we still need something better than good. We need it to be big, huge, monumental."

That is when Chris walked into the library. Like he'd heard the call and he was ready to answer.

His eyes found mine immediately, warm and twinkling, a smile lifting one corner of his mouth. I watched him as he navigated the obstacle course of tables and bookshelves, a flutter beginning in my stomach. That flutter had been taking up entirely too much space lately, and only when Chris was around. It was concerning. But my concern didn't stop my smile growing wider with each step he took.

"Like him?" Horace asked.

No one answered him, and it was then I realized the entirety of the room had their eyes on us. When he reached me, Chris didn't hesitate. He wrapped his arms around me and hugged me so tight my feet left the floor, forcing me to wrap my arms around his neck.

Someone sighed.

When he set me down, he kept one hand at my waist and the other moved a strand of my hair from my face, tucking it gently behind my ear. Then he kissed me. It was soft and quick, a brushing of lips. But still, when he pulled back, my eyes opened slowly, reluctantly.

"Hi," I said, my voice breathless.

"Hi."

"Oh, my," Sarah said, her voice dreamy. "Reminds me of my Will. First thing he did when he entered the room was kiss me hello."

"Thought I'd come over a little early in case the meeting let out sooner than you expected," Chris said.

I frowned, my head such a jumbled mess I had no idea what he was talking about.

"For dinner, remember?" With a smirk, he tapped my nose. "We had plans."

"Oh. Right. Yes, um, yes. We're just finishing up here."

He found a seat at the same table as Horace, nodding a hello to him. "Don't rush on my account."

"As I was saying," Mrs. Katz said. "We do need something big to draw a crowd. Something"—she stood and began to pace —"that no one would expect from a little library in the middle of nowhere." At this, she stopped in front of Chris and smiled down at him, hands laced behind her back.

Horace slapped a hand on the table. "Like a meet-and-greet with a famous football player?"

"I'm about to say words I never in my life I thought I'd say." Mrs. Katz didn't look happy about it either. "Yes, Horace, what a good idea."

Horace grinned.

"I'd be happy to help any way I can." Chris said. "How much money do you need to raise?"

"A lot," Horace said. "A hundred thousand dollars."

Chris leaned forward. "I could just donate the money."

Several gasps made their way around the room.

"No!" I said much too loudly and then took a calming breath. "I mean, that's an amazing offer, but the library needs to learn to stand on its own. We might not always have you around to rescue us."

"But, Mae, that would solve all our problems, wouldn't it?" Sarah asked.

I didn't want to rely on Chris, not when I knew his presence was fleeting. It would be hard enough to cut him out of my life, but I didn't want to be responsible for breaking the hearts of the entire town.

"We'll handle it." I could feel Chris's eyes on me, but I refused to look his way. I would not bend on this.

"I'm sure we cannot handle it," Melinda said.

"I agree," Horace chimed in. "We could use his help."

Sighing, I turned to stare at Chris. "You can help. But you will not donate a hundred thousand dollars to the library. Understood?"

Chris nodded, looking far too serious and innocent. I should have known he was already up to something.

"Well," Mrs. Katz cut in, smiling broadly at Chris like he'd just named every single capital and state in alphabetical order, "it's settled then. Welcome to the committee, young man."

FORTY-FIVE

Did you just see that? (As he points in the direction he came from.)

No, see what?

I just slid into your world with a pickup line, and you never even saw it coming.

—*NONIE S.M.*

Three days later, Iris stomped into the library with an expression on her face that warned of danger and possible violence.

"You heard from Dad yet?" she asked by way of a greeting.

"My darling sister, it is nice to see you, too."

She hopped up on the circulation desk and crossed her arms. "Well?"

"One, get off the desk, and two, I haven't heard anything."

She narrowed her eyes. "How do I know you're even calling? Maybe you're just telling me you are."

"Really, Iris? *He* won't respond and somehow, it's my fault?"

Her shoulders slumped. "Fine. I just..."

"What?"

"The school wants to know how many tickets I need for graduation. They're limited, or whatever." She brushed a chunk of black hair out of her eyes impatiently. Her voice broke with her next words. "I just want to know, okay? I don't understand why he can't call back."

I put my arms around her, and she allowed it. (I swore I heard angels singing.) "I'm sorry, Iris. I'll call again. I'll do whatever I can to get him here, okay?"

While she didn't hug me back, she also didn't move away. "Yeah."

"I mean it."

She nodded against my shoulder, and I swore I heard a sniffle. A tiny piece of my heart broke off at that sound. I rubbed her back. We were having a moment. An actual sister moment.

After a beat, Iris pulled away and discreetly swiped at her cheeks. "I have to go pee before I meet with Aidan."

Without waiting for me to respond, she jumped off the desk and trudged to the bathroom, shoulders bent in despair. And while the situation made me ache for Iris, it made me angry, too.

I was going to kill my father for making my sister cry.

I called four times in the next two hours. The first two times went to voicemail immediately. The second two rang and rang. I didn't leave a message until the last call.

"I'm looking for Dale Sampson. This is Mae. Look, Iris wants you to come to her graduation. I don't know why. You've been a crap dad. But Iris wants you there anyway. You owe her that much. Think about your kid for once in your damn life."

I spent the entire afternoon alternately staring at my phone and fuming at myself for staring at my phone. If he didn't call back, it was on him. Not me, not my mother, not Iris. He was missing out on knowing us.

After I kicked everyone out at closing time, Aidan lingered and helped shut down the computers.

I wanted to go home and eat my feelings. No, take a hot bath. No, no. Eat my feelings while taking a hot bath.

Aidan slouched by the door, his expression troubled.

"You okay there?"

His head jerked. "Oh, yeah, sorry. Actually. I had a question."

I waited.

Cheeks pink, he opened and closed his hands at his sides. He said nothing.

I waited some more until I couldn't take it anymore. "What did you want to ask?"

He cleared his throat. "Do you know if Iris has a date to the prom?"

Now I was speechless.

Aidan and Iris?

The two did spend a lot of time together. Aside from their two tutoring sessions a week, she'd met up with him a couple of times on the weekends "to study," which was a huge lie. I'd found the movie ticket stubs.

But I'd seen them together, Iris doing her worst while Aidan was surprisingly unaffected and uber patient. Which only annoyed Iris more.

"You don't have to look that surprised." His cheeks flared red. "I like her. She's cool."

"You two are so different."

His smile was small. "I like that."

"So, ah, prom?"

"I thought I'd ask her to go. You know, as a friend, or whatever. Nothing serious but, well..." He scrubbed a hand down his face. "She's Iris and, I don't know..."

"She is pretty terrifying."

He huffed a laugh. "Yes, exactly."

"She's not so scary once you get past all the talk. She's kind of... cuddly underneath." It would take someone special to burrow through under all Iris's bluster to get to that soft part of her. But she was worth it.

It was her way of protecting her heart. I did the same thing, but my methods were different. I almost felt sorry for the guy who figured out how to get past all my defenses. I'd had a lot more years to build up my layers. My heart probably had fifty-seven padlocks, maybe a booby trap—at least one involving dynamite, chain mail, and a really angry guard dog that showed up after I broke up with Peter.

What guy wanted to make all that effort?

My phone buzzed in my back pocket—a text from Chris. I fought the smile that usually came when I discovered he'd texted me. After staring at his name for a beat, I put the phone away to read later.

I gave Aidan an encouraging smile. "I think you should ask her. What's the worst that could happen?"

He held the door open for me. "Are you kidding? She could eviscerate my heart, laugh in my face, chop me up into small pieces and mail me back to my parents."

"Or she could say yes." I locked the door behind us.

"Yeah, that might be the scariest thing of all."

My phone buzzed yet again. I knew without looking it was Chris. A strange, warm feeling curled in my stomach; it wasn't bad or good, just persistent like it was trying to tell me something. Like maybe I'd already met someone who'd managed to slice through all my armor. Maybe he was closer than anyone had ever been to capturing my heart.

I blew out a shaky breath and patted Aidan on the back. "I know exactly what you mean."

FORTY-SIX

Giiirrrlll, you be breaking Old Testament laws!
Look at you workin' it on the Sabbath.

—PEARCIA B.

Next day, I left two more angry messages for my father. He didn't return either of them. Which made me angrier.

In fact, the whole day ended up being a craptastic crapfest of epic proportions. First, my favorite t-shirt, the one that read *FEAR THE LIBRARIAN*, had a giant hole in it. Second, Iris used up all the hot water before I could get a shower in. Third, my mother spent twenty-five minutes going over wedding ideas. Fourth, Kevin got something stuck in his craw and decided to shred one of my curtains for fun. Fifth, I hadn't slept all night.

What I did do was lay awake, wondering what the hell was happening to me. Mostly, I thought about Chris. I thought about how he could get under my skin in less than three seconds. How he still managed to take care of me even when I tried to keep my distance. How I pushed and pushed but he remained unflappable, solid as a rock. How he had become my friend.

I thought about that stupid kiss many, many times. Friends didn't kiss friends like that. They didn't. I could say otherwise but I knew it hadn't felt that way.

What was I supposed to do with all of these *feelings*? I didn't have time for feelings. Feelings led to irrational things. And the worst part about these feelings? The questions. Was Chris feeling feelings too? Where the feelings mutual? What if they weren't? What if they *were*?

And threaded through all that was fear. Honest-to-goodness fear at even the thought of opening my heart to someone, of giving anyone the ability to hurt me again.

I missed my Before Chris life. It was rough but uncomplicated. I worked and worked some more and survived and that was enough.

At some point, I drifted off to sleep for a couple of hours, but even after I got up and dragged myself to work, the thoughts didn't stop. That afternoon, Chris texted and then called and then texted again. I couldn't bring myself to reply or answer.

In short, I was a coward.

By the time Peter Stone moseyed on into the library fifteen minutes before closing, I was not in the mood for his pettiness.

"What do you want?" I asked. See? Not in the mood.

Peter leaned an elbow on the circulation desk and gave me a cat-in-cream smile. "I thought you'd be a whole lot happier, seeing as how you found a way to get what you wanted."

"Look," I said, my voice hard, "I'm tired, I'm irritated, and yours is the last face I want to see. So tell me what you want. Did you come on a quest to start banning books? Are you hoping for a good old-fashioned book burning and barbecue?"

Peter (wisely) took a step back, hands raised. "I didn't mean anything except I thought you'd be happy. Wanted to let you know the check came and it's already deposited."

I rubbed my forehead. "I don't understand what you're talking about. What check?"

His eyes widened in surprise. "The donation from Chris Sterns to the library. Surely you knew about it."

I went still. No, I had not known about it. In fact, I remembered sitting in this very library and making him promise he would not donate. There'd been witnesses and everything.

"How much?" I asked.

"That's kind of funny, actually. I called him twice to make sure it was right—a hundred thousand dollars and a cent."

Of course it was. I was going to kill Chris. "I don't want that money."

Peter looked nothing short of dumbfounded. "Of course you want that money. You've worked hard for it."

I froze, my blood beginning to heat. "What?"

"You found a man with money. Wasn't that the plan? I almost feel responsible seeing as how I introduced the two of you." Then. He. Winked. At. Me.

Alright. Chris may survive. Because I was going to kill Peter instead.

"Are you accusing me of using my relationship with Chris to save the library?" I stalked around the counter until I was only a couple feet away from him. "Is that the kind of person you think I am?"

It was at this point Peter figured out he may have said the wrong thing. He pulled at his collar and took a step back. "That's not what I meant. You misunderstood me."

I moved closer and Peter backed up again. He might be a couple of inches taller, but we weighed about the same and frankly, I was scrappier. I might have been able to take him. Especially with the mood I was in.

"Get out."

"You did the same thing to me. Made me like you, got what you wanted, and then broke my heart."

"What I wanted?" I whispered.

"Well, this job at the library."

I never thought seeing red was a thing. Turns out, it was. "I got this job at the library because I am highly qualified. The only thing I did wrong was thinking for even one moment you were worth any time I ever gave you."

His expression mulish, he crossed his arms. "You're just mad because you had a good thing and couldn't keep it."

I cursed; Iris would have been proud. "Are you kidding me? You had girlfriends in four other towns, you idiot. You know, we have a support group now for all the women who were stupid enough to date you. I'm the treasurer this year. We're saving up for matching tattoos. They'll say something like, 'Peter Stone is a giant cucumber.'"

As far as insults, it hit the mark. I would have to thank Ali for her creativity.

Peter's face went through a wide range of emotions—fear, anger, embarrassment, fear again, and back to anger. For a split second, he even tried to get a backbone. "You can't talk to me that way. I'm the mayor."

"Out!" I yelled.

My hand itched to throw a book at him. I stalked toward him, and he walked backward, tripping over the return cart but saving himself before he met the floor.

His back hit the door. With as much pride as he could scrimp up, he pulled it open. "I can't wait for the council meeting. I'm going to crush you."

The door slammed shut behind him and I locked it even if it were a few minutes early. I leaned my forehead on the cool wood and tried to pull in deep, calming breaths. It didn't work. The more I thought about it, the angrier I got. Peter was a lost cause, and I was a little embarrassed I'd used any emotion on him.

But Chris was another story.

FORTY-SEVEN

Are you Siri? Because you autocomplete me.

—JULIA B.

"And where might I find Chris right now?" I asked, trying to keep my voice calm.

It should be noted I was not calm. Oh, I tried. I'd gone home, stalked around the house like a caged animal, changed into shorts and a t-shirt and gone for a walk in the hopes I'd feel better after. But I was looking for a fight. Peter and my father were out of the running. That only left one person.

Piper gave me a hesitant smile. "He's out in the barn."

"I'm gonna go pay him a little visit."

"Should I be worried? You look a little steamed up."

"A little steamed up," I muttered under my breath as I stomped out the front door, around the side of the house, and across the yard to the old red barn. "You have no idea."

I whipped open the door to the barn and marched in, letting it slam behind me. The inside of the barn was nothing like I'd expected, and it momentarily threw me off my mission.

From the outside, the barn looked old and faded. But on the inside, it had been completely renovated into what was probably a first-class gym. There was an elliptical, a treadmill, a rowing machine, that sort of thing. But also weight machines, the large ones with lots of moving parts that looked like someone could get tangled up in them easily.

Okay, *I* would probably get tangled up in them easily.

A clink of metal on metal snapped me back to attention. "Chris Sterns, where are you?"

"Mae? What are you doing here?" His voice came from somewhere in the back behind some fancy arm thingy.

I tramped toward him. "What do you think I'm doing here? I was minding my own business at work today when Peter shows up, and do you know what he had to tell me? Do you?"

At this point, I'd arrived almost in the back corner of the room and that's where I saw him sitting on a weight bench. Shirtless.

Get your act together, Mae. Who cares if he doesn't have a shirt on? Not you. You are here because you want to yell at him. Remember that.

I snapped my spine into place and marched over to him. By the time I reached him, he'd stood and was using a towel to dry the sweat off his face. And neck. And chest.

I kept my eyes very purposely on his. "Do you know what Peter just told me?"

He winced. "I'm guessing it was something—"

"He told me," I snapped, cutting him off, "you donated a whole lot of money to the library. After I very clearly told you not to."

The towel paused. Right on top of his six-pack. I wasn't going to look, I swear. But apparently my eyes had a different idea. It was all right there, out in the open. How was I not supposed to look at it? All golden skin and defined muscles. And a little scar below his left shoulder which I now itched to touch and ask about. When my eyes finally made it back up to his face, and I'm embarrassed to say how long that took, he was smirking.

"Are you enjoying the view?"

I felt my face heat with embarrassment. "Put your shirt on."

His smirk transformed into a grin. "Why? Is it bothering you?"

"No, it is not." I took a step closer, just to prove my point. "It's that I need to have a serious conversation with you, and I don't want to do it while you're half-naked."

"I think it bothers you." He wrapped the towel over his shoulders.

"I need to talk to you, and I don't want to have to stare at your sweaty chest the whole time. It's gross," I said, with all the outrage I could muster, which was a lot.

"You know what I think, Sprinkles? You're hanker sore."

I blinked. "Hanker sore? That's not a thing."

"Sure is. It's what you are when you find someone so attractive, it makes you mad. You're hanker sore over me." He took a step closer now and my heart rate kicked up. With one finger, he poked my shoulder. "You are hanker sore."

I sputtered, feeling panic rise in me. That was exactly what I was. I did find him attractive, and it did make me angry.

I took a deep breath. "I am not."

"You are hanker sore. Mae is hanker sore," Chris taunted, continuing to poke at me with both his words and his finger.

"Oh, grow up." I batted his finger away. "Put your stupid shirt on. Now."

"Nope."

What I said next would forever follow me the rest of my life. On my deathbed, someone will lean over and remind me of the stupidest thing I ever said. This would be it.

"Fine. If you won't put your shirt on, I'll take mine off."

Before he had a chance to even work out what I'd said, I'd

whipped my ratty t-shirt off and stood in front of him wearing a pair of shorts and my third-best bra.

I needed to plan these things in advance. Then I could have been wearing my best bra.

Really it didn't show any more skin than a bathing suit top. Or my outfit at Chicky's.

The smile slid off his face and I could see a small tick in his jaw as his eyes crawled from my face and lower. I actually heard him swallow. A surge of satisfaction ripped through me. There was power in knowing I affected him too.

"Now, let's talk," I said sweetly, and dropped my shirt at our feet. "I asked you not to donate that money."

His eyes snapped to my face. "Fine. I'll put my shirt on, and you can put yours on and we'll talk."

"Nah, I'm good."

With a frown, he bent and picked up my shirt. "Look, I'm sorry. I was being a jerk. I shouldn't have teased you. Let's put our shirts back on and talk."

I shrugged. "Why do you care anyway? A minute ago, you had no problem with it."

"A minute ago, I was the only one without a shirt on." He took a step forward. I'm not sure if he expected me to back up, but I held my ground, even if I did have to tilt my head back some to see his face.

"So?"

"So?" he said, his voice growing louder by the second. "Put your shirt back on."

He dangled the shirt in front of me, the back of his hand brushing against my chest. A sizzle ran through me at the contact. I gasped, which only made me more determined to not back down.

"I don't care if it's ridiculous. I'm not putting it back on." I poked him in the chest. "You are not the boss of me, Sterns."

Yes, I sounded like a third grader with authority issues.

He leaned closer, smirking. Oh, I wanted to wipe that smirk off his face. "I kind of am your boss, if you think about it."

"Oh, really?" Somehow my finger-jamming had turned into my entire hand pressed flat against a warm, solid chest. His heartbeat matched the same chaotic rhythm of my own. "Maybe I need to talk to HR about filing a sexual harassment complaint since my boss can't keep his damn shirt on."

He leaned closer, glaring down at me like a miffed-off Greek god. The only sound was our breath sawing in and out. His hand clutching the shirt skimmed down my arm, so light I wasn't sure if he meant to do it.

But then his eyes dropped to my lips, and his smile was slow and a little wild; my breath caught.

"Mae." That's it. Just my name.

He took a step toward me, crowding me. And when a 6'5", 280-pound professional defensive lineman decides he's going to get up in your space, there's nothing you can do but go with it.

I shuffled back. My heart pounded. Not in the "I'm scared of what he's about to do" sort of way; it was more in the "I'm excited for what he's about to do" sort of way.

"What are you doing?"

Another step. "I haven't been honest with you."

"A-about?"

Yet another step. "That kiss?"

I knew that kiss well. My back hit the wall. "Yes?"

One of his hands landed on the wall by my head. "I wanted to do it."

I swallowed. "W-we said we were going to forget that happened."

His other slid into my hair. "Alright. You forget that one if it makes you feel better; this one, though? You remember."

I sputtered, but words seemed impossible to form. Not that I had time to say them.

There was nothing soft or teasing this time. It was his

mouth on mine, his lips firm and demanding and greedy, taking the gasp that escaped me, my breath, my ability to remember my name. He crowded me, pressing me against the wall.

I reached for him—arm, neck, hair, whatever I could hold onto. One of us groaned, him or me, maybe both of us.

There's a rational part of the brain; it makes logical, well-thought-out decisions. It kept me from doing idiotic things.

That part of my brain broke.

Which left the irrational, illogical, impulsive, stupid, stupid, *stupid* side in charge. And oh boy, was it.

It said things like, *We should start naming our children right now.*

Well, not right now. Right now, we should keep kissing him.

He broke the kiss, his chest rising and falling. His mouth opened and I slapped a hand over it.

"Do not say a word. Just keeping kissing me," I said.

He smiled the most satisfied, primal smile, and I wanted to kick him. Instead, *I* kissed *him*.

"Oh, I didn't mean to interrupt."

We both jerked at the voice and turned to find Piper standing not fifteen feet away, her back turned to us. I scrambled out from under Chris's arm, more than a little horrified. What must she think of us shirtless and sucking face like teenagers on prom night?

HOW DID MY LIFE GET HERE? Maybe that will be the name of my autobiography one day.

"I'm so sorry." She took a few shuffling steps, careful to keep her back to us. "I wanted to talk to you both about something, but it can wait."

Chris stepped in front of me. "You didn't interrupt anything."

"Nothing at all." I snatched my shirt from his hand and pulled it over my head. "Just in the middle of a discussion."

"Ooo-kay." Slowly, Piper turned around, keeping her eyes pointed at the ground. Just in case, I guess.

"Clearing up a few things about this whole *fake* engagement." I emphasized the word fake as though it were written in neon lights with arrows pointing at it. "How it will end soon, so we need to be careful about respecting each other's wishes and not overstepping."

"Yeah," Chris mumbled, wandering several feet away. "What she said."

"And Chris now," I continued, keeping my attention on Piper, "realizes his mistake and that he shouldn't have tried solving a problem I asked him not to solve. I don't need him to fix anything for me. This is just business between us, right, Chris?"

"Yes," he said, but it sounded more like "Yeth," because he was pulling his shirt over his head.

Piper's eyes darted between us, her expression caught somewhere between what-the-hell-did-I-just-walk-into? and I-do-not-have-time-for-this.

"So"—I pasted on a smile and turned to Chris—"I'm sure you'll give Peter a call and clear this up immediately."

Eyes narrowed, he put his fists on his hips. "Sure."

"Great."

"Fine."

More weird staring between us.

As casually as I could, I strolled past Piper and headed to the door. To freedom. To forgetting whatever the heck had just happened and getting back to my normal life. You know, my normal life that involved a fake engagement to a famous football player who I *kissed* kissed mere seconds ago.

I almost made it before Chris called out, "Hey, Sprinkles, your shirt's on backward."

FORTY-EIGHT

Did you Windex your pants? Because I can see myself in them.

—CHELSEA C.

Later that evening, I received a voicemail from a number I didn't recognize.

"Maebell, it's your father," he began, his voice gravelly from a lifelong smoking habit. "I got your messages and I think we should get together. Just the two of us. I feel like we have a lot to talk about. Call me at this number."

The Bluebell Café was a hole in the wall in the small town of Brookshire. On a Thursday night, only a handful of customers were cozied up to the mismatched tables and chairs that dotted the restaurant.

I checked the time for the seven hundredth time. It was 6:45 p.m. He was fifteen minutes late.

I'd told Mama I had to run into Houston after work to pick

up some donations for the auction. She had fussed about the weather—stormy gray clouds were rolling in and we were expected to have a long night of thunderstorms— but I told her I would be fine.

The truth was that I was meeting my father.

My leg jiggled with nervous energy. I pushed the menu aside and straightened the salt and pepper shakers, then moved on to the sugar packets. My phone vibrated. I snatched it up, hoping it was my father telling me he was coming. Or cancelling. I'm not sure which of those I wanted to happen more.

Instead, it was Chris.

Dreamboat: *About last night...*

I set the phone down. I didn't want to talk about last night and whatever had happened in the barn. I'd dreamed about it every time I closed my eyes. Even now, I flushed thinking about it. I kept replaying the part just before Piper had interrupted. Except in my dream, she didn't.

Dreamboat: *On a scale from 1–10, you're a 9. I'm the 1 you need.*

I rolled my eyes.

Dreamboat: *Nothing?*

Dreamboat: *I know you're upset about the donation.*

Dreamboat: *I talked to Peter and took it back.*

Dreamboat: *I wanted to make things easier for you. You don't let anyone help you carry the weight.*

Dreamboat: *You know I can tell you're reading these, right?*

Dreamboat: *You can't avoid me forever, Sprinkles.*

I started to reply but it was then my father slid into the booth across from me.

"Well, look who I found," Dale Sampson said. He smiled his charming smile. My stomach rolled.

"What do you want?" I asked.

My father ran a hand through his hair and leaned back. He'd aged in the three years since I'd seen him, but he'd been blessed with the sort of face that looked good young or old. His blond hair may have faded to gray, but it only made his blue eyes more noticeable.

"That's not the greeting I expected from my daughter."

I shrugged. "You're not the father I expected, so I guess we're even."

A waitress stopped at the table, a middle-aged woman who looked tired.

He smiled. "Well, hello there, pretty lady."

She blushed. "What can I get you?"

My father ordered a full steak dinner. I ordered nothing.

After the server left, I asked, "What do you need to talk about?"

He wasn't here for a friendly catch-up, I knew that. There had to be a reason he'd only wanted to meet with me.

"Is it such a bad thing I wanted to see how my girl was doing?"

I shifted in my seat. "You haven't bothered to see how I was doing in three years. Why the sudden change?"

"Just thought it was about time," he said, his voice jovial, but his eyes were hard. "Besides, you were the one contacting me."

"Mama and Iris also tried to contact you. I didn't see you calling them back." I took a sip of my tea. "What do you want?"

The waitress stopped and dropped off a cup of coffee. My father added cream and sugar and stirred it slowly before taking a sip. He stared at me over the rim.

"I've heard congratulations are in order."

My breath caught. Of course, he would have heard about the engagement.

"Thanks," I said, going for nonchalant. "You're not invited to the wedding."

He smirked, added a bit more cream to his coffee and stirred. The tinkling of the spoon sounded impossibly loud. "Who's going to give you away? That's my job, after all."

"Mama will. Or hell, the mail carrier. He's way more reliable than you ever were."

His mouth tightened at the corners but otherwise he seemed unaffected. "I'd sure like to meet this fiancé of yours."

"I'd rather you didn't." I pushed my glass away and took a deep breath.

"I have this opportunity to invest in some condos in Florida he might be interested in, you know."

"No."

"What about—?"

"No. You're not meeting Chris and you're definitely not talking to him about any of your scams."

The thought of Dale Sampson going anywhere near Chris gave me hives. My father would work any angle he could to get money out of Chris, and Chris... he liked to help people. No, he was too good to be in the same room as my father.

"We can cut the niceties. The truth is that I don't want you anywhere near me or Mama or Iris. But Iris wants you at her graduation. That is the only reason I called."

His eyebrows rose in surprise. "She's already graduating?"

"She'll be eighteen in a couple of months." I shook my head. "I guess I shouldn't expect you to know that. But for some reason, she has it in her head you aren't all that bad. She's wrong, of course."

"So that's the reason for all the phone calls?" His eyes drifted to a spot over my shoulder.

"Yes. She has her heart set on you being there."

He smiled. I turned and saw a pretty, older woman with big blonde hair blushing at his attention. Ugh. "I could probably make it."

"That's the thing, *Dad*. If you aren't going to come, don't bother saying you will. I'm tired of covering for you. I've run out of excuses. You can only have so many aunts die. I think you're up to eight now."

"She is my kid."

"So am I. I'm okay never seeing you again."

He was quiet for a long moment. "You remember when we'd go play miniature golf, just the two of us?"

There had been moments, although few and far between, when my father had almost been a dad. Our miniature golf adventures had been a sort of tradition. As we moved from town to town when I was a kid, one of the first things he'd do is find a nearby course and take me. And we did have fun.

I frowned. "Where did that come from?"

"I was thinking about it the other day." His gaze was intense. "I wasn't all bad, you know."

Those miniature golf trips were perhaps the only memories of my father that had not been tarnished by all the other things he'd done. Evidence that a tiny piece of him had at least tried.

"You had your moments," I admitted reluctantly. "Iris is still willing to give you a chance. I don't know why but she is. If you say you're coming and don't show up, you might blow it with her forever. Maybe you should leave things the way they are. I'll tell her I couldn't get ahold of you. She doesn't need to know any differently."

The blonde strolled by our table, boldly trailing the tips of her fingers on my father's shoulder.

"You know what?" He stood and ran his fingers through his hair. "I forgot I have an appointment in half an hour, but tell Iris I'll be there."

"You don't even know what day it's on."

But he was already gone. From the window, I watched him catch up to the blonde in the parking lot.

FORTY-NINE

Are you a coconut? 'Cause, damn, you shredded and sweet as hell.

—*KARA R.*

The storm started fifteen minutes after I left the café. The sky split open and rain poured in buckets, making it difficult for my windshield wipers to keep up. Downward zags of lightning lit up the world almost on top of each other.

The flat tire happened five minutes after that. One minute I was inching my way down the interstate and the next, the whomp-whomp-whomp could be heard even over the sound-track of rolling thunder. With no choice, I took the nearest exit off the freeway, a desolate scrap of land at the corner of the freeway and a state highway.

White-knuckled, I pulled over into a patch of dirt, dropped my forehead to the steering wheel, and gave into the rage burning in my chest.

No matter what I did, how hard I tried, nothing ever went the way it should. Nothing.

Why? Why today? Why me? Most days, I tried not to ask the whys. If I thought too much about it, it made me so angry.

I was angry now and I was blessedly alone somewhere off the freeway in a broken car.

So, I did what any sensible person would do in this situation —I screamed.

A long, loud scream. There may have been beating on the steering wheel with my hands. Maybe, "How is this my life?" was yelled to no one in particular. I sat there in my car in the middle of nowhere with a flat tire in the pouring rain and screamed.

The last couple of days had been a lot. I deserved this scream. When my throat started to ache and the rage seemed to have dissipated enough so I could think clearly, I convinced myself it was time to change that tire.

About five seconds after digging the jack and spare from the trunk, the rain became a good old torrential downpour. The lightning ripped through the sky, one bolt on top of another. If anyone was going to get hit by lightning, it would probably be me. This was not a good idea. I knew I should wait it out rather than attempt to change that tire but I was desperate to get home, crawl into bed, and never speak to another living person again.

The patch of dirt I had parked on quickly became one giant mudpuddle. I slipped twice and caught myself before I went all the way down. After I managed to get the car jacked up, I removed three of the four lug nuts before I ran into a problem. The fourth one wouldn't budge. No matter how much force I put behind it, nothing happened.

I kicked the tire—not a smart move—and climbed back into the car to consider my options. It quickly became apparent I only had one.

With a sigh, I picked up my phone and called.

. . .

When Chris's truck pulled up, there was not a part of my body that wasn't soaked through. I shivered from the temperature drop brought on by the storm but still, I stood in the rain, intent on removing that damn lug nut.

"Hey." He reached for the tire iron in my hand, his hair already plastered to his head. "I got it."

"I think I almost have it." I pulled as hard as I could. It didn't budge.

"Let me do it."

"No," I yelled, clutching the tire iron like it was my firstborn child and Chris was the goblin king. "I got this."

I didn't have it.

But Chris stood back and watched me struggle for a solid three minutes. I knew I'd been the one to call him. I knew I couldn't get that lug nut off. But for some reason, I could not relinquish that tire iron to him. It was madness.

Maybe I was finally losing it.

One more huge effort on my part, but my foot slipped out from under me. I fell hard on my backside, covering half of me in a coat of slimy mud and the other half in splatters and spots like a very sad Dalmatian. Stunned, I froze.

A hand appeared in front of me, big and solid. "Come on."

I wanted to smack it away. I didn't want to need help. But I didn't have any other option, did I? Finally, I let him pull me up.

"Why don't you go get in my truck? You can dry off some. I'll take care of this," he said close to my ear so I could hear over the roar of the storm.

"I'm covered in mud."

"It can be cleaned."

I pointed at the tire. "I can get that. I know I can."

He took a step back and put his hands on top of his head, eyes burning with intensity, his shirt plastered to his chest from the rain. "Please go to the truck and let me do this."

"But—"

"Go sit in the damn truck," he roared.

I gasped and held out the tire iron. "Okay. Fine. You don't need to yell."

"Now," he growled.

I made my way to his truck, my shoes squelching in the mud with each step. There were two towels on the seat. I used one to sit on and the other to dry off as best I could. He'd left the engine running and the heat on full blast. Still, I was shivering when he finished and climbed in next to me.

"It's done." After pushing his wet hair out of his eyes, he reached into the back seat and pulled out a gym bag. From it came another towel and two dry t-shirts. He tossed me one. "Put that on."

I was too cold to argue but I twisted around as best I could to try for a modicum of modesty. My poor *I Like Big Books and I Cannot Lie* t-shirt was a sopping wet, muddy mess.

"Give it," Chris said, his voice gruff, when I turned back. He stuffed it into a plastic bag and tossed it all in the back seat.

Staring out the front window, his hands wrapped around the top of the steering wheel, the knuckles turning white. Frustration radiated off him in waves.

"You have got to be the most exasperating person I have ever met. And you've met my sisters. Still, you beat them all out. You are confusing, stubborn..." His voice trailed off. "Why did you call me if you didn't want my help?"

I rubbed at the tightness in my chest. My voice was very small. "I didn't have anyone else to call. Mama can't help. Iris wouldn't know what to do. Ali doesn't drive." I turned to stare out the window and sniffled. "You're the only one."

"I'm sorry," he said quietly.

I shrugged and wiped my nose. "I'm used to it. It's always been that way. I can depend on me. I guess I don't know any other way."

A beat of silence. "You could learn."

"I don't want to learn. I—I just want my life to go back to the way it was be-before you came along. Sure, it was a lot of work, and I was tired, but it was predictable. I had a plan and I followed it." My breathing sped up and my nose stung, and my eyes felt hot and, oh, no, I was going to cry. "And then you... and I don't know up from down most days... and it's messing with my head and... and..."

One second I was sitting in my seat and the next I was hauled over to Chris's lap like a rag doll. He was so freaking strong.

"What are you doing? I'm covered in mud."

"I don't care," he muttered. He pushed my head down on his shoulder. "Be quiet."

So, I was. Not because he told me so. Just because I needed to get myself together. I pushed my face into his chest.

"Are you crying?" he asked.

"No," I sobbed, my voice muffled. "I'm fine."

"Stubborn," he muttered.

I didn't have it in me to argue with him. So, I sat there, his arms around me and one hand idly playing with my hair. It felt nice, soothing, his body warm and strong and capable. I didn't want to leave this strange and lovely moment of peace. And that was the whole problem, wasn't it?

"You yelled at me," I said, a little like a petulant three-year-old.

"You needed someone to yell at you." His fingers had moved on from my hair to outline the shape of my ear.

"Excuse me?"

"You can't be the boss all the time." His thumb was tracing my jaw now. Stupid opposable thumbs. Stupid, gentle, lovely opposable thumbs.

A shiver skittered down my back. "Being the boss is easier. I'm in charge of what happens."

He grunted. "No one can be in charge of everything all the time. Life throws us curveballs."

"Ugh. A sports analogy?"

With a chuckle, his hand moved back to my hair. "I apologize. Let me try again. Think about Millie. Her being born with a heart defect changed all our lives. There were times when we thought we might lose her, or she was in another surgery or she got sick with a regular old cold that turned into something worse. Those aren't things we're in charge of. We have to handle them and do the best we can. Not to throw out another sports analogy, but you gotta roll with the punches sometimes."

"The punches hurt," I muttered.

"No kidding."

"Thank you," I whispered.

"What was that? You need to speak up. Wait. Let me get my phone out and I can record it."

I smacked him on the shoulder. "Thank you for helping me."

His arms tightened and he pulled me closer still. A hint of calmness, of rightness curled in my chest, whispering this is where I should always be. It was terrifying how good it felt.

Softly, he kissed my temple.

We stayed like that until the rain stopped.

FIFTY

If you and I were socks, we'd make a great pair.

—AMANDA H.

Dreamboat: *I bet you smiled when you saw my name pop up on your phone.*

Me: *That wasn't a smile. It was a grimace of pain that I had to read that.*

Dreamboat: *Ah, there she is. You must be feeling better.*

Dreamboat: *Hey...*

Currently, I was in Adult Fiction, where I'd been culling out mis-shelved books. Last night had seemed like some kind of weird fever dream. Had I really curled up on Chris's lap and cried? By the time I'd got home, I'd been exhausted in all the ways a person could be. I'd taken a hot shower and, for the first time since the pool house, I'd slept hard. But between the Barn Incident and last night, I had no idea where Chris and I stood.

Me: *Yes?*

Dreamboat: *Are we okay?*

Me: *I think so.*

Dreamboat: *Good.*

Sometimes texting was the absolute worst form of communication. Was that a *hey, it's real good* or a *eh, good*? If texting was supposed to make things less awkward, it was not working.

"Attention. Can I have everyone's attention, please? Gather 'round."

I poked my head out from the stacks to find Iris standing in the middle of the library, arms spread to the ceiling like a prize fighter.

"What's going on?" I asked, walking to her.

She bounced on her feet. "Where's Aidan?"

"Right here," he said, coming from the children's section.

A huge grin spread across Iris's face when she saw him. She ran to him, put her hands on his cheeks, and kissed him right on his mouth. When she stepped back, he blinked, looking dazed but not altogether unhappy.

"Hi?" he said.

"We did it." She pulled a packet of paper from her backpack and presented it like she was a magician and it was her rabbit. "We did it."

Without waiting for his reply, she waved the paper in the air and ran around in a circle like she was doing a victory lap.

"Okay. Iris, I need to ask you something and I want you to be honest," I said. "Are you using drugs?"

She stopped directly in front of me. "Not yet."

"Not funny."

"Ta-da." She presented me with the packet.

I took it from her and realized it was the math test she'd taken earlier in the week. "You got a B plus? No way."

"Yep. It brings my grade up to a very solid C minus and I still have the final to go. That means unless I completely give up, I'll be able to pass. I can't believe it. We did it, Aidan."

Iris and I turned to look at him, but the poor guy hadn't moved a muscle.

"Hey?" Iris said. "You okay?"

"Um, yeah," he said, his cheeks pink. "This is great news."

"The very best." She giggled—giggled!—then turned to me. "Heard anything from Dad?"

I shook my head and lied straight to her face. "Sorry. Nothing."

With a sigh, she stuffed her test in her backpack. "You'll keep trying?"

"I promise," I said, and resisted the urge to cross my fingers and hide them behind my back.

"Well, I have to run. Stuff to do." She took off for the door and then stopped, turned back and rushed to Aidan. When she got to him, she threw her arms around him. "Thank you. I can't believe I passed that test."

"No problem," Aidan squeaked out, his arms pinned to his sides. He cleared his throat. "See you tomorrow for tutoring?"

With a nod, she released him and headed to the exit.

"Be home by midnight," I called to her back.

"Yeah, yeah." And then she was gone.

"Hurricane Iris." I shook my head. "You okay over there?"

Aidan blinked and jolted out of his Iris-induced trance. "I think so?"

"Have you asked her about prom yet?" I said as I headed to my office.

Aidan followed and faceplanted on the circulation desk. "I almost did and then chickened out."

I grabbed two water bottles and set one next to him. "Looks like you might need to cool down a little."

Straightening, he grimaced. "That was weird. She was weird. She did kiss me, right? I don't think I've ever seen her smile when it wasn't after she made fun of me."

I walked around the desk and slung an arm around his shoulders. "You must understand. The love language of the Sampson sisters is sarcasm. If she hated you, it would be 'please this' and 'thank you that.' She insults because she loves. Just ask her out."

The look on his face was part miserable, part hopeful as he wandered away.

* * *

"I brought you a chocolate croissant." Ali dropped a bag from my favorite bakery in town on the reference desk.

I picked up the bag and took a whiff of the world's best pastry. "You only bring me chocolate croissants when something is wrong."

Pressing her lips together, Ali nodded. "That's because something is wrong."

I stood and pulled my phone from my pocket, my heart thumping. "What? Is it Mama? Iris? I don't have any missed calls."

Ali plopped in a chair and threw her feet up on a table. "Nah, nothing like that."

Slowly, she tore off a bite of her croissant and stuffed it in her mouth. Closing her eyes, she chewed slowly, a blissed-out smile making an appearance.

"Ali!"

She opened one eye. "Alright. Alright. I was just enjoying this last minute of peace before you freak out."

"I am not going to freak out."

"You're freaking out right now and you don't even know what the news is."

I rounded my desk and smacked her feet off the table. "Just tell me. I won't freak out. I swear."

Ali rolled her eyes, but she set her croissant down and dusted off her hands. "You're totally going to freak out."

"Ali!"

She pulled out her phone, tapped around on it, and handed it to me. "This was released earlier today. Maybe have a seat."

On the screen, a video was playing with a person clearly hiding their identity. I immediately understood this was the anonymous source. Above his head in large letters, it read ANONYMOUS SOURCE HINTS CHRIS STERNS AND HIS FIANCÉE AREN'T ALL THAT THEY SEEM.

I sat with a huff and turned the volume up on the phone.

"...aren't exactly on the up-and-up," the man was saying in his altered voice. An engagement photo of Chris and me flashed on the screen.

"Can you tell us more about that?" a voice off-screen asked.

Anonymous squirmed in his seat, the rat. "I don't want to say too much except that I don't think there'll be a wedding."

"And why is that?" the interviewer asked.

"I have a feeling they'll be breaking up very soon."

The interviewer gasped. "Does this have to do with the woman in the video?"

"No, it doesn't. It's something else entirely." Anonymous faced the camera and even though it was impossible to tell because of all the security measures, it seemed like he was talking directly to me. "I'm saying Chris Sterns is not the guy the world thinks he is."

I tossed the phone on the table with a thunk, anger

churning in my stomach. "What a bunch of crap. None of that is true. None of it."

Except it was true.

Ali took another bite of her croissant. "So, everything's okay with you two?"

"Yes. W-we're in love and we're getting married."

"Excellent. Because I have a plan."

I groaned.

"No, this is a good one. I might be able to figure out who this anonymous source is. If we find out his name, isn't there legal action that can be taken?"

I had no idea, but finding out who it was would go a long way to making this all stop for Chris.

"I could help," said a voice behind us.

I jumped and put a hand on my chest. "Aidan, I need to put a bell on you."

Ali stood. "What do you mean, you could help?"

Aidan didn't quite meet anyone's eyes. "I'm pretty good at that kind of stuff."

"How good?" Ali stuffed the rest of her croissant in her mouth and waited.

"Good enough to know how to find him without anyone knowing what I'm doing."

"Wait. Is this illegal?"

Aidan winced. "Only if you get caught."

"Did you get caught?"

He nodded, clearly annoyed. "They only caught me the last time because I got careless. Even though I kept reporting how the basketball team was cheating on all their tests. Over and over, and no one did anything. So, I maybe found a way into the school server and changed their grades."

Ali nodded, looking proud. "So, you used your powers for good?"

"Yeah, that defense didn't work on the judge either."

"Was it worth it?" I asked.

Aidan tugged at his shirt collar. "I don't know. I like it better here in Two Harts, and I met you and"—he blushed—"Iris."

My heart squeezed and I had the brief but strong desire to hug him. But I thought that might embarrass him more than he already was.

"This is awesome," Ali crowed. Leave it to her to break up a touching moment.

"No!" I glared at my best friend. "I can't let him do this. He could get in big trouble. And this time he might get more than community service hours."

"Oh, you beautiful, strong, rainbow-colored lady water buffalo." She nudged my shoulder. "What's the rule?"

"Ali..."

"We don't ask, and we don't tell." She grinned at Aidan. "Get to work, kid."

FIFTY-ONE

Girl, you are so like Batman.
Only the world's greatest detective could have found
a boy wonder like me.

—PROFESSOR POPINJAY

That Saturday morning, the Save the Library Committee, along with Aidan, and Iris, gathered at the crack of dawn to set up for the auction later that day. Mrs. Katz produced detailed instructions which required reorganizing the library for an "optimal auction experience."

"No, I did not say put that table there," Mrs. Katz said. "Did you hear a thing I said?"

Horace bared his teeth. "I turned down my hearing aids. I got tired of listening to your caterwauling and yelling."

Mrs. Katz clutched her clipboard to her chest with her crossed arms. "If this is the kind of help that I can expect from you, you can find your way out the door."

Horace stomped up to her. "You are a mean old woman."

"It takes one to know one."

He sputtered, his face turning a shade of red his doctor would likely be concerned about.

"Calm down," I said. "We're all on the same team. Let's just put the table where she wants it, okay?"

With a final glare at Mrs. Katz, Horace followed me. Together, we finished setting up the tables and I kept the two of them from killing each other. Barely. We had another close call over where to put the pens, to the left or the right of the bid sheets. I think Horace was about three seconds away from using one of those pens as a murder weapon.

"Those two need to do it and get it over with." Iris shoved hair out of her eyes.

"Gross. Mrs. Katz was my sixth-grade teacher."

She shrugged. "Their sexual tension is through the roof."

"Seriously. Gross." I put a hand on my hip. "And what do you know about sexual tension? You're still a baby."

The look she gave me was anything but toddler-like.

For lunch, Ali showed up with a boatload of food from the Taco Truck. "I have brought sustenance and my gracious presence."

The volunteers fell on the food like someone yelled 'brains' at a zombie convention. When they were through, I was left with a partially unwrapped fish taco and eight tortilla chips (yes, I counted).

"Thanks for this," I said. "We were all getting a bit cranky."

"No problem." She stretched out her legs in front of her. We were both sitting on the floor, leaning against the circulation desk. "Is the librarian gonna get mad we're eating in here?"

I shrugged. "She's willing to overlook it today."

"She's such a badass."

"I know, right?"

"Where's Chris? I thought he was supposed to be here?"

"He will be. Later. He's got something going on he couldn't tell me about."

She shoulder-bumped me. "Maybe he's going to surprise you with something amazing. Oh, I know. A surprise wedding. He's gathering up everything you'll need. You'll get married in a little ceremony under the stars. No big muss or fuss. Just a quiet little wedding."

I stared at her. "That is very... specific."

"Eh. I've been watching that show again. The one where they spend a bazillion dollars on one stupid wedding? Gives me the hives just thinking about it." She waved a hand. "Just put a ring on it and be done."

I laughed. "Sorry to burst your bubble. I'm positive Chris isn't planning a secret wedding."

"You never know. He could surprise you."

She had no idea how true that was. Chris Sterns was the biggest surprise of my life. I wasn't exactly sure what I was supposed to do about that though.

The rest of the afternoon was a blur. I sent Iris and Aidan over to the Sit-n-Eat to help Ollie decorate for the dance. Or rather, do all the decorating.

"You can have the dance here," Ollie had said. "But I ain't making it pretty or nothing."

At the library, we arranged all the auction items we'd spent weeks procuring. Aidan's idea had been a good one and we'd gotten several donations from wedding vendors. I had to imply I'd be using their services for my future wedding; I only felt a pinch of guilt. Once the engagement was called off, there wouldn't be a wedding to service anyway.

The doors opened at 6 p.m. and we all stood around with bated breath.

And waited.

And waited.

By 6:30 p.m., only three people had shown up, Mama and Sue, and Cody Spear, who had a reputation for being a tight-wad. Which we found to be true when he'd tried to bid on a two-night bed-and-breakfast package well under the minimum bid, and argued with Mrs. Katz for fifteen minutes about the unconstitutionality of minimum bids.

"Where is everyone?" Ali asked, frowning.

"I don't know. We'd heard Peter was threatening people not to come but I didn't think they'd listen to him." I sat down, feeling sorrier for myself than I had in a long time. "I don't know what I'm going to do if this doesn't work. We don't have much more time until the council vote."

"Hey." She patted my shoulder. "It's going to work out. Have you heard from Chris?"

I shook my head. "Not since this morning."

The last week we'd barely had time to text, let alone see each other. Piper kept him busy doing as many things as he could to take the attention off the latest drama. He'd had to fly to Nashville midweek to talk with the board of the Children's Heart Fund. They were still waffling on whether they'd like to continue their relationship with him, given the recent events.

More than that, I think both of us were ignoring the real question: if two people make out in a barn, does it really count?

How had my life gotten so complicated?

"He'll be here," Ali said with confidence. "Chris has always come through for you before."

"Hmm?"

"Well, it's true, isn't it? Has he ever let you down yet?"

Had he? We hadn't known each other that long but I couldn't think of a time he hadn't done exactly what he said he was going to do. And some things I hadn't expected at all.

"I mean, I don't think I've ever seen anyone try to take care of you as much as he has and you do not make it easy," Ali said.

My face must have shown my surprise. "What?"

Ali shrugged. "Don't give me that look. Do you know how hard it is to be your friend sometimes? You never call me for help. It's always the other way around. You take care of your mom and your sister, the library, and probably a whole passel of woodland creatures I don't know about because you're just that good. Who gets to take care of you?"

I stared at her, a little in disbelief. "That's not true."

"Totally true. I love you and hate you for it. You have your life together. I can't even keep a cactus alive."

My chest tightened. "Cacti are stupid."

"I know, but that doesn't mean I should murder them." She gave me a pointed look. "Now, text Chris and ask him when he'll be here because you need his help."

"Yes, ma'am." I pulled out my phone and tapped out a message.

Me: *Where are you? We've already started.*

Dreamboat: *Running late. We'll be there soon.*

Me: *Who is we?*

When he didn't reply, I shoved my phone back in my pocket. He would be here. Ali was right. He'd always come through for me. I guess I'd never given him credit for that. I guess I just always expected people to let me down; it was my default mode.

"Damn it," Sue yelled and stomped over in her boots. "Just got a text message from Connie. She's over at the pizzeria. The entire menu is seventy-five percent off."

My eyes narrowed. Peter. This reeked of him, that petty jerk.

Sue held up her phone. "Connie said to hurry because the sale is from six to eight p.m. and the line is real long."

The announcement seemed to suck all the air out of the room. The same hours of the auction. That wasn't a coincidence. It was a pointed, deliberate attack.

"That man's a real bastard." Sarah Ellis looked as fierce as a woman of eighty-seven could look. "I hope you revoke his library card."

Several others agreed.

I turned to the one person who might be devious enough to help. "Ali?"

She already had her game face on. "Oh, I am on it."

As I watched her stomp out, I said a little prayer for the pizzeria. If it burned down in fiery flames later this evening, I would have no doubt she'd be responsible for it.

Mrs. Katz marched to the front of the room. "The whole town cannot be at that restaurant. Get your phones out and start calling everyone you know who's close enough to drive in. Call in favors. Bribe them. Whatever you have to do."

The whole room went to work. I was four calls in when the door opened, and Chris arrived.

And he was not alone.

FIFTY-TWO

Are you a magician?
  Because every time I look at you, everyone else disappears.

—TENNAYA B.

Chris brought us help in the form of three of his fellow teammates, all of them giants with ready smiles. Between the four of them, they filled up our tiny library. They didn't come empty-handed, either; they brought their checkbooks, and they weren't afraid to use them.

"Why?" I asked Chris as I watched Sherrod Young, the insanely popular quarterback for the Oklahoma Stars, bid an ungodly amount of money for a floral arrangement.

"The flowers? Sherrod has to apologize to his wife a lot." Chris grinned. "He says stupid stuff all the time. Once, in an interview, he said that his wife was *just* a stay-at-home mom. He had to sleep at a hotel for three weeks and buy her a very expensive necklace to go back home."

I laughed. "Not the flowers. Why are these men here?"

He shrugged. "I asked them and they're my friends. Plus, they owe me one."

I leaned in and lowered my voice. "Were these the guys with you in Vegas?"

Chris nodded. "They feel bad for how that all went down. So, it only took a little guilt-tripping and one call to Sherrod's wife."

I gazed at him for a long moment, running Ali's words through my mind. An emotion I didn't want to name made me feel almost buoyant. Chris Sterns was a good man; likely the best man I knew. For the first time in a long time, the weight I carried seemed lighter, manageable. Maybe this wouldn't all come crashing down in a fiery inferno.

"Thank you."

He tapped the tip of my nose, his smile warm. "Anything for you, Sprinkles."

"Don't call me Sprinkles." I turned back to the activity in front of me. But slowly, I slid my hand in his and held on tight.

It was soon after word got out that Chris Sterns and his friends were at the auction that people began to arrive. Although that may have also had something to do with the rats.

A rumor that rats were spotted in the kitchen of the pizzeria spread like wildfire. In fact, someone even had a photo. Sure, it was blurry, and it was a little hard to tell if it had been taken in the restaurant, but the good people of Two Harts weren't willing to risk getting the plague for discounted pizza.

For the next hour, the people came. The library grew full of laughter and excitement and, most importantly, the sound of pens scratching on paper as they wrote out bids.

Did we raise $100,000? Of course not. But it was a start, and I was hopeful. I couldn't remember the last time I'd really, truly felt hopeful.

After the auction ended at eight, people wandered over to

the Sit-n-Eat for the dance. Mama pulled me aside and pressed a bag in my hand.

"What's this?" I asked.

"I brought you a little something to change into," she said. "For the dance."

"You didn't have to do that." I waved a hand at my t-shirt and jeans. "I'm fine like this."

Mama smiled. "You are that, Maebe, but I thought it would be fun for you to dress up a little. Sue took me shopping at the outlet mall and helped me pick it out."

"Mama, you didn't need to spend money on me."

"Of course I did. You're my child and I want to give you things. Sometimes it seems like it's always the other way around." She wrapped a hand around my wrist and adopted her "do not argue with me" voice. "Now, you're going to go get that dress on, put a comb through your hair and maybe a little lip gloss and come dance with your fiancé. Understood?"

"Yes, ma'am."

She patted me on the cheek. "That's better."

In the bathroom, I put on the yellow wrap dress I found in the bag. It fell to just above my knees and flared when I twirled. Mama had also brought me a pair of sandals, earrings, and yes, lip gloss. I combed out my hair and left it down.

Standing back as far as I could in the little bathroom, I checked myself out in the mirror. I thought of what Chris might say when he saw me, and I smiled. Then I stopped smiling because I shouldn't care what Chris thought of me. Then I sighed because I didn't know what to think anymore.

The warm night air washed over me as I walked the two blocks over to the dance. Before I even saw it, I heard the music and the murmur of the crowd. When I turned the corner, I gasped.

The Sit-n-Eat had been transformed into a wonderland. The parking lot had been blocked off and the wide wooden porch had been strung with fairy lights. Tables were scattered around the edges, topped with stacks of old books and mason jar vases of flowers as centerpieces. Simple, yet special.

Maybe it was the soft lighting or that we'd all dressed up a little or that the auction had been such a success, but the atmosphere was jubilant. All my favorite people were there—the library committee members; Horace and Mrs. Katz were dancing together, and they seemed to almost enjoy it. Ali; who chatted it up with one of Chris's teammates; Mama, Sue, and, across the way, dressed in jeans and a button-down shirt and laughing with the high school football coach, was Chris.

Like he could feel me, his head turned and his eyes met mine; he smiled slowly. I waved back and tried to ignore the strange mix of emotions inside me. Nervousness, excitement, and something else I wasn't ready to say, even to myself.

Maybe I was a little drunk with all those emotions because when a slow song came on and Chris wandered over and held out his hand, I took it. Probably also why I let him hold me close. Probably why I closed my eyes and buried my nose in his shirt, to remember his smell, and the feel of his hands on my back.

A memory to keep forever.

"The dress suits you," he said quietly.

I pulled back enough to see his face. "Can I ask you something?"

"Anything, Sprinkles."

"Don't call me Sprinkles," I said, but my heart wasn't in it. "That thing you say, 'It suits you,' I heard your dad say it to your mom."

"There's a story behind it."

The song changed but we didn't separate. A beat passed, then another.

"Are you going to tell me the story?" I finally asked.

He grinned. "It goes like this: Mom and Dad met in college

when they both took a required art class their freshman year. Mom liked Dad right away, but Dad has always been a little shy, kind of quiet. And you've met Mom; she never stops talking."

I smiled at the affection in his voice.

"One day, she asked if he wanted to get lunch and he said yes. And that's how it went for the next three years. Mom invited him places; Dad accepted, and so on. But it was purely as friends. Drove Mom crazy. She didn't mind he was quiet, but she did mind that he held his feelings so close. About the closest thing he said to pretty words was, 'It suits you.'"

"For three years?"

"Three whole years." Chris grinned. "In all that time, Dad had never asked her out or even made a move on her. So, Mom got fed up. One day, she laid into him, told him she was tired of never knowing where she stood with him, and she was done."

"Uh-oh."

"But, and this is the important part." He pulled me even closer. "Dad looked right at her and said, 'I tell you I love you all the time, I just don't say those words. But you suit me just fine.'"

My heart dropped to my feet and then slowly climbed back up. Like a roller coaster, except I had no idea where the top or bottom were. I was going in blind.

Chris cupped my cheeks with his hands and tilted my face, so I had no choice but to meet his eyes. "You're freaking out."

"I-I-I am not freaking."

I was totally, completely, undeniably freaking out. This might be the freak out of all freakouts in a few seconds. The roller coaster had reached the summit and I might puke on the way down.

"You're freaking out, Sprinkles."

I flushed. "I am not."

"I expected that." He smiled, his eyes warm. "You're terrified."

"Excuse me?"

"You're scared. Like a skittish horse."

"I am not a horse." I stomped my foot like, well, a horse.

"It's okay, I'm patient."

"I don't need you to be patient. Because I'm not scared and I'm not freaking out and everything is fine. You surprised me. Can I not be surprised when... when... you said the thing you said?"

I watched his smile turn into a grin and realized he'd done it again, taken me from certain meltdown to annoyance.

"I just have to prove it to you," he said, more to himself.

"Prove what?"

He kissed me, slow and sweet like time was merely a suggestion, his thumbs idly tracing my cheekbones. It went on and on, warming me from the inside out. That kiss went a long way to making me forget what I'd been freaking out about to begin with.

When he pulled back, my eyes blinked open, and I uttered the only eloquent thing to express my feelings. "Whoa."

"Yup. Whoa." He took my hand and led me off the makeshift dance floor. "We'll talk about it. I'm sure you'll come around to my way of thinking. I have a PowerPoint presentation even."

Maybe he was right. Maybe there could be more between us. Maybe we were suited for each other. Maybe...

But something caught my eye in the crowd and my stomach dropped.

Because that's when I saw my father.

FIFTY-THREE

"It's a good thing I have a library card. Because I am totally checking you out."

Still can't believe he said that to me once upon a time. Now we've been married for seven years.

I can also confirm: he did not have a library card.

—NAOMI B.

I gave Chris some lame excuse about needing to use the restroom but, instead, followed my father's head through the crowd. Hastily, I checked for Iris or Mama, hoping they hadn't seen him.

Good ole Dad managed to avoid stopping to talk to anyone. He wandered away from the crowd and I followed. When he looked back once, I realized that was what he'd intended all along.

I caught up to him at the next corner. "What are you doing here?"

He grinned his stupid charming grin. "I came to see you, of course."

"You saw me. Now leave."

He wrapped a hand around my upper arm. "Now don't be like that. I just want to talk a little."

"I saw you last week. You didn't want to talk much then."

"Look"—his voice hardened—"you and me need to talk about your fiancé."

The way he said fiancé made my stomach drop. I didn't like the way he was watching me like I was the prey, and he was about to attack.

"Unless you'd like me to go talk to him myself? Because I could do that." He turned on his heels and began to walk back the way we came.

"Get back here," I whisper-yelled and marched toward the library, expecting him to follow.

I unlocked the door and flipped on the lights. He followed me inside. I anticipated he'd start talking right away but, instead, he took his time walking around and glancing at the auction items and bid sheets.

"Huh. Made some good money."

"Getting ideas for your next scam?"

He walked past me, his expression thoughtful. "That's a great idea, actually."

I drew in a deep breath through my nose. "What do you want?"

"Oh, right." He unzipped the jacket he was wearing and pulled a stack of papers from an inside pocket. "I happened to come across these."

He tossed them on the counter and moseyed over to look at more auction items like he had all the time in the world, like he knew he had the upper hand.

Swallowing the urge to scream, I stalked over and glanced at the packet. I recognized it immediately. It was the contract, the one I'd been asked to sign, the same one that outlined in specific details how my engagement to Chris was to be handled.

"How did you get this?" Only five people knew of this arrangement—Chris, me, Piper, Doug, and Chris's attorney.

My father made a little sound in the back of his throat. "Didn't even deny it. Very telling."

"What do you want?"

"Me?" He pressed a hand to his chest, trying—and failing—to look innocent. "I don't want anything. I just thought you should know this was out there."

"When did you start doing things out of the kindness of your heart? For that matter, when did you get a heart?"

My hands opened and closed at my sides. The urge to hit him was overwhelming. But an even stronger urge to get him out of Two Harts and away from Chris and Iris and Mama was stronger.

"It would seem a lot of people would love to get ahold of this information." He pulled out the chair behind the reference desk and took a seat, propping up his feet and knocking over my Jane Austen bobblehead. "Funny thing. There's a couple of gossip rags that would love to get their hands on this."

"You can't."

"Get this. One of them is offering me fifty thousand dollars. That's an awful lot of money, you know."

I could not let this happen. It would ruin Chris. After he'd already had months of someone trying to ruin him. He didn't deserve this.

"You wouldn't do that, would you? I know we don't have a great relationship but I'm still your daughter."

He shrugged and removed his feet from the desk. "I could be persuaded to forget about those offers, but..."

"But what?" I asked warily.

He propped his elbows on the desk and cradled his chin in his hands. "A man's gotta eat. So, if I had a better offer then I might consider it."

A chill ran through my body. I stared at this man I was

related to and wished with all my heart I wasn't. "You are trying to blackmail me? Where in the world am I supposed to get money like that? Do you think I can run down to the bank in the morning and withdraw sixty thousand dollars?"

He sucked in air through his teeth. "A little higher, honey."

I leaned my arms on the desk. "I can't pay that kind of money."

The door to the library opened. Because of course I'd failed to lock it.

"I knew you were freaking out, Sprinkles. I shouldn't have let you go."

Because of course it was Chris.

"I know you can't pay that kind of money." My father's smile was evil personified. "But he sure can."

Chris paused by the door, his eyes flicking from me to my father and back. "Who's this?"

My father stood and slowly adjusted his jacket before casually strolling by me. "You can keep that copy. Don't worry. I have others. I'll be in touch."

"Please don't do this," I whispered, even though a little part of me died saying it.

When he got to Chris, my father held out a hand. "Chris Sterns, congratulations on your engagement."

Even puzzled, Chris was still a gentleman. He shook his hand. "Thank you. I didn't catch your name."

"Oh, I didn't give it to you." With a wink, he patted Chris on the shoulder. "You have my condolences. My daughter has the personality of a bridge troll, so good luck with that."

Then my father left the building. As usual, he came, he destroyed, and he left.

"What the hell is going on?" Chris asked, frowning at the door. "That was your father?"

I nodded and scooped up the stack of papers, but I was shaking so badly, I dropped them. They scattered everywhere.

With a groan, I sank to the floor and scrambled to pick them all up. Maybe I could keep this from Chris somehow.

A pair of enormous tennis shoe-clad feet appeared in my field of vision. "What is all this?" He crouched beside me, tucked a piece of my hair behind an ear. The concern on his face made my heart squeeze.

I leaned into his hand and closed my eyes. Because I knew what I was about to tell him would change everything. This had been a fantasy, a living, breathing romance novel with a living, breathing hero but it had to come to an end. Happy endings didn't happen in real life, at least not for me.

"We need to talk," I said.

FIFTY-FOUR

Do you know what the Little Mermaid and I have in common?
We both want to be part of your world.

—*JULIA B.*

Piper went into hyperdrive. "How serious is he? Would he do this?"

"He would probably gnaw off his own hand for that kind of money." I flopped my head back on the couch.

After I'd explained what my father wanted, Chris had called Piper immediately and she'd met us at the Wilson place an hour later. Even though it was almost midnight, she'd come dressed to impress in a deep-blue power dress, killer heels, and her game face. She must roll out of bed ready to take on the world.

"The timing of this sucks. Chris is supposed to be interviewed tomorrow"—Piper peeked at her watch and winced—"make that today, with Phoebe Mayfield at KRRE about the Children's Heart Fund fundraiser. This will overshadow it, and after he just got back in their good graces."

It wasn't fair. My father, and by association, me, could ruin it all for Chris.

"Mae, can you call your father and tell him we'll have an answer by tonight? That will buy us some time, I hope."

"What are our options?" Chris asked. He was sitting in the chair across from me, his mood unreadable as it had been since I'd told him all of it.

"If we ignore him..." Piper began.

I cut her off. "He'll sell it, and he won't feel bad about it at all."

Chris pressed his lips together in a thin line. "Nice guy."

"The best," I muttered. "I'm so proud."

"In that case, he sells it to the highest bidder, we could deny it." Piper picked up the copy of the contract my father had left. Our signatures were clear and legible. It wasn't the original, but it was a copy of it. "But this looks pretty damn legit. I'm good, but I don't know if even I can talk our way out of this."

Chris leaned forward and rubbed his forehead. "And it'd just be another lie."

Piper paced the room. "Our other option is to give him what he wants. Pay him the money. But I have a feeling if we do that, he'll just keep coming back."

Like cockroaches and bad movie remakes.

My eyes drifted to Chris and my heart twisted. Wasn't that part of the problem? I was part cockroach, biologically speaking. As long as I was connected to Chris, my father would have a connection to him too.

"Piper's right. You cannot pay him," I said, my voice firm. "What if you blamed it all on me somehow?"

"What do you mean?" Piper asked.

Chris shifted in his chair. I felt his eyes on me, but I ignored the pull to look at him. Refused to remember that just two hours ago, we'd danced, and he'd said things that terrified me in good ways.

"You say that I duped Chris. I agreed to the engagement, but it was all just an excuse to blackmail him." Nervous energy forced me out of my seat. I circled the room. "Think about it. You make me the bad guy. Make people feel sorry for Chris. He gets to go on with his life, keep working with the charity."

Piper thought about it before nodding hesitantly. "That could work. I mean, we'd have—"

Chris cut her off, his voice low. "What about you?"

"I'll go back to my life. I have work and Mama, and Iris will need help with college next year. It will be like it was... before."

There'd be backlash. I'd probably be the most hated woman in Two Harts since JoBeth Cockran ran off with the Cupcake King leaving his wife with six kids to raise on her own. But it wouldn't last forever.

Chris's gaze was piercing. "That sounds terrible."

"I know this will surprise you, but there is life after Chris Sterns."

But if I were honest, it *was* going to be terrible. Because I'd gone and broken that stupid contract. This wasn't just a business arrangement anymore, and it hadn't been for a long time. My foolish heart liked Chris's smiles and his stupid opposable thumbs and the way he got under my skin and listened to me and somehow managed to be a soft spot for me to land when I didn't even know I needed one. So, yeah, it was going to be horrible.

But I didn't have a choice. I had to do this. For him.

"Piper"—he didn't take his eyes off me—"can I talk to Mae alone?"

"Yeah, sure." Her gaze bounced between the two of us, brow creased. "But let's make a decision soon."

After she left, I wandered back over to the couch and sat, keeping my voice brisk. "What did you need to talk about?"

He stood up and stalked over to me, coming to a stop so

close, I had to crane my head back to see him. "Are you kidding me right now?"

"I know this isn't turning out the way we planned, but now we can quit all the lying. You get to go back to your life." I ignored the twisting pain in my chest. "That's what was always going to happen."

His death stare grew in deadliness. I flopped back onto the couch. He bent and boxed me with his arms, one hand on the couch arm, the other on the back of the sofa by my head.

"Who's lying now?" he asked.

"I have no idea what you're talking about. We need a plan. I have a plan. The plan is good."

He brought his face closer to mine. "You do like your plans, don't you?"

"Yes."

"You know what else you like? Being a martyr." He flung that out there like a red cape in front of a bull.

I flushed. "Excuse me?"

"You are a martyr. You live in this town spending all your time, all your energy, taking care of people," he said, his voice growly.

"I do not like the tone of your voice right now, buddy."

"Your mother, your sister, Ali, and the library—it's all your responsibility. No one else. God forbid if you ask someone for help. I bet I'm just another checkmark on your list, right?"

I grabbed a fistful of his shirt. "Why is that wrong? You're supposed to take care of the people you love, you idiot."

Too late, I realized what I had just implied.

Chris's smile was pure satisfaction and I felt it in my toes. "Oh, Sprinkles. I heard it. You can't take it back."

"You heard nothing," I snapped.

"Shut up," he said about two seconds before his mouth was on mine.

This kiss was angry, and that suited me just fine. I was

angry, too. I was not a martyr, and I hadn't meant to imply that I loved—

Chris pulled back and scowled. "Stop thinking."

"You can't tell me to stop thinking."

"I can when it's messing with me kissing you." One second, he was standing above me, the next he was on the couch with his hands on my shoulders. "Stop thinking and kiss me this time."

"Fine," I said a mere half-second before our lips met again. He was really good at this kissing thing, and I lost myself in the small, soft touches that turned bolder. The way he tasted like the cinnamon gum he always had in his pocket. How the hair at the back of his neck tickled. He kissed me until all the anger drained out and I felt warm and a little drunk.

He pulled back slowly, his eyes soft. "This is the way I like you best. Just-kissed. But I also like you best when you're sarcastic or when you don't let me get away with anything and when you scrunch up your nose because you're annoyed at me."

"Chris..."

"No, wait. Listen to me. I've worked my ass off to play football. I've worked hard at being a good son and brother. I've worked hard to help those kids in the hospital. I've worked hard to be a man of integrity. I've worked hard my whole life, and it paid off. I've always thought no one could outwork me."

He turned to me, his face earnest and so beloved I felt my eyes grow hot with tears.

"Until I met this librarian in a random small town who works circles around me. The craziest part? No matter how hard she works, it's never enough but she never gives up. It's humbling. I am humbled by you, and I am amazed every day by your tenacity and perseverance. I am in awe of how fiercely you love people. I want to be one of those people. I want to be able to take care of you sometimes. Not because you need someone to take care of you, but because I want to. Because that's what we do when we love someone."

"Chris," I whispered, swiping at a tear on my cheek. "Please stop making this so hard."

"I'm not letting you get away with this," he said, stubbornly.

"Me?"

"Or him. Not him either."

"I don't see any way out of this."

"If you want something bad enough, you find a way. Might not be logical, but it's the truth." He gazed into my eyes intensely, but I got the feeling he was seeing something else, feeling for solutions to a very messed-up problem. His smile appeared slowly but it came just the same. "Listen to me. Don't do anything, okay? I have a plan."

"What?"

He stood, determination written all over his face. "Promise? Just sit tight. Don't contact your dad. Just wait, okay?"

"Okay," I said slowly, standing. "I'll wait."

"Good." He pressed a short, hard kiss to my mouth. Grinning, he tapped my nose and he was gone.

FIFTY-FIVE

Oh, no! The cops are here.
    Someone must have reported that you've stolen my heart.

                                                    —ELENA S.

Piper: *Chris's segment airs tonight at 6:20 p.m.*

Me: *What's the plan?*

Piper: *Just watch.*

I hadn't slept much at all, or eaten, or left my room more than necessary. I tried to read a book, but my focus was all over the place—the library, Chris, Mama, Chris, Iris, Chris, Chris, Chris. Bit of a one-track mind, it seemed. Mostly, I curled up on my bed and discussed the finer art of respecting each other's personal space with Kevin.

But that evening, I pulled myself together enough to sit on the couch with Mama and Sue and Iris. My stomach felt like it was trying to fight its way out of my body.

The segment started right on time, first with a produced piece about Chris's work with the Children's Heart Fund and a little about why he was so passionate about helping kids and families affected by congenital heart defects.

"Oh, he is such a sweet man," Mama said. "You got a good one there, Maebe."

"He is a snack," Sue said. "Just wanna take a bite out of him, ya know."

"Sue," Mama said, "that's my future son-in-law."

"Well, he shouldn't be allowed to be seen in public looking that good."

"He's okay," Iris mumbled. Which was high praise in Iris-speak.

He did look good in his dark jeans and button-down shirt with the sleeves rolled up so he was showing a scandalous amount of forearm.

The interviewer, Phoebe Mayfield, who'd become every woman's favorite reporter after calling out her ex-fiancé in a blistering set down on TV, smiled brightly at the camera. "Chris, I'm so glad you could join us today."

The camera panned out and showed Phoebe and Chris sitting across from each other. Chris nodded, his face serious. "I'm glad to be here, but I wondered if I could ask a favor?"

Phoebe smiled. "Of course."

"I have something I need to say. Would you mind if I made a statement right now?"

"Oh, yes," she said, her expression curious. "Go right ahead."

"Thank you." He turned so he directly faced the camera, fingering a notecard in his hand.

I held my breath, my leg bouncing.

"I'm not sure who'll be interested in all this, but lately it seems like everyone is concerned with everything I do. Today, I need to make a confession. It starts with a party in Vegas for my birthday. The video that was released began a whole chain of events I'll try to explain. The rumor mill has tried over and over to claim I am in a secret relationship with the woman in that video. That is false.

"While I do know this woman and have for a long time, I am not releasing her name out of respect for her, so please don't ask. And if you have any kind of journalistic integrity, or a heart, you will not publish anything that someone might try to sell you.

"When the news came out, it looked like a lot of people were more than happy to make up rumors about our supposed relationship. Those rumors jeopardized my work with the Children's Heart Fund. You saw from the video why it's so important to me. To counteract the bad press, I came up with a plan. It was to give you all something good to focus on."

He paused and took a deep breath, his smile tight.

"Do you need a minute?" Phoebe asked.

"No, just a little courage, I suppose. Doesn't matter how old you are, it's hard to admit when you've done something stupid."

Phoebe smiled encouragingly.

Iris sat up and leaned toward the TV. Mama and Sue's eyes were glued to the screen. When Mama reached over and took my hand, I held on for dear life.

"The plan was to get engaged, real fast. So, I found a woman I greatly admired and asked if she'd be willing to help me out and she agreed. What I'm saying is our engagement is fake."

"No!" Sue said.

"Oh, honey," Mama said, her voice so sad.

Chris continued. "I deeply respect the woman who agreed to help me. She is not to blame in any of this, so please don't bother her. We had a business arrangement and a contract, all looked over by an attorney.

"I learned from my father that before anything, it's important to be a man of your word. I lost sight of that the past couple
of months, and I need to apologize, especially to my youngest
fans. Sometimes adults make mistakes, too. What's important is
to realize your mistakes and bad choices then make it right."

He looked down at the notecard in his hand and back up at
the camera. My heart clenched to see how troubled his eyes
were.

"So, this is me making things right. I need to ask for your
forgiveness. I made some bad decisions. I hope you all can look
past this, but I understand if you can't."

I swear he looked directly at me at that moment, a piercing
gaze meant for me only.

"I've learned that all things come to light eventually. We
can try to hide them, even from ourselves, but eventually we'll
have to deal with them."

He paused and set the index card down on his knee. His
gazed fixed on the camera with such intensity, I could feel it like
a caress. I couldn't tear my eyes away from his face any more
than I could gnaw my arm off.

"And since I want to be completely honest, I guess I should
also admit something else. While all of this may have started as
a fake engagement, my feelings are very, very real."

A strangled groan erupted from my throat, but it was
drowned out by the collective gasp from the other three people
in the room.

He turned to Phoebe. "Thank you for letting me get all that
out."

Phoebe placed a hand on his arm, her eyes shiny. "Thank
you for being so open. I know that had to take a lot of courage. If
you'd like to see the full interview with Chris, come back
tomorrow at five thirty p.m. Now, back to you, Tom."

I clicked the television off. The room was doused in silence, the air heavy with the questions they were anxious to ask. But all I could think about was what Chris had just said.

"Holy shit," Iris said.

For once, Mama didn't correct her.

FIFTY-SIX

If you were a booger, I'd pick you first.

—*MELANIE S.*

Their questions came fast and furious. I couldn't blame them. After all, I had a lot to explain. But I was still half stunned from Chris's pronouncement.

My feelings are very real.

My brain refused to focus on anything except that. Even when Mama tapped me on my shoulder to get my attention.

"Maebell Sampson, you have a lot of explaining to do," she announced, crossing her arms over her chest.

"I do," I said. "I'll explain everything."

"I take back what I said about you being boring. This is a telenovela-level drama right here," Iris said, her blue eyes round with respect. She held her fist out and I tapped it back without thinking.

"I think now is a good time to start." Mama pointed to the recliner. "Sit. Start talking."

And I would have, honest, but my phone vibrated with a text.

Dreamboat: *Did you see it?*

Heart pounding, my fingers shook as I typed back.

Me: *Yes. I don't know what to say.*

Dreamboat: *You don't have to say anything yet. I'm on my way to you right now. I need to see you.*

I shrieked, my heart pounding. "He's coming here. Right now. What do I do?"

"How about put real clothes on?" Iris pointed at my sweat-pants and oversized t-shirt.

"Great idea." I grabbed her by her cheeks and planted a kiss on her forehead.

I rushed to my room and hunted through my closet, tossing more than half of it on my bed as discarded options. My mind raced, pulled in two directions at once. One part of me joyful, excited to see Chris, at even the remote possibility the two of us could figure out some way to be together. The other part was more logical. It twisted the situation around like a Rubik's Cube, trying to see it from all angles, finding the problems that didn't have easy solutions.

Finally settled on a blue dress with lace overlay and my trusty boots, I plopped on my bed and stared at the door and twisted my hands in my lap, trying, and failing, to get my thoughts under control.

Someone knocked on the door and I yelled, "Come in."

"How are you doing?" Mama carefully made her way to sit beside me. "This is a lot to take in. I have so many questions."

"I know," I whispered. "I promise I'll let you ask them all soon."

She wrapped an arm around my shoulders and squeezed. "You should be more excited. That boy loves you."

Swallowing the lump in my throat, I picked at a stray string on my dress and pushed out the words. "I'm scared."

Mama made a small noise of sadness. "Remember what I used to tell you when you were scared of the dark?"

I smiled. "Being scared is halfway to brave."

"That's right. So, it's time you moved on to brave, Maebe." She leaned over and kissed my cheek. "Things happen when you're brave. Sometimes good, sometimes bad, but at least you're moving toward something. I worry you've gotten so stuck in this life you've forgotten how to be brave."

I blinked against my burning eyes. Maybe Mama was right. Being brave was all I had control over, really.

Someone shrieked in the living room. "He's here. He's here!"

Mama stood and tugged on my hand. "Come on, honey."

I followed her but when I was almost at the door, Sue stopped me. "I'll open the door. You just stand there and look pretty."

The door opened and a hand jutted forward with three small bouquets of flowers. Chris stepped into the house and passed Mama, Sue, and Iris each one. "For you, ladies."

Mama and Sue gushed over the flowers and the man. Iris shot me an expression that almost looked like excitement. My whole body vibrated as I waited for him to notice me.

"You are so sweet," I heard Mama say.

But then I lost track of the conversation because a text message came through on my phone.

It was from my father, and it changed everything.

FIFTY-SEVEN

Did you call in your order? Because this is a pickup line.

—*CHAD Z.*

I'm not sure what sound I made—a gasp, a scream, maybe—but the room went silent.

"What's wrong?" Chris asked, suddenly beside me, his eyes concerned.

"We..." I cleared my throat. "We need to talk. Right now."

Without another word, I took his hand and pulled him toward the front porch.

"Is everything okay?" Mama whispered as I passed her.

With a shake of my head, I pulled the door closed. It was just Chris and me now. The edges of my heart felt jagged, and it was a little hard to breathe.

Chris cupped my cheek. "What's wrong?"

I couldn't say it out loud, so I handed him my phone and turned away, wrapping my arms around myself. The text wasn't long, but it packed a punch.

Dale*: Tell that pretty fiancé of yours if he thinks he's won, he hasn't. 'Cause I know all about Eleanor Sterns and how she likes to get a little wild and crazy. I know about her little boy too. I got proof. I think there are a lot of people who'd be interested to know about Chris Sterns' sad, drunk sister, don't you?*

As if all that wasn't bad enough, he'd attached pictures. One of Ellie with her little boy. Another in which it appeared Ellie was sitting in a bar, drink in hand, surrounded by a group of male admirers. And yet another of Ellie with dark sunglasses, her hair messy and her clothes wrinkled, walking down a sidewalk.

Every one of those photos could be totally innocent, but taken out of context or with a media spin, most any story could be told. Ellie was already dealing with so much; she didn't need her name out there too.

"Son of a..." Chris muttered.

I perched on the edge of the porch railing. "That's my dad."

Chris handed me my phone back, his jaw ticking. "It changes nothing. I'll pay him what he wants, and he'll be out of our lives."

"You don't understand." My voice sounded strange even to my own ears. "You can try but it won't work. He'll always be after you." I held up my phone. "This is the proof right here."

"No," he said firmly.

"Yes." I mirrored his tone.

He planted himself in front of me, his expression earnest. "We have done all we can. If he's never going to stop, he's never going to stop. And if I have to go through that, put Ellie through that, I'd rather do it with you by my side." His fingers brushed my cheek. "I'd rather do my whole life with you by my side."

"Chris," I whispered, my nose beginning to sting.

"We can figure this out. Together."

It sounds so easy, so tempting. A fairy-tale ending. A happily ever after.

"You would resent me. Maybe not at first. But when, not if, my father finds a buyer, he'll sell all the information he's dug up on Ellie and eventually you'll grow to resent me. If for some reason you didn't, Ellie would and the rest of your family, too. Any life with me by your side," my voice broke, and I swiped at the tears that had begun to fall, "would only drive a wedge between you and your family. It would break my heart twice. It —it's not worth it. It's just better to break this off now."

I slipped off the railing and shimmied around him, walked to the other end of the porch to put some distance between us.

He stalked toward me. "There you go again. Martyr Mae, swooping in to sacrifice herself for everyone else. I'm a big boy; I can take care of myself. I don't need your sacrifice. I just need you."

"I have to do this," I said quietly. "Don't make this harder than it already is."

"It should be hard for you to walk away," he said, suddenly inches from my face. "Because you know we belong together."

"Life isn't a romance novel. As much as I love to read them, they're fiction. Happy endings don't really exist. I will not be the reason you don't get to do all the things you've worked hard for. I will not be the reason your sister's life gets turned upside down."

He took a step back, his eyes going sad. "You know what the real problem is. You're scared. I understand, I do. But I am not your father, and I am not Peter."

I rubbed my forehead, at the headache that was building, and avoided looking in his eyes. "I'm being realistic. I'm not scared."

Terrified. Confused. Defeated. All of those things.

Chris's head dropped. He rubbed the back of his neck.

After a long moment, I saw his chest expand as he drew in a deep breath.

"Okay, okay," he muttered, more to himself than me. He cupped my cheeks, turning my face so he could see my eyes. "I've done all I can do, said all I can say. I don't know how else I can convince you. I'm not giving up on you. I just think you need time to get your head figured out. When you do, day or night, whenever, you let me know. I'll be waiting."

I sniffled. "What if I never get there?"

His expression turned fierce. "You will. I have faith in you, in us." He touched his forehead to mine. "It's going to break my heart to walk away right now."

"I'm sorry. It's for the best," I said, trying to convince myself as much as I was convincing him.

He stared, his eyes roaming my face like he was memorizing it. He pressed a lingering kiss to my temple. "It's the best for who?"

But he didn't wait around for me to answer. He was just gone.

Which was also probably for the best, too.

FIFTY-EIGHT

If you were a vegetable,
you'd be a cute-cumber.

—JULIA B.

A numbness spread across my chest as I walked back into the house. Mama, Sue, and Iris were all sitting on the couch, eyes fixed on me with concern. Iris moved over and patted the empty space. I sat, all four of us squished in, no one quite sure what to say.

A sob escaped me. Then another. And instead of asking their questions, they wrapped their arms around me and let me cry.

Afterward, when I'd calmed down enough to speak, I told them everything. All of it. The medical bills. My job at Chicky's. The deal I'd made with Chris. Dad's threats. The text message I had just received. I even told them about Ellie after swearing them to secrecy.

When I finished, it was clear I'd stunned them all into silence. Even Iris.

I swallowed. "I'm sorry."

Mama narrowed her eyes. "Iris, go to my bedroom closet. On the top shelf, under the electric blanket, is a manila envelope. Bring it here." Iris heard the steel in her voice and scurried to do as asked.

"That man is something else," Sue muttered, looking as angry as Mama.

"Your father..." Mama growled and took a visible breath. "Get him on the phone and tell him you want to meet with him. Tonight."

"I'm not sure that's a good idea." The thought of facing him made me equal parts exhausted and disgusted. All I wanted to do was crawl into bed and lick my wounds.

Before she could reply, Iris returned with a thick, oversized envelope and handed it over to Mama.

"Oh, it's a fantastic idea." Mama tossed the envelope on the coffee table. It landed with a dull thud.

"I don't see what the point is." Everything seemed pointless at that moment. Chris was gone. My brain knew I'd done the right thing in sending him away; my heart, on the other hand, felt like it would never work properly again.

"Don't you worry, honey." Mama patted my cheek. "I will take care of this."

"How?"

She pointed at the envelope. "With that. I can't make everything better, but this thing with your father? That I can fix."

"What is it?"

Her smile was small and wholly diabolical. "Insurance."

Dad agreed to meet at the same café where I'd met with him before. In fact, he was already seated when Mama and I arrived, hunched over a cup of coffee. When he saw us, he stood, surprised to see I'd brought Mama with me.

"Lucy, it's good to see you." Smiling, he leaned down to give Mama a hug, which she rebuffed.

She slid into the booth. "I can't say I could say the same."

"Mae, I didn't know you were bringing your mother," he said, an edge to his voice.

"Surprise."

"Don't bother getting on at her. I insisted." Mama pulled out the envelope and dropped it on the table.

Dad's gaze flew to the packet and back to Mama's face. "What's that?"

Arching an eyebrow, Mama leaned forward. "This? It's how I'm going to make sure you never, ever threaten my children's happiness again."

His forehead wrinkled. "What does that mean?"

"You know, I spent almost half my life thinking you were a good man who just made bad decisions. I stuck with you through a lot of the stupid things you did. I watched you lose jobs and waste money, but there was always a little part of me that thought you weren't all bad. I thought, given the choice, you would choose the right thing when it mattered." Her eyes narrowed to blue slits. "Apparently, I was also an idiot."

Dad opened his mouth but Mama put a hand up to stop him.

"No. I'm gonna say this and then we're leaving. This will be the very last time you ever see my face." She opened the envelope and began pulling things out. "This is evidence of several fake IDs you created. That's illegal, of course." A packet of paper. "These are the credit card accounts you opened from applications you stole from strangers' mailboxes. Did you know stealing mail is a federal offense? I didn't know that until this nice man came to the door one time and identified himself as an inspector with the United States Postal Service." A business card joined the items on the table. "He was very interested in talking to you. Don't worry, I covered for you."

Good ole Dad was starting to look a little green. "Lucy—"

"This one is my favorite though," she said, talking right over him. She withdrew a USB drive. "Four or five years ago, the last time you stayed at the house, I knew you were into something but I couldn't figure out what. Leaving all hours of the night with strangers, sometimes in one of those serial killer-type vans. So, Sue rigged up a video camera and wouldn't you know it? We got real nice pictures of you and your new friends with a lot of animals, and I'm not talking about cats and dogs. Did you know the U.S. Fish and Wildlife Services are the ones who take care of idiots who traffic animals? Me, neither. But luckily, another nice agent came and talked to me. Left a card in case I had anything I wanted to tell them."

Dad's face was downright frozen now. He reached out a hand and, for a split second, I thought he might try to grab everything and make a run for it.

Mama must have suspected the same. "Go ahead. Do you think I'm foolish enough to only have one copy?"

"What do you want?" he asked, his voice shaky.

Mama held up a finger. "You will erase any damaging photos and information you have concerning Chris and Mae and Chris's family." Another finger. "You will never again show up to my house or any place in Two Harts. Period." Yet another finger. "You will leave us alone. Send a postcard if you have something to tell us."

Mama handed me the envelope and I hastily stuffed everything back in it. She stood and flung her purse over her shoulder.

"If you decide to break any of these rules, this information will immediately find its way to the right authorities." She leaned in close to my father. "Don't try me, Dale Sampson."

As she passed, my father gave Mama a long look, one that Mama returned. And I felt it. Whatever hold he'd had on her all these years, Mama had severed it completely. Dad flinched.

When we got back in the car, Mama let out a shaky breath. "Oh, my goodness. I can't believe I did that." She held up a hand. "Look how much I'm shaking."

I stared at her in awe. "Mama, you are a badass."

A blush colored her cheeks. "Watch your language, honey. But yes. Yes, I am."

That night, I sent Chris a text.

Me: *It's taken care of. Those photos will never be seen. It's safe now.*

Although I saw that he'd read it, he never replied.

FIFTY-NINE

If you were a Transformer, you'd be Optimus Fine.

—DAVE F.

I woke up each day and I pretended I was fine. I smiled at Mama. I argued with Iris. I had lunch with Ali. I met with the library committee to discuss the upcoming council meeting. I read a book. But not a romance; my heart couldn't handle it. I told everyone I was fine.

Mama played a game with me where she pretended I wasn't lying to her. It went something like this:

"How are you feeling?" Mama would ask.

"I'm okay," I'd say.

The truth was I felt like I was walking around with an open wound and no Band-Aid in the world could help it. So, I pretended. Except when I crawled into bed and Kevin plastered himself to my side and I stared at the engagement ring on my finger and cried stupid, useless tears.

When the morning came each day, I reminded myself that

I'd made the right choice, the smart choice, the only choice, the best choice for Chris.

But sometimes when I got to work, I sat in my car and cried for fifteen minutes.

Ladies and gentlemen, I was not fine.

* * *

The first check came by certified mail two weeks later.

"Do you know what it is?" Mama asked.

I shook my head and stared at the legal-sized envelope, almost afraid to open it. Despite Chris's request to leave me alone, it hadn't stopped the emails, requests for interviews, a publisher reaching out and asking me to write a tell-all, and more than a few pieces of hate mail. Thankfully, the public's reaction to Chris after his confession had been surprisingly positive and I'd read more than one article that praised him for his willingness to speak the truth.

"It can't be too bad, it's just an envelope." Mama pushed it toward me. "Go on, open it."

"It's from a lawyer. It could be really bad." Inside was an accounting sheet for "services rendered" and a check for $100,000. I held it out to Mama.

Her eyes widened. "So, he came through."

A surprising wave of anger ripped through me. "I'm not keeping that. It's going right back where it came from, thank you very much." I snatched it off the table and stuffed it back in the envelope.

The next day before going to the library, I stopped at the post office and mailed it right back to the attorney with a note:

To Whom it May Concern,

I received this payment by mistake. Services were not rendered.

Thank you,

Mae Sampson

A week later and, to my great astonishment, it came back.

"I need your help." Iris sounded more annoyed than anyone who needed help should sound.

I pressed the cell phone to my ear. "Go on."

"The car won't start."

"Where are you?" She named a town thirty minutes away. "Why are you there? It's after midnight. Which I seem to remember is your curfew."

"Suggested curfew."

"It's amazing how you hear things so much differently than me."

She sighed. "I need your help. Please."

I resisted the urge to squeal with delight. *Please?* Oh, my. She was desperate.

"I'm on my way."

Thirty minutes later, I pulled into the empty parking lot of a steakhouse and found Iris sitting on the hood of Mama's car. I pulled in next to her. The parking lot was otherwise empty.

"Why are we in a steakhouse parking lot at one in the morning?"

Iris hopped down from the hood. "Because this is where I work."

"What?" I stumbled climbing out of my car. "When did you get a job? You never said anything."

She rolled her eyes. "Keeping secrets must be a family trait."

To say Iris had taken the news of Dad's involvement poorly was an understatement and somehow I was the one she'd decided to take it out on. She refused to talk about it at all except in a passing snide comment. It was exhausting. Normal Iris was a lot to handle; Angry Iris was taking your life in your hands if you dared approach her.

"What do you do here?" I asked, turning to look at the low brown building.

"I'm a server."

I blinked. "You mean, for customers?"

"Yes. I've been here almost a year."

"That's why you're late all the time? Why didn't you say something?"

"Because I knew you'd be all 'School is your job, blah, blah, blah.'"

"Was that supposed to be an imitation of me?" I arched an eyebrow. "Because it sucked."

"Well, you suck," Iris shot back.

I took a deep, calming-ish breath. "Go pop the hood so we can jump the car and get out of here."

"Whatever." Iris stomped to the driver's side and practically tore the door open. "How do I pop the hood?"

"Seriously?"

"Just tell me, okay?" she snapped. "It's not like I had a dad to show me how to do this stuff."

Ouch. I crossed my arms. "Okay. Are we doing this now? Fine. Let's do it. I get it. You hate me."

She threw her arms in the air and yelled to the stars. "I don't hate you, you idiot. I hate *him*. I hate that I'm related to *him*. I really hate that he tried to hurt one of the most important people in my life."

I gaped at her.

Iris swung around to face me, her face red. "You know what

else? I haven't seen him in so long I can't even make an accurate replica for a voodoo doll. And that Pisses. Me. Off. I hate that you and Mom kept so many things from me. You didn't trust that I was mature enough to know what kind of person he is. I'm almost an adult and I'm smarter than you think." She stalked closer. "I knew about your job at Chicky's."

I sort of sank into the side of my car. "No."

"Yep. A kid from school went there with his dad and saw you. When he asked me about it, I played dumb but I started to wonder. I followed you one day and figured it out."

"Oh, Iris."

"Nope." She wagged a finger in my direction. "Do not get all teary-eyed and emotional. You've cried a million times the last couple of weeks, and I hate that, too. You don't cry. You're... you're Mae. You can handle anything."

I sniffled. "I'm not sure I can handle anything anymore."

"You know what makes me the most upset though? You were happy."

I pulled in a shaky breath. "I was pretending."

"You were not pretending." She came closer. "Maybe you started out pretending. But you loved him... still love him. And he loved you. It was so obvious, even I could see it."

And I hadn't.

The tears slid down my face, unchecked. "Now I'm crying and it's your fault."

After a hesitation, she wrapped her arms around me. "Sorry."

I nodded against her shoulder. When I got under control, I untangled myself and we both leaned against the car in silence.

"Aidan asked me to the prom," she said suddenly.

"He finally did it. What did you say?"

"Obviously I said yes. He's adorable."

I laughed.

"You want to go dress shopping with me?"

"I'd love to."

"Cool."

"We should probably jump your car. I want to go home and go to bed."

"Fine." Iris walked back to the driver's side of her car. "But, seriously, how do I pop the hood?"

SIXTY

So... if I told you that you had a beautiful body,
would you hold it against me?

—*KEN S.*

Next morning, Mama was up before me.

"Come eat breakfast with me," she said.

I grabbed a yogurt and a granola bar and slid into a chair across from her at the table. After unwrapping the bar, I broke it into smaller chunks.

Mama touched the back of my left hand. "You're still wearing the ring."

With a start, I held out my hand. "I guess I forgot I had it on."

I hadn't forgotten; I just didn't want to take it off. I know, pathetic. My heart twisted as I slipped it off and set in on the table between us. Mama picked it up and held it to the light, turning the stone a rainbow of colors.

"It's so beautiful. I looked up what an opal is supposed to represent. Do you know?"

I shook my head.

She lightly ran a finger over the stone. "Hope and love and goodness. Isn't that lovely? Those are things a marriage should be built on."

"Piper picked it out," I said, not quite meeting her eye. "She probably had no idea it meant something like that."

Mama set the ring down carefully. "Maybe so."

"Is that how it was with you and Dad at first? Hope and love and goodness?"

Mama looked at me with surprise. I was surprised too. I rarely ever brought up my father unless it was followed by a lot of very not nice things.

"I wouldn't say that. It felt exciting and dangerous. I was a stupid girl, just out of high school. He was six years older and so handsome and interested in me, of all people." She sighed. "I wasn't like you, honey. I think you were born fully grown, always had a good head on your shoulders. It was intimidating being your mother sometimes."

"Really?"

"Oh, yes. I wasn't even twenty when you were born. I had no idea what I was doing. Your father and I had left Two Harts, so I didn't even have my own mama to help me." Frowning, she stared into her coffee cup. "I know things weren't easy for you, Mae. I—I have a lot of guilt about that."

"Mama—"

She held up a hand. "No, no. Let me get it all out. I am sorry that my decisions affected you. I'll never regret marrying your father because he gave me you two girls, but I will always regret how my actions made things so much harder for you."

"I don't blame you for anything," I whispered, my nose stinging.

Mama smiled sadly. "Maybe you should be a little angry with me. I should have chosen you girls over what I thought was love. Because looking back, I'm not even sure it was love, just a young girl infatuated with a handsome man. But I worry you and Iris have never had an example for what real love and marriage look like. Or worse, you won't be able to recognize it when it's right in front of you."

"We turned out okay."

"You did"—she patted my cheek—"but I feel partly responsible for this whole engagement mess. If I had been a different mother, if I hadn't had this stroke." She shrugged. "Life could have been easier for you."

I sniffled. All these tears the last few days. It's like I was making up for years of never crying. "I like my life just fine."

She laughed quietly. "No more lying. Life kind of sucks right now."

She wasn't wrong. "I love you, Mama."

"Love you more." She gripped my hand. "You'll have to give the ring back."

My stomach twisted and I pushed the yogurt away. "Of course. It's not mine. Not anymore."

Not that it had ever really been mine.

Later that day, I tortured myself over whether to contact Chris about the ring but, in the end, I chickened out and texted Piper. It was several hours later before she replied.

Piper: *The ring is yours to keep. Chris picked it out specifically for you. He said if you needed to sell it, he understood but he hoped you would keep it.*

Me: *I thought you picked it out.*

Piper: *Nope. He spent a solid week looking for just the right one. Said it had to be an opal.*

Me: *I didn't know.*

I slipped the ring back on my finger and allowed myself to sleep with it on for one more night. Then the next morning I carefully stowed it away in my jewelry box for safekeeping.

SIXTY-ONE

Hey, baby. Are you tired?
    'Cause you've been running through my mind all day.

—SAM

In May, I returned to my old shift at Chicky's. Shane even seemed happy to see me. Which didn't last long. By the end of the evening, I'd had two complaints about my attitude and one drunk guy who was sure I'd purposely spilled a beer on him.

It sure wasn't an accident, buddy.

On my second night back, Amanda found me and told me my presence was requested. "Don't worry. No handsome football players."

No, it was worse.

"Oh, the gods have smiled down on me today," Iris crowed and held up her phone. "Smile, Mae."

"Honey, don't you look cute in that uniform," Mama said. "But that shirt's a little revealing, isn't it?"

"Eh, leave her alone," Sue said. "She can pull it off."

"I could talk to your boss about letting you wear something more appropriate," Mama offered.

"Please don't."

Iris held up the phone. "Damn, this picture is amazing. I'm going to get it blown up to poster size."

"Iris, watch your mouth," Mama said. "And put your phone away."

I sighed. "Oh, boy, you came to Chicky's."

"Of course, honey. We wanted to see where you worked."

"Don't worry. We'll leave you a good tip," Sue said.

"Ha," Iris said. "My tip is that this place needs better servers."

"Thanks for the support." I smiled. "Now figure out what you want to eat so you can get out of here."

The next week, I found out that every single one of my mother's medical bills had been paid in full. Every. Single. One.

That jerk. That beautiful, sweet jerk.

That week, I worked up the courage to text him:

Me: *I do not want your money.*

Me: *I just mailed the check back for the FOURTH time. Stop sending it.*

Me: *Seriously. Don't send it back.*

Me: *Or else.*

Me: *And I'll find a way to pay you back for Mama's medical bills.*

Then, much later, in the middle of the night when I
couldn't sleep:

Me: *I miss you.*

He did not reply.

The city council held all their meetings on Tuesdays at 6 p.m.
sharp in the auditorium of the high school, which seated two
hundred people comfortably. I arrived at 5:30, anxious and
jittery. I didn't relish throwing myself on the mercy of the
council but this was my last shot to pound some sense into
them.

Except for a handful of people setting up the stage, I was
the only person in the auditorium. I sat in the very front row,
stuck in my earbuds, and pulled up some music while I
reviewed my notecards. Over the last week, I'd spent hours
going over the points I wanted to make.

The plan to arrive early had seemed like a good one two
hours ago. But now, the longer I sat there, the more nervous I
became. I rechecked the order of my notecards, smoothed out
my hair, adjusted the volume of the music, and slapped on a
little more lip gloss.

Eventually, the council members trickled in. Mr. Jersey
looked like he was half asleep. Stephen O'Donnell was fiddling
with his phone. Sabrina Olsen sat nearest to Peter, smiling at
something he'd said with her scary toothy smile. These people
held the fate of the library in their hands, and it was a terrifying
thought.

Maybe I'd been stupid not to take Chris's donation. I could
have avoided all this, but this wasn't his problem. It wasn't even
mine. I could go elsewhere and find a job. The library had been
here longer than most of them and would be here long after.

The people of Two Harts needed the library and they needed to fight for it.

Because when something is important to you, you fight for it.

My heart lurched in my chest at that thought. I tucked it away for later.

Someone tapped me on the shoulder. I looked up to find Mrs. Katz, Horace behind her. The two of them had become a matched set of late, showing up for lunch at Ollie's or stopping by the library together. Much like a bonded pair of cats, they seemed just as inclined to get their claws out or cuddle up for a nap. It was fascinating to watch.

"Well, move over so we can sit with you," Mrs. Katz said.

I popped out one of the earbuds. "I didn't know you were coming."

She frowned. "Of course I came. I'm on the agenda to speak against the library budget cut."

"Me too." Horace whipped out what looked to be a small novel's worth of paper. "Typed out all my notes, too. Didn't want to forget anything."

"Horace, can you sit down, please? I can't see," a voice behind us said. It was Sarah Ellis, white hair neatly curled, pearls in place, smiling her grandmotherly smile. "I'm going to be speaking too. I plan on telling that bastard Peter Stone how I really feel."

"Me, too," someone else said.

"Same here," another voice said.

It took me several seconds to realize what I was seeing. I stood and faced the back of the auditorium. Almost every seat was taken. So many of the faces I recognized. People I'd grown up with, who came to the library for books or to use a computer or to ask me how to get the Facebook app on their phone. A few of them waved at me.

"Where did they all come from?" I whispered.

"What does that mean?" Mrs. Katz asked. "Goodness sakes, they came from Two Harts. They know how important the library is to this town and they know how important you are. You needed help. You have help. They're here for you,"

"For me?" My voice squeaked. "I—I don't know what to say."

Mrs. Katz shook her head. "You young people have no manners. You say thank you."

I couldn't help myself. Later that night, I texted Chris:

Me: *The city council voted down the budget cuts.*

Me: *It was amazing. So many people came to support the library.*

Me: *The council caved under the pressure.*

Me: *Anyway, I wanted you to know.*

SIXTY-TWO

Can I tie your shoes?
'Cause I don't want you to fall for anyone else.

—ELENA S.

Somehow, I managed to survive the next few months. Iris went to the prom with Aidan. He reported later that she'd danced several times and had even smiled in the pictures. She also graduated high school and, while Dad was smart enough not to show up, he did send her a postcard to say congratulations.

Mama got stronger and, with her medical bills paid off, it helped make paying for more therapy manageable. So much so, I dropped down to two nights a week at Chicky's and allowed myself one whole day of rest. Which was mostly spent doing chores and laundry.

As for Chris? I began texting him each night even though he never replied. I understood why. I'd hurt him. He'd been willing to figure out a way and I'd been... scared, just as he'd said. It was the only word that made the most sense. I thought time would make it easier to move on. Heck, I'd moved on from Peter in roughly twenty-three seconds, the amount of time it took me to walk in on him with another girl, throw a crystal ashtray at him, and slam the door.

Chris, though? He wasn't so easy to get over. I tried to cover it up, but others could see it. They spoke gently and patted me on the back or gave me unsolicited hugs. For three weeks straight, one of several sweet elderly women would stop by at the library and leave me a sugary treat—homemade cookies, cupcakes, a muffin.

Mrs. Katz informed me they'd all started a Break-up Dessert Train for me. "Because it's a little easier to get through with something sweet."

I didn't argue.

One summer day, I traipsed over to the Sit-n-Eat to meet up with Ali. Ollie shuffled over to me a few minutes after I sat down. "Is the other one coming?"

I laughed. "Every time, Ollie. Yes, she'll be here."

A shadow of a smile flashed on his face. "Alright then. Two orders."

"Thanks."

This was the part of the conversation where Ollie always shuffled himself off to the kitchen and magically reappeared with food. But he didn't move. Instead, he peered at me from under his bushy eyebrows.

"How you doing?" he asked.

I don't know which of us was more surprised he'd asked me such a question.

Maybe because it was so very surprising, I found myself giving him an honest answer. "Lonely, sad, wondering if I made a terrible mistake."

Ollie nodded like he understood. "I was in love once. Long time ago."

Again, we stared at each other in disbelief.

He shrugged and continued. "It wasn't an easy love. Some

people think being in love has to feel good all the time. If you ain't happy, then it can't be real. I thought that too back then. But that is not how life works, is it? We can't be happy all the time. If we were, we wouldn't appreciate it when we are."

This was the most I'd ever heard Ollie say in a week, maybe a month, maybe my entire life. "What happened?"

His eyes seemed to be looking somewhere else. "We split and she left. That was close to sixty years ago. Never, not one day, have I not thought of her and wondered what would have happened if I'd gone after her. Instead, I stayed around here and took over the restaurant."

"I'm so sorry. That must have been awful."

His dark eyes narrowed. "Do you get what I'm saying here?"

"I— No." But maybe I did.

"Don't let it get away from you too." Then he shuffled off to his kitchen-cave without a glance back at me.

A few minutes later, Ali slid in next to me at the counter. "What's that look on your face?"

I blinked. "I just had the strangest conversation with Ollie."

Ali laughed. "A conversation? Like an actual back-and-forth with words?"

"Like I said, it was strange."

"About what?"

"Nothing." Ollie's story was his own and not for me to share.

Ali cheered when Ollie brought the food around and wasted no time digging in. But all I could do was stare at my food and replay Ollie's story.

"What's up?" Ali nudged me with her shoulder. "You aren't hungry?"

"I think I made a mistake," I whispered.

Slowly, Ali set her fork down and turned toward me. "About?"

"Chris. I miss him."

Ali wrapped an arm around my shoulders. "I know you do, honey."

"I've been texting him. Every night. Just little things about what's going on around here. A photo of Iris at graduation. Keeping him up to date on Mrs. Katz and Horace's love life." I straightened and tried on a small smile. "He's never written back. Not once. He told me that he'd wait for me. Do you think maybe he's finally figured out we aren't meant to be?"

Eyes narrowed, Ali flattened her mouth into a thin line. When she finally spoke, it was not with her inside voice. "Are you kidding me right now?"

"Why are you yelling at me?"

"Maebell Sampson, you sent him a text? A text to tell him you missed him? Come on. That man has not given up on you. No way. You've read how many romance novels?"

My mouth dropped. "How do you know about that?"

She rolled her eyes. "Hello, dummy. We've known each other since we were ten. You're good at keeping secrets but not that good. You should know from reading them that you're going to have to put a lot more effort into making things right. Way more than a text."

"You think?"

"Uh, no. I know." She picked her fork up and resumed eating. "You better make it good too. He deserves it."

"Excuse me," I sputtered. "Whose side are you on, anyway?"

"Chris's side," she pointed her knife at me, "and your side. Because you're both on the same side. We all know that. We're just waiting for you to figure that out too."

Later that night, when I couldn't sleep, I texted Chris:

Me: I sent the check back AGAIN yesterday. Please stop. I don't want it.

Me: Ollie told me a story today.

Me: The most words I've ever heard him say.

Me: Do you really think everyone gets a happily ever after?

SIXTY-THREE

Our love is like diarrhea,
I just can't hold it in.

—ELENA S.

I found a woman sleeping in the library.

She was in the children's section with a little boy of about three who was also asleep. I didn't recognize her, although it was hard to see her face the way she was curled around the child. It didn't feel right to wake her.

Two hours later, the little boy wandered over, his big blue eyes sleepy and confused. Something about him seemed so familiar, but I couldn't place him.

"Haffa go potty." He rubbed a hand through his dark hair.

"Let's go wake up your mommy."

He took my hand and we walked to his mother.

"Miss," I said quietly, hoping not to startle her. "Miss."

She startled anyway and immediately went into a panic. "Oliver? Oliver."

The little boy's face scrunched. "Mommy, I right here."

"Oh, my goodness." She snatched him up in her arms and held him close until he squirmed and complained he wanted to get down.

"Is everything alright?" I asked.

She set Oliver down and stood, brushing her hands off on her faded jeans. It was the first time I got a good look at her face. I gasped.

"Ellie?" I whispered. She looked just like the photo Chris had shown me. Long blonde hair, oversized blue eyes, very pretty in a girl-next-door way.

"Surprise." She twisted her hands at her waist.

"H-how?" Without too much thought, I hugged her. With a sigh, she returned the hug.

She pulled back and smiled. "I'm sorry. I know this is kind of sudden, even a little weird, right? We drove all the way here from Los Angeles the last few days. I'm so tired that my head's all jumbled up. And driving with a three-year-old. Phew. The potty breaks alone. And then just all of West Texas. Who would even live there?"

She paused, blushing slightly. "Sorry. I'm making this weirder now."

I smiled. "What in the world are you doing here?"

"I don't know." She bit the corner of her lip. "I've been talking to Chris, who tells me he's fine but then I talk to Betsy and she says he's miserable and I hated that thought. I guess I wanted to tell you I'm sorry. I feel like my foolish actions are the reason for all this."

"He's been miserable?" I leaned against a bookcase.

"That's what she said but in more words. You know Betsy, she's a talker."

"Oh." My heart did a small flip.

"I just hate that him protecting me turned into such a huge mess. And I was so tired of L.A. It was a foolish dream of mine when I was a girl, going out there. I was such a baby. Only eighteen. Plus, I have Oliver now." She ruffled the boy's hair. "So I packed us up and we drove... here. Seems a strange place for me to come, now that I think of it. Sorry, I talk to myself sometimes. And other times, no one can follow what I'm saying. Sometimes I get lost in what I'm trying to say." Her forehead crinkled. "Short and sweet, what I wanted to say was I'm sorry."

I grinned. "In a way, you're the reason I met Chris, so maybe I should be thanking you?"

Her head tilted to the side. "Either way, I'm happy to meet you, Mae Sampson."

"And I'm happy to meet you, Ellie Sterns."

Oliver tugged on her leg. "I go to the potty. Now."

Ellie gave her son a firm look. "What do we say?"

He sighed. "Pwease. I go to the potty now."

"I'm sorry," Ellie said. "I should take him."

"Of course." I directed them to the bathroom and wandered back to my desk.

I was starting to think my life was likely never going to go back to the way it was before Chris. Some things might still be the same, but I was not.

My texts to Chris that night were all about his sister:

Me: I met Ellie today. She's lovely.

Me: Found her and her little boy, Oliver, sleeping in the library. Isn't it funny? The same way I met you. I didn't yell at her though.

Me: She's staying in town at the hotel for a few days to figure out a plan.

Me: Just thought you'd want to know.

SIXTY-FOUR

Babe, you're like a whoopee cushion.
Fun to squeeze but embarrassing at social functions.

—PROFESSOR POPINJAY

Two things were delivered to the library addressed to me on a sizzling hot Friday in August. The first I recognized immediately as the Check I Did Not Want. No matter how many times I sent the thing back, it was returned. Over and over. With a growl, I tossed it on my desk to deal with on Monday.

The second was from an agency of some kind with a Dallas address. I opened the envelope slowly and pulled out the contents. Photos.

Not just any photos either. They were the engagement photos Chris and I had taken in his parents' backyard, photos I'd never seen. A note slipped out from between the photos and fluttered to the floor.

Mae—

Thought you'd want these.

No signature. I took my time to flip through them, although there were only five in total. All of them were the photos taken before, during, and after the kiss. One of them had a sticky note attached to it that read, "This one."

My breath caught when I saw it. In it, one of Chris's hands rested on my cheek. One arm wrapped around me, his head dipped, mine reaching toward him. The curve of a smile just touching the corner of my mouth.

It was a photo taken a second before. A second before something magical happened. A second before everything changed. A second before a kiss.

Nothing about it seemed fake. Not the way his thumb rested on my cheekbone or how my fingers curled into his shirt.

It was a photo of two people in love.

Later that day, Aidan found me in the Y.A. section. I sat on the floor surrounded by piles of books as I attempted to fix a shelf on one of the bookcases.

"I am smarter than a shelf. Truly I am." It should be noted this shelf was proving to be genius-level frustrating.

"I have a name," Aidan said.

I frowned. "A name for what?"

"A name for Anonymous. Took me forever. I had to do a lot of—"

"Nope," I cut in. "I don't want to know how you did it."

He grinned. "Oh right, I forgot. Well, I have the name of the anonymous source. Looks like he lives in New York City."

"New York? Well, that narrows it down to eight million people."

He cleared his throat. "There are emails between this guy

and your dad. Looks like that's how your dad got a copy of the contract."

I stood, mindless of the books that toppled over. "Does this guy have a name?"

"Yeah—it's Douglas McGill."

My pulse skidded to a halt and started back in double time. "No."

"Do you know him?" Aidan asked.

"That's Chris's agent."

"What?" Piper bellowed.

I winced and held my phone away from my ear.

"That rat," she huffed, only slightly quieter. "Are you willing to help me hide a body?"

She sounded a lot more serious than I was comfortable with. But, at the very least, it would be justifiable homicide as far as I was concerned. I would totally be a character witness at her trial.

"Will you make sure Chris knows about this?"

"You know what? I sure will. I'm doing it in person. He has a pre-season game tomorrow in Atlanta. Afterward, he's giving his first press conference since the television interview. Doug is with him. Don't worry, I'll get him." The thread of violence in her voice convinced me she was not lying.

"Good." I hesitated. "How is he? Chris?"

"He's... okay."

"Great. Good. Okay is good."

Piper barked a laugh. "You two are something else. Did you get the photos I sent you?"

"Those were from you? Thank you. I love them."

And him. I love him. I love him so much; it hurts not to see him. I thought of Ollie and his lost love. I thought about spending the rest of my life in Two Harts pining for someone who never even knew how I felt about him. I thought about all the plans I'd made and how maybe just this once it was time to do something spontaneous. Even if it was terrifying.

Because living life without Chris was even scarier.

"Piper, do you think you could get me into that press conference?"

SIXTY-FIVE

Life without you is a broken pencil. Pointless.

—*JULIA B.*

I didn't have a plan.

Word had spread fast through the Two Harts' grapevine that Mae Sampson was flying to Atlanta to profess her undying love to Chris Sterns. And once *that* got out, the whole town ascended on the library like Target shoppers on Black Friday.

"What is going on?" I asked no one in particular.

"They're here for you, idiot," Ali said.

Mrs. Katz glared at me over the top of her glasses. "You think we're going to let you do this on your own?"

Alright then.

It quickly became apparent that next-day plane tickets cost the earth. Even worse, the only flight with an available seat got to Atlanta by way of Newark and took over seven hours.

"Should I be doing this?" I asked, again to no one in particular. "It's so expensive."

At least five different people yelled, "Yes!" including my own mother.

"Folks," Horace said, "we're taking up donations. We need eleven hundred dollars to get Mae to Atlanta."

In less than an hour, the money had been donated, and the ticket bought.

The next morning, after very little sleep, Sue, Mama, and Iris dropped me off at the airport.

Mama hugged me tightly. "Remember halfway to brave is scared."

That was good news, since I was terrified. Never mind seeing Chris. I had to get through the plane ride on my own.

For the first leg of the trip, I sat next to a mother traveling alone with her two-year-old and six-month-old children. She'd purchased two seats for the three of them and it became apparent this poor woman was in way over her head. Which was how I ended up bottle-feeding a baby.

Then I learned something very important: the amount of spit-up one small eighteen-pound human can produce is truly astounding.

Especially when said small human does it all over my shoulder, down my back, and a into a large chunk of my hair.

Damage done, the kid fell dead asleep in my arms. Which was kind of adorable and almost made up for the puke. At least it took my mind off the whole "flying in a tin can" fear.

Once at our layover, I had just enough time to switch out my shirt for a clean one (thankfully, I'd only packed a carry-on) and try to wash my hair. Except that in my haste to pack, my one change of clothing—my return ticket was tomorrow—I'd forgotten to pack a clean shirt. Who does that? Me. The only thing I had was a sleep shirt Sue had gotten me for Christmas. It read *I'm Great in Bed. I Can Sleep for Hours.*

Given the choice between the vomit shirt and my nightshirt, the answer was clear.

Next, I tackled my hair. Which resulted in me washing off half a face of makeup and crouching under a hand-dryer. It should be noted that it did not work. But it was fine. Surely, I'd have a bit of time to put myself together once I made it to Atlanta.

But then after we'd boarded the next flight, it departed over an hour late due to mechanical issues.

Mechanical. Issues.

So Bill, the middle-aged guy in the seat next to me, held my hand when we took off. He told me I reminded him of his daughter and she was a nervous flyer too. He started talking about all the best places to eat at while I was in town. The last thing I wanted to hear about was food when I'm pretty sure my stomach was trying to remove itself from my body.

I was never flying again without Chris. So, he was going to have to say yes.

When we landed, I wanted to kiss the ground but I didn't. Because gross. I did text Mama to let her know I'd arrived safely. Piper and her rental car were already waiting for me in the pickup area.

"Are we late?" I asked by way of greeting as I slid into the car.

Grinning, she shook her head and shot out into traffic. "They were in the fourth quarter when I left. As long as we don't run into any traffic, we should be great."

So, of course, we ran into traffic. The kind of standstill traffic that brought out the road rage in better people than me. I took a deep breath and reminded myself this was for Chris.

"You're looking a little rough," Piper said once she took a close look at me.

She was not kidding. But it was what I had to work with. I tried to smooth down my hair and attempted to replace the makeup I'd accidentally washed off, but finally gave up. It was hopeless.

Piper swung into a parking spot at the stadium and called a friend to check the status of the press conference. I texted Mama with an update and imagined everyone in Two Harts huddled around my mother's phone waiting to see what I said. It made me smile.

"It started ten minutes ago. We need to hustle."

Piper got us through all the security checks and to the room in which the conference was being held. She paused outside the door to calm herself and straighten the jacket of her deep-purple power suit. Then she looked at me and winced.

"It's bad?"

She tried to fluff my hair and wiped her hands off on my nightshirt. "He probably won't even notice. He'll just be excited to see you."

"You think?"

"I know." She surprised me and gave me a hug. "Are you ready? Do you know what you're going to say?"

"Yes. No. I don't know." My stomach dipped. "I think I might throw up. What do I do?"

"That's easy. Don't throw up." With that, she grabbed my wrist and opened the door.

We came in through the back of the room. In front of us, a sea of video cameras and photographers stood and in front of them, several rows of chairs occupied by reporters. In front of them all, a long table where six men sat. I caught a glimpse of Sherrod next to an older man who I knew was the Stars' coach, and I thought I recognized a shoulder that belonged to Chris.

My whole body was strung taut with tension. I forced myself to take slow, deep breaths. Shook my arms out and tried to figure out the best way to weave around all these people.

Should I yell his name? Throw something to get his attention? Like, myself at his feet? What if he ignored me? What if he wanted nothing to do with me?

Before I could do anything, a commotion broke out at the side of the room. It only took a second to realize Piper and Doug were arguing. Or Piper was arguing. Doug stood with his arms crossed and his nose in the air. At first, it was hard to understand them but when the room cottoned on to what was unfolding, they went silent.

"...can't believe you," Piper bit out. "You are scum. To go on television in a disguise and imply the things you implied about your own client."

"I did nothing wrong. I only wanted to give him more opportunities for endorsement deals. Just needed to dirty his reputation a little bit."

"You are an idiot!"

I scampered toward them just in time to see Piper ball up her fist. She pulled it back but must have thought better of it, seeing as how she was surrounded by cameras. With a growl, she dropped her hand.

"What's going on?" Chris asked, cutting in between Doug and Piper. I stared at him, taking in every little detail. For the first time since April, it felt like I could take a deep breath.

"It was him." Piper pointed at Doug. "He's the anonymous source. He's the one giving out all the gossip."

"You don't know that," Doug snapped, cowering behind Chris.

Chris whipped around to face Doug. I couldn't see his face, but his voice sent chills down my spine. "Is this true?"

Piper leaned to the side to glare at Doug. "Oh, I can prove it, you rat. How could you even think about bringing the woman in the video into all this? I cannot believe you went after her. You are despicable."

Doug's eyes skittered around the room wildly, probably

looking for a way to escape. "What? No, I didn't. I wanted no part in that. I told him not to."

"Chris, can you tell us what's going on?" a reporter yelled out. Everyone ignored him.

"But you didn't stop him, did you? You are a monster." Piper balled up her fist again.

"Don't listen to anything she says," Doug said. "It's all lies."

"You son of a b—"

"Whoa, there"—Chris gently put his hands on Piper's shoulders—"let's take this to another room."

"You're right." Piper straightened, yanked down the sleeves of her suit jacket. She glared at Doug.

Chris pointed to a door at the side of the room. Piper marched toward it, leaving the door open. Doug, looking more than a little panicked, followed behind, his shoulders stooped.

"I'll be in soon," Chris said.

Piper popped her head out. "Mae, I'm sorry to ruin your moment."

"Mae?" Chris spun around and his eyes found me immediately. He froze.

"Oh," I squeaked, coming from behind a video camera and into the light. "It's okay."

Piper winked at me, muttered something to Chris, and closed the door. A few seconds later, I was certain I heard Doug yell, "You punched me!" But maybe that was only wishful thinking on my part.

Slowly, I walked toward Chris. He was so still, watching me closely.

When I was ten or so feet from him, I waved. "Hi."

"You're here."

"This is my grand romantic gesture," I said, fully aware my hair smelled like airport hand soap, and I was wearing only half a face of makeup.

He closed the gap between us. His hair was wet from a quick shower after the game, and his face looked thinner.

I frowned. "Have you lost weight?"

"A little." A few inches separated us now, and I itched to reach out and touch him. His eyes traveled from my head to my toes and back. "Nice shirt."

"It's a nightgown."

He grinned. "Thanks for dressing up for the occasion."

I swallowed. The only thing I wanted to do was throw myself in his arms. But I hadn't come all this way for nothing. "Are we being recorded?"

"Yep," one of the camera people replied.

"Come on." Chris glanced around the room before he grabbed my hand and pulled me toward the front of the room.

"Chris, Chris," the reporters shouted. "Do you want to make a statement?"

He stopped so fast, I ran into him. Still smiling, he wrapped an arm around my shoulders and grabbed one of the microphones on the table. "Here is my statement: It was a great game. But now, ladies and gentlemen, I'm going to go enjoy this grand romantic gesture in private."

The room erupted in laughter. But he was on a mission. He tossed the mic to Sherrod and we were moving again toward a door in the front corner of the room. It opened on to a long, wide hallway where people were milling around. He pulled me along, opening and closing doors as we went until he found an empty room. The door shut behind us and he flipped on the light to reveal we were in a small supply closet.

I put some distance between us—the whole two feet the room allowed—and held up a hand. "Don't distract me with your smiles and twinkly eyes. I have things I need to say."

He tried (and failed) to rein in his smile. "I'm listening."

I pulled the check out of my bra where I'd stuffed it to keep it safe. "I don't want your money. I've returned it every time and it keeps coming back. Our contract became invalid."

He frowned. "How?"

"Because it was a business arrangement. No feelings allowed, remember?" I ripped up the check into tiny little pieces and tossed them in the air.

Chris nodded.

"I screwed up. I had feelings. I have feelings. So many feelings, and I was scared of the feelings, like you said. I'm still scared of the feelings. I know I kept saying that happily ever after isn't real. The thing I kept getting stuck on was the 'happy' part. But it's the 'ever after' part that's important. Because we won't always have happy times. Sometimes we'll be angry or sad or hurt. Sometimes life will be hard. But the 'ever after' part means it's us together. Forever."

Chris studied my face, his eyes warm.

I took a deep breath. "I love you. You're the only person I want to do 'ever after' with."

Smiling softly, he took a step toward me, tucked a piece of my hair behind my ear.

"I need you to say something," I whispered. "I'm kind of dying here."

"Do you believe in love at first sight?" he said. "Or should I walk by again?"

I closed my eyes. "You're going to torture me right now?"

He crept a few inches closer, his eyes twinkling. "If you were a chicken, you'd be impeccable."

I laughed. "This is my punishment."

"Are you a time traveler?" He picked up my hand and tugged until I half fell into him. He smelled so good—soap and cinnamon gum and Chris. "Because I can see you in my future."

I grinned and curled a hand into his shirt. "I think you have to kiss me."

One of his eyebrows arched. "Is that so?"

"Yes." I nodded solemnly. "That's what comes after the grand romantic gesture and a declaration of love. You don't want to disappoint people when we retell this story, do you?"

One of his hands settled on my lower back, the other slid through my hair to the back of my head. His eyes dropped to my mouth and my heartbeat sped up. "Sprinkles, the only person I'm worried about disappointing is you."

"Don't call me Sprinkles."

"You suit me just fine," he whispered against my mouth.

Then, finally, he kissed me.

EPILOGUE
CHRIS

A girlfriend and I had gone to a hotel in the Catskills back in January of 1968. We were sitting at a table in the bar and this guy who looked a lot like Buddy Holly came up to our table and said, "What are two nice girls like you doing at a place like this?" He was looking at my girlfriend, but when we got to talking, it turned out that he lived in the same apartment complex I did! We got married five months later and had fifty-two years together before he passed away.

—ENID G.

"Hey, Sprinkles, you remember that question you were saving for later?"

Mae scrunched her nose in the adorable way she always did when she was confused. Or annoyed. I liked to make her do it as much as possible. For fun.

"I have no idea what you're talking about." She turned a page in the book she was reading.

"Sure, you do. That time we went to the Taco Truck, and I was very manly and beat you at the hot sauce challenge."

That got her attention. She set her book aside. "Excuse me? I do not think so."

This was the best part—when she got all riled up. Her face turned all pink, and it made her freckles stand out even more.

"No, no. I remember. I beat you fair and square."

Mae stood, causing the porch swing to shift and knock her in the back of her knees. The swing was a new addition at the Wilson place. Except it wasn't the Wilson place anymore. It was mine. But nobody in this town was inclined to call it the Sterns place. It would probably take a hundred years before that caught on.

I'd bought it flat out six months ago after Mae had pronounced her undying love to me in a supply closet while wearing a nightgown. What more could a guy ask of a grand romantic gesture, I say.

Moving to Two Harts hadn't been much of a hardship. Strangely, Ellie had decided to stay too. She'd found a job and a little apartment to rent in town and for the first time in a long while, she seemed to be settling into her own.

Staying here meant Mae could still help out her mom. Lucy had done well in therapy and had taken a very part-time job at the drycleaners in town. She said it made her feel "human" again to be working. Iris still lived at home and commuted to the community college for now, still not quite settled on what she wanted to be when she grew up.

As for the house, I had begun the critter removal almost immediately. Although we were still on the fence about the moose. Mae felt some kind of kinship to him. I didn't want to deal with the hassle of getting that sucker out of the house.

I had one more year on my contract with the Stars. When it was up, I was retiring. I still planned to go to medical school, so we'd have to leave Two Harts, at least for a while, but we'd figure it out. Like Mae had said, doing ever after together meant we'd find a way to make it work.

"That is not what happened at all." Her eyes narrowed.

"How about we agree to disagree?"

"You know you only say that when you know I'm right and don't want to admit it." She took a few steps toward me where I was sitting in a sturdy wooden chair on the other side of the porch. It was such a nice day in March. Perfect for lazing around and for asking questions. Important questions.

"Why?"

"Why what?" I asked innocently.

"Why do you want to know about my last question?"

"So suspicious." And smart.

She hummed and took another few steps toward me. She was close enough now I could reach out and grab her hand if I wanted to. But I didn't. It was more fun to get her to come to me.

"Well, to be honest, I did have an ulterior motive." I smiled up at her. "I was sort of hoping you might let me have that question."

Her eyebrows shot up. "Oh, really?"

I nodded solemnly. "Yes."

She came even closer, all shrew eyes and long, pale legs. I did like those legs an awful lot. "You're planning something."

"You don't know that." She was right.

She put her hands on the arms of the chair and bent over me, so close now I could lean forward and kiss her. Which was mighty tempting, but I had an objective here. I needed to finish that first. Then kissing.

Priorities.

"Alright, you can have the question," she announced.

"That easily?" Now I was suspicious. But never look a gift horse in the mouth, they say. Catching her off balance, I wrapped my hands around her waist and set her on my lap so her feet dangled off one side and she was forced to lean into me or risk falling over.

She grinned and linked her arms around my neck. "Hi."

"Hi." I started to get distracted because her mouth was this close, and it didn't seem right to leave her lips there all alone. With a frown, I pulled my head back.

"I want to use my question now," I announced.

"Go ahead."

"Now remember, you have to answer honestly."

"Of course."

"Because this is a real important question, okay?"

She rolled her eyes. "Ask the question."

"Do you know what today marks the first anniversary of?"

"That's your question?" Her nose scrunched in thought. I wanted to kiss it. But I resisted. I should be in the running for Saint of the Year. "No, I guess not."

"On this day, exactly one year ago, I was minding my own business in the Two Harts Public Library—"

"You were *sleeping.*"

"That is debatable. Anyway, this bossy librarian came over and started heckling me."

"Heckling?" She laughed.

"I'm telling a story here. Sssh."

"It was an important day. Did I know that librarian would turn out to be the best thing that ever happened to me? Not at the time. Mostly I just liked when she whisper-yelled at me. It was sexy."

She smacked my shoulder. "You're so weird."

I picked up her left hand. Her ring finger was bare. Shortly after we'd gotten back together, she'd given me the ring back and told me to hold onto it until the day I wanted to propose for real.

Today seemed like a good day to do that.

I pulled the box out from where I'd hidden it next to my leg. Mae straightened, her eyes lighting up.

"The first time we were engaged, it was all twinkling lights and fancy gazebos and photos. All that stuff is nice but it's not real." I popped open the jewelry box. "Real is you and me sitting on this porch together exactly where I hope we're sitting fifty years from now."

Those blue eyes of hers were growing shiny with unshed tears.

"Chris," she whispered.

"I've already spoken to your mother, of course. And I cleared it with Ali and Iris, too, to be on the safe side. I think I may have promised both they could be maid of honor. I'll let you figure all that out."

She giggled.

I cleared my throat. "Maebell Sampson, would you do me the great honor of becoming my wife?"

"No contract this time?"

I shook my head.

"No pretending?"

"All real, all the time."

She plucked the same opal ring I'd picked out almost a year ago, the one I'd made Piper search high and low for, and slid it on her finger. "I would love to marry you."

"You know, you do suit me," I whispered against her mouth.

"I love you, too."

A LETTER FROM SHARON

Dearest Reader,

Thank you so much for reading *The Fake Out*. If you'd like to keep up to date with all my book news, just sign up at the following link. Never fear, your email address will never be shared, and you can unsubscribe at any time.

www.bookouture.com/sharon-m-peterson

People often ask me where I get my ideas, and the honest answer is everywhere and nowhere. Sometimes it's a snippet of conversation, a news story, or a line from a song. But please know these characters live in my head for months, so, in many ways, they feel real to me. When they show up on the page, I'm just writing down what the voices in my head are telling me to write. They never do what I expect them to do. Frankly, they are the boss of me.

Basically, what I'm saying is that being a writer is awesome.

But the most awesome-est part is getting to connect with readers. I mean that, truly. I'm still wrapping my head around the idea that you—yes, you, dear reader—chose my book out of so many other choices. I know time is precious; thank you for using it to get to know Mae and Chris.

I'd love to hear what you think. Reviews are a great way to share that, and they make such a difference helping new readers to discover one of my books for the first time. If you ever have questions, want to chat, or need a random picture of a baby animal to brighten your day, please feel free to find me online.

You might have noticed those pickup lines at the beginning of each chapter of *The Fake Out*. Guess where they came from? Readers just like you who follow me on social media. I asked and they answered. Which I think emphatically proves that: a) I have the best readers; and b) my readers are capable of epic levels of cheesiness. Thanks for helping your girl out.

You can find me on my Facebook page, tweeting nonsense on Twitter, not curating my aesthetic very well on Instagram, adding too many books to my TBR list on Goodreads, making awkward videos on TikTok, or my website.

Remember that being scared is halfway to brave.

Go do something amazing today,

Sharon

sharonmpeterson.com
goodreads.com/user/show/68003715-sharon-m-peterson

facebook.com/SharonMPetersonAuthor

twitter.com/stone4031

instagram.com/stone4031

tiktok.com/@stone4031

ACKNOWLEDGMENTS

I know most of you will skip over this part, even though it is arguably the most important. See, this book wasn't just written by me. It took the support, talent, and love of so many people to put it in your hands.

Many, many thanks to my agent, Nalini Akolekar, who has been a constant support and has worked tirelessly to get my books into the world. I'm forever grateful that you believed in me, sometimes when I did not believe in myself. Thanks also to the rest of the gang at Spencerhill Associates.

To my editor, Billi-Dee Jones, thank you for championing my quirky stories and characters and helping to get them out in the world. To the whole team at Bookouture, you've created such an amazing environment for authors to bloom. Thank you for all you do.

To Tonya Joza, who patiently answers my bazillion questions about Hypoplastic Left Heart Syndrome, or HLHS, and for sharing what it's like to have a child with HLHS as well as your journey of the hope your family has in God's protection and healing. I'm truly blessed to know you and your family.

To Christie, for telling everyone you know about your friend who writes books and for being a friend who has always been like family. To Noydena and Mat, for always being willing to answer my weird, random tech questions. To the rest of the gang—Andrea, Stephanie, and Shawn—thank you for letting me vent (a lot), for your encouragement, and for funny memes just when I need them. And Brian, I promised you FDR. So here he is.

To Google, for always knowing the answer to the most random questions I ask. You truly make my job easier. Plus, I'm sure I'm on a government watchlist somewhere because of you.

To Melissa Weisner. Thank you for being a listening ear and for answering countless questions. So many questions. Your patience knows no end.

To the ladies at the Eleventh Chapter. I'm so grateful to be part of a group of women writers who support each other in so many ways. You all rock!

To Courtney Lott, who has been cheering me on since the very first word of my first book, read countless drafts, and is the queen of encouragement. I could never, ever have finished writing my very first chapter without you.

To Maria Gonzalez-Gorosito, who, along with a group of moms who barely knew me, surprised me with a new laptop when mine broke. It remains one of the most remarkable gifts I've ever been given. It wasn't just a laptop you gave me; you gave me the courage to write. You're going to be thanked in every book, so just get used to it.

To the ladies of the Ink Tank. Your constant support and the safe place you've provided for me to vent/scream/cry/lament/laugh/celebrate is such an important part of my writing life. You are all amazing.

To Tracey Christensen. Thank you for always telling me the truth even when I might not want to hear it. Your wisdom and friendship have truly been a gift from God. I'm so very glad I know you, my friend. HONEYMOON BABY, forever!

Thank you to the members of the Women's Fiction Writers Association and the League of Romance Writers for giving writers support and opportunities to grow.

To my mom and Aunt CC, thank you for being my cheerleaders and believing that I could make a dream like this a reality. Love you bunches.

To my sister Gabbie, who will never get to hold one of my books in her hands. I miss you always; love you forever. And I fully expect you to sell a copy of this book to every single angel in Heaven.

To Daniel, Benjamin, Gideon, and Katherine. I am incredibly blessed to be your mother. Thank you for putting up with a mom who makes you repeat everything you say at least twice because my mind was somewhere else the first time you said it. You are in my heart always.

To Carl. You've put up with my exhaustion, my tears, my anger, my disappointment, my excitement, my crazy ideas, my ramblings about made-up people in made-up worlds, and way too many pizza dinners. You've never wavered in your support of me. Ever. I love you.

To the many, many others I can't even begin to list here, but you know who you are. Your endless support, encouragement, and prayers have kept and continue to keep me going daily. Thank you for always believing in me.

Lastly, thank you to the readers. Aside from having really good reading taste, you all have been incredibly welcoming and kind to me over the last year. I'm humbled each time someone reaches out to me, writes a review, or spends time reading one of my books.

In *The Fake Out*, I had two characters with health conditions, and I hope I've handled each with care.

For Mae's mother, Lucy, I researched strokes and spent some time in chat rooms, reading and asking questions. There are many types of strokes, and they can affect patients in many ways. Every stroke victim's story and recovery is different. If you'd like to know the signs of a stroke, you can find them here on the American Stroke Association's website: *https://www. stroke.org/en/about-stroke/stroke-symptoms*

Millie, Chris's youngest sister, was born with a congenital heart defect called Hypoplastic Left Heart Syndrome, or HLHS. If you'd like to know more about congenital heart defects, more information can be found on the American Heart Association's website here:

https://www.heart.org/en/health-topics/congenital-heart-defects

Printed in Great Britain
by Amazon